MATTHEW S. COX

I0553255

OUT OF MIND

Progenitor Series Book 2

OUT OF MIND

PROGENITOR BOOK 2

MATTHEW S. COX

DIVISION ZERO PRESS

Cover art by: Jackson Tjota

Cover Layout: Alexandria Thompson

Title Page/Interior art: Ricky Gunawan

ISBN (ebook): 978-1-950738-34-2

ISBN (paperback): 978-1-950738-35-9

CONTENTS

1. Eight Months   1
2. A Period of Adjustment   9
3. Never a Snitch   19
4. Some Chance at Happiness   33
5. Extra Credit   38
6. A Series of Problems   58
7. Trust   70
8. Hiding   80
9. World Changing   95
10. Merely a Dream   105
11. Friends   117
12. Old Habits   133
13. Trash   136
14. Stupid Creatures   153
15. Storm   160
16. New Species   171
17. Malicious Intent   183
18. Emissary   199
19. A Question of If   210
20. Reprieve   217
21. From Bad to Plasma Beams   222
22. Going Down   230
23. Extinction Event   238
24. Final Stand   243
25. Disassembly   248
26. A Hidden Threat   257
27. Street Rat   266
28. The Cosmos Commands   272
29. With a Bang   279
30. Uncharted Territory   284

Acknowledgments   287
About the Author   288
Other books by Matthew S. Cox   289

1

EIGHT MONTHS

U ncertainty clouded every aspect of Sima Nuvari's life—from school to her new clothes to the purplish-blue trees in the distance.

Nothing on this planet, Mirage, felt real enough to quell the constant doubt gnawing at her. Whenever she caught herself starting to accept things, the worry it would all evaporate in an instant pounced. For the first few weeks after finding safety in the colony, every time she settled down in her new bed, she expected to wake up in a trash-filled alley or underground in a Crash, surrounded by fellow street rats. This place couldn't be real. Every night brought the anxiety she'd open her eyes the next morning to find another kid overdosed like Draz.

At least the nightmares of other teens 'floating' her, throwing her into a river of sewage to dispose of her body, stopped. Every successive day she found herself still on this strange planet, still with parents and a safe home, chipped away at her worry. If the Earth Government Security Force really had strapped her down somewhere and pumped virtual reality into her head, they'd gone all out programming the simulation.

If Sima tried hard enough, she could pretend the park and playground area near the residence complex actually existed. Which far-fetched story happened for real? Had the EGSF dragged her some-what unwillingly onto a colony starship and sent her to another planet where she and three children almost didn't survive an escape pod malfunction? Or did they sell her to some corporation for mind games?

Both options sounded ridiculous when she stopped to think about it.

Some weird virtual reality experiment wouldn't have so many boring parts… or provide an actual education. All the schoolwork she'd been doing felt genuine enough. Little by little over the past eight months, Sima tried to set aside her fear this… second chance would turn out to be a dream. The planet Mirage and its strange plants, stranger wildlife, and Earthlike climate didn't shock her near as much as people treating her with respect. Not once had anyone looked down at her for being an Outcast. She hadn't needed to beg glint to buy food or try to find a hidden place to sleep so gangs couldn't find her.

In a way, being stranded in the wilds, believing herself the only living human on the planet, then discovering small children—who she'd expected to watch die—had been a good thing. Without those experiences, she might have been too hostile, surly, distrustful, or closed off to cope with adoptive parents. She'd been so thrilled 'her' kids wouldn't die, she suppressed the false tough persona she'd created around the child she used to be. If it helped keep 'her' kids safe, she'd risk lowering her guard and trusting someone. Add to it, the overwhelming relief of learning the four of them *weren't* the only humans on the entire planet. Her nightmare scenario of burying three small children, then spending however many months she had left before dying alone would never happen.

Sima hadn't given her new parents, Manoj Akbar and his wife Pai Chen, any nasty attitude or defiance. They'd been nothing but nice to her and the kids. It embarrassed her somewhat how readily she'd metaphorically clung to them for protection. Perhaps child-ish, definitely an alien feeling to even have a parent who appeared to care about her. Street rat or not, Sima had the intelligence to see her situation clearly. Two total strangers had agreed to adopt all four of them, sight unseen. The colony administration didn't *have* to honor her demand she not be separated from 'her' kids, but they did so.

Mirage gave her a second chance *not* to end up dead, a prostitute, or incarcerated.

Watching Austin, Juan, and Lissa run around playing with other children their age still struck her as surreal. On Earth, Outcasts—even the six-year-olds—rarely smiled and certainly never giggled. They did plenty of running, however... but not for fun. The three little people she'd taken care of out in the wilderness for weeks now felt closer to siblings than her children. She still had a serious protective streak for them, but between her new parents and Dr. Bystrova—the psychologist—Sima allowed Manoj and Pai to take over 'parenting' so she could focus on her education. The doctor wanted her to 'be a child herself,' but she had no idea where to even start. Even before she ran away from her bio-mother's apartment, she'd been taking care of herself as long as she could remember. 'Play' and 'fun' never really existed in her world.

She still could scarcely believe the little blonde girl zooming around the park almost died in her arms from destroyed lungs. Lissa, who'd turned seven only two weeks ago, possessed limitless energy as well as optimism. Except for his twelfth birthday a few months ago in January, Austin acted so normal she could pretend he'd never been an Outcast at all. Granted, he didn't spend much time on the street compared to her. His father had been an EGSF officer with a good life—right up until he went crazy and killed his wife and then himself. Austin hadn't spoken much of it, other than to say his father survived being shot in the head, but his whole personality changed... turning violent and paranoid. The birthday party reminded Austin of his former family. He'd spent half the day crying on and off, but having some of his new friends over made him feel better.

Juan, still eight, would be turning nine in June. He, too, acted like the whole near-death of a crash landing and being chased by quill cats never happened. Every so often, he went through a sad moment, whenever thoughts of his father came out of nowhere. The man abandoned him in a nicer area hoping someone would take him in. Juan spent the first seven years of his life in *La Propagación*, a sprawling slum where merely walking to school could've ended his life due to a stray bullet or even someone taking deliberate pot shots at any moving target for laughs.

Sima had her doubts regarding the man's motives. Juan believed his father hoped 'nice rich people' would adopt him. She suspected the guy got tired of having to worry about a kid and dumped him. Rich people didn't swoop in out of nowhere to adopt poor kids left alone. Anyone who *would* grab a kid off the street to take home was someone the kid did *not* want grabbing them.

Dodging those kinds of creeps had almost been a full-time job for Sima at first, along with begging.

But none of it mattered anymore.

Squinting, she peered up at the sky. During the day, it looked exactly like Earth. Not until night, when the sky held two moons, did the planet remind her she'd gone somewhere far, far away. Colonists named the pink one Perys and the much smaller orange one Ember. She didn't care for 'Perys' as it sounded too much like 'perish' to be reassuring. Starting from around five in the afternoon, Ember became visible at the northern horizon. Despite the nightly reminder of being at the far end of a two-year-long space flight, she couldn't summon the slightest bit of sorrow at the idea of never seeing the planet of her birth again.

Earth has forgotten all about us. She let out a long sigh. *Wait... no. They can't forget what they never cared enough to know about.*

The sounds of happy children and attentive parents seemed the most alien part of this place.

She fidgeted at the silver bracelet on her left wrist while watching her siblings enjoy the playground. The Omnicomputer, despite containing an AI, turned into more of a friend than a tool. It communicated entirely by text, which appeared on a projected holographic screen floating a quarter-inch above her arm when active. It didn't even bother her anymore the device refused to unlock itself until her eighteenth birthday. Juveniles and prisoners had much in common, primarily someone else managing their lives for them.

Her often overly literal companion saved her life at least twice, saved all of them, really; she couldn't hate it. Omni no longer felt like a shackle, rather a tiny guard dog she didn't have to feed and would never pee the rug. Austin got one the day he turned twelve and didn't even complain about not being able to take it off. They didn't weigh much, and on a potentially dangerous world, wearing a tracking device could save his life. Their parents could override the lock, as could the Security forces, if need be for whatever reason. Children under twelve weren't expected to ever leave the safety of the city, so the need for an Omnicomputer to assist or track them wasn't considered as pressing. Sima figured it came down to a combination of not being able to make them small enough for younger kids, and not wanting to spend the resources replacing them when a kid grew out of their first one.

Many of the adults in sight still wore jumpsuits in various colors associated with their duties: security in blue, medical in white, science in green, engineering in brown, and so on. Kids and 'unskilled' workers wore grey. However, the conversion of the *Progenitor* spacecraft into the Progenitor Colony progressed well. Some manufacturing had started up, making normal clothing available. Sima didn't really care about fashion. After four years of wearing rags on the street back on Earth, then weeks stranded in her underwear on this planet, having intact clothing at all felt like a serious win. Didn't matter what it looked like.

The parents got them all 'normal' clothes as soon as the option became available. They still had jumpsuits, though. Sima tended to wear hers for school or any extra credit projects she took on. As the number of students around her wearing jumpsuits declined, she'd probably swap to 'normal' clothes for school so she didn't stand out. For a day in the park, a basic top and a skirt over leggings worked fine.

Sima smoothed her hand over the black fabric, still worried a random EGSF officer might come out of nowhere and give her attitude for stealing it. Obviously, clean, new clothing didn't belong on an Outcast. Whenever she spotted a Security officer, she fought the urge to cringe, look away, or run. Even if she hadn't done anything, merely existing felt like a crime. It never took much to get an EGSF officer to harass an Outcast.

She still couldn't get used to seeing the police here smile.

I don't look like a street rat. Even an EGSF officer wouldn't bother me unless they ran my ID.

Perhaps living in a tiny city surrounded by alien death cats and forty-foot-tall flamingos rearranged people's priorities. Everyone worried too much about dying to *natural* causes—as in Mother Nature—to make trouble for each other. Given the newness of the colony, people worked together for mutual survival. She didn't expect it to last forever. As soon as people started to feel safe, they'd become complacent. Except for the street kids rounded up and crammed into the ship at the last minute, everyone else who'd made the trip to Mirage had undergone screening. If the place had any criminals, they'd come from the former street rats. Maybe the authorities hoped sending the little ones would give them time to educate the criminal intent out of them. Few young Outcasts could truly be called criminals, resorting to stealing or pickpocketing primarily as a means of survival. However, enough time spent in the company of worse people made for the sort of education not available in school.

Put enough people in one place long enough, crime will happen. I shouldn't think this is some kind of perfect utopia. Governor Harland wouldn't have established a security force if he didn't expect crime at some point.

Again, she looked up at the kids and parents at the playground, then beyond it across the small park to other citizens walking by. Irrational fear of 'crime' being something she had to worry about flared up and faded away in less than a minute. The utter idiocy of her being scared of 'crime' after spending four years surrounded by spree killers, drug dealers, thieves, prostitutes, violent gangs, and probably worse made her laugh.

What happened to me...? It's so weird being part of society instead of outside it. Good weird.

She'd deliberately left her tablet at home, deciding to take a break from studying and enjoy some idle time watching the kids play. Lissa remained on the clingy side with her, but their relationship took on a more sisterly vibe. Sima appreciated their new parents for taking the pressure off her. Dad had been right. She really *wasn't* ready to take care of kids since she had to take care of herself—and needed the support of a mother and father.

Sometimes, while alone in her room right before falling asleep, Sima would get so furious at her birth mother, she'd cry. Living with Pai and Manoj showed her what life *should* be like, and it worsened the resentment she had toward the awful woman responsible for her existence. She let her thoughts drift, trying to sort out how she felt about the new parents. It didn't feel totally accurate to say she loved them, but 'like' didn't work either—not strong enough. She definitely respected them.

Yeah, I'd probably be sad if something happened to them. She bit her lip, arms folded, watching Lissa dangle upside down off a climbing dome of metal bars. The boys ran around with a pack of other kids playing a soccer-like game. The smile on Lissa's face—even upside down—made Sima grin back at her. Almost every time she saw the child smiling, she choked up a little, remembering the moment the girl stopped breathing. If she hadn't been sent to Mirage, she'd be dead. The EGSF officer even had to carry the then-six-year-old onto the ship, as she'd been too weak to walk.

That's how a mom should feel. Sima randomly thought about someone telling her Pai or Manoj had been killed in an accident at work. Surprisingly, she found the imaginary message painfully depressing as well as frightening.

The soft patter of digital text came from her left wrist.

Sima twisted her arm so she could see the glowing green letters appearing on the holographic screen.

‹Almost time to return to your residence. Your father wants me to let you know he has started on dinner.›

"Thanks." Sima smiled at the thought of him cooking.

He always made spicy food, which she adored. Lissa and Austin didn't care so much for the hot stuff, so he always prepared a tamer portion for them. Whenever he got going in the kitchen, he muttered random funny things or made silly faces. She could only describe him as 'cute,' and totally into the Dad thing. Both he and Mom genuinely adored being parents. She couldn't figure out why they didn't have kids of their own before… beyond possibly spending too much time at their jobs.

Okay, maybe I do kinda love them. She gazed up at the overly blue sky, waiting for the police to come grab her for impersonating a Citizen. After a few minutes and no security officers bothering her, she sat up out of her slouch, stood, and waved to the kids, calling them over.

I'll probably never feel normal like everyone else. Best I can do is try to stop caring about the past.

2

A PERIOD OF ADJUSTMENT

F ollowing some predictable foot-dragging and delay, the boys trudged over.

It helped that most of the other kids they'd been playing soccer with had to go home as well. Much easier to walk away from a rapidly dispersing group of children than be the only two who had to go home for dinner. Once it became clear the game would end regardless of whether or not Austin and Juan remained, the boys stopped dawdling. Leading the kids back to their residence from the park could hardly be considered dangerous, but it afforded her a small chance to enjoy feeling protective of them. She much preferred it to guiding them on a trek through the wilds of an unexplored planet while a quill cat stalked them. However, despite being inside the colony, a chance still existed dangerous wildlife could come out of nowhere.

She turned seventeen only five days ago, not expecting anyone to notice or care. In truth, she'd forgotten her birthday. Somehow, the EGSF found her records from before she ran away. Her bracelet reminded her about it, but failed to convince her to tell anyone. The day hadn't felt special in any way for the past sixteen years.

Though, it didn't matter.

Her family refused to ignore it.

Realizing a few months short of five years separated her from Austin made her feel somewhat silly for thinking of him as *her* kid, plus got her feeling like a bit of a child herself. Still, as the oldest, it had been her job to protect the rest. Safe in the colony—or as safe as one could be on Mirage—she tried to let her guard down and be a kid. Alas, while she had the opportunity to do so, she lacked the ability. Dr. Bystrova reassured her no one could 'switch off' four years of hypervigilance overnight. That she trusted Mom and Dad already surprised the doctor as much as it surprised Sima.

She credited determination and anger toward her birth mother. The woman had done so much damage to her life already she refused to let her mess it up any more than she already did. Being as normal and happy as possible felt like the best victory-slash-revenge possible.

The kids' sneakers clattered on metal plates, repurposed pieces of the *Progenitor's* outer hull turned into a sidewalk. At first, she didn't have a clue why they bothered building a network of paths around the colony—until the first time it rained and the downpour turned the area into a treacherous, slippery, muddy mess. No one bothered building roads yet, as the colonists only had a few dozen Nomad six-wheelers and some smaller rovers to drive around in. Not only did such vehicles not require roads, none belonged to individual citizens. Decades in the future, someone might start manufacturing gee-vees... but the entirety of human habitation of the planet existed within a roughly two-mile-square area. No one had anywhere to drive to, and most gee-vees couldn't handle going off road. People wouldn't need them on Mirage until or unless humanity spread out to multiple cities separated by distances impractical to walk.

The park and playground sat at the end of a 'street' running between several residence buildings. In the time Sima and the kids had been stranded out in the wild, the other people on the ship established the city's basic infrastructure via expanding dozens of prefab modules. Most of the 'ready-made' structures detached from the ship became housing for the 8,292 people on board. The capacity planners didn't expect an additional 251 street kids, but being kids, they'd all been adopted or assigned to caretakers who'd been 'budgeted' into the housing plan.

Within one week of landing, everyone had a home. Rich people back on Earth would consider the residence quarters small. To Sima, the place felt massive, easily four times the size of the little apartment her bio mother lived in. She even had her own room. The boys presently shared a bedroom. Lissa had one to herself as well. Upon agreeing to take in the four of them, Manoj and Pai got reassigned to one of the largest family residences.

Having a clean bedroom to herself still felt as though she'd become wealthy overnight. Being able to take a shower or grab clean clothing whenever she wanted thrilled her more than glint raining from the sky. Speaking of glint, she had some money without having to beg for it. Sure, they just made it up out of thin air... but 500 credits was 500 credits. The colony administration created an account for every resident. Those who had money from Earth kept their finances. People like Sima who didn't have anything received a starter account. So what if someone arbitrarily typed in 500 credits and the money meant nothing anywhere else but this place? Not like Sima would pop back to Earth any time soon. Besides, money back on Earth had been made up, too. It didn't stand for anything more valuable than numbers in a computer somewhere—even the plastic 'coins' enabling untraceable transactions had microchips in them pointing back to digital currency somewhere.

She eyed other colonists going by on both sides of the street, another old habit. No one came anywhere near as close to threatening as the people she used to live among. One more weird thing on top of all the other weird things Mirage required getting used to: no crowds. Most days, so many pedestrians milled around the areas she haunted on Earth, she had to press herself against the wall of a building *not* to constantly be touching someone.

Another oddity came from the food. Since arriving in the

colony, she'd eaten things pulled from the ground mere hours before the meal. Nothing frozen. Nothing freeze-dried. No processed goo in silver packets. Nothing flown in by aircraft from halfway around the planet. Workers established farms in outlying fields. Ninety-two percent of the crop seeds they brought with them took root in Mirage soil. In addition, the research she unwittingly gathered on various fruits and native plants here helped supplement the citizens' diet. Their savior vegetable, what Lissa referred to as a 'space cucumber' had become something of the 'universal food' named the titan squash.

Surprisingly, Sima hadn't become completely sick of those strange raspberry-ish super tart fruit pods they'd all lived on for most of their feral time.

Other than being small—and made from a disassembled starship—the colony looked as modern as any of the nicer places on Earth… and much cleaner. The uniformity of the people in terms of social strata lent an air of otherworldliness as well, making her continue to suspect everything to be a weird virtual reality experiment. Her brain couldn't process seeing a society without rich people, Citizens, poor people, Outcasts, and gangs. Sure, some of the colonists had important jobs—bosses or managers—but no one possessed tons of wealth or flaunted it around. Progenitor Colony lacked beggars, gangs, or obviously indigent people. Everyone had an OT—occupational task—and contributed in some way to the continued survival of the colony.

Mom referred to it as 'camping with air conditioning.'

Watching people had been a survival instinct that kept Sima alive for four years. She couldn't help but size everyone up on the way home. Despite the relative normalcy of everything, she didn't expect it to last. Given enough time, cracks would appear. Perhaps not for decades, but they'd appear. Small mannerisms of people, the way they looked at her, carried themselves, or behaved, told her who would have been trying to get high, breaking into places, starting fights, forming gangs, or doing worse back on Earth.

Everyone smiled, but they also ran on 'we're inches from death' mode.

No idea how long it would take before the general population of the colony stopped worrying about *if* they would survive, but eventually, people would get lazy. When people got lazy, problems happened. How would Governor Harland deal with the first person who refused to work their OT? Would they deny someone food if they couldn't afford it?

No matter what happened here, Sima resolved herself never to end up in that position again. She survived the streets of Earth at twelve with nothing but the clothes she ran away in. The education her new parents and this colony let her have would make sure she kept right on surviving.

And if she could grab a little happiness on the way, she'd risk it... even if it felt like she did something wrong by smiling.

Everyone's too busy trying not to die. They don't have time for the BS of drugs.

The idea of illegal narcotics here almost made her laugh. Sure, some of the chemists might be able to make drugs, but they also lacked the ingredients for them. Governor Harland even declared alcohol a 'waste of resources' for the time being. While not 'banned,' using food supplies to make booze could get someone in serious trouble. Already existing liquor brought from Earth, no one cared about. When civilization here stabilized, they'd permit alcohol production.

Someone's definitely going to do it by themselves before it's allowed.

The kids ran, cheering, to the front door of their residence complex. One giant pod held twelve 'family-size' quarters, four per story, and ten somewhat smaller 'mid-range' apartments intended for couples with two or fewer children. Sima lived on the third floor, back left corner from the entrance.

She still tensed up whenever she entered the building. Maybe in another few months, she'd stop looking over her shoulder for a cop coming to throw her out of an area intended for Citizens only. Seams, hinges, and various mechanical components in the walls revealed it as a collapsible prefab structure. The building made the journey here collapsed to a mere fraction of its present size. Much like the *Progenitor* itself, it had become a permanent structure. Workers had welded everything in place so it couldn't collapse again, intentionally or by accident.

Sima and the kids took the magnetic elevator to the third floor, then ran down the hall. The strong fragrance of spices embraced her the instant she walked into her apartment. Dad brought cases of them from Earth. Everyone who officially went on the trip got to bring along up to fifty pounds of 'non-vital' possessions. Her new father used almost all of his weight allotment on herbs and spices he wouldn't be able to obtain on Mirage for many years, if ever. Tonight smelled like what he called 'masala,' probably chicken.

"Dad?" called Sima while the little ones ran down the hall to the left. "We're back."

"In here." He leaned out of the kitchen, wearing a 'hug the cook' apron over his dark orange work jumpsuit. As soon as he made eye contact with her, his smile broadened. "Did you have a nice break?"

Sima tossed her bag on the sofa on the way to the kitchen. "Yeah. Nice to just sit for an hour and not do anything."

She helped out by keeping an eye on the main portion of food while he tended to the less spicy batch for Lissa and Austin. Such a small thing, but his willingness to do extra work to make the kids happy ended up being a major reason she came to trust him so fast. They chatted about their respective days. She had a relatively normal day of seemingly endless schoolwork while he discussed mundane operational things regarding the colony's electrical power.

A few minutes later, Mom arrived home, having been working a bit late. She had a bad habit of becoming occasionally absorbed in her job and losing track of time—the only person Sima ever met who considered work fun.

"Sorry I'm late." Mom breezed into the kitchen, hugged Sima, kissed Dad, then looked around. "Where's everyone else?"

"Their rooms." Sima poked the chicken masala. "Looks done."

Dad peered into the rice cooker. "Perfect timing."

"C'mon guys," called Mom into the hall. "Dinner."

Soon, the dining room filled with the voices of three loud children and Dad's subdued laughter. Sima smiled at the scene around her as she always did, despite questioning how much she belonged to it. After her third bite of spicy food, it occurred to her the nagging sense of getting away with something had changed without her realizing the exact moment she stopped feeling like an Outcast who snuck into another family's house. A mixture of anger at her biological mother simmered beneath an uneasy knot of worry. How long would it take—if ever—for her to stop feeling like a guest? Had she become too old for adoption? On Earth, people didn't officially become Citizens until turning eighteen. When they sent her to Mirage, Sima only had a year and nine months left of legally being a 'child.' It almost seemed pointless to bother adopting her. She wouldn't even have the chance to adjust to being part of a family before she turned eighteen and didn't require parents anymore.

Require. She stirred the bright orange chicken masala around in the rice. *Legally. What if I need them for other reasons? Dr. Bystrova thinks I have 'issues.' Abandonment... attachment... if it's an issue, I've probably got it.* She caught herself being envious of Lissa. Being adopted had to be so much easier for a child her age. Even Austin... all three kids adjusted to the parents fairly easily. Both boys knew what 'normal' parents should be like. Lissa didn't, but at her age, she didn't have much memory of the past and had plenty of childhood left ahead of her. And even her druggie parents paid more attention to her than Sima's mother before they blew themselves up.

I'm embarrassed. She let a long breath out her nose. *Too proud to accept I really am a kid or too scared something will go wrong?*

"How was school?" asked Mom.

The kids all erupted in chatter at once. Lissa had fun and couldn't wait for tomorrow so she could go back. Austin offered an 'it's okay,' which meant nothing particularly good nor bad happened. Juan complained about his language teacher constantly trying to 'correct' him whenever he used wrong words. Generally, everyone on Earth spoke GANSEC, a chimeric language assembled primarily from major languages used prior to the End of Nations centuries ago. The change happened many generations before Sima existed, so she didn't know much about the old languages. Evidently, some people—predominantly the poor—incorporated regional words into their dialect.

Juan, being from *La Propagación,* had a handful of what he called 'Spanish' verbs and nouns in his vocabulary. He liked them. His teacher didn't.

"Everything all right, Sima?" asked Mom. "You look like you're deep in thought."

Crap. She knows. "Yeah. I'm okay. Just trying to adjust to everything. Nothing bad." She managed a weak but mostly sincere smile. "Sometimes, I still think I'm going to wake up and find out I dreamed all of you."

"So do I." Dad ruffled Austin's hair, then patted Juan on the shoulder before grinning across the table at Lissa and Sima. "I'm glad the four of you are happy."

Mom leaned forward. "If you think they're pushing you too hard, we will insist they back off some. You've taken on a lot of work."

"It's fine." Sima tried the trick Dr. Bystrova mentioned and visualized her anxiety as smoke she could exhale. "It's not the schoolwork that's bothering me. I like it... more than I used to, even before. Just... I'm kinda embarrassed."

"Embarrassed?" asked Dad. "For enjoying academics?"

"Yeah." She shrugged, stabbing her fork into the contents of her plate. "Talking about 'smart things' is like asking for a beating."

Austin whistled. "If you're smart, gotta keep it to yourself. They think the smart kids are easy to pick on."

Mom patted Sima's arm. "You aren't on the street anymore. There's no need for you to pretend to be 'hard' anymore."

"I know." She gave her mother side eye. "We're billions of miles away from Earth on an untamed planet. How messed up is it I'm *safer* here?"

Her parents chuckled.

"Real messed up, but true." Austin stuffed another overloaded spoonful into his mouth.

Sima continued reassuring her parents her stress didn't come from academics. At first, she couldn't quite say exactly why she'd been growing increasingly anxious in recent days, but a circular, random conversation about generalized anxiety over dinner brought clarity. Somehow, she'd become seriously attached to her parents without realizing it—and dreaded something would go wrong. Whatever part of her remained a frightened child, the part she had to hide away in a locked vault for the past four years, had finally dared to poke her head out at some point within the past few months.

By some miracle, Sima Nuvari *trusted* adults—at least these two.

She stared at her mostly empty plate, vaguely aware of the conversation hanging on a moment of expectant silence.

"Sima?" Dad tilted his head. "Are you all right? You stopped talking in the middle of a sentence. Everything's just so what?"

The kids, Mom, and Dad, all looked at her as if waiting for her to say something.

A rush of warmth filled her face. Admitting vulnerability hadn't happened in a long, long time. She glanced at Lissa, who beamed at her. The girl's smile had such power, Sima couldn't help but smile as well.

"Umm, I... this. All of this. You guys." Sima bowed her head. "It's too perfect. I'm afraid to let myself settle in and accept you and Mom really want me. Want us. It's like... as soon as I let my guard down and think this is real, I'm going to wake up on a VR table. Or, something bad's gonna happen."

"I highly doubt we are characters in a virtual reality simulation." Dad winked at Mom. "But if we are, when you wake up, please let the people running the simulation know they did an amazing job on Pai."

Mom smirked at him, then cracked up.

"Me, too," whispered Austin. "But... I wanted to be happy. Even if it's pretend, I can be happy until they pull us out."

"It can't be pretend." Sima sat up, wide-eyed on a sudden wave of hope. "They wouldn't program you to be worried about waking up out of VR."

"I'm not a program." Austin picked up a bit of chicken, faked tossing it at her, then ate it.

She ducked anyway, laughing.

Kid's got a point. If I'm going to be unplugged eventually, I might as well try to be happy until they do it.

3

NEVER A SNITCH

Most kids Sima's age—at least the ones she knew back on Earth—didn't care about school.

They viewed it as somewhere between a job and prison. The dumber ones considered being on the street as freedom... right up until they overdosed, got chewed up by the EGSF, or murdered by a gang. Worse, some joined the Blanks. Society considered them another gang, though Sima regarded them as a cult. Blanks called themselves the 'Prophets of Naught.' All sorts of creepy rumors circulated about what they did to their members, most of which involved using certain mind-altering drugs to destroy free will and erode personality to an almost android-like state. The wilder stories claimed once a person 'advanced' far enough in the Blanks, they scooped out their brains and replaced them with computer chips. Her 'friend' Callie once said they worshiped technology and made a 'god' out of AI.

Sima used to flee from them with as much fear as she held for the Scathers.

School, however, never frightened her. Up to age twelve, before she ran away from home, she'd thrown herself into her schoolwork as an escape. It helped she'd gotten lucky enough to come out of the genetic lottery with above average intelligence. Probably came from her father's side. Fortunately, she hadn't inherited his butt-headedness.

Sima leaned back from the monitor, rubbing her eyes. While she adored learning, sitting in front of a terminal for such long periods wore on her. The colony administration hadn't assigned her to an OT yet to allow her to catch up on lost schoolwork. Initially, she'd tested at a roughly eighth-grade level despite abandoning school in sixth. Part of it came from luck and deductive reasoning on the multiple-choice test. Some questions—like the algebra—she had to make blind guesses at since she'd never been exposed to it before. Street kids didn't often care about the 'value of x.'

The past eight months of ten-to-twelve-hour days started to pay off. In essence, she *did* have an occupational task: learning. Her job at present was to become a useful contributor to the colony. She'd poured herself fully into it. A month ago, she began attending day classes as a high school sophomore. By age, she should be a junior, but by education, she technically shouldn't even be in high school yet. They almost started her as a freshman, which wouldn't have bothered her *too* much. She had tons of experience pretending to be younger.

Here, she confused the other kids.

Roughly thirty percent of the eight-some-odd-thousand 'official' colonists were under eighteen. Those Citizen kids regarded the Outcast orphans as generally dumb, uneducated, and violent. Few had the nerve to openly make fun of them, expecting them all to be gang punks armed with knives. Sad to say, a handful of her contemporaries lived up to the stereotype, at least insofar as being uninterested in education. Sima's intelligence and generally normal behavior had many of the Citizen kids mistaking her for one of them, not a street rat. When or if they found out the truth, they limited their derision or worry to odd looks. At least the teachers banned the use of the word 'Outcast' since it no longer applied on

Mirage. Being called rats or street rats didn't seem much of an improvement, even if it lacked all the baggage of official contempt 'Outcast' carried.

Ironically, Sima lived up to one part of the stereotype: she *did* carry a knife at all times.

When her eyes stopped itching, Sima resumed working.

Skipping the 'not-academically required' classes like art, music, and physical education allowed her to mostly catch up to where she should have been. They'd initially given her a plan that skimped on history—for sake of helping her become 'useful' to the colony more quickly—but she worked those instructionals voluntarily. At first, she'd attended a separate class with other kids needing remedial education, a small group of nine attending twelve-hour sessions all week long. Many more than nine kids needed catch-up work, but the school kept the groups small so teachers could cope with everyone being at a different grade level. It also involved a ton of independent work via tablet.

Now, she'd caught up enough to where she only needed to attend the remedial sessions two nights, on Tuesday and Thursday, instead of all week long. Five students remained of the original nine in her group. Four of them had 'graduated' on to ordinary school already, mostly due to their having become Outcasts recently and not missing as much formal education as the others. She knew only a little about each of the kids around her. Between having so much work to do and no interest in nor ability to make friends, she'd kept to herself. Despite knowing it irrational, she'd spent too much of her life viewing other teens as rivals competing for food to change her thinking any time soon. Socialization could wait until after she sorted herself out academically. Of course, when she finished the remedial work, they'd probably give her a part-time OT... unless the psychiatrists thought she needed 'play time' to make up for the childhood she never had.

She wouldn't necessarily mind the idea, but also wouldn't go out of her way to ask for it.

Stefan Novotny, a tall seventeen-year-old in the front row, asked Mr. Eiger—the teacher who'd been running the remedial sessions—another question. The first time Sima saw the boy, she braced for problems. Tall, muscular, and broad-shouldered, he appeared to be grown man with a baby face... and his short-buzzed hair made him look way too much like an EGSF cop. Much to her surprise, he wasn't as dumb as his facial expression suggested, and rather soft-spoken.

The girl seated next to him, Veronica Ruiz, rolled her eyes. She didn't enjoy school, more put up with it. At fifteen, she'd probably place out of the remedial class to ninth grade—assuming she passed, which remained a legitimate question. The girl didn't come off as dumb, merely thought education pointless. Garret Cole, the boy sitting next to Sima on the left, was the youngest in their group at fourteen. He had long blond hair, blue eyes, and only a third-grade education. The boy also became frustrated easily and made a habit of whispering to Sima for help since she'd already developed a reputation as a 'smart kid.' Some of it came from actually being smart, but most from her attitude of wanting to learn. Not many of the former Outcasts appreciated going from having the whole day to do whatever they wanted to an organized schedule. Some, like Stefan, *wanted* to learn but struggled at it. Sima had zero problem giving up total freedom in exchange for not having to worry about *if* she could eat or *if* she would wake up in the morning.

The third girl in the class, Anita Kendall, kept to herself like Sima did and focused on her work... except when Robert Banff, another fifteen-year-old, threw small things at her hoping to get them stuck in her frizzy hair. For the first few days of the class, Sima expected a knife fight lurked one tiny thrown object away at any moment.

Fortunately, everyone settled into their mutual acceptance of each other's company. Vanessa no longer shouted at the teacher. Robert no longer fell asleep. Garret no longer cried quietly to himself as soon as he couldn't understand something. Sima didn't bother to care if any of them hung out as friends after school. These classes ran so late she'd always go straight home after.

Mirage followed a surprisingly Earth-like orbit around the local sun. Being slightly larger, it took the planet twenty-four hours and six minutes to complete a rotation. For simplicity's sake—or sheer laziness—the people in charge decided to keep Earth's twenty-four-hour day and have a six-minute 'nowhere' time separating each day. Its solar orbit came close as well, slower by two days—which they decided to simply add to February. Predictably, the two planets (Earth and Mirage) hadn't synchronized their orbits in terms of seasons. Earth January lined up with Mirage July.

Sima's birthday had been August 22nd, but here, it legally changed to February 22nd. She'd officially turned seventeen two months ago. Since she had never known a birthday as a significant event, adjusting to the new date took zero effort. Her bio mother never even acknowledged it. Her adoptive parents, however, upon learning this, made a *massive* embarrassing deal about it. Bad enough, every colonist knew her at least in passing as the 'kid who survived in the wilderness,' Mom and Dad talked the entire education department into hosting a 'thing' for her birthday. She had handmade cards from first graders saying how sad they were she'd never had a birthday party before and hoped she would be happy for her first one.

Mortifying. But also kinda nice in a way.

"Sima?" asked Mr. Eiger.

She opened her eyes. "Sorry. Staring at the screen so long."

He smiled. "It's all right. How are you handling the material? Any questions?"

"She never has questions," muttered Garret.

"What's she even doing here? She can't be no Outcast." Vanessa made a dismissive face at her.

Huh? Sima stared at the younger girl. A momentary surge of defensiveness welled up, but before she shouted, it burst into a bizarre feeling of relief. Not an Outcast. *Maybe she's right... I didn't end up working for Magdalena or joining a gang. What kind of loser pretends to be twelve to beg for glint?*

She looked up at the teacher. "Umm. No questions I can think of. This is kinda easy."

Mr. Eiger spent a few minutes discussing the material on her screen, grade nine biology, mostly cellular structures and functions. He appeared impressed, nodded at her, and moved over a desk to work with Garret.

Everyone else except for Robert and Anita stared at her in perplexed shock. Clearly, the science stuff went way over their heads.

A little more than an hour later, the period ended at 10:00 p.m. Eight months in, the remedial classes had become mostly Mr. Eiger supervising them all working individually on their terminals. One couldn't exactly teach a traditional class when the kids operated at a wide variety of grade levels. Fortunately, the extremely long day contained multiple breaks. She figured the teachers handling the remedial classes couldn't wait for them to finish, since their entire lives consisted of wake up, go to school, go home, sleep, then do it again. Like the students, *they* had almost no free time either except for weekends. On the positive side, such grueling schedules wouldn't last forever.

Sima shut down her terminal and got up. Her bracelet emitted a faint pulse, a signal it sent a message to her parents to notify them of her leaving the school. They didn't care for the class running so late, but due to being on a colony, offered only minimal protest. On Earth, Sima wouldn't have dared go out after dark if she could avoid doing so. Here, she didn't mind as much, though still kept looking over her shoulder.

A small population didn't guarantee no one would ever be dangerous.

Fortunately, she didn't have *too* far a walk to get home. The rear portion of the *Progenitor* had become an eight-story building containing the governor's office, security headquarters, reactor and power control systems, hospital, and all educational classrooms.

People called it the Center. Construction generally spread out to the southwest from the Center due to open fields—and there having been a two-mile-long spaceship sitting there while workers unloaded and set up all the prefab structures. Only a few structures made from repurposed materials occupied ground where the *Progenitor* formerly existed. The grass had even recovered. A river bordered the colony on the east, forest to the north.

After they'd unloaded all the prefab buildings and other supplies, workers cannibalized most of the ship's former hull, interior, wiring, and framework into the colony's infrastructure. Eventually, they'd break down the ion engines into... something. For now, they stuck out from the rear side of the Center, making it look like an enormous toy spacecraft some overly energetic child broke.

No one really cared about aesthetics.

Sima rode the elevator down from the sixth floor, then followed the other kids out the main doors. The area where the now-missing portion of the starship used to sit remained empty, effectively becoming a courtyard in front of the Center. Long metal beams jutted out of the irregular face of the former starship on either side, 'hugging' the open area, giving the giant building a C shape. Some wiseass even left a mangled hunk of debris—from the spot where escape pods had been knocked off the ship by space debris—in the middle of the area as an 'art object' or perhaps a memorial to the people who died.

None of the kids spoke much, everyone exhausted and eager to go home and sleep.

The others broke off to head toward their residence pods in different directions. She guessed none had a 'family of six,' so lived in smaller units in a different area from her building. The colony didn't have many of the large ones.

A man in a blue jumpsuit and light armor walked out into view from between two metal buildings up ahead. Despite not having any contraband on her or doing anything even close to against the rules, she instinctively froze in her tracks, staring down. It took her a second to remember she didn't look at an EGSF officer, but a soldier. Progenitor Colony Security existed mainly to protect everyone here—including her—from *outside* threats, not sit around bored all day and amuse themselves by abusing Outcasts. While she might never be able to trust anyone even remotely similar to an EGSF officer, with a bit of effort, she could see herself getting over her fear response.

If I stop acting like a criminal caught in the act whenever I see a cop by thirty, I'll call it a win. She smirked. *If I make it to thirty, that'll be a win, too.*

Eyes closed, she sighed out her nose, focusing on all the ways living here was better. Family. No begging. Good food. No gangs... and an entire other planet away from her birth mother's creepy boyfriend.

The security man noticed her hesitation and changed course toward her.

Oh crap! She took a deep breath and thought about the soldier named Winters, part of the team who found her and the kids out in the middle of nowhere. He'd been the total opposite of the EGSF. Concerned about them, caring... *Not the same. These guys are different. Even that detective rescued Flora—I mean, Alina—from Mag's.* She frowned. *Or he did it to pump up the quota of kids on the ship. Did I really start to think he cared?*

"Miss Nuvari?" asked the man. "Is everything all right?"

"Yes, sir."

"What are you so nervous about?"

"Umm." She forced herself to make eye contact. "You know how the EGSF treated us back on Earth, right?"

The man, who couldn't be more than four or five years older than her, sighed hard. "Yeah. I know. One of the reasons I volunteered for this mission."

"I just got out of class. I'm going home." She started fumbling at her pockets, turning them out so he could see she didn't have anything illegal on her.

"It's fine." He waved her off. "Just checking to make sure you're okay. Need an escort home?"

Sima stared at him until her brain finished rebooting. "Umm. Duh. You're not going to search me. Ugh. Sorry. It's all right. It's not far. I can get home."

"It's no bother, really. But I understand the uniform makes you nervous, so I won't insist." He smiled. "We're here if you need anything. Stay safe."

"Thanks." She summoned a hasty smile and hurried off.

Wow, can I be any more obvious? She pressed a hand to her throat, shivering at the memory of having a fake bomb around her neck. Agreeing to help a guy smuggle contraband across the city had to be one of the dumbest decisions she ever made. If the EGSF caught her, it would've been better if the necklace really could explode. Life on Earth had multiple options for a street kid her age—and they all ended poorly. Even the toughest Outcasts turned into frightened children when confronted by the EGSF... except for the crazy ones who wanted to die.

Pattering text from the bracelet made her look down at her arm.

‹You received three messages. I held them for you since you were in class.›

She smiled at the small holographic screen as the bracelet played a 'good night' message from Austin, Juan, and Lissa. They did this every night she had a late class. A few minutes later, after Lissa waved and reluctantly stopped the recording, Sima kept staring at the kids' paused faces, grinning. It felt *so* weird to have other people caring about her.

I'm addicted to Pixie... just not the chemical one.

The light from the holographic screen flickered out as she dropped her arm to her side. She stopped short, surprised to find unfamiliar scenery around her. To reorient herself, she turned in place, trying to get a feel for where in the colony she'd strayed. It looked as though she'd walked on autopilot while absorbed in the video, missing the spot she should have turned. Large metal structures surrounded her, the area they referred to as 'the Mall,' which contained every store on the entire planet. Not saying much, as only about eleven stores existed thus far.

Of course, at 10:09 p.m., all had closed for the night except for a 'bar' called the Rec Room and a pair of, essentially, fast food places. One, named 24-6, never closed. The other, simply called Noodles, stayed open to 11:00 p.m. The ship brought some stores of alcohol along, but the vast majority of it on Mirage came from colonists' 'personal space' allotment. Due to scarcity, liquor ended up becoming extremely expensive. Most people who went to the Rec Room did so to relax and play games, not so much for drinking. Then again, for the time being, money didn't matter *too* much. Basic needs like bare subsistence food, jumpsuits, and housing were issued to everyone. Nice stuff, like non-jumpsuit clothing, toys, games, real food, and so on, had to be purchased. Someone could blow all their money on pointless crap and not end up an Outcast.

"Dammit," whispered Sima, sighing at the wrong turn keeping her out—and awake—later than she wanted to be.

Rather than go the long way around the whole Mall, she headed deeper in, cutting right to go straight across to her residence pod roughly a half mile away on the other side. She followed the main concourse between the larger stores, cornered past the electronics shop—and stopped short for the second time that night, a few steps from crashing into a small group gathered in the alley.

An unusually short but muscular guy, another man with snow-white hair in a brush cut, and a tall dark-skinned woman stood back like guards while a thin guy in a brown jumpsuit tried to loom at a late-thirties man with platinum blond hair, who looked as nervous as a Citizen trying to obtain drugs from an Outcast for the first time.

Sima knew in an instant she'd stumbled upon a bad situation. Back home, a scene like this meant drug deal and interrupting one usually resulted in a panicked chase. At best, most gangs loved a self-delivering young girl to have fun with. At worst, they'd suspect her of being from a hostile gang and try to kill her. Rarely, they'd ignore her, but it did sometimes happen.

However, she no longer lived on Earth. Fear took a back seat to curiosity.

The overconfident thin guy glared expectantly at the blond man. Except for everyone wearing clean jumpsuits, they reminded her of E86ers, one of the tamer gangs that mostly sold drugs and mugged people for glint. 'Involuntary donations' as some of them called it.

"A hundred credits for two bottles? You sure this is real vodka?" asked the nervous buyer. "What did you make it from?"

"Gotta ask Cedar. She's our brew master." The leader indicated the woman.

Cedar folded her arms. "Trade secret. It's as close to vodka as we can get here. Probably closer to being moonshine if you want to split a hair."

"It'll get you messed up just the same," said the short guy.

Booze? This is about booze? Sima clamped a hand over her mouth to stop herself from laughing.

Everyone spun to look at her. The white-haired dude caught her off guard—both his eyes glowed bright red. She leaned back in alarmed surprise. Few Outcasts had the glint to afford body modification. Light shining from his eyes could only be from electronic replacements. Cybernetics. That meant he probably hadn't been an Outcast. Some gang members *could* afford parts, but not in their mid-twenties. Still, people with implants could be *extremely* dangerous. A guy who had both eyes replaced might have concealed blades, poison needles, or any of a dozen different means to hurt her.

Red-eye and the woman lunged to grab Sima. She jumped away, avoiding their reach, scrambling backward. The others rushed over, cornering her against the wall. The 'buyer' stood where he'd been in paralyzed shock, gawking at her. She didn't feel *too* threatened by this group. None had visible weapons, and they didn't radiate malice the way Earth gangs tended to do. Still, she kept trying to retreat despite her back pressing against the wall.

The thin guy stepped up on her. "Seems we have an unexpected visitor."

She glanced at his chest, specifically a reflective white strip bearing the name 'Kurosawa.'

"Think this one knows why it's a good idea to keep her mouth shut?" asked Cedar. "Or is it going to take some... encouragement?"

Sima shifted her gaze to the woman. Taller, more muscular, probably six to eight years older than her, but definitely not an Outcast. Her jumpsuit didn't have a name patch, one of the generic grey ones. Despite the woman's physical advantages, Sima had seen scarier twelve-year-olds. Drugs plus desperation plus no sense of self-preservation could make even a kid terrifying when they're waving a knife around. *This* woman, who Kurosawa referred to as Cedar, definitely sounded fearful of being caught. However, the idea of illicit trading in *alcohol* of all things struck Sima as hilarious, though she managed not to laugh, or even smile—mostly.

"Doesn't look like this one realizes the gravity of the situation," said Red-Eye.

"Oh, I realize it fine." Sima rested one hand on her hip, all her weight on the opposite leg, copying the dismissive pose her former associate Callie always used whenever an idiot got too close. "It's taking all my self-control not to laugh."

The buyer giggled nervously.

Kurosawa glared.

"Give me a break. You guys are dealing alcohol?" Sima rolled her eyes. "And acting like it's serious?"

Snarling, Kurosawa grabbed for her shirt collar. Sima ducked his arms, then shoved him into the wall while simultaneously pulling her knife off the back of her belt. The skinny man crashed chest first into the metal. She leaned her weight into his back, pressing the blade to his neck. The instant metal touched his skin, he went still, palms flat on the wall—almost in a posture preparing for an EGSF officer to search him.

"Gonna give you some useful information," said Sima in a low voice. "I used to be an Outcast. Spent four years expecting to die at any minute. As street rats go, I'm pretty tame. Most of the people I used to live around would've just slit your throat for touching them and kept walking."

"Put the knife down, kid," whispered Cedar. "This doesn't have to get bloody."

Sima shoved away from Kurosawa, took a step back, and slid the knife back into its sheath. "I didn't say it as a threat. Same people would kick my ass for *not* cutting him." She looked over at the others. "I'm not a violent person. There are a couple hundred ex-Outcasts in this colony. You shouldn't threaten people over something as vape as selling vodka."

Kurosawa pushed away from the wall, spinning to resume glaring at her. His mood appeared evenly divided between wanting to hit her for making him look foolish and being impressed at her maneuver.

Nerves knotted her stomach. Laughable or not, four adults getting it in their head to kick her ass would *not* end well for her no matter how inexperienced they might be. Life as an Outcast was eighty percent image, twenty percent follow-through. Granted, her 'image' had been trying to come off as childlike to squeeze more glint from begging. She'd never tried the 'tough girl' act before. But... three facts worked in her favor. One, back on Earth, she'd never charged a giant alien panther armed only with a small axe. Two, these people wouldn't know what an actual dangerous Outcast looked like. Third, and hopefully true, the trouble they'd get in for roughing her up would be worse than any reprimand for wasting supplies on alcoholic drinks.

Clinging to thought number three, Sima pushed her nerves aside and started walking off, pretending to be unconcerned with whatever the people might do.

"Look, I'm late. Keep your heads screwed on. *Pff*. Vodka. Give me a break. Try selling Pixie, or Black Mist, or Nightmare Fuel, or S-94. You ever have something on you the cops would shoot you on sight for possessing? Didn't think so. Worst thing'll happen to you guys is the admin saying *bad, don't do that again*. I'm not a 'go to the cops' type of person. Whatever you're doing isn't my problem."

Kurosawa and his 'people' simply watched her go, none made a move to chase after her or said a word.

Sima strolled away, refusing to look back or speed up. She couldn't give off any sign of being afraid of them. The alley hung in awkward silence for the twenty seconds it took her to reach the end and go around a corner. Once she had a solid building between her and the 'gang,' she let herself walk faster.

Gonna pretend this never happened. Hope they do, too.

4

SOME CHANCE AT HAPPINESS

Sima stretched out on her bed, working on a self-paced electronic instruction module.

The warmth of a recent shower still clung to the air. Damp hair gave her an excuse to delay going to sleep. Her parents didn't insist on a childish bedtime for her, though if they caught her up past midnight, they'd pester her about going to sleep. She didn't plan to stress herself out, merely needed to give the adrenaline from her almost-fight a chance to go away. No point lying down and closing her eyes until it became *possible* for her to sleep.

Besides, the more EI modules she completed, the sooner she could move to a normal schedule.

A soft knock at the door preceded Dad poking his head in. "Is it okay if I come in?"

She almost said 'Sure, it's your house,' but bit her lip. Neither her birth mother, her creepy boyfriend—or probably her actual father—would've asked. They'd have barged in on her like she was a little kid. "Yeah."

Smiling, Dad pushed the door the rest of the way open. He gave a brief look around before approaching the bed. "I couldn't help but notice something was bothering you when you walked in before. Is everything okay?"

"It's not a big deal compared to some of the crap I've had to put up with." She stared *through* the screen, no longer seeing words as much as a hazy field of letters.

"Sima?" Dad sat on the edge of the gel mattress. "I know something is bothering you. Would you like to talk about it?"

It took her a moment to process everything. When it hit her she had someone—a parent—concerned enough to check on her... and someone she *could* confide in, emotion got the better of her. As soon as she started crying, he gently grasped her shoulder. She didn't remember the age at which she learned her bio mom didn't care and couldn't be relied on for any protection or comfort, but she'd probably been younger than Lissa. Little by little, she untangled the knot of grief, anger, resentment, relief, hope, and joy.

No point to be pissed over stuff I can't change. Stuff that's over.

Dr. Bystrova got her to realize she'd spent her whole life surrounded by threats or rivals. At no point did an adult exist in her periphery she trusted. Understanding her past on an intellectual level made it seem as if she read about someone else's life. Seeing this man she now called Dad being here in her room purely because he thought something bothered her pushed her into a headspace she'd never contemplated before.

"Sorry." Sima gathered her composure and rolled over to sit up.

"There's no reason for you to apologize." He smiled. "You are going through a great many adjustments. Being on a different planet is not the biggest one."

She chuckled while wiping her face dry. "You're right, something is bothering me but it's not why I started crying. Never had like parents before I could talk to. Used to keep everything inside. Didn't even have a friend I trusted enough."

He choked up a little.

She couldn't tell if he became emotional over her deciding to trust him or it came from pity. At the moment, it didn't matter. "So, umm. Yeah...." After a long exhale, she told him about stumbling into Kurosawa and his three friends. "… can't believe they're dealing alcohol like it's Nightmare Fuel or something. So ridiculous."

Dad's expression went pensive.

"Told them I didn't care and wasn't going to tell the Security team." She fidgeted at her hair. "Not planning to. Really isn't my problem. Only booze. Besides, they're clueless. They'll get caught without my help."

"I agree." He patted her back. "If they didn't specifically threaten you, something this minor isn't worth any disruption to your life."

She grinned. "Thanks, Dad."

"I'm not trying to replace your lost father, but I—and your mother—are here for you no matter what you need."

"Oh, go ahead and replace him." She scowled off to the side. "The woman who gave birth to me was only his mistress. As soon as he learned she got pregnant, he dumped her. She spent the next twelve years punishing me for making her easy ride go away. I don't even know what the man's name is or what he looks like."

"I… see."

"Don't be sad." She leaned against him. "I've never called anyone Dad before you. Never even been in the same room as the guy, so you've got full rights to the name 'Dad.' It still does kind of feel awkward to use 'Mom' and not mean it sarcastically. And wow, I still can't believe you guys took all four of us."

"Well." Dad wagged his eyebrows. "I came from a family of nine."

Whoa. What sort of crazy people have nine kids? She whistled in awe. Overpopulation aside, being able to afford caring for so many couldn't have been easy. "None of your brothers or sisters are here?"

"No." He shook his head. "I'm the youngest. Only two survived the war. I was only about eight then."

She blinked. "You're not that old. The End of Nations happened a really long time ago."

"Not that war."

"Umm." Sima peered up at him. "How could there be war after that? Earth became one government."

"Small, regional wars happen all the time. People who aren't close enough to see for themselves never hear of them. An impressively large group of Separatists attempted to wrest control of the area in which we lived. The fighting lasted for two years and a few months."

Sima looked down. "I'm sorry."

Dad spoke of his family. Two of his older brothers died in combat, fighting for the EGSF. One died when a Separatist-stolen EGSF combat aircraft was shot down and landed on his home. The other four brothers died randomly over the course of the conflict to stray bullets or errant explosions... all bystanders. Both of his sisters remained alive because they'd spent the entire duration of the war hiding in the basement with him and their mother.

"Is it wrong of me to hate Earth?" asked Sima.

"Don't blame the planet." He patted her arm.

"Duh. I'm blaming the people on it." She scuffed her feet back and forth across the carpet, unable to decide which side was wrong.

As a child, she'd been angry at the EGSF for not protecting her from her mother. After she ran away, she soon came to fear them, especially once she'd seen firsthand how they abused Outcasts. On the other hand, she agreed with the Separatists idea that the Earth Government had big problems... but their methods made them no better than the corruption they claimed to oppose.

"It must've been hard for you to leave your sisters behind."

He nodded. "Yes, but they understood. My expertise was needed, and Pai was so excited at the opportunity to research the biological specimens on this planet I couldn't say no and force her to stay on Earth. My sister, Bina, is too old to make the trip. My other sister, Naira, is happy on Earth."

Ugh. How could anyone be happy there? They must have a ton of glint. "We can't even send messages back home. I, umm, didn't even care about that until now. Sorry you have no way to talk to your sisters."

"It is an unfortunate circumstance. You are like Pai. No one there she cares to speak with." He winked.

"Is Mom trying to forget her life on Earth ever happened and pretend this is reality?" She kept scooting her feet back and forth, staring down. "I'm afraid it's all fake and I'm going to wake up."

He put an arm around her. "You sound frightened."

"I guess." She leaned into him again. "I want this to be real so bad I'm worried it isn't."

"It's real." Dad squeezed her hand. "Maybe you should consider slowing down and getting some air. You've been working so hard these past months. There is no need for you to burn yourself out."

Sima let a long, slow exhale drift out of her nose. "I know. Could plead trauma and stuff, ask for time. It's okay. Academics are fun for me. It doesn't feel like work."

"In that case, don't overindulge." He smiled. "For now, though, I suggest you go to sleep."

She glanced at the clock, which showed 12:02 blinking. The flashing numbers indicated the clock displayed the six-minute nonspace between days. "Ack! Yeah... Ugh."

"Ugh?" He tilted his head.

"I'm up too late. Waking up tomorrow is going to be hard. Night, Dad."

"Night, Sima." He stood. "I don't expect those people with the homemade liquor will bother you, but do stay careful. If anything happens, please let me know."

While yawning, she gave a thumbs-up. "I will."

After he left, she changed into her nightgown and burrowed under her bedding. She expected to stare at the ceiling half the night, her mind racing in circles between the anxiety of stumbling across a 'gang' selling alcohol, dreading everything would turn out to be VR, and the oddity of having a father—but before she knew it, she fell asleep.

5

EXTRA CREDIT

O ver the next few days, Sima caught herself slipping
somewhat back into her old habits.

She avoided being alone in secluded places and
constantly monitored her surroundings. Unlike Earth, the Progenitor Colony didn't have Scathers who might randomly kill her for
the fun of it, nor powerful underworld figures who'd send
someone to stick a knife in her back because she saw something she
shouldn't.

Merely a few desperate workers craving cheap booze.

It didn't seem likely they'd be watching her, but it didn't matter.
She had no intention of ratting them out. Her paranoia worried her
more than Kurosawa and his three friends. By her reasoning, if
anyone *did* follow her, they had enough skill at doing so to avoid
her noticing. Sima preferred to think no one followed her rather
than let her imagination torment her with phantom assassins.

The morning of April 16th (Mirage) started with an unusual
scene. Mom buzzed around over breakfast in a fit of excitement and
worry. Sima had applied and been accepted for a one-time tempo-
rary OT, serving as a research assistant on a short trip out away
from the colony. Being both a medical doctor and a botanist

allowed Mom to set aside her parental fears for Sima's safety and become excited at the learning opportunity.

Dr. Vivek Desai, one of the Progenitor Colony's biologists, wanted to collect plant samples from a location thirty or so miles away he'd previously scouted via drone.

Saturday offered something tastier than the beige nutrient porridge they usually ate on weekdays to save time when everyone had to rush off to school or work soon after waking up. Some genius figured out how to make jelly from those fruit pods and get rid of the bitter aftertaste. Another—or maybe even the same— person devised a way to process the 'space cucumbers' Sima and the kids found into bread, or something close enough to bread to count.

She'd never had jelly on toast before arriving here. Despite being sick to death of those raspberry-tart fruit pods, she adored the preserves.

"You should be proud!" Dad beamed at her.

"Yay!" cheered Lissa. "Don't get eated by the night scratch!"

Austin and Juan stared at each other, then Sima.

"There's night scratches there?" asked Austin in a hesitant voice.

"No. We're going in the opposite direction from where we crashed." Sima pointed at the wall as if she knew off the top of her head.

The Omnicomputer screen activated, presenting a corrected directional arrow.

Sima swung her arm around to point behind her to the left.

Everyone except Mom laughed.

"We know so little about those… quill cats?" Mom scratched her head. "What their range is, distribution, diet, and so on."

"I know what their diet is," said Lissa.

Sima's heart practically leapt into her throat… until the child grinned.

"Bad kitties!" Lissa shook her head. "Not like Orange. Orange is a nice kitty. I hope he's okay."

"I'm sure he is." Sima forced a smile, preferring to think some random nice person found and adopted Lissa's former cat. The girl had at least seen the animal alive after the Pixie lab exploded. It hadn't so much been 'her' cat as a stray she fed sometimes.

"I still think you should be proud." Dad smeared jam on a second piece of toast. "Seventeen and you're working with Dr. Desai."

"It's not that big a deal." Sima waved him off. "I was the only person who applied."

Mom laughed. "I doubt that. I'm sure he selected you because of your experience. You are a bit of a celebrity in the lab."

"I didn't do anything special. Just lived like a cavewoman for a little while." She shrugged. "Not like I studied the plants or made any breakthroughs. Only had as much education as Austin."

The boy furrowed his brows. "What's that supposed to mean?"

"You went to school until age eleven. I went to school until age twelve. We had about the same amount. It means I'm not a biologist or a botanist."

"Oh." He nodded.

"You will be." Mom grinned.

"Probably." Sima smiled, pretending an indifferent shrug. She often talked with her mother about science, as she found it fascinating. As the price for being safe on Mirage was eventually getting an OT and working—which she had zero problems with—she may as well do something both fun and beneficial. "Good chance. I'm definitely *not* going to join the Security team."

Her parents chuckled.

"Well..." Sima stood. "I better get going. Wouldn't want to be late and make a bad first impression."

DR. VIVEK DESAI somewhat reminded Sima of her adoptive father.

Both men had the quality of not taking themselves too seriously. While Dad struck her as 'cute' sometimes, especially in the kitchen,

Dr. Desai seemed like the 'cool' teacher who'd help some kids set off a smoke bomb in the principal's office if no one was watching. Good thing for everyone involved he taught biology and not chemistry. He looked unremarkable, neat, and professional like any other researcher. She figured him a few years shy of fifty, a little older than Dad.

When she'd gone to the Center to meet him at the lab facility, he'd been formal and serious, to the point she'd started to dread the day ahead of her. On the walk across the building to the vehicle garage, she'd expected him to be a complete prig. She'd also been expecting to go out in a Nomad, one of the giant all-terrain vehicles the soldiers used to retrieve her and the kids from the wilds.

Instead, they approached a small rover. The strange vehicle resembled a beetle, due to having a rounded front cabin attached to a boxy body the size of an ordinary gee-vee riding high on six enormous white tires. Every vehicle she'd ever seen on Earth had rather small tires, not even as high as her knees. These came up to her chest, as fat as they were tall. Where an Earth vehicle would have had cargo space or extra passenger seating, this one carried an assortment of scientific equipment, storage bins, and a modest load of survival supplies. Along the top rested a retractable robotic arm, likely intended to collect samples or perform basic tasks in atmospheres too dangerous for humans. The bubble-shaped, two-seat cabin looked like it belonged more on a helicopter... one of the small, silent, electric ones the EGSF used to spy on people at night. Only, those didn't have seats or people inside them. Merely cameras.

Sima approached the passenger side door and grasped a simple pull handle at her eye level. Getting in required climbing a three-rung ladder. Clear material extended down to the base of her seat, making her feel as if she sat inside an enormous glass egg. Despite the oddity of being able to see the two front wheels below and in front of her, she trembled from excitement. Leaving the safety of the colony behind scared her to a point, but this experience would be a huge boost to her future. If she made a good impression on the professor, it could open opportunities for her.

Deep breaths, Seem. Just need to worry about two things. Don't say anything stupid. Don't get eaten.

Dr. Desai's demeanor changed entirely once he hopped in and closed the door. The strict, professional scientist gave her a look somewhere between excited boy and crazy friend about to do something recklessly fun.

Sima swallowed a little saliva and pulled her door shut with a soft *whump*.

"I apologize in advance if I put this thing upside down." He fiddled at a few buttons, as if having forgotten how to turn it on. The fourth control he poked made the console light up. "Aha! There it is." He spent a moment fussing at a navigation system until a map came up, then gripped the control sticks and nudged the rover into motion. "Only my second time driving one of these."

"This is only my third time in a vehicle at all, so I can't criticize." Sima chuckled. "It's got six giant wheels and a low center of gravity. You'd really have to work hard to mess up so bad it rolls over."

"Good observations. Still, I should hold off on the rum until we get back." He glanced at her. "You didn't bring any, did you?"

Uhh. Does he know about Kurosawa? She gripped her knees. "Uhh… no."

"Relax. I'm merely making a joke." He smiled. "I don't indulge much. One drink a week."

"Oh." She raked her fingers at her hair, chuckling. "Right."

"The secret to sticking to my regimen is a huge glass." He winked.

Assuming he joked, she kept laughing. The man didn't look or smell like an alcoholic.

The rover wouldn't set any land speed records, but it did move faster than a person could run. Based on the creep of their dot on the map screen, she guessed it would take them about an hour to reach the sample site. Whether or not the continuous whirr of electric motors drove her nuts by then remained to be seen.

"For what reason did you apply for this excursion?" asked Dr. Desai.

"Extra credit."

He snickered. "I cannot say I've ever met a student before willing to accept potentially dangerous extra credit work. Except for the geologists. Will never understand their fascination with volcanoes and things that explode at random. I prefer my science of the less incendiary type."

"Yeah. Me, too." She tapped her fingers on the armrest. "But, I think all the science on this planet is going to be dangerous for a while. Even if we're only going to be picking flowers, we have no idea what might be there."

He nodded in an exaggerated manner, then looked over at her. "Yet you still wanted to go."

"Yeah. It's probably stupid of me. I already played chicken with a quill cat... more than once." She whistled. "Really ought to spend the rest of my life hiding in a safe, warm place." She paused. "Nah. Too boring."

"I see. Boring is definitely bad. Are you *sure* you want to pursue work in a science field? There are *lots* of boring parts. It's basically seven hours of drooling on yourself for every thirty seconds of heart-stopping excitement... wait, no, that's archaeology."

"I thought archaeology was two weeks of drooling for every ten seconds of thrill."

Dr. Desai cackled. "I believe your estimation is closer to correct."

She grinned, gazing out the side window at fields of rolling blue grass and distant blue-purple trees. "Has anyone figured out why chlorophyll on Mirage is blue?"

"In basic terms, it reflects blue light and absorbs green. *Why* it does this, we're uncertain still. This system's solar radiation is comparable to that of Earth, but not entirely identical. We know a single chromosome being different can result in huge changes in an organism. It's going to take us a while to determine how much of an effect a few minuscule variances in the sun here has."

"Umm. It's not dangerous to *us* is it?"

"Not that we've seen. Seeds brought from Earth are growing. Green chlorophyll does not appear to be putting them at any measurable disadvantage… but there must be some reason for it."

She nodded.

"I understand you have some hands-on experience with the local flora."

"One way to say it." She smirked. "I found one plant with leaves sharp enough to use as throwing weapons. Long, green ones too brittle and rigid to make garments out of, but they're really fibrous. Couldn't weave them into a skirt. Maybe they could be mashed up, and the fibers used to create fabric." She proceeded to tell him about her experiences while living wild, sparing the embarrassing parts and focusing on plants and creatures.

He seemed enthralled by her story of the massive ichor-stained vines Lissa used to paint herself purple.

"I do hope you are interested in pursuing biology. I think you will do quite well in the field." He whistled to himself. "Usually, people your age are obsessed with sports, musicians, or what color to paint their nails. It's a pleasure to see a young woman interested in scientific research."

She gave him side eye. *Does he not know where I came from?* She exhaled out her nose. *Stay calm. I am not an Outcast pretending to be a Citizen. Earth was nothing but a bad dream.* "Giving serious consideration to it."

"Your mother is Pai Chen, correct?"

"Yes."

"She works with my team sometimes. Her group is doing great things. I'm sure she's proud of you."

Okay, he has *to know I'm adopted. No way does he think she's my bio mom. I don't look at all like her. Maybe he doesn't care.* "She is." Sima smiled, feeling weird and warm inside her chest. "I'd rather work in an academic field, anyway. Maybe I applied for this job because

I've been out there already and feel like I have something to contribute. Didn't look at anything under a microscope, but I've seen a variety of plants which aren't growing anywhere near the colony."

"Excellent."

"Oh... be careful near the giant red flowers. We're a little big, but one of them tried to eat my brother."

"Eat him?" Dr. Desai gawked. "I am insanely curious how that came to be."

"Early one morning, he was half awake and saw this gaping giant flower that looked like a boy toilet, and, well... the flower objected. When I found him, just his feet stuck out of the top of this huge flower."

Dr. Desai laughed so hard he had to stop driving for a moment.

"The base has all these long vines. They grabbed us, moving like an octopus. Really strange for a plant to be able to move."

"That is absolutely fascinating. I cannot wait to get a specimen of one in my lab."

Sima pointed back over her shoulder. "We're going to need a larger vehicle."

"They're that big?"

"About as tall as an eleven-year-old boy, plus roots underground."

He whistled.

She folded her arms. "And this plant is going to resist being 'sampled.'"

Dr. Desai chuckled. "Ahh, new world, new wonders."

They crested a hill in the meadow onto a long, downhill slope. A mile or so ahead at the bottom, a flock of the huge flamingo-like birds walked in a single-file line, heading toward a lake. Dr. Desai brought the rover to a stop, hastily grabbed a video recorder, and began filming.

Sima leaned forward, face near the plastic windscreen, watching the tall, graceful animals striding off. Even at a lazy stroll, they appeared to be covering ground faster than the rover could move.

"The kids called them 'aurak' because it sounds like their noises. Those birds are intelligent."

"Fascinating," whispered Dr. Desai.

"When we were stranded, Austin found an injured aurak. After he pulled the quill cat spines out of it, the bird showed gratitude. It even let him climb on for a ride. Couple of days later, one of those cats attacked us. I thought we were in big trouble, but the same group of birds came rushing over and chased the cat off. They remembered. The whole flock understood we helped one of their friends, and the mother—I think—swam over to thank us."

"Amazing... there is clearly some manner of predator-prey relationship between them." He smiled. "Cats do love to chase birds."

Sima raised an eyebrow at him. "Doesn't work so well when the birds are big enough to step on the cats."

He laughed.

"I'm not sure we should expect any animal on Mirage to behave in a certain way because it resembles an Earth animal. It is kinda weird how similar they are, though."

"You are correct." Dr. Desai nodded once, seeming impressed. "This is *not* Earth. Making assumptions is the last thing a true scientist should do. It's fine to start off with expectations, but observed evidence must alter our expectations to fit reality."

She twirled a bit of hair around her finger. "Yes. Strange as it is, the cat that pestered us for a couple days acted basically like a giant housecat going after mice in a box. Why would a planet so far away from Earth have animals so similar to ours? Sure, no cat on Earth has venom-tipped quills, but.... You know."

Once the aurak moved off too far to be worth video recording any more, Dr. Desai resumed driving. A screen in the center of the console displayed a map of the area, showing a glowing dotted line to the location selected for sampling. "The similarities play into a theory I've had since my college days."

"You still teach, don't you?" She blinked.

"I meant my time as a college *student*. The End of Nations destroyed an unfortunate amount of scientific data collected prior to the *big* war, but some remnants I studied made me suspect an outside force seeded ancient Earth with life. In fact, it may have transformed an otherwise dead planet into one capable of sustaining life."

She gave him side eye. "You mean like God?"

"No… nothing magic. I'm talking about aliens." He gestured at the windscreen as if to say 'look at this.' "It is not beyond imagination to theorize the same civilization responsible for getting things started on Earth visited other worlds. Mirage is unbelievably similar in so many ways. The minor differences we are seeing could be attributable to the process of transforming a dead rock into a vibrant biosphere. Minute variations in the composition of the starting state of the planet prior to their arrival caused the process to run ever so slightly awry. Hence, blue chlorophyll here."

"It's almost as if the same source made both."

"Something to that effect, yes." He looked over at her. "You think a god did it?"

"When I was little, I sometimes asked a god to tell my mother to care about me or protect me from whatever scary man she brought home. If any sort of god is real, they never listened. Many kids my age had it *way* worse than me. What kind of god would let the big war happen, and do nothing to stop famines, plagues, all sorts of evil?" She continued twirling her hair around. "If it exists, he, she, or it is cruel and I'm not going to worship it. Or, I dunno. Maybe it is real but doesn't even know we exist. Humans don't care what happens to bacteria."

"Hmm. Curious."

"What is?" She peered through her hair at him.

"Have you ever wondered why a significant portion of people on Earth maintain belief in a supernatural being of extreme power, often with magical abilities despite never having seen any proof of its existence… yet the minute someone like me starts suggesting aliens exist, we're called crazy."

She snickered. "Probably because if aliens did it, it means the god they want to believe in *didn't* do it."

"Not necessarily. Who's to say the god they want to believe is real didn't make aliens, too? If a god existed and made humans, it stands to reason it would have made any other being out there. I do not understand the human exceptionalism."

"Hmm." Sima shrugged.

"Perhaps it is defensiveness. Ahh well. My field is not psychology. Still, if you calculate the sheer number of planets known to exist by a tiny chance of life happening, the answer is much higher than zero. It is a statistical certainty living organisms exist on planets other than Earth, yet it's viewed as nonsense... even among respected scientists."

"Umm, Dr. Desai?" Sima bit her lip.

"Yes?"

"My first day on Mirage, I found a cave that looked like someone used to live there. If we are the first humans here, it means aliens *definitely* exist."

The soft electronic patter of the Omnicomputer typing out a text message came from her bracelet.

"And my bracelet just corrected me to say *we* are the aliens here." She raised her forearm so she could look at the screen. Sure enough, it wrote exactly what she expected. "I know. I know... but if we were still on Earth, civilization here would be alien to us." Sima let her arm fall into her lap. "Once the kids were with me, I took them back to the same place thinking it would be fun to show them. Juan managed to open a door by a secret switch and fell down into an underground complex."

Dr. Desai stared at her. Fortunately, they cruised over open grassland, so his not looking where he drove didn't matter for the time being. "Why has no one mentioned this?"

She held her hands up in a 'who knows?' manner. "I gave them the information my bracelet scanned. Some of the walls down there had writing on them. One of my teachers, Ms. Taylor, is working on translating it in her free time."

"Hmm." He kept staring at her. "You've piqued my interest. Once we are back at the colony, I will have to see this scan data. I'm also quite interested in taking a closer look at these... what did you call them, aurak?"

"Yes. We shouldn't treat them like normal animals and capture or experiment on them. It's ethically wrong since they are intelligent enough to comprehend being helped, and then aware enough to help us in return. They demonstrated the capacity to understand intent behind actions as well as the ability to remember us."

Dr. Desai offered a slow nod. "It is worth less invasive experiments. Attempting to visit and communicate, for example. Besides, it would be too much work to build bird cages that size."

She chuckled.

For the next twenty-seven minutes, Dr. Desai peppered her with questions about the alien facility she and the kids had been stuck in for a while. The last time she'd thought about the place, she never wanted to go anywhere near it again, but after a brief discussion, she agreed to lead him there at some undetermined future date. As the navigation map pointer neared their destination, they entered a swath of forest consisting of the familiar bluish-violet trees and fruit pods.

Dr. Desai stopped the rover when the foliage became too thick for them to travel deeper into the woods with the vehicle. "It appears we must walk from here."

"How far is it?" Sima pulled up on the handle to open the door on her side.

"No specific point. I wanted to visit this general area. Looking to gather a variety of samples of plant life. Hopefully, we can obtain some specimens not available within walking distance of the colony."

Sima slipped out and dropped to the ground in the space between the front and middle tire. She hurried around to meet the doctor at the back. He opened the cargo hatch, grabbed two sample kits, and handed them to her before grabbing two more and walking off.

"You're going to leave the door open?"

Dr. Desai kept walking. "Expecting someone to run by and steal from us here?"

"Oh. Right. Yeah…" She gazed around at the woods. *Way to go, Seem… act like an idiot in front of the man who's going to be teaching me in three years. Real smart. Maybe three years… probably won't take his class my first year after high school.*

She stared into space for a moment, stunned at the realization she would be able to take college classes. Most Citizens on Earth stopped after grade twelve unless their families had money or political power. Sometimes, a kid could distinguish themselves academically enough to get the attention of a university, but generally, only the upper social classes attended. If she'd had a stable—or at least safe—home, she probably could have scored her way in.

But none of it mattered now.

She could learn whatever she wanted.

Thrilled, she jogged after Dr. Desai.

They walked deeper into the woods, examining various plants. Sima pointed out the brittle, gossamer strands she'd tried (and failed) to make clothing out of as well as some of the bushes with 'ninja star' leaves. Dr. Desai appeared quite impressed at the sharpness of the edges as well as the hardness. She mostly took photographs and observed as he collected samples. The fruit pods grew near the colony, so he paid them little attention as they'd been well documented already.

Sima described the chest-high roots covered in indigo ink—none of which appeared to be growing in this area. Her Omnicomputer bracelet hadn't been able to determine the purpose of the dye, or why a plant would 'sweat' it. Dr. Desai guessed the substance served as the plant's sap or tasted horrible as a deterrent to being eaten.

"Didn't try tasting it. People live longer when they don't lick strange substances." Sima spotted a spread of tiny red-orange flowers growing low to the ground a distance away. "Doctor? New plant. I never saw those little flowers before."

"Excellent. Would you mind taking some pictures of them? I'll be there as soon as I finish this seed extraction."

"Sure."

Sima hurried over to the new discovery. A series of individual plants, roughly twelve inches tall, grew close together to create the appearance of a 'carpet.' Each one sported approximately twenty small flowers growing among soft, blue leaves. She crouched and started taking photographs, zooming in close on the different parts.

"I've seen pictures of a similar plant from Earth, except the flowers were white." She held one of the blooms open to get a good image of the inside.

Pattering text came from the bracelet, along with a mild electrical shock.

"Ack!" yelped Sima, nearly dropping the camera. She opened her mouth to call the bracelet a jerk for zapping her, but stopped herself. It wouldn't have done so if it didn't *need* her immediate attention for a serious reason, so she kept her mouth shut and turned her arm to read the holographic screen.

‹Danger! Thirty-seven feet straight ahead.›

Sima lifted her gaze from the small glowing screen, over a smear of blue and orange—at a dark shape among the trees. A creature with four luminous green eyes watched her from the shadows. The upper pair being larger and wider-spaced than the second set told her exactly what watched her.

A quill cat.

"Doctor?" whispered Sima. "We've got a big problem."

"How big?" asked Dr. Desai in a relatively casual tone.

"About six hundred pounds." She swallowed. "It's looking right at me."

He froze, turning only his head to glance at her. All the joviality fled from his face. "Get back to the rover."

"If it's exactly like a cat, it's going to chase me if I run." Sima rose to stand, side-stepping to her left.

The cat crept forward. Five shiny, metallic claws peeked out from between tufts of blue fur on its lead paw. Narrow silvery quills studded the pod at the end of its swishing tail.

She stared at the pattern of thin white stripes on its furry cheeks, its huge pink nose, and flashed back to the last time she'd been face to face with one of them. She and the kids took refuge in a root dome under a giant tree, surrounded on all sides by quill cats. At the time, she believed no other people survived the 'crash' of the *Progenitor*. She expected to die no matter what she did, but refused to let the beasts lay one claw on any of the children while she still drew breath.

Charging *at* one of them with a starship fire axe had been sheer desperation.

At the moment, she didn't have a fire axe, merely an eight-inch knife. Nor did she have the unshakable resolve to protect kids in immediate danger or the fatalistic expectation of inevitable death. Austin, Juan, and Lissa remained safe in the colony. She had a future… a family.

The quill cat narrowed all four of its eyes.

Acting tough hadn't mattered much last time. She couldn't scare it off when she had the overwhelming need to protect the kids crushing her fear. It already stalked after her. Walking away calm wouldn't help. Sima had two choices.

Run… or die.

She bolted toward Dr. Desai, who pulled a handgun off his belt. Sima ducked as he fired a few shots. The cat snarled, but didn't sound hurt. She half crashed into him, grabbing his left arm and trying to pull him along. He fired rapidly to the rear as they ran side by side toward the rover. The heavy thumping of a charging cat came up behind them.

Too slow!

If she let go and sprinted, she could easily outrun him. The cat would probably take the easier meal and let her go. Sima couldn't do it. She struggled to pull Dr. Desai faster.

Something whistled overhead.

Why did he stop firing?

She spared him a split-second glance. He'd given up looking behind them, entirely focused on trying to run.

Out of bullets?

The second time a faint whistle went over their heads, she caught a flash of silver reflecting sunlight—a quill.

She yelped, ducked, and pulled him to the left. "Weave the trees!"

They slalomed around trunks as big as portable bathrooms. Every time a hollow *thok* sound announced a quill striking wood, she zigzagged. The cat chased in a series of small jumps, flinging a quill at them each time it landed.

Finally, the rover came into view in the less dense woods ahead.

"Get the door!" yelled Dr. Desai. He stopped running ten feet from the rover and spun, firing wildly in the direction of the cat—which skidded to a stop, flicking its tail up.

Sima sprinted the last few strides to the driver side door.

As soon as she grabbed the handle, Dr. Desai dove into her from behind. A *clank* came from a quill bouncing off the rover above her. She shoved the door open, but the doctor didn't let go of her, his body more rigid than anything.

Crap! He's been hit.

She squirmed around to face him. A little awareness remained in his eyes. He had the distant far-off gaze of a drug addict riding the strongest part of a high. Dr. Desai weakly reached his left arm up to grab the handle on the rover's frame by the opening. His right side already appeared fully paralyzed.

Evidently spooked by the gunfire, the cat remained a short distance away, swishing its tail, likely waiting for its intended dinner to fall over and stop moving.

"Thank you for not being a big guy." Sima shoved Dr. Desai up into the cab.

As soon as she moved, the cat dashed forward.

She screamed and jumped in on top of the doctor, slamming the hatch closed two seconds before the cat crashed into it. Several hundred pounds of angry feline hit the vehicle hard enough to fling

Sima into the passenger seat. She bounced off the cushion and slid headfirst into the well below the console, feet in the air.

The rover rocked back and forth from the cat's assault. She grabbed the wall for support while twisting over to sit right side up. Dr. Desai lay slumped face-down over the seats. One long silver quill stuck out of his back by his right shoulder. She didn't know if the thin spike delivered all the venom in an instant or if leaving it in him would worsen the dose, but still hastily yanked it loose and tossed it over the seatback out of harm's way.

Claws raked the rover, accompanied by ear-piercing screeches of scraped metal. She gasped in fear at the sudden realization they'd left the rear hatch open, but fortunately, no opening or hatch connected the cabin to the cargo area. Even if the cat decided to squeeze into the back, it wouldn't be able to get at them. After making its way completely around the rover, it attacked the cockpit. Frantic paw swipes left white gouges in the windows. Sima stared at the marks, shivering in fear, watching the cat methodically attack the door in a manner suggesting it understood the concept of a hatch—perhaps even recognizing the handle's purpose. She didn't think cat paws would be able to operate it, but she also didn't want to take chances.

Sima smacked the button for the lock, then ducked down to huddle on the floor under the console. Given most of the floor under her happened to be transparent didn't help matters. Anywhere she went in the cabin, the cat could see her. Like a hamster trapped in a plastic ball, she held still and hoped her shelter withstood the punishment.

At least with the locks engaged, even if the cat managed to pull the handle in the correct manner, it had no chance of getting inside. Her worry became the plastic window bubble and the doors. The material scratched rather easily, though its great thickness gave her some confidence it could withstand any beating a large cat could dish out. When she fought to get Juan and Lissa out of their stasis pod, she'd battered a window only as thick as her finger, and it proved remarkably difficult to break open using an axe. The rover's canopy roughly tripled the stasis pod lid for thickness.

Hope it's the same stuff.

For a few terrifying minutes, Sima jumped and cringed at an endless barrage of paw slaps, bites, and lunges. It did *not* fill her with confidence how much the rover rocked each time the beast pounced at it. She kept still, hoping the cat would tire of its futile assault and go away. After about twenty minutes, it gave up and began pacing back and forth in front of the rover. She sat still, not daring to even breathe too loud.

"Dr. Desai?" she asked maybe ten minutes after the cat stopped attacking the rover.

He emitted a weak moan and murmured something about the sample cases.

She blinked. "What?"

A shadow moved under her. She peered down through the bubble floor at the cat passing by underneath. Being inches away from such a deadly creature made every hair on her body stand on end. The dark blue tail drifted behind it like a serpent swimming in the air, glimmers of silver—unlaunched quills—peeking out from the tuft at the end. The cat meandered off into the woods, not looking back.

Whew.

Another moan came from Dr. Desai.

Sima started to glance at him, but the patter of electronic text diverted her gaze to her arm.

‹I believe he said 'We forgot the sample cases'›, typed the bracelet. ‹I also believe he intended it as humor.›

She bowed her head, too wound up on adrenaline to laugh or cry. "Did you send a distress call?"

‹We are too far away for my transmitter to reach. The rover's transmission dish is broken. I believe that's it on the ground over there.›

"Dammit!" She exhaled. "At least it gave up. I can probably drive this thing."

Wham!

The rover jolted, lurching toward the driver's side. Sima screamed—mostly out of surprise. She caught a brief glimpse of the quill cat going overhead as the rover rolled off its wheels. Up became down. Being on the floor already, she tumbled over the curved wall, ending up on the roof, which had become the floor. Something metal and painful bounced off her left knee and clattered to the plastic bubble window beside her leg. Dr. Desai flew face first into the passenger-side door like a dropped mannequin, then crumpled into a heap partially on top of her.

"Oof," grunted Sima. "Crap! This is not good."

Dr. Desai moaned.

Text patter came from the bracelet.

It's going to say something obvious. Despite knowing she'd regret it, she twisted her arm to look.

‹I believe he said 'Ouch.'›

Sima rubbed the sore spot on her knee. As soon as she noticed the handgun next to her, the likely culprit, she picked it up before thinking about it. For an instant, she froze in panic. EGSF officers would kill any Outcast they saw with a gun. Even someone innocently trying to turn it in to them because they found it. In the back of her mind, she'd just committed a crime punishable by death.

Not on Earth anymore.

She exhaled.

A tiny green display on the back end of the weapon showed 02. Though she'd never so much as laid one finger on a firearm before, she'd seen them used often enough to have a general idea. Point it at something and pull the trigger.

"Two shots left… definitely not enough."

A patch of fog formed on the clear barrier, the quill cat's nose almost touching as it sniffed. Sima cringed away, pressing herself into the mostly upside-down seat behind her. A similar cat trapping her and the kids in an escape pod the size of a small cabin had been scary, but that experience seemed like a pleasant vacation compared to a small, clear bubble.

Shaking, she raised the gun in both hands, staring over it at the huge cat less than two feet away from her. So close, but unable to hurt her. *It can't get us in here. It can't get us in here.*

It snarled, pawing at the window. Each swipe of its claws left five thin, white scratches.

"Go away! Please don't make me hurt you. I will, but I don't want to." She rested her finger on the trigger, as frightened of the weapon as the cat.

The holographic screen appeared under her left arm.

‹Do not fire at the window. The resin will trap the bullet. Save your shots in case it finds a way inside. Make them count. You'll need to hit it in the brain at close range to kill it using a small personal defense weapon. Those rounds will likely not have the power to reach its heart.›

Great. I am so screwed. She looked around at the cabin. Due to its design, a brick-like body perched atop a wide wheelbase, the rover hadn't quite ended up on its back. The driver side wheels still touched the ground.

I *can worry about how to get home later…*

She squeezed the pistol grip. "Bad kitty. Go away. Don't make me have to tell Lissa I killed another one."

The quill cat roared and lunged at the glass.

6

A SERIES OF PROBLEMS

S ima screamed, flinching away from five hundred pounds of
cat slamming into the windscreen.

The rover didn't move much. After another rapid
barrage of paw-slapping the canopy, the cat sat on its back end,
curling its tail around its front paws, staring at her and giving off a
noticeable air of annoyance.

She couldn't help but be reminded of an evil cartoon lion from
an ancient movie, all the intelligence—and ability to speak—of a
person in the body of a cat. Each passing minute she gazed into its
four glowing green eyes, the more certain she became the beast was
furious at her for escaping into the rover. It may not have possessed
the intelligence to operate door handles or comprehend the
purpose of a vehicle, but it appeared to grasp the concept of shelter.

Irony sometimes had claws as sharp as the cat's. Sima hadn't
watched movies since she'd run away from home. She'd survived
four years in a world every bit as dangerous as Mirage, owning no
technology more advanced than a Dreamland-connected tunic she
couldn't even use for anything more than clothing. The global
information network didn't do Outcasts much good unless they
possessed the skills to hack up a fake Citizen account. Here she sat,

surrounded in a literal shell of the best technology humanity had...
and it couldn't help her against a wild animal.

This is backward. The animal's supposed to be in the cage at the zoo.
She glanced down at the pistol, then lowered it. No sense pointing
it at the quill cat. Wasting a bullet into the windshield would
accomplish nothing. A meager two shots probably wouldn't help
either, but if she had to use them, it wouldn't be at long-range.
Even a girl who'd never touched a gun before had a reasonable
chance of hitting a large quill cat from two feet away. Also, if the
canopy would trap a bullet, she felt much better about its ability to
protect her from the cat.

Dr. Desai emitted a pained moan.

A flicker of greenish light came from her arm. The Omnicomputer bracelet displayed a message: ‹He is either apologizing for
placing you in a dangerous situation or expressing discomfort at
being folded in half.›

"Sorry." Sima set the gun on the floor—formerly the roof.

She struggled to reposition him as close to lying comfortably on
his back as possible. The rover cabin didn't quite have enough
width laterally for him to stretch out across the seats. Seeing as how
the vehicle had almost rolled upside down, they had less available
room. She propped him seated up against the bottom of the driver-
side door, then arranged his arms at his sides.

He gave a grunt of gratitude.

The beast continued watching them, its nose an inch from the
windshield.

She tried not to give the creature any satisfaction by acting
scared. As much as her brain allowed, she ignored its existence and
focused on watching Dr. Desai to make sure he didn't stop breathing. When Juan suffered a hit from a quill, he'd come close to dying
a few times. Without immediate danger, the thought of having to
give an adult man rescue breathing made her feel awkward.
However, if he stopped breathing, she'd certainly forget all about
the awkwardness until after.

Please don't stop breathing.

"I know you're awake and can still see and hear."

He emitted a faint moan.

"The cat's right outside. I think it tried to tackle the rover. We're kinda upside down, but it can't get us. A different one of those cats hit my little brother with the same venom. You're going to be okay. He was fine. Uhh, I mean, he almost stopped breathing a few times, but he's only eight, and malnourished. Or was."

Dr. Desai wheezed.

She fidgeted the handgun's safety on and off repetitively. "You're probably happy you collected a sample of the quill."

His lip twitched, perhaps an attempted smile.

"We're thirty-nine miles away from the colony. No one's seen one of these cats yet, so they haven't gotten close… at least in the meadow. We should probably document this as the closest one has been sighted to us. Think they're afraid of the city or did we simply get lucky and land somewhere they don't go?"

He emitted a feeble bird-like squawk.

Sima blinked.

‹I believe he means no aurak have been seen from the city.›

"Oh. Umm. Maybe. The cats *try* to hunt them, but I think the birds usually win. When one of those cats chased Austin up a tree, an aurak stormed over and the cat ran off."

Dr. Desai gave an urgent moan.

Text patter came from the bracelet.

‹He is most likely annoyed he cannot speak. Certain prey species with herd mentality have been known to turn aggressive against predators if threatened. A single cat fleeing from attacking aurak does not prove the dynamic of their predator-prey relationship. It would be nice for you to say this aloud so Dr. Desai is not frustrated.›

Sima read the message out loud.

He grunted approvingly.

"Those furry deer-like creatures are in the meadow near the colony. If I was a quill cat, I'd hunt them instead of birds big enough to step on me like a bug. Or those little piglet things." Sima peered out the corner of her eye at the windscreen.

No cat.

"Ooh… he's gone." She cautiously looked around.

The 'cockpit' style of the cabin made for a terrifying cage, but it also gave her a wide field of view. Unless the cat slipped around directly behind the rover where she couldn't see, it finally gave up.

"I'm not sure if they're really smart or if I imagined it. Maybe it *is* sneaky enough to hide and try tricking us. Going to wait a little more."

Ugh. How long are we going to be stuck here?

She peered up at the passenger side wheels dangling in the air. Except for one yellow warning light marked 'orientation alert,' nothing on the console gave any indication of a malfunction or serious damage. As far as she could see, the rover took the roll in stride. Then again, it had probably been designed to handle environments far worse than Mirage.

You'd think they'd have given it a tougher transmission dish. Stupid cat broke it off like a toy.

"How many planets have we visited?" asked Sima. "Don't answer. I know you can't. People must have been going into space for a long time. It's kinda silly to think they just made the *Progenitor* right away after discovering this planet."

‹Humanity has been engaging in manned space flight extending beyond our solar system for 284 years. Mirage is the first attempt to establish a permanent colony, or any installation larger than two-dozen scientists. Travel time is the limiting factor. My data mentions three scientific expeditions launched before you were ever born, which have still not reached their destinations.›

"If they're so far, how does anyone know they didn't get there yet?" She chuckled. "What did they do, make a wrong turn?"

‹We do not know their status, merely that the expected duration of their trips, assuming no errors or problems, exceeds thirty years one-way.›

She whistled. "Thirty years to go to a planet where they're

going to be stuck inside a pod or a rover like this because the atmosphere isn't breathable? Who would *want* to do something like that?"

‹Scientists.›

"Is it a one-way trip?"

‹I do not have the specific parameters of their missions. However, their research would do no one any good if it stayed out there. Consequently, my assumption is they will return.›

"Whoa. Thirty years to get there, spend a year or whatever there, then thirty back? That's still crazy."

Dr. Desai wheezed.

"Eep!" She scrambled onto all fours, instinctively moving to start rescue breathing, but stopped a few inches from lip contact when she noticed he still appeared to be conscious. "Are you having trouble breathing? Make two noises for no."

Dr. Desai grunted twice.

She sat back on her heels. *Whew.* "Hoping it's not as bad for you as it was for Juan since you're a lot bigger than him."

He groaned.

"I'm not calling you fat. He's tiny… or used to be. The boys have put on weight since we found the colony. Lissa's still too skinny. The boys look healthy now."

She leaned against the inverted seat, rambling about her new family merely to have something to talk about and to reassure herself. Thinking of them bolstered her nerve. Even if the paralytic toxin in the quill had zero chance of threatening Dr. Desai's life, it would render him unable to move for somewhere between four to eight hours. Mom, being a medical doctor, studied the reports from all the tests they ran on Juan after his initial arrival.

Not wanting to stress Dr. Desai too much, she didn't mention how long he'd be unable to move. She also didn't want to spend eight hours sitting there.

"This thing's made to explore hazardous environments. Are there cameras on the back?"

Dr. Desai grunted in a tone of 'no idea.'

Sima poked around the controls. It didn't take long for her to find an entire panel dedicated to 'exterior view cameras.' Four buttons switched between cameras, and a tiny joystick allowed her to pan each one around. Alas, camera three had an amazing view of dirt, its housing likely being at the rear driver's side corner, and thus, embedded in the ground. Its opposite, camera four, had a good elevated view to the rear.

She panned back and forth as far to either side as the camera could move. If the quill cat still observed the rover, it would have to be at least sixty or seventy meters away, hidden in trees. It sounded reckless to think about, but she felt confident in her ability to dart back inside if she saw it coming. As an added precaution, she stuffed the handgun in her jumpsuit's pocket.

"Okay. Time to go home." Sima stepped on the side of the driver's seat, stretching to reach the passenger door overhead. Pulling the handle did nothing. *Crap! Something broke when we rolled!* Grunting, she struggled at the lever above her in increasing desperation for a minute or three until she noticed the bracelet's holo-panel glowing above the underside of her left forearm.

‹Lock.›

"Oh. Right." She sighed, and sheepishly pushed the button to disengage the door locks.

The door—now basically a roof hatch—proved to be surprisingly light. She had no difficulty pushing it upward out of her way and climbing to sit on the outside hull between two giant barrel-shaped wheels. They looked massive, but weren't solid. At least, she assumed so. Had tires this size been solid, the rover would've been far too heavy for the quill cat to knock over. Considering the width of the wheelbase, it shocked her the beast had managed to roll it at all.

He must've been mad. Or she.

After a few minutes of not having a cat come running, she stood atop the rover and looked around. Trees surrounded her on all sides, thicker to the right. Some broken 'sword leaves' showed where she and the doctor had come running from. She unofficially named the giant aloe-like plant 'sword leaf' due to it having long, tapered leaves reminiscent of a blade. Despite their appearance, the leaves proved to be brittle. A human walking into it would snap them easily.

"Bracelet, do you see the cat anywhere?"

‹No. But, I do not have eyes.›

She flashed a nervous smile. "You know what I mean."

‹I am not detecting it in any manner my sensors are capable of.›

"Great."

Sima sat again, then slid down the curved hull to the ground. "Might as well try the stupid thing first."

She braced her hands on the rover's roof and pushed, trying to brute force it over onto its wheels. Unfortunately, she succeeded only in forcing her feet half an inch deeper into the relatively soft ground, not even making the rover wobble. Light-headed and somewhat winded, she gave up after a brief struggle.

"Yeah… not happening. This thing is heavier than it looks." Sima backed up so she could take in the totality of the scene. "Don't panic. Like Dr. Desai said, life is simply a series of problems needing to be solved. Some are easy, some aren't."

An inquisitive grunt came from inside the cabin.

"You wrote that in your bio page," said Sima. "I read it before applying."

Dr. Desai gave a pleased grunt.

‹There is a fine line between respect and brown-nosing.›

"I am not too proud to resort to that. However, I'm not quoting him for extra credit. I'm quoting him because he's right. This rover not being on its wheels is just a problem I need to solve. We're not going to be stranded out here until we starve. And I'm not being hopeful when I say it. Worst-case scenario, as soon as Dr. Desai can move again, we walk home. Even if we get eaten by the cat on the way, it's not us starving here."

‹That is the most pessimistic optimism I've ever heard.›

"Most people refer to 'pessimistic optimism' as realism," said

Sima. "I don't want to be realistic. I want to be hopeful, but wishing never fixed anything. Heck with it."

She looked around again, saw no sign of the cat, and stormed off toward the damage trail in the foliage.

Patter.

She looked at the bracelet's display.

‹Where are you going!?›

"To recover the sample kits we dropped."

‹!!!›

"We drove all the way out here and almost got eaten by a cat. What's the point if we just leave everything we came out here to get behind?"

‹The point is, you continue to be alive. Please do not make me resort to zapping you until you return to safety.›

"Don't. It's not far, and I can run faster than Dr. Desai. Let me know if you sense the cat."

‹This is under protest. You are needlessly exposing yourself to danger for... plants.›

"I guess I'm a scientist." She jogged into the forest. "Grabbing four sample cases is a lot less risky than a thirty-year space flight."

‹Did you not think those people were crazy?›

"Crazy is relative. It's one thing to gamble your life for science, it's another to do so while throwing sixty years away."

Sima grabbed the first two sample cases and ran them back to the rover, setting them inside the still-open rear hatch. All the gear clamped securely in mounts, so despite the vehicle being rolled, everything stayed where it belonged. The sample cases, as well, had 'sockets' they clicked into. Sima slid them in place one after the next.

Against the protest of the bracelet, she ran back for the other two. As soon as she grabbed the last one, a *snap* came from the woods nearby. She somehow resisted the urge to freeze in panic, going directly to a full sprint without even looking toward the source of the motion. Heavy trampling raced away from her, deeper into the woods.

Realizing it must have been some other animal—perhaps one of those fuzzy pig-like creatures—she relaxed, but didn't slow until she reached the rover. Her heart beat so rapidly she became light-headed again and her hands trembled. Expecting the cat to show up at any second, she hurried the cases into their sockets, then pushed the hatch up to close it.

"Wow, umm. I must be scared out of my mind."

‹If so, why did you risk going back for the cases?›

"Because doing *something* is less scary than standing here doing nothing but thinking." She walked around the rover, studying it. "How am I going to—?"

Snap.

Sima spun to her rear, pulling the gun out and aiming at… a curious fuzzy blue piglet.

At least, she thought of it as a piglet. Despite being the size of a baby Earth pig, the creatures didn't seem to get any bigger. Fur, large eyes, and a face more like a hamster made them far too adorable. For all she knew, it possessed a toxin so deadly merely touching it could kill her. But it *looked* harmless.

"Ugh…" She exhaled, letting her arms—and the gun—fall limp at her sides.

Within seconds of turning her attention back to the problem of the rover being undrivable, she noticed the robotic arm. Two beams, each about seven feet long and joined by an elbow folded against each other, tucked against the roof. A box at the front end had three lenses of varying size as well as multiple tiny robotic manipulators, all collapsed into recesses. At a guess, she identified a welder-slash-cutting torch, a gripper claw, a scooper, and two others she couldn't discern the function of.

"Is this arm strong enough to push the rover back onto its wheels?"

‹I do not have the requested data. However, we have an easy means of discovering the answer.›

"Good point." She climbed into the rover, wasting no time

closing the door and re-locking it. "I'd rather be inside here anyway."

She twisted herself over sideways, trying to look at the console as close to right-side-up as possible. Amid all the various buttons and displays, she eventually located controls for the robotic arm positioned in front of the passenger seat. They appeared quite similar to the two primary sticks used to drive, except the left control stick had a smaller micro-joystick on top.

"Found it." She looked around at her situation. "If this arm is strong enough to push us upright, we're going to bounce around."

Dr. Desai sat roughly half on the roof, half on the driver's side door. He wouldn't have too far to fall. Sima doubted she had the strength to lift him into a seat hanging overhead, so she'd have to be gentle with the arm controls... assuming it worked at all.

Taking inspiration from Lissa, she did a handstand, pushing herself into the inverted passenger seat. After bracing her feet against the console to hold her butt in place, she secured the seat-belt and shoulder harness.

"Yep. Completely backward. Human in the cage at the zoo... now I'm strapping myself *into* an upside-down seat." She gave the left side of the harness a tug, pinning her shoulder against the cushion. "Yeah, they definitely designed this thing for a really rough ride. Someone would probably stay in the seat if it bounced down the side of a mountain."

Dr. Desai grunted in acknowledgement.

"Are you agreeing with me these were made for hostile environments or saying you like the idea of using the arm?"

He made the same noise, which she took to mean 'yes to both.'

"All right. Hope it works." She grabbed the sticks.

Moving them didn't do anything.

"Drat. Oh, duh. Helps if I activate the system." She pushed a red button, which lit up.

Protesting groans from an electric motor came from behind her somewhere. The rover rocked upward a little.

"Bracelet, do you have any files on how the controls work? The sticks aren't labeled." She held her arm up, waiting for the screen to appear.

‹Connection established. One moment, reading files... done. The controls operate based on the multifunction module at the end of the arm. Think of it like moving an object around in three-dimensional space more than controlling an arm. Left stick moves the unit forward, backward, left, and right. The right stick controls up and down as well as rotation. Twisting the sticks angles the MFU around like a human wrist.›

"Hmm. Okay." She pictured the arm folded up against the rover's back. "I'll need to push the end up and lean it somewhat to my right so it doesn't slip."

She gingerly eased the left stick forward. Unhappy whirring came from the motor in the back. The rover shuddered... but the ground in front of her began to rotate. A small screen between the control sticks showed a view from the multifunction unit at the end of the robotic arm, another close-up of dirt and vegetation.

Motor whirring took on a more and more pronounced whining quality as the mechanism strained to shift the weight of the rover. Red warning lights flashed 'load excess' at her. She added a bit of rightward push to keep the arm from buckling, easing the left stick further forward to push faster.

Gotta do this before the motor burns out.

Dr. Desai slid over the driver side door, coming to rest against the seat.

"I think it's working!" rasped Sima. "Any second now, we're going to—"

She screamed as her prediction came true.

The weight of the passenger-side wheels pulled the rover past the teetering point. It fell onto all six wheels hard enough to bounce the other set off the ground. Blur filled the screen as the MFU whipped around. Sima swung the robot arm left, trying to shift the center of gravity so the rover didn't bounce/roll upside down the other way.

Fortunately, the left-side wheels only caught a little air before the vehicle settled flat on all six of its tires.

Dr. Desai ended up headfirst in the gap between the seats.

"Ack! Sorry!" Sima hastily unbuckled herself to pull him up off the floor.

She still lacked the strength to lift him completely, but managed —after a valiant struggle—to haul him into the passenger seat and secure the harness. He grunted appreciatively. That done, she flopped in the driver's seat and buckled herself in.

"Another pair of sticks… how do these work?"

‹Simple. Each stick controls the wheels on its respective side. Push both forward to go forward. Pull both back to reverse. If you move them in different directions, we rotate. Moving each set of wheels at slightly different speeds is how you do gradual turns.›

"Just like a video game." She exhaled. "I can do this. Sorry, Dr. Desai. I've never driven before and I'm not eighteen yet, but you're kinda out of it, so… hope I don't get in trouble."

He groaned in a way she took to mean 'don't worry about it.'

Seriously. I don't think anyone cares about gee-vee licenses up here.

A warning buzz sounded when she pulled both sticks backward a little bit.

"Ack!" She cringed, instinctively letting go of the sticks. "What did I do wrong?"

Dr. Desai grunted in a 'how should I know?' tone.

She searched around the console until spotting another flashing yellow warning light. "Caution arm? What?"

‹Look up.›

Sima peered up through the bubble windscreen. The robotic arm stuck almost straight into the air. Except for a tuft of sod on the boxy MFU at the tip, it didn't appear damaged. "Oh. Guess it doesn't like driving around with the arm loose. I should fold it up."

The panel had a convenient 'auto away' button, which she pressed. As the robot arm retracted to its rest position, she backed into a turn. A few seconds after hearing the *clank* of the mechanism locking itself down, she pushed both sticks forward and began the drive home.

7

TRUST

Two hours later, Dr. Desai managed to smile.

Sima stood beside his bed in the medical facility, having a highly one-sided conversation explaining they made her undergo a mandatory examination due to being in a 'vehicle accident' as well as a violent attack. She hadn't suffered any injuries worse than bruises—the worst being where the gun hit her on the side of the knee.

It felt wrong to simply leave him alone. Also, the medics required her to remain in the med center until one of her parents arrived to sign her out. Being told she *had* to stay there irritated her to a point. How much difference did going from seventeen to eighteen truly make? Even if she had most of a year to go before legal adulthood, teens didn't wake up experiencing a sudden blast of maturity the day they turned eighteen. It sounded so ridiculous to tell a girl who kept herself and three children alive out in the wilderness for weeks she couldn't walk across the colony to her residence alone.

Of course, *having* parents who cared enough to come get her defused much of her resentment. She didn't want to think how her bio mother would have reacted to being told to pick her up from a hospital on Earth. The woman probably would've ignored the call. *If* she showed up, it would only have been out of fear of breaking the law and ending up in jail.

The medics expected Dr. Desai to regain control of his muscles in a few hours.

Sima marveled at the potency of the toxin. Only a single quill hit him, causing total paralysis in a matter of seconds. Unlike Juan who'd instantly become a statue, Dr. Desai's larger body mass caused him to retain some use of his left arm and leg for a few seconds, as well as the ability to grunt. The medical doctors estimated two quills would have threatened his ability to continue breathing. Three would definitely have killed him via suffocation. One nearly killed Juan. She didn't understand biochemical processes enough to know the math necessary to figure out how close the boy came to death—nor did she particularly want to.

Maybe those cats really do *hunt aurak. The venom is so damn potent because it's intended for enormous birds.*

She started discussing the idea of the cats possibly being a predator of aurak, citing the high potency of their venom. "Do you think their claws have metal in them or are they just shiny? I'm thinking they probably do since they're capable of scratching the rover's windows. It's fascinating they produce keratin with such a high mineral content."

"Sima!" called Mom.

Her parents and the kids rushed in. Lissa ran the fastest, diving into a hug. Juan crashed into her a second later. Austin strolled in more hesitantly, seeming worried—until he saw her standing there in good shape, then darted up to her. Both parents hurried to embrace her, squishing the two smaller children into her briefly.

"What happened?" Mom looked her over. "They told us you almost got killed out there... but you don't appear hurt."

Dad stared at her for a long moment of silence, looking as if he hadn't slept in weeks. "We didn't know what to think when they notified us. The attendant made it sound serious."

"Couple bruises." Sima explained everything.

At the mention of a quill cat attacking them, Lissa squealed in alarm. The boys thought it 'awesome' she got to play with the rover's robot arm.

"... please don't be upset with Dr. Desai for taking me to a 'dangerous place.' Nothing we've seen yet gave us any idea one of those cats would be so close to the colony. I was focused on opening the door and didn't see the cat right behind us. It would've shot *me* with the quill if he didn't jump in the way to protect me."

"You would'a been okay." Juan grinned. "Didn't make me stop breathing."

Austin's side eye said, 'You almost did... a few times.'

"Why's this place have only bad cats and no good kitties?" asked Lissa.

"There might be small cats here. We just haven't seen them yet." Sima ruffled the girl's hair, earning a grin.

"Can't bring cats from Earth 'cause they'll mess up the place." Austin slouched. "Dogs, too."

"How's cats gonna mess it up?" Lissa blinked.

"Ecosystems," said Austin.

"But we brought people here. We're gonna mess it up." Lissa flailed her arms.

Dad chuckled. "As a species, we never seem to care all that much about the damage we do to an environment. We are trying to be as unobtrusive as possible."

"Someone else lived on this planet before we found it." Sima glanced out the window at the sparkling silver buildings, bluish foliage, and perfect sky. "Hope we don't make the same mistake they did."

SIMA and her family stayed with Dr. Desai until he regained the ability to move his face and talk.

Her parents thanked him for jumping in front of the quill. Since it appeared to require significant effort for him to speak, Mom and

Dad didn't belabor the discussion of what happened, though the three of them decided to make a formal suggestion to the governor that any future expeditions away from the colony include armed Security officers.

The idea people with combat rifles might kill the wildlife out there bothered Sima, but not as much as it horrified Lissa. However, Sima—and certainly Dr. Desai—preferred one dead quill cat to a near death experience and hours sitting in a stranded rover. While she respected wildlife, giant cats became far less cute and adorable when they tried to eat her—and almost succeeded.

Eventually, they left the medical facility as it drew close to time for dinner. By then, Dr. Desai had regained modest use of his arms. His enthusiasm for studying the local plant and animal life didn't seem the least bit dampened by the quill cat venom. According to him, a biologist didn't become a 'real' scientist until they'd been bitten, stung, or poisoned by at least half the specimens they tried to study.

Lissa and Juan buzzed with excitement over dinner as they made their way across the Center and outside. Sima shared their happiness at no longer having to worry about food, more relief than the thrill the little ones experienced. For her bio-mom's faults, the woman at least made sure they had food, even if she left Sima to cook for herself. Meals hadn't become a matter of *if* rather than *what* until she ran away. She'd overheard a few teens at the high school complaining about not having certain foods they loved on this planet. Such a complaint marked them as obvious Citizens. She couldn't imagine someone refusing to eat available food because it didn't 'taste good enough.'

"What did you do with the quill?" asked Mom.

"I tossed it behind the seats in the rover. No idea what happened to it. Wasn't exactly worried about anything but Dr. Desai when we got back. I don't think I even told the Security people about it. Probably still there. Why?"

Mom nodded. "I'd like to study the venom… if there is any left in the quill. Perhaps we can develop an antidote to help relieve the paralysis much faster. It's likely we will need to study the entire animal before such a development will become possible."

"They might be smarter than we think, too." Sima shivered. "The way it looked at me... it's like it knew it couldn't get me and got mad."

Dad patted her on the shoulder. "Are you sure you're not imagining it? Cats and dogs often do things that appear intelligent."

She shook her head. "No idea. You're right, though. I shouldn't base my opinion entirely on one assumption made while scared out of my mind."

"Are they gonna shoot the kitties?" asked Lissa, sounding sad.

"One of them tried to eat you." Austin nudged her. "They aren't nice cats."

"I know." She grinned. "But I'm little. It 'fought I's a mouse. Won't when I'm bigger."

Juan pointed at Sima. "One tried to eat Seem and that guy in the hospital bed."

"They attack auraks." Austin grimaced. "They're kinda like Juan... will eat anything they see no matter how big it is."

Juan laughed, rubbing his belly.

Lissa stuck out her tongue.

———

A MOMENTARY WAVE of emotion paralyzed Sima as soon as she entered their residence.

For a brief period that morning, she thought she might never see her home—and family—again. A sudden, powerful possessiveness welled up inside her. She had a *home*, a room to herself, a place to feel safe.

I'm going to be living here until I'm forty.

The idea embarrassed her as much as it reassured her. Sima figured her brain overcompensated for years of feeling vulnerable and afraid. Most likely, she'd adjust in a few years once she processed 'past trauma' as Dr. Bystrova called it. Someday, she might become interested in a boy and maybe even do the whole family thing. Looking after Lissa, Juan, and Austin ignited a little spark of motherhood. She didn't exactly want to rush out and have a kid tomorrow but wouldn't necessarily object to the idea, either.

Only problem being, in order to do so, she'd need a boy.

Other students in her 'normal' high school classes—specifically the girls who'd been Citizens their whole lives—often talked about their boyfriends. Not once in her life had Sima ever even entertained the idea of having one. Outcasts around her hooked up for sex all the time, but few tried for any sort of relationship. Nobody expected to live long enough to bother getting attached. Every time she tried to sleep in a Crash or an alley and heard grunting or moaning, she became highly uncomfortable.

Seeing or hearing people being intimate always made her think about bio-Mom's creepy boyfriend who pinned her against the kitchen counter and tried to touch her when she was twelve.

Dr. Bystrova had been surprised to hear Sima say she didn't blame herself for any of it. Her fear came from expecting the same behavior from all men. Though... she'd been alone with Dr. Desai all day and he'd been completely awesome. Also, her new Dad would never do anything like that. Even the detective back on earth, Ral Marr, became angry when she told him about seeing 'Flora' at Magdalena's brothel. More and more, she kept seeing evidence her bio-mother's creepy boyfriend had been an anomaly, not the norm. Still, it didn't mean such anomalies were rare.

Somewhere in the vast tangle of mental crap going on between her ears, she associated the creep—and by extension anything sexual—as the reason she ended up an Outcast. Here, though, she had a stable home, a family, and perhaps even a chance to heal.

The idea of someday taking the chance and trusting a boy no longer frightened her. She'd have to be careful, and also didn't feel any particular urgency. A mountain of academic work she needed to climb came first.

"Sima?" asked Dad. "Everything all right?"

She snapped out of her mental fog, realizing she'd been

standing two steps inside the door for several minutes. "Yes. Fine. Just thinking."

He smiled, then headed off down the hall.

The kids sat in the living room like any Citizen family, playing games on the Wondercube. Only two could play at a time, so Lissa entertained herself with dolls while the boys played. Juan also played with dolls—albeit space men figures—while sitting out. Austin used a handheld video game while the two younger kids took their turns on the game.

They look so normal. She pressed a hand over her heart, overcome with gratitude. No one looking at the three of them now would know they'd ever spent weeks essentially living as tribal primitives, half a step ahead of starvation or predation at any minute. Worse than their experiences after crashing, their lives on Earth before. Except for the occasional comment about missing her cat, Orange, Lissa acted as though she had no memories whatsoever of growing up in a home with Pixie addicts. Her parents hadn't been intentionally cruel or neglectful beyond making such a hazardous chemical around her... and all the associated problems going along with being high more than sober.

Austin remained wary of the Security officers—a feeling Sima shared—and it had taken him the longest of the three kids to trust their new father. He no longer came off as visibly suspicious of Dad, though didn't show the same degree of affection as the other two. Sima wondered if it had something to do with his bio-father murdering his mother, then trying to kill him, too. As she 'legally' counted as his sister, not his parent, no one told her anything about his sessions with Dr. Bystrova.

Juan attached himself to their new dad the most of the three kids. He still sometimes cried over his bio-father abandoning him in hopes he would find a better life out of *La Propagación*, but as far as the escape pod crash went, he appeared to have discarded the memories and trauma entirely. Lissa occasionally complained in jest about having to wear clothes, but only did so to make Sima laugh. The girl didn't have any issues being civilized.

Looking at them here, playing video games, she could scarcely tell they'd been through such a harrowing experience. Another sudden bout of possessiveness and worry gripped her when Juan laughed at something in the game. Hoping his bio-father never came to Mirage and wanted him back made her feel guilty and like a horrible person. If it happened, she'd have to let him go, but dreaded how much it would hurt.

Sima watched the kids for a few minutes, thrilled they'd all bounced back to happiness after everything. *They're tougher than me.*

Mom peered in from the kitchen. "Sima? Do you want to help with dinner?"

"Sure." She exhaled out her nose and headed to the kitchen. The sight of Mom smiling at her set off a sudden wash of anger toward her bio-mother for never caring.

"Sima?" asked Mom.

"Sorry." She pushed rage aside. "I really need to stop thinking about that woman."

"Which woman?"

"My roommate from birth to age twelve." Sima frowned.

"Ahh." Mom put an arm around her. "Anything you want to talk about?"

She shrugged. "Not really. I'm being dumb and emotional because you wanted me to help out with dinner."

"Your mother didn't teach you how to cook?"

"Bitch taught me how to cook by forcing me to do it for myself. She never wanted to cook *with* me, or show me how. I'm lucky she let me use some of the food she bought. Probably afraid of getting in legal trouble if she starved me." She stared down. "As far as I'm concerned, *you* are my real mother."

"Better late than never, I suppose." Mom gave her hand a squeeze.

"Not your fault. There's too many people on Earth. I'm no more special than any of a billion other kids. Lots of them had bigger problems than me."

Mom hugged her. "Someone else having it worse doesn't make what you experienced any less traumatic."

"Now you sound like Dr. Bystrova." Sima chuckled while slicing a 'space cucumber' into bite-sized blocks.

"She's right. You had a harrowing day and yet you don't seem terribly fazed by it. I'm concerned."

Sima looked up from the cutting board, making eye contact. "I'm not disassociating or anything. What happened today wasn't half as scary as crash landing and thinking myself the only human on a whole planet, or charging *at* a quill cat with an axe to stop it from hurting the kids. Yeah, it was scary, but I've been *more* frightened of some people back on Earth. The Scathers' murder pit freaked me out more than the quill cat today."

"What's on your mind?" Mom examined a packet of noodles, made from wheat grown in the *Progenitor's* hydroponic farm.

"Still trying to process having a real family. Dr. Bystrova has almost convinced me there's nothing inherently wrong with me that made the other woman reject me."

"You should listen to her. There isn't anything wrong with you. The woman had serious mental issues. I understand you'll need time to trust us. Please don't feel any pressure or like we are trying to take 'your kids' away from you."

"I *do* trust you and Dad." Sima smiled at the massive vegetable. Though it had a somewhat eggplant-like shape, the biologists determined it more closely related to squash. Lissa worked as hard as a seven-year-old could work to promote calling them 'space cucumbers' instead of titan squash.

"That's not where my anxiety is coming from. Everything is too perfect. I'm afraid something is going to go wrong."

"Perfect..." Mom gathered some seasonings from the cabinet. "Mirage is far from perfect."

"Compared to being an Outcast, it is." She chuckled. "It's so weird to think I was afraid to get on the ship."

"The unknown is terrifying. Always has been." Mom gestured at the spices, indicating Sima should try to remember the correct amounts of each to add. "That's why we are here: to help bring the unknown into the known."

Sima moved closer to her, eyeing the jars. "Science... do you ever regret taking the wonder out of the world?"

"No. Consider how vast the universe is. For everything we understand, there are an infinite number of things we have yet to see. The universe is full of wonder."

All three kids burst into laughter at something in the other room.

Sima chuckled. "It sure is."

8

HIDING

Six days after the trip with Dr. Desai, Sima sat in class on a Friday afternoon, gazing into space.

The majority of the other twenty-one teens in the room grew up as Citizens, never having to beg for food or sleep under a pile of trash to keep gangers away. For the most part, they didn't make any issue of her being a former Outcast, likely due to her not having 'the attitude' expected of one. A few seemed afraid of her, one or two looked down their noses, but said nothing. She ignored them. No amount of explaining would ever help as much as trying to put the past behind her and be as normal as possible.

She'd finished the test quite early, so had about half the class period to idle. Due to the test going on, she couldn't use her tablet or Omnicomputer bracelet to read or do any other classwork while she waited for the period to end... so daydreaming happened.

April twenty-second... and a Friday.

Distant memories of being in school as a child drifted around in the back of her mind. Unlike her peers, she hadn't looked forward to going home at three in the afternoon or got excited for weekends. As far back as she could remember, she preferred school to her bio-mother's apartment. She didn't have any particular affection for weekends here, either. Unlike all her Citizen classmates, she spent most of her weekend time working on self-paced learning modules to catch up. While she enjoyed the learning, it robbed Saturday and Sunday of feeling like a mini-vacation, turning them into the same as every other day of the week.

One of the history instructionals mentioned school used to stop for June, July, and August in some areas. Historians had no good explanation for why, but theorized it had likely been a product of seasonal child labor hundreds of years ago when kids had to work on farms during the summer. The massive war culminating in the End of Nations destroyed a tragic amount of history. Ever since the Earth Government established itself, GANSEC became the official language and school ran year-round. No one presently on Earth— or their great grandparents—lived during a time when any sort of 'summer break' existed. It struck Sima as a little cruel to teach kids about a three-month break in seventh-grade history, as if taunting them with a vacation they couldn't have.

Governor Harland proposed the idea of reintroducing it on Mirage, primarily so high-school-aged students could spend a few months as interns in various OTs while younger kids would help out on the farms springing up on the outskirts of the colony. Hydroponic growth machines in the Center—what remained of the starship—couldn't keep up with the demand to provide *all* the food for almost nine thousand people.

No decision had been made yet. Her classmates complained about the idea, as they thought a 'summer vacation' should be a vacation, not merely a change from education to employment. Sima found herself agreeing with them. Sooner or later, everyone had to work an OT. At this age, they needed to learn.

Question being, what did she want to do for her OT upon becoming an adult?

Having at least a half hour of time to do nothing but think, she spent the remainder of the class period mulling over her future. By the time the teacher, Mr. Meru, announced the end of class, she'd narrowed her interest down to either biology or robotics.

"Anyone who hasn't finished yet can stay and keep working if you want," said Mr. Meru.

Two students remained seated as everyone else got up to leave, their expressions relieved.

The teacher approached Sima as she headed for the door. Though he had similar salt-and-pepper hair to her bio-mother's creepy boyfriend—and also looked as if he came from the same region of Earth as her, he gave off no signs of being a threat.

"Ms. Nuvari?"

She stopped. "Yes? Something wrong?"

"No. Not at all." He smiled. "You've been a little distracted lately. I'm merely concerned you might be pushing yourself too hard."

Ugh. Why does everyone say that?

"Oh. No, I'm fine. The schoolwork is actually fun for me. Feels like I'm thriving." She swiped her hair off her face. "If I look distracted or worried, it's from adjustment issues. After the escape pod crash and knowing what the future held for me on Earth, I'm totally thrilled to be able to drown myself in academics."

Mr. Meru nodded once, then chuckled. "More than academics. I hear you barged into Governor Harland's office to insist he prohibit hunting of those enormous birds."

She fidgeted. "Not sure it counted as 'barging' in, but I did go to his office. I'm kinda surprised they listened to me since I was only sixteen at the time."

"You had experience with the creatures."

"Yeah." Sima told him about the birds' display of intelligence and gratitude. "They are *definitely* smarter than people would think of birds being. Umm… can I ask you something?"

"Certainly. Not only is it my job, I love helping young people understand things." He sat on the edge of the desk. "What's on your mind?"

Sima shifted her weight from one leg to the other. "Do you think I should focus on biology or robotics? I've been thinking of biology mostly because I 'lived with nature' for a while out there, but some of the robotics stuff in the course materials is really interesting."

"Hmm. When considering the OT you are going to spend most of your life engaged in, it's important to take into account both one's aptitude for it as well as how rewarding it is. Who would you trust more: the most gifted doctor in the world who utterly despised medicine or a decent doctor who adored what she did and couldn't wait to get to the medical complex every morning?"

"Depends. As a researcher shut away in the lab, the gifted person would be okay. As a patient, I'd rather see the one who loved what she did."

Mr. Meru grinned. "You are a bit young yet to demonstrate measurable aptitude in either field. If you can't tell which one you enjoy more, it means one of two things. You like them both equally, or you haven't seen enough of them to make a decision. I suggest you delve a little deeper into both and see what clicks. You might even find a third option you prefer."

True. Dad works in power engineering. Maybe I'll end up on the reactor team.

"Good idea."

A loud clatter arose from the right.

She glanced over at an athletic brown-haired boy named Corbin clumsily getting up from his desk. "I'm leaning toward biology, but there's something about robotics that's tempting me. Should probably get home before I'm missed."

Mr. Meru checked something on his tablet, barely suppressing a wince at seeing Corbin's test score. "Have a good weekend."

"You too, Mr. M," said Corbin on the way by.

Sima leaned out of the boy's way. Once he passed, she smiled at the teacher. "Thanks. Same to you."

She headed out into the hall, following Corbin only because they both went to the main entrance. If the school had any sort of sports teams, he'd likely have been their star. *Handsome, check. Strong, check. Smart? Not so much.* Considering she didn't pay much attention to her classmates, that she considered him a bit of a jerk had to mean something. Not only was he one of the kids who occasionally sneered at her for being a former Outcast, he also gave other 'smart' students a hard time, cracking jokes as if being into academics was something to be ashamed of. It made little sense why someone like him—who'd obviously come from a well-off Citizen family—to be here. His parents probably had important jobs. For all of Earth's flaws, rich people didn't have too bad a life there. Of course, she merely assumed Corbin's family had money due to his superior attitude.

Once outside, she veered left while he went right... and she didn't waste another second of thought on his existence.

SIMA'S WEEKEND shot by in a blur of self-paced instructionals and children.

Both parents ended up working all weekend, trusting Sima to resume her role as 'mom' to Austin, Juan, and Lissa between breakfast and dinner. The kids spent most of both days playing outside with friends they'd made who lived in the same residence pod as well as the one across the metal sidewalk from it. Sima sat nearby dividing her time between watching them and studying via tablet. After dinner, they stayed in and played video games until bedtime —while she studied via tablet on the couch.

Her weekends might have lacked the joy of being a day off due to catch-up classwork, but all the studying made Monday less of a downer. The kids walked together to the Center, splitting up to their respective classrooms once inside.

Life in the colony struck Sima as spacious despite the population being a few hundred short of 9,000 people. She had no idea of exact numbers, but on Earth, city had taken over every inch of usable terrain where construction was possible. Except for bodies of water, swamps, bogs, mountains, or other places nothing could be built, dense urbanity covered the planet. In the same amount of land Progenitor Colony took up, perhaps 50,000 people would live on Earth. Seeing more than three feet of space between pedestrians she begged from would've been unusual. Here, the only people walking closer than like fifty feet to each other were families or friends.

Not that she had any interest in being a pickpocket, but any of the other Outcasts who used to live by stealing would have a damn hard time of doing it here. Wading into a stream of pedestrians where everyone couldn't help but bump into each other constantly made filching glint a breeze. Not many people could tell an innocent bump apart from theft.

Monday started like any other day since she'd rejoined civilization... until lunch.

Then, it got weird.

As she did most days, Sima shuffled through the line, received her portion of food from the smiling cooks, and proceeded to sit near the corner of the cafeteria by herself. Unlike the grade school she remembered, no teachers 'patrolled' the cafeteria here. Either they trusted high school kids to behave themselves, or the change happened due to this being a colony on another planet. It didn't seem likely for too much trouble to stir up among the first-generation students who still remembered being on Earth. If anyone tried to start a gang here, they'd certainly be dealt with swiftly. Besides, Citizen kids didn't end up in gangs. *They* had futures they didn't want to throw away.

Every so often, other students would sit at her table, but never close enough to talk—until Monday, April 25th, 2410.

The day a boy sat right next to her.

Since she already had a fork in her hand, she resisted the urge to reach for the knife hidden behind her back. Eight months living like a normal person tempered her Outcast habits enough to where she didn't stab him in the neck as a reflex, though she had to concentrate on not doing so.

"Hey, you're in my class, right?" asked the boy.

Definitely not Corbin. Too high-pitched, not arrogant enough.

Sima shifted her gaze off her food tray to her left. A thin boy with black hair smiled hopefully at her. She recognized him from a few of her classes: Koji Ito. Despite being seventeen, he gave off about as much of a threatening presence as eight-year-old Juan. She didn't know him—or any of her classmates—too well, but doubted he'd come to ask for help understanding schoolwork. Like her, he tended to finish tests fast and sit there daydreaming.

"Yeah," said Sima, in a tone halfway between 'what do you want' and 'go away.' *Oh, crap. He's going to ask me to have sex, isn't he?* She bit her lip.

"Sorry, dumb question. Pretty obvious." Koji awkwardly scratched the back of his head. "Umm, so were you really stranded way out there in the forest alone?"

She stared at him for a moment, caught off guard. For sure, she'd expected the next thing out of his mouth to be 'wanna ride' or whatever slang term the people in his District back on Earth used for sex.

Duh. Normal people don't go straight from 'Hi, what's your name,' to naked... only people who'll be surprised if they're not dead in three hours.

"You okay?" asked Koji. "I'm sorry if it's not something you like thinking about."

No... not why I'm starting to blush. She broke eye contact. No way did she want to talk about weeks spent running around the woods in her underwear—or nothing—with a boy. Bad enough the soldiers saw her. At least they hadn't found her swimming naked.

"It's fine. Scary, but not as bad as Earth."

"Earth? You lived where Seps started fights?" Koji tilted his head.

"Not exactly. We had Seps, but they were more like the scary things in the dark no one wanted to talk about." She picked at her food, waiting for him to figure it out... and feeling somewhat proud of herself he hadn't known her to be a former Outcast.

He picked up half his burger. Though it consisted mostly of mushroom and titan squash, it smelled like meat. "What was it like out there? I went into the woods for a couple days with my dad to camp. So amazing and peaceful. It's really sad Earth doesn't have natural beauty like this anymore."

"I guess. Umm, it was kinda scary. I mean, we all thought the *Progenitor* exploded in orbit and we were the only people left alive."

"Wow. That's sad. I guess you'd have no way to know. Any idea why your escape pod malfunctioned?"

She looked at him. "How do you not know what happened?"

"Uhh." Koji stared at his burger. "I do. Sorry. Just trying to think of something to talk about. Not really good at it. Meteorites or some kind of little rocks stuck in orbit hit the ship."

"Yeah." Sima decided to eat her hummus sandwich as an excuse not to have to say anything for a moment. *Why does he want to talk to me? That's weird.*

Koji held out his left arm, showing the holographic screen of his Omnicomputer bracelet. "Look."

Still chewing, she glanced over at a photograph of an aurak from below. Whoever took the picture stood next to its leg, aiming up. Dark blue leathery hide nearest the camera bore thousands of deep wrinkles, blurring out to smoothness as the leg stretched up to a humorously round body thirty some odd feet above.

"Did you see these guys? They're called auraks."

Sima nodded. "Yeah. Austin rode on one's back."

"Oh." He seemed a little deflated.

Ugh. Maybe I should let him think I have a boyfriend already.

"Thought you'd be impressed by the picture."

"It's a good picture." She stared into the end of her sandwich. "They're called aurak because my little sister named them that."

His mood brightened. "Really? How'd she come up with the word?"

"It's how she tried to pronounce the noise they make." Sima blushed a little, but reproduced the bird call at a low volume so only Koji could hear her in the cafeteria.

"Wow, that's almost funny. Named for something so simple and obvious."

"Austin's my brother," said Sima out of the blue… regretting it as soon as she spoke.

Koji nodded. "Yeah. I know. You guys were on the news the day after they found you. Even before, they mentioned picking up a signal out there about a couple children in an escape pod. Like the whole colony stopped breathing until they found out if the signal came from real survivors, an Omni bracelet on a dead body, or only a glitch."

"Are you serious?" Sima stared at him. "No one said anything to us about it."

"Don't know why. People were cheering all over the place when they announced the soldiers made contact with four kids. Maybe they thought it would be better for you not to be a celebrity or something."

"Fine with me." She took a bite of her food to stop herself from saying she preferred to be left alone. Not that she didn't prefer it, but it felt rude to say.

Koji spoke enthusiastically about he and his father camping in the forest over the weekend. He leapt from topic to topic as if his brain raced faster than his tongue could handle, speaking of plants, animals, the astonishing quiet, clear sky, and so forth.

"Yeah… it's nice here. Earth is a mess." Sima shrugged. "The sky wasn't bad where I lived before. Everything else mostly sucked, though."

"Where did you live before?"

"Earth."

"I mean, where on Earth?"

She waved dismissively. "District A019F4, I think. I don't really remember."

"You don't know what it used to be called before the End of Nations?"

"No, don't be stupid." She gave him side eye. "You know the government deliberately destroyed all that information to stop separatist thoughts. I'm sure they even hate history classes mentioning individual nations used to exist before."

He nodded. "Yeah. My family aren't Seps, but we have kept old knowledge. My district used to be called Kyoto. I've seen pictures from centuries ago, before everything became city. It used to be beautiful on Earth, too."

A shaft of fear raced down her spine. Perhaps not for a Citizen, but an Outcast speaking a pre-End-of-Nations name for a city would surely get them labeled a Separatist, and likely shot on sight. The Earth Government's brutal suppression of anyone even talking about the old ways definitely made her distrust them and believe the government knew it did something wrong... but she also chickened out from challenging it. No point hastening her death.

"Don't be scared. It's not illegal up here."

Sima gave him a flat look. "How do you know this is 'up' compared to Earth?"

"Spacecraft go up into the sky." He laughed. "Once you're in space, there is no up or down. It's all three-dimensional relativity."

"Right." She nibbled on her sandwich. "What do you think about aliens? Or, before my bracelet corrects me, non-human sentient life?"

Her bracelet displayed ‹Lmao.›

"It probably exists. Just because we haven't seen any doesn't mean it's impossible for life to have developed somewhere else. It's like opening one closet in one apartment on Earth, not seeing any shoes inside, and saying shoes don't exist because they're not in this one closet."

"We found evidence of another civilization here."

Koji's eyes went wide. "Really?"

She hesitated momentarily, unsure at what point her guard lowered or when talking to him changed from unwanted awkwardness to okay. It didn't feel worth dwelling on, so she dismissed her reservations and began telling him about the cave she found and the underground complex she and the kids stumbled into days later. He gawked the whole time.

"Ms. Taylor mentioned they'd discovered abandoned alien ruins." Koji blinked.

"Yeah. I was there. We are in the same class, remember? She's trying to translate the writing I took pictures of." She managed not to smile at herself. "My bracelet scanned all the writing we found on the walls. So bizarre."

"Bizarre? Sure, aliens and all."

"Technically, we are the aliens on this planet. But… it's bizarre because the wall writing looked like something a primitive culture would do, but we also found high tech objects."

"Huh…" Koji stared into space, seeming lost in thought. "Maybe it's like how some people have swords and stuff on their walls as art? Objects from a really long time ago as decoration."

She tilted her hand in a so-so gesture. "Maybe if we found tablets hung up, but this looked like they wrote directly *on* the walls."

"Could be the site had significance to them like a temple? Or maybe it was just old. What if you found like ancient ruins other aliens were in the process of excavating like archaeologists?"

"Umm. Maybe, but the doors still worked. Juan hit a button and it opened."

"Where did they get power from?" Koji whistled. "Amazing."

"Honestly? I'm not sure if it had power or simple gravity pulled it down. No idea how long ago the beings who used to live on this planet died out."

Koji flashed a conspiratorial grin. "What if they didn't?"

"Ack." She shivered. "Don't even say that."

"Why?" His eagerness gave way to a look of concern.

Sima opened her mouth, but stopped short of telling him of her constant fear this new 'perfect' life would be ruined by something bad happening at any moment. If everything turned out to be virtual reality, talking too much about aliens would give the people running the simulation the idea to throw them in. "Just, because. It's not smart to tempt fate."

"Didn't think you were superstitious."

"I'm not. I'm a pessimistic optimist."

He laughed. "What does that even mean?"

"Means I hope for nice things but expect reality to suck. When nice things happen, I don't trust them to last."

"Sorry. Must be rough getting kidnapped."

"What?" She glanced over at him.

"You know... fake arrested and put on a colony ship."

He knows I'm an Outcast. Warmth flooded her face.

"Don't be like that." Koji nudged her. "Nothing to be ashamed of. You're not at all like what they say. Maybe you got stuck being homeless, but you're not really an Outcast inside."

Sima stared at her lunch tray. Any attempt to speak would end in tears. Of course, she figured a boy trying to talk her into sex would say whatever he could to make her trust him. However, nothing about him gave off insincerity. He truly sounded as if he didn't perceive her as an Outcast, merely a normal kid who was stranded on the street. Perhaps she'd been wrong about Koji. His disappointment when she mentioned Austin didn't come from the assumption she already had a boyfriend but from her lack of awe at the photo of the aurak... from being 'topped.' He got a picture. Her brother rode one.

Also, Koji totally wanted to talk about the world outside the colony. Discussing animals, plants, and exploration excited him like Juan going on and on about cartoon characters. Certainly, Corbin would never use a term like 'three-dimensional relativity' in casual conversation.

"You should totally go on the field trip Ms. Taylor is organizing," said Koji, perhaps sensing her heavy mood.

She scrunched up her nose. "Field trip?"

"It's been on the board for a month."

"Oh. I don't really pay attention to social stuff."

"Heh. Not really social. It's academic. She's trying to get approval to bring some interested students out to investigate another alien site."

Both Omnicomputer bracelets displayed messages protesting the use of the term 'alien' to refer to the prior civilization on Mirage.

"I know." Koji shook his wrist. "It's just easier to say 'alien.'"

"Another site?" Sima raised an eyebrow. "Or the same one we found?"

"Umm. It's only eighteen miles southeast of the colony. I think your pod crashed farther away."

"Yeah." Sima looked at her bracelet's screen. According to her map, their pod crash-landed 164.8 miles north-northeast of where the *Progenitor* landed. It took only a couple hours to walk from the escape pod they'd made a home out of to the alien cave. Definitely not the same place. She showed him her map. "Here's where I landed. Cave's here... and this is the pod I found the kids in."

"What's the red X on the other side of the river?"

Sima winced. "Another escape pod... everyone died."

"Ugh. Sorry. I can't imagine seeing something like that."

"Yeah... not fun." She sighed. "Not the first time I've seen dead bodies."

"Wow. Umm. Should I ask or not?"

She shrugged. "I'm as over it as I'm going to be. Sometimes, people would die in their sleep from Pixie or other drugs. I've seen the EGSF shoot people, too."

"Wow. Sorry."

"Don't be. It's done and nothing will change it. I'm on Mirage now. So... field trip, huh?"

He cringed. "Darn. I... you just almost got killed. Kinda dumb of me to mention going out of the colony again."

"Nah." She fidgeted crumbs around the tray. "Dumb was me going back into the trees to recover the sample kits when the cat might've still been out there."

"Wow. Brave."

She shrugged one shoulder. "Maybe. More like I wasn't really thinking straight. I mean, we went out there to take samples of plants... and this quill cat shows up. Figured the trip shouldn't be a total loss. Didn't see the cat anywhere. Couldn't figure out how to get the rover back on its wheels right away, so I just went to get the samples to keep myself from freaking out. My bracelet wasn't happy."

‹I was not.›

Koji looked at his arm. "Mine says you should've listened to yours."

"Does yours always say obvious things?"

"Umm. Not really. They're AI, so they have unique personality traits."

She brushed a hand over the bracelet, oddly happy to learn she had a unique friend. It vibrated in response. "What's yours like?"

"Nerdy, like me." He laughed. "Yours?"

"Smart, super sarcastic, but really loyal and helpful." Sima blushed, realizing he'd probably take her comment as a reflection of herself. Perhaps the Omnicomputers adjusted their AI to suit the personality of their humans.

Koji smiled in a way that confirmed he applied the description to her, too.

"So, field trip." Sima slapped the table. "Might as well have another near-death experience this month."

"You *want* to go back out there?"

"I almost got killed about thirty times before the EGSF stuffed me on a spaceship... and another dozen or so 'almosts' before we made it to the colony. My parents and Dr. Desai are going to ask Security officers to accompany anyone leaving the colony. It *was* kinda reckless of us to go out there alone. This planet is hardly 'domesticated.'"

"Right." Koji sat up straighter, as if he hadn't thought of actual danger before. "Good idea. Still, it might not be totally safe... but I'm going to go if the trip happens."

"I think I will, too. Really curious about the old civilization."

"You really are brave."

She kept fussing at the crumbs. "You know how like from computer class a memory buffer can overflow from maximum and go back to zero?"

"Yeah."

"That's me and fear. On the street at twelve, I got *so* scared it stopped being scary... if that makes any sense. It's nice being safe in the colony, but..." Her mind leapt back to the day she ran away from home, the images... sounds... smells... everything as clear as if it happened five minutes ago. Not as if she had any better options for dealing with a creep when her own mother accused her of trying to 'steal' and seduce him. At age twelve, seeking refuge in the streets had been her only option.

"But?" Koji tilted his head.

Sima held her chin up. "I'm not going to spend the rest of my life hiding. I've already wasted too much time doing that."

9

WORLD CHANGING

Sima caught herself losing focus in the middle of class Tuesday morning.

Admittedly, language class didn't excite her the way science or math did, but she still strived to work as hard as possible. Not only did a higher overall grade score help her with university acceptance, she felt she owed it to 'everyone' to work hard in exchange for the second chance. On the rare occasion she became fatigued with schoolwork, she thought about the other possibility—her body being thrown into a sewer back on Earth by a bunch of people who didn't know her, after they'd looted her of everything useful.

Momentary loss of focus to daydreams happened before, and generally, didn't surprise her. However, the subject of today's wandering thought *did* worry her: Koji. She'd enjoyed talking to him, however briefly, during lunch yesterday. He'd smiled at her a few times over the second half of the day and stood next to her while she approached Ms. Taylor about the field trip.

Predictably, the teacher had been *thrilled* to have her interested in going. Of course, the woman knew she'd seen the first site and had been tempted to invite her along, but didn't want to make her feel obligated. No, she had bigger problems.

Sima Nuvari caught herself thinking about a boy.

What am I doing? She rubbed her eyes and tried to pay attention to the teacher. *A new planet is scary enough. I don't need an even more drastic change to my reality. Boys are trouble.*

Her thoughts drifted from the creep to random boys she'd seen among Outcasts. The ones who stood out in her memory had been scary. Probably five times as many had been reasonably nice, but as the human mind tended to do, hers focused on the bad parts. Koji, however, seemed nice. He wanted to talk to her for the sake of talking to her, not merely as a means to an end—of getting in her pants. For all she knew, he had no such interest at all. Nothing he'd done or said gave any impression he even thought of her that way.

Except for Callie, she hadn't made any real friends on the street. As a younger kid before running away, she had a few school friends, none of whom she talked to after ending up an Outcast. She'd been too ashamed of what the man tried to do to her to let anyone she knew see her. Even Callie didn't fully count as a friend —more an associate of convenience and mutual protection. The older girl trusted Sima about as much as a thief trusted another thief they'd been forced to work with on a big job. Ironically, the girl's distrust came from Sima's refusal to steal or run contraband. She'd been terrified of the EGSF and didn't want to give them any excuse to treat her worse. To Callie, an Outcast who refused to break any laws had to be up to something. Fortunately, they'd met when Sima had been fourteen, so she *couldn't* have been a government spy. The EGSF had many flaws, but using actual children as undercover agents wasn't one of them.

Still, she tried to process the idea of having a friend.

On Earth, she'd resented children. Little kids made her life difficult by being cuter than her and glomming up all the begging. She constantly had to relocate to spots without kids younger than her to have any hope of eating. Her entire attitude changed as soon as she found Juan and Lissa trapped and suffocating in a broken stasis pod. Austin hadn't been in danger of suffocating, but he had been stuck inside his pod—a death sentence via slow starvation.

Having three kids to protect didn't equal friends. She couldn't confide in them or talk about certain subjects. She couldn't confide in Callie either, but would have talked to her about 'certain subjects' if she'd had a boyfriend. Could she talk to Koji about such things as a friend? Didn't feel right somehow. She *definitely* couldn't talk about boys with Dad. Maybe Mom, but not Koji. For that, she'd need to make friends with another girl her age.

Again, no big rush to do so.

She'd have been happy to never say two words to Koji, too…

Which totally explained why she randomly thought about him in the middle of language class.

Catching herself thinking about him sounded an awful lot like those 'certain things' she couldn't talk to the kids about. Maybe she'd ask Mom later… or bring it up in her next session with Dr. Bystrova. The doctor said during their first or second meeting she had 'maladaptive social structures' or something to that effect. Essentially, she viewed everyone as a potential threat and resisted social contact. Sima disagreed. She had, after all, offered no protest to Mom and Dad adopting her, nor did she push them away emotionally. Sure, it took her months to stop feeling like some random kid they rented a room to, but she *did* let them into her world. Granted, she'd done so mostly out of a desire to protect Lissa, Juan, and Austin.

Maladaptive sounds so evil. I'm not that bad. She sighed out her nose. *I am also not paying attention.*

KOJI JOINED her for lunch again Tuesday afternoon.

She didn't think much about him being there talking to her for fifty minutes about plants, animals, aliens, and other random science stuff until the period ended. On the way out of the cafeteria, she realized it annoyed her they had to stop hanging out. She didn't let it bother her too much. Another month or so and she'd be fully caught up with ninth-grade level work and wouldn't need to worry about remedial class modules anymore.

Then, she'd have free time to hang out with a friend.

Until they assigned her an OT.

But even adults working OTs had personal time. She didn't need to stress over time yet. There'd be plenty in the future, once she finished school.

Sima slipped back into the routine of the day. Being Tuesday, it would be long. She wouldn't leave the school building until after dark. Once 'normal' high school ended, she'd go to Mr. Eiger's room for the remedial class as she did on Tuesdays and Thursdays for an additional eight hours of instruction. Spending thirteen hours here—from nine in the morning to ten at night—took a lot out of her, but she'd volunteered for it... and kept her grades up. Better to catch up as fast as possible.

If she passed the test in a few weeks, she'd 'graduate' to normality and be free of the overtime classes. Poor Garret would be lost without her sitting next to him to ask for help, but she didn't feel too guilty about it. Schools had official teachers for a reason, after all.

She set aside thoughts of free time, Koji, friends, and any other distraction.

Spite for her former mother pushed her to excel.

THE DAY TOOK an unexpected swerve twenty minutes into her last period algebra class.

"Can I have your attention please?" asked Mr. Meru.

Silence fell over the room.

The teacher smiled. "Relax. Not a surprise test. This is fun and exciting. Everyone, please get up and follow me."

Confused, but curious, Sima followed her classmates out into the hall.

"What's up?" whispered Koji.

She looked back at him. "No idea. Maybe a movie or something?"

"Don't know. Weird, they haven't said anything special was on the schedule. What's with the surprise?" Koji dodged a larger boy attempting to 'trip' into him.

Sima shot a sideways glare at Corbin. "I don't really like surprises."

"They can be fun sometimes." Koji stuffed his hands in his pockets.

She almost said something like 'Not where I came from,' but kept quiet, not wanting to ruin his mood. Also, who cared where she came from? New planet; new rules.

Mr. Meru led them to the stairs. They went to the ground floor, then out to the courtyard in front of the Center, where every other student and all the teachers gathered. The sight of everyone in one place set off a twinge of worry in Sima. It hadn't occurred to her before, but the people in charge used the largest remaining intact piece of the *Progenitor* for all education from six-year-olds to the end of university, as the hospital, security headquarters, the governor's office, and worst of all, the power reactor. They couldn't exactly move the reactor as it powered the starship. However, a reactor had to be dangerous, right? In history class, she'd read a bunch of stories about them 'melting down,' blowing up, or otherwise causing catastrophic damage. If *this* reactor had a serious failure, it could wipe out every single child in the colony, assuming it failed during school hours.

I'm being a moron. She pinched the bridge of her nose. *If this thing explodes, it's going to vaporize the entire colony, and probably a few miles around it. Won't matter if we're in the building or at home. Wait... does this kind of reactor even explode if it fails big, or just release a ton of radiation?*

A none-too-quiet murmur of hundreds of voices came from the assembled students. No one seemed to know the reason they'd gathered everyone outside. Deciding not to question it, she took advantage of the break in math class to talk to Koji about aliens and Ms. Taylor's field trip.

Minutes later, various adults emerged from the Center, joining the students in the courtyard, mostly gathering in clusters sorted by jumpsuit color. No doubt people who worked together grouped, but it still struck her as funny to see people arranged by the hue of their outfits.

"Hey, Koji..." Sima nodded toward the various engineers, scientists, doctors, and security officers. "Do you think they're evacuating the Center and not telling us there's a problem?"

He looked around, studying the groups. "Probably not. Everyone's too calm. Even Governor Harland is here and he's smiling."

Sima spotted him once Koji pointed him out.

Governor Lincoln Harland stood in a small group beside the former captain of the *Progenitor*, Anlon Yos, who had become the head of the security team, as well as an older man in a white jumpsuit she didn't recognize, and another man wearing a dark orange jumpsuit... who resembled a late-forties version of Koji. The governor had a relatively young face for a man with grey creeping into his afro. Sima had no idea how old he was or what his OT had been before governor. No one else she'd seen wore a black jumpsuit, so it had to mean 'politician.' No sooner did she think about the black jumpsuit being weird, two younger people, a man and a woman, also wearing black suits, hurried out of the Center to join the governor's group... so perhaps black jumpsuits denoted colony administration.

She looked around, hunting for groups of dark orange jumpsuits in hopes of seeing Dad. Most of the adults all stopped talking around the same time and gazed skyward.

Mr. Meru pointed up. "Look there."

The din of kids talking quieted. Other teachers pointed at the sky, too.

All this for a meteor shower or something? She stopped trying to find her parents in the crowd and looked where the teacher pointed.

A single orange, glowing object streaked the blue, trailed by a billow of whitish-grey smoke. She squinted, trying to get a better idea of what it might be.

"Some kind of comet?" whispered Sima.

"Kinda looks like it." Koji held both hands over his eyes as a shield. "I think it's on fire."

Several minutes passed of staring at the seemingly motionless object in the air, shrouded in billowing smoke and flame. Despite there being a couple thousand people in the courtyard, no one made any noise. Even the handful of grade zero kids—five- and six-year-olds—kept quiet. Gradually, the flaming meteor grew larger, as if it flew directly toward the colony.

Umm. Is that meteor going to hit us? She eyed the adults. None of them appeared at all concerned. Most had been watching the sky before the teachers told anyone to do so. *They knew something was going to happen.*

"It's coming right for us," yelled a teen boy.

"There is no need for alarm," said Governor Harland, his voice amplified on speakers. "What you are seeing is the *Progenitor II*, a sister ship to ours."

A collective 'whoa' came from the students.

"Another ship?" Sima gawked, picturing a giant space-faring ORC collector vehicle packed with orphans. Obviously, Omni Recycling Corporation didn't make starships, but the concept fit. Citizens occasionally put Outcast children in ORC bins. Sometimes, they couldn't escape before the collector vehicles arrived… but fortunately, the people operating them checked for anyone sleeping in the bins before loading the contents into the crushers.

Ironic, the most compassionate people on Earth collected the trash.

"Apparently, yeah." Koji whistled. "They would've had to take off before we got here."

"Obviously." She laughed. "It's like a two-year trip. The ship launched eight months after ours. Do you think the people in charge knew it was on the way?"

Koji nodded. "Yeah. They would've had to. I don't think they can build a colony ship fast enough to be a surprise. Even if it hadn't been finished when we launched, the command crew had to know it would be following us."

The fireball went out, drawing gasps from the crowd.

For a few minutes, no trace of anything appeared in the sky. Then, a glimmer of silver. A noise like a distant waterfall grew in volume until it became obvious as the roar of massive engines miles away. All the students, teachers, and people who worked in the Center watched the metal brick in the sky come closer in enthralled silence.

Sima only got a brief look at the exterior of the ship when she'd been dragged on board. After arriving in the colony, its sheer size became more apparent by virtue of the amount of separate buildings the colonists broke it down into during the time she and the kids had been stranded out in the wilds. According to the official documentation, the ship had been two miles long, 120 meters wide, and eight stories tall —averaged.

The *Progenitor II* descended from the sky in a deafening roar. Despite being so far off, it appeared too massive to possibly be able to fly. It continued growing bigger and bigger until Sima reflexively leaned back, fearing it would crush her as the nose drifted perilously close. It eventually came to a midair standstill 300 feet off the ground, then turned broadside. Antennas and other narrow tubes sticking out of the front end passed overhead, casting a shadow on the courtyard.

Sima felt like a flea on the floor watching a door swing open above her.

Silence held the crowd until the second ship stopped rotating and drifted away, shrinking gradually over several minutes before stopping again and settling to the ground.

"Our new neighbors are landing one mile from us," said Governor Harland. "In the coming months, they will do as we did and break down the ship into a colony. Our eventual goal is to merge into one city. Humanity on Mirage increases this day by 11,204 souls."

Adults began cheering.

Most of the kids did as well, including Koji. Sima stared at the distant dark blue metal wall. The immense, mostly rectangular, ship sitting on the meadow a mile away looked more like a barrier than a spacecraft. It offered no possibility of going back to Earth. Like the *Progenitor* before it, the ship didn't have the fuel necessary to escape the planet's atmosphere—or make a return voyage. The last of its fuel burned ensuring it landed safely instead of crashing.

Everyone on board knew they'd taken a one-way trip.

In spite of this fact, it felt somehow wrong to take a perfectly good starship apart. The most expensive toy on the planet wouldn't do anyone any good without fuel, so they really had no valid reason to leave it intact. Its components had been designed to become a city. Not breaking it down amounted to wasting it. Besides, the vast majority of its length consisted of packed-up buildings and framework to hold them.

We were still sleeping in cryo stasis when they left Earth. It took us two years to get here.

As the noise and wind from the *Progenitor II* died down, Mr. Meru gathered his students for a return to the classroom. Without a word, Sima fell in line among her classmates and walked, struggling to comprehend two full years going by while she lay frozen. The trip to Mirage felt instantaneous. One minute, she had a panic attack in a stasis chamber, then the drugs knocked her out. Next thing she knew, she woke up in a crashed escape pod.

But two years had passed.

Two years of stuff happening back on Earth without her. Did the detective get in trouble for helping Alina? Did Magdalena still run a brothel? Better question: did Magdalena even run a brothel at all, or merely pretend to? She'd put Alina—as Flora—in the front room, dressed provocatively to set a trap for anyone who'd dare pay to touch a thirteen-year-old. While she had only the girl's word to go by, it sounded as if Magdalena used her as bait to personally murder creeps. Did any of the girls working there serve as real prostitutes? Probably... too many stories. No reason for Magdalena to kill men patronizing adult women.

What happened to her mother? In two years, did the woman finally do something stupid enough to get killed by one of the men she tried to siphon money from? Maybe she gave up trying to find a rich man. Time marched on, after all. She wouldn't stay pretty forever. As an ultimate irony, perhaps her bio mother ended up working for Magdalena. No... the woman hadn't been an Outcast. She had a real OT and earned money, merely wanted more, wanted to be wealthy enough not to need an OT at all. Having a kid got in the way.

Sima clenched her fists, hoping her running away hadn't made the woman happy. She demanded her bio-mom have *some* shred of emotion for her daughter, but wouldn't hold her breath. Her reaction to Sima's disappearance had probably been 'took long enough.'

And what of Callie? Oema? Theof? Demona? Pim? Or any of the other young Outcasts she shared a Crash with for the last few months prior to the EGSF tossing her on a spacecraft? Wondering what happened to the few people she knew made her sad for a moment. The unexpected glumness came more from the idea life went on without her, and no one likely noticed her absence or cared.

Screw it. I hate that place. This planet is my home.

10

MERELY A DREAM

R emedial class turned into a slog for the first time.

Between maudlin thoughts of the past, the material being boring, and Garret, she had trouble concentrating. The boy didn't mean to distract her, but the desperate way he kept glancing at her whenever he became confused made him appear childlike—at least in her mind. He had the same 'please help me' stare half the smaller Outcast kids used while begging. Part of her wanted to scoop him up and comfort him like a kid half his age, but part of her wanted to show him a quill cat up close, so he stopped being frightened by not immediately understanding schoolwork.

By the time the class ended at ten, she gave serious consideration to requesting to test out of it early. Nothing she worked on in 'normal' high school stumped her, though parts were challenging. Going over eighth-grade level coursework purely to put marks in the computer bored her to tears and seemed pointless.

Everyone appeared to be asleep, parents included, when she arrived home. She briefly looked in on everyone, but didn't disturb them, content to get ready for bed and go straight to sleep. Unlike most days coming home from late class, it didn't take long for her brain to stop spinning and allow her to pass out.

SIMA OPENED her eyes to a white ceiling and painfully bright light.

She tried to shield her eyes, but her arm jerked to a stop an inch from her waist with a metallic *clink*. Heaviness saturated her body, making it difficult to move. Fog clung to her thoughts, everything fuzzy and indistinct as if she'd been drugged. Having no other way to escape the glare, she closed her eyes and waited for her head to clear. Every breath carried an unfamiliar antiseptic smell.

After a moment, she became aware of cold metal around her ankles as well as wrists. Panic killed the last of her grogginess. Sima lurched up to sit in bed, finding herself upon a foam mattress in a featureless white cell. Her bare feet stuck out of the leggings of a glaring hot-pink detainee jumpsuit. Large black letters spelled 'JUVENILE' down both arms. Handcuffs secured her wrists to a thick, black nylon belt cinched too tightly around her waist. A larger chain descended from the belt to keep the hobble chain connecting her ankles from dragging on the floor.

The EGSF restrained her the same way when she'd first been processed, as if she were some manner of dangerous killer. Of course, they didn't really fear her… merely wanted to be cruel and make their contempt for her obvious. She hated the shackles, but if the EGSF intended to torment her, she preferred chains to a beating… or worse.

Whatever drug she'd been given left her feeling dizzy and off balance. Even seated on the bed, the room swayed side to side as if her cot had become a small boat on the ocean.

"What…?" She squirmed at the restraints, trying to wipe her eyes but unable to reach.

Frustrated, she leaned forward. A curtain of jet-black hair fell around her face. The glaring overhead lights made the pink of her jumpsuit legs look like lasers floating above a background of nuclear white.

What happened?

She gazed around at a small holding cell, only half again as wide as the bed. A tiny toilet, also white, occupied the corner at the foot end away from the only door out. The space had no windows, only a tiny four-inch square ventilation opening at the center of the ceiling.

"How am I here?" She grunted, trying unsuccessfully to pull her hand out of the cuff. "Is... No!"

Her worst nightmare had come true. Mirage had been exactly that... a mirage. No wonder the planet had been so damn close to Earth. The EGSF made it up in a virtual reality simulator. She strained at the handcuffs, desperate to feel around her head for needle marks or any sign of whatever technology they'd used to insert her consciousness into a computer. Being unable to check set off the irrational fear she might be bleeding horribly from the back of her head.

Screaming, she thrashed at the restraints until collapsing limp, out of breath, on the bed, staring down the perfectly white foam mattress at her feet. A scrap of shiny silver chain draped out from under the pink leggings between them.

Mom... Dad... not real. She closed her eyes, overcome by sadness, as if she'd watched her whole family die. *I knew it.*

Wracking sobs shook her. It didn't matter no one would care how she felt; she cried anyway. Some evil scientists probably watched her grieve people who probably never even existed. The pain of loss grew to the point she tried to wish herself dead. When that failed to work, she sobbed more.

"I don't care if it's fake. Put me back in!" shouted Sima past tears.

She absentmindedly grabbed at the handcuffs as if she might snap them off... and noticed the Omnicomputer bracelet was gone. It may have also been a bit of metal locked on her, but she missed it like a family member.

It would say something obvious now like... I dunno, I shouldn't cry when I can't reach my face.

She sniffled.

When she woke up in the pod, she hated the stupid bracelet.

The wiseass thing said she wasn't 'stuck' in her underwear because she could take them off. Ironic she found herself literally stuck in a pink detainee jumpsuit. High security transport restraints made it impossible to remove the incriminating garment. She could say she was stuck wearing it and the bracelet couldn't make a smartass remark.

Sima broke down crying again. Did those bracelets even exist? She'd never seen one before waking up in the escape pod. One of the ship's techs must have put it on her after they hit her with the knockout drugs... or not. None of it really happened. Maybe they brought her to a fake ship and what she assumed to be stasis pods were, in fact, virtual reality pods. Perhaps the original white cell the EGSF put her in had been a VR chamber, and the whole trip to the *Progenitor* never really happened.

Of course. How could a two-mile-long starship propel itself into space? Didn't they manufacture large ships in orbit and ferry people up to them on shuttles? Admittedly, as a street kid, she hadn't seen many spaceships or heard anyone talk about them. Planetary exploration didn't matter to people who'd be thrilled to have a non-moldy dinner. She had little true understanding of how they worked. Despite that, it sounded ridiculous for such a massive ship to be able to fly inside Earth's atmosphere. She started to think about the *Progenitor II* gliding to a hovering stop. The same engines allowing it to float probably could allow it to take off, but it didn't matter. Obviously, the ship hadn't been real. Virtual reality could do whatever the people who made it wanted. Spaceships, aliens, even magic—or most unbelievable of all, a real family.

Tears rolled down her face, dripping onto the front of her neck. She instinctively tried to wipe her cheeks; both hands jerked to a halt with a *clink*.

"Argh! Let me out!" Sima rattled the cuffs. "This isn't fair! I'm not dangerous! I didn't even do anything wrong."

She glared at the wall, furious. Why the hell had the EGSF left her chained up in a cell? Did they expect her to freak out upon realizing her ideal new life had all been a lie, or did they expect she'd try to harm herself?

Detective Marr is gonna be mad at them for putting me in cuffs again. She sat on the edge of the bed, tapping her foot on the plain concrete floor. *Unless... he probably lied to me, too. Pretended to be nice. Yeah, sure. He really went to Magdalena's and got Alina out of there. Sure. Cops don't care about us. Kids or not, we're just Outcasts to them.*

Sorrow over the loss of her family melted into fear during what felt like an hour of total, isolated silence. They'd let her out of the simulation. What would they do with her now? *Why* did they have her secured in shackles? They obviously didn't intend to set her free or they wouldn't have kept her locked up. Dread she'd be sent away for cruel medical experimentation got her shaking so hard the chains rattled.

She *hated* the clinking, hated being so vulnerable.

These chains are so loud. Sima tried to stop shaking and bundled up the tether connecting her leg irons to the belt to keep it from making noise. Her breathing became noticeable. Whatever facility they put her in sat in absolute silence.

"So weird."

Another seeming hour passed.

I'm going to go crazy from solitary confinement before anyone cuts me open. This is cruel.

She tossed her head back to fling her hair over her shoulders... and noticed the door to her cell was ajar. Open two inches.

"Whoa... the cell isn't soundproofed... the place really *is* dead silent." She paused, then raised her voice. "Hello?"

No one responded.

Clinging to a spark of hope, Sima dropped the bundle of chain, rose to her feet, and twisted, trying to look for the clasp on the belt. She figured it would be at the middle of her back, the most impossible place for her to reach with her hands locked to the exact opposite point on the belt. Even if she could spin the overly tight nylon around her waist, she couldn't move her hands any closer to the clasp. Maybe she could back up against a corner of a desk or something and pop it open, depending on the style of clasp. More likely, she'd have to find a good knife capable of cutting the heavy nylon.

Making an escape attempt in her present state sounded about as dumb and reckless as going to collect botanical samples in a forest while a quill cat prowled around… but a failed escape attempt *probably* wouldn't kill her. Sadistic as they were, the EGSF officers wouldn't view a shackled juvenile inmate as a threat to their lives. They might beat her, but she doubted they'd kill her.

Sima peered down.

An irritatingly short hobble chain connected her ankles, reducing her stride to a mere eight inches. All four shackles had obvious keyholes… so if she could find a desk, she could theoretically locate a key. Until she got out of the chains, she could pretend to be wandering lost. Maybe they wouldn't think she tried to escape. Only an idiot would try making a run for it when they could barely move.

She shuffled over to the cell door and pulled it open. No one out in the hall said anything. No alarms went off. Sima poked her head out, peering left. Dozens of similar cell doors lined both sides of an otherwise empty corridor. A haze of smoke clung to the ceiling. Every breath tasted like burning plastic. Some of the lights appeared broken, dangling on wires.

Sima looked right. More of the same.

Whoa… did the Separatists attack? Did I pop out of VR because it broke?

Emboldened by the apparent abandonment, she shuffled into the tomb-silent hall, fearing the clinking of her restraints would ruin her escape. She had no way to muffle it, so merely hoped the jangling metal only *seemed* loud compared to the eerie silence.

All the cells around her appeared unoccupied.

Five doors away from where she woke, signs of gunfire became apparent. Holes, gouges, and burns marked the walls and floor. No blood, though. Lights flickered, far weaker out here than in her cell. The smoke behind her thickened, obscuring the corridor from sight more than three doors away. It made no sense at all, but she half expected to see a quill cat stalk out of the fog. The same feeling she had in the rover of being stared at by a large predator made the hairs on the back of her neck stand up. Dangling, broken light tubes, smoke, and the total silence elevated her fear to almost terror.

Something seriously bad happened here, and she could barely move.

If crazy Seps, monsters, zombies, or something came out of the fog after her, she'd be as good as dead. Tiny shuffling steps wouldn't let her run away from an angry elderly person using a walker, much less a large cat or crazy anti-government terrorist.

"Wake up, Sima… those cats aren't real. They never were." She sniffled. "None of it. You gotta get out of here."

Steel bit into her ankles as she speed-shuffled along.

"Grr! I freakin' hate handcuffs! So much."

A loud *bang* went off above her head, along with a brief flash of light—then darkness. She reflexively dropped into a crouch, screaming because she couldn't raise her arms to shield her head. No pain. Silence. A thicker haze of smoke fell around her.

She timidly peered up. A light had blown out, leaving a small section of corridor dark.

"Oh, crap…" She shuddered. "What happened here? Yeah, I think the EGSF didn't *let* me out of VR. What if the Seps attacked and broke the computer? Do I have some kinda wireless thing in my head?"

With a grunt, she lurched to her feet and kept going.

"Gotta get out of here… not gonna get far in this pink abomination and chains." She grumbled for a few steps. "Screw it. Gotta try."

She peered into cells on either side as she made her way down the corridor. Not one had anything in them.

Wow. How big is this building? Feels like I've walked a mile already. She scowled. *It's not long. Stupid chain. I definitely need to find keys or I'll have no chance. Gotta ditch the jumpsuit, too. I won't make it half a block outside in this thing before the EGSF pounces on me.* She frowned.

Won't be the first time I've been stranded in a hostile environment in only underwear.

The bizarre idea she'd *rather* be seen in public in her underwear than a prisoner jumpsuit nearly made her laugh… though the giggles came from nerves rather than genuine humor. The repetitive jangle of chain from shuffling as fast as she could manage without tripping herself verged on hypnotic. Someone should have seen her on security cameras by now. Why hadn't any cops come rushing after her? Could the Seps truly have killed everyone?

Why did they leave her there? How much time had passed? Did eight months of Mirage consume mere minutes in the real world?

Finally, a door emerged into view out of the smoke at the end of the corridor.

Sima rushed—as much as the ankle chain allowed—forward, twisting her body at the last second before impact, shoulder-bumping the door open and stumbling into a room containing six desks. It looked like the area where she'd met Detective Marr. Personal computer terminals, desk kitsch, more cuffs, batteries, and other office supplies lay strewn about. A fight of some kind had definitely happened here.

Searching desk drawers with her hands stuck to her belly proved maddeningly frustrating. At least, she doubted anyone would stash handcuff keys in a lower drawer. Still, she looked anyway. Those, she could pull open using a foot—one bonus of not having shoes. Desk by desk, she rummaged, panic increasing. How long could she freely roam around the building before some guard noticed she'd escaped her cell?

Frustration boiled over into tears when she failed to find a key in the last desk.

After a momentary breakdown, she collected herself and shuffled to the next nearest door. Bumping it open revealed another hallway of cells and a dead end. Deciding not to bother wasting time going that way, she moved to the third door. Unfortunately, it didn't hang ajar and she couldn't reach the doorknob, her fingertips missing it by less than a full inch even if she stood up on her toes.

Sima muttered a few choice words under her breath while dragging a chair across the room to the door. Bracing one knee on it allowed her to lift herself enough to get a grip on the knob and open the door a half inch before it bumped against the chair.

"Dammit."

She curled her fingers around the edge of the door, then attempted to slide off the chair while bumping it out of her way, nearly falling when one chair leg got hung up on the chain between her ankles. Sima refused to let the door slip from her fingers and slam shut, kicking at the chair to disentangle herself from it. Once she caught her balance, she flung the door out of her way and hobbled forward—but stopped short, stunned by the sight in front of her.

The room had no exits, containing a heavy steel table and two chairs. Beside one chair lay Lissa, slumped on her side, partially curled into a fetal position. She, too, wore a pink detainee jumpsuit as well as full restraints... her hands secured to a belt, her tiny ankles locked in shiny cuffs. She appeared sickly and gaunt like when Sima first found her. Bloody froth dribbled from the child's mouth and nose onto the floor, already having formed a large puddle.

The little girl did not appear to be breathing.

A strong smell of cherry hung in the air.

Pixie...

All the strength left Sima's legs. She fell to her knees beside Lissa, struggling to reach out and grasp the child's hand. The cruelly tight restraint belt made it impossible, keeping her arms pinned against her stomach. Blinded by tears and her hair in her face, Sima flopped on her side and scooted forward, straining at the steel cuffs until her fingers made contact with Lissa's little hands.

Cold.

"Monsters!" shouted Sima, before grief overcame her and she bawled, tightening her grip on the small, lifeless hand. "You are all fucking monsters!"

Mirage never happened. Maybe Lissa had been in the simulation as well, like two people playing the same video game together. She might know Sima… or might not. Regardless, the child really existed —not a piece of computer programming—and she died because the bastards in the EGSF didn't think an Outcast orphan was worth the cost of lung replacement cloning. Except for the bloody discharge from her mouth and nose, she didn't have any visible injuries. Sima pictured her sitting in the chair suffering an interrogation, then collapsing to the floor and convulsing to death as her lungs melted into slime. Had the security officers done anything but watch and laugh? Maybe they hadn't even been interrogating her… if the Seps attacked, they might've put her in here and run off to fight.

"Liss… wake up. Please." She tugged at the girl's limp body.

Like a dropped blonde doll, Lissa's bright blue eyes stared glassily into oblivion, her mouth slightly open.

Even if this child never knew Sima, *she* still remembered weeks of desperately trying to protect her. Weeks of being mom to a girl who adored her. Months of being a big sister to the happiest, most unflappable, most innocent child imaginable. A child who, facing almost certain death on an alien world, spent her time weaving flower anklets and smiling.

A child the damned EGSF murdered.

All interest in escape crashed out of Sima. The stupid handcuffs wouldn't let her pick the body up and cradle her, so she lay on the floor behind her, pressing herself against Lissa, as much of a 'hug' as she could manage.

Nothing mattered.

She'd lay there until she either starved or the EGSF showed up to take her away. Perhaps ghosts existed and she could be with the girl again in some way soon.

"I'm sorry, Liss."

A low growl came from the doorway.

"Whatever," muttered Sima.

The growl happened again, louder, a rippling reverberation underscoring it… a great cat, not an angry security officer. Confusion at such an odd sound short-circuited her grief. Sima lifted her face away from Lissa's hair.

A quill cat stood partially in the doorway to the interrogation room, surrounded by wisps of smoke. Its dark blue fur made it appear almost like a silhouette. Sima locked stares with its four glowing green eyes, then glanced down at the chain between her ankles, her wrists trapped against her stomach. The cat blocked the only way out of a room with one exit.

"I'm so screwed..." She started to shake in fear, but stilled herself. Being eaten by a quill cat would be a quicker end than starvation. She'd join Lissa. Neither one of them deserved to die, but it happened. Sima hated Earth. She wanted off it one way or the other. "Come on then. You got me. I can't get away from you this time. Do it."

The cat snarled.

She stared defiantly at the large furry monster, waiting for it to maul her. Somehow, she managed not to soil herself.

It kept looking at her as if savoring the moment of victory... almost as if the same cat that trapped her in the rover caught back up to her. It occurred to her she *did* stare at the same cat. The pattern of thin white lines on its face matched perfectly.

She hadn't soiled herself. *How* long had she been in VR while wearing a jumpsuit? No tubes stuffed in places tubes didn't belong. No diaper. How had she even been connected to VR in a tiny prison cell?

Crippling sorrow vanished in an instant. "Wait. *This* is the dream!"

The cat snarled, stepping closer.

Sima scrambled to her feet and glared at the beast while shaking her chained hands. "Come on, bitch! You're not real. Go ahead! Bite me! You can't hurt me. You're not real!"

Roaring, the quill cat pounced, tackling her to the floor. Sima's cheek smacked into the concrete—which abruptly turned into beige carpeting.

Stunned by the hit to the face, she didn't try to move for a few seconds.

"Ouch."

Gradually, she became aware of having one foot up on a soft mattress, her legs tangled in blankets. The uncomfortable tightness around her waist vanished. Her right arm lay sprawled in front of her eyes, clearly free of handcuffs. With a grunt, she pushed herself up to sit on the floor of her bedroom.

On Mirage.

Home.

She hugged the Omnicomputer bracelet to her chest, choked up. It felt like she'd been told a dear friend died... then discovered it a cruel prank.

This has to be real, right? I had a nightmare. Virtual reality didn't glitch out. The other ship landed today and it made me think of the EGSF loading me onto the first one. Guess I fell out of bed when the 'cat' jumped on me.

"What time is it?" She tilted her arm so she could see the bracelet's screen when it opened.

"Really late," whispered a tiny voice from the doorway.

‹The current time is 03:19 a.m., Wednesday, April 27, 2410.›

Sima peered up at the doorway.

Lissa stood there in a nightgown, bleary eyed and half awake. She didn't look gaunt or sickly, merely too skinny. "Why are you screaming? Who's not real?"

At the sight of the girl alive, not dead on the floor of a prison, her liquefied lungs leaking out of her face, Sima lapsed into happy sobs.

"What's wrong?" Lissa crept into the room. "Why are you crying?"

Sima reached for her.

Lissa obligingly ran into a hug.

"Just a bad dream, sweetie." Sima squeezed her close, as if her arms could protect the little girl from all the evils of the universe. "A really, really bad dream."

11

FRIENDS

I t had been a while since Sima had a nightmare, especially one so vivid and horrible.

Lissa gladly played human teddy bear, spending the rest of the night in Sima's bed. Even clinging to the child for a continual reminder nothing bad happened to her didn't allow sleep. When the parents found out she'd had a nightmare so bad she stayed awake all night, they declared she would remain home from school —and see Dr. Bystrova.

Sima didn't mind talking to the doctor, but she stressed out over missing class. At least being Wednesday, she wouldn't miss a remedial session. Eventually, she accepted her parents might have a clue... and it wouldn't do her any good being in class after not sleeping. Anything the teachers said or she looked at on the screen would disappear in a haze.

She spent two hours in the doctor's office talking about the nightmare and what it potentially meant. Sima didn't need a psychiatrist to tell her she had a great deal of hate and resentment toward the EGSF and had become extremely protective of Lissa and the other kids. They mostly discussed her insecurities about Mirage being real, the fear she had about everything. The woman compared her to a street kid finding a fresh meal packet in the street and clinging to it so no one took it from her. Only, instead of a single meal pack, she'd found a new life.

Even with Dr. Bystrova's assurances the trip to Mirage really happened and the colony was neither dream nor virtual reality, the nightmare hit her so hard she spent the next two days questioning reality.

SIMA ENTERED the resource room at the education center after class the following Wednesday.

It had been a week since the *Progenitor II* landed. Thus far, other than having a giant metal object visible in the distance, the only real change she noticed took the form of an increase in the number of people in the Mall around the stores, and frequently seeing unfamiliar kids in the hallways at the Center.

Their lost, angry, and often confused expressions revealed them to be Outcasts going through the 'welcome to Mirage' process she underwent eight months prior, when the administration arranged her adoption to Manoj and Pai. Most likely, adults who came over on the second ship would adopt Outcast kids from their ship. No one had said anything about how many orphans the EGSF crammed on board. For all she knew, the entire ship might've been unwanted street kids. Earth certainly had enough of them to fill a starship as big as the Progenitor class several times.

It seemed quite unlikely they'd send *all* kids, though. The existing colony couldn't handle taking on eleven thousand juveniles, even well-behaved ones. Sending an entire ship of Outcasts would virtually guarantee the colony descended into anarchist chaos. Since all hell hadn't broken loose yet, she assumed the *Progenitor II* followed a similar plan as her ship, being mostly official colonists with any extra space taken up by 'trash.'

No point worrying or wondering about it. Sima had issues of her own to deal with, namely, ridding herself of the need for remedial education. She wanted to go from lagging behind to pulling ahead.

Alas, people filled the mini-desks and terminals, most being university students. Some teens and even a handful of adults also used the room. While everyone had access to the same information store from their portable tablets or even Omnicomputer bracelets, the resource room offered three advantages: large screens, quiet for studying, and a handful of librarians to help out wherever possible.

She spent a moment wandering around in search of an open seat. When she finally spotted one, she rushed over to sit—and noticed the person sitting there before her was still logged in.

Grr.

While she could be rude and log the person out to steal the terminal, she didn't want to get into a fight over it. So… she sat there waiting. If whoever left the terminal logged in had merely gone to the bathroom or went to ask a librarian for help, she'd give up the seat when they returned. But, sitting there kept anyone else from taking the only potentially open workstation.

Only one application appeared active on the screen, the basic email client. Evidently, enough people asked about contacting Earth, someone built in a notification to the interface stating they had no way whatsoever to communicate over such a great distance. Feeling a little mischievous and a lot restless, she poked around. The account looked as if it hadn't been used before, everything still at the default settings, plus a few icons for games appropriate for a tween. According to the profile, it belonged to a twelve-year-old boy named Caiden Luna, but he hadn't added a picture of himself or even a profile icon yet. The email client contained no messages in the inbox. One appeared in the sent folder, timestamped a mere minutes before Sima arrived at the resource room.

This is the real deal. Our guy came through. Sorry it took so long, but it took forever for things to... make their way through the usual process. Only got the memory fob back this morning. What the heck is in the food here? Not using any hardware they can trace to me. Fob was rigged to nuke itself after download. Paranoid bastards. Didn't pay fifty grand not to have a stupid backup.

THE EMAIL CONTAINED AN ATTACHED FILE. She tapped it, and a message popped up.

Unable to parse encrypted file. Unrecognized format.

"HUH... weird. That doesn't sound like anything a kid would write. Strange. Fake profile?"

She sat there another thirty seconds, tapping her finger on the desk while scanning the room. No one paid her any unusual attention or appeared to be on their way back to the terminal. Every other spot in the room remained occupied. Shady as this looked, Sima didn't want to go prying into someone else's business, and had a lot of work ahead of her if she expected to pass the exam on Friday.

So... she logged the account out, then logged in as herself.

Wednesday wasn't an official 'late' day, but no one said she couldn't work independently.

HOURS LATER, Sima decided to call it a night.

Except for a few trips to the bathroom and the cafeteria for dinner, she spent the past seven hours in the same chair mopping up every self-paced instructional she could until they all felt boring and easy. She had no doubts whatsoever she could pass the eighth-grade equivalency exam on Friday and become an official high school student with no further need to attend remedial sessions.

The emotional high of accomplishment squished the last bits of nagging fear left behind from her nightmare.

She logged out of the terminal, gathered her tablet, and made her way out of the resource room. Both librarians left a few hours ago, making her the last person there. Only a few Security officers plus the people running the power system remained in the Center. Walking around alone after dark still put Sima on edge. No matter how safe and secure the colony appeared to be, she couldn't let her guard down. It might never become even half as bad as Earth here, but it would only take *one* bad person in the wrong place at the wrong time. The colony had grown to roughly twenty-thousand people. Simple statistical probability said they already had at least a few dangerous ones. No point trying to train herself to relax. The longer the colony existed, the greater the chances for crime and violence.

Staying vigilant made sense, even if it did feel like an overreaction for the time being.

At least there are no Seps or EGSF or Scathers or Blanks here.

Walking roughly a mile from the Center to her residence unit didn't involve trying to make it through sectors where the inhabitants might randomly shoot at any moving target for fun. She wouldn't be stopped by the authorities for being out at night.

The colony definitely caused *less* fear than post-sunset Earth.

Still happy about the upcoming exam and feeling ready for it, she mostly set aside her anxiety and headed home. Even at night, the air retained a good deal of warmth, a sign summer approached. She'd crash landed in late August (Mirage). Into the early weeks of September when she lived wild with the kids, it had been so hot, even traipsing around naked felt as if she'd overdressed for the weather. No human had yet experienced *real* summer on this planet. She, and most of the scientists predicted day temperatures between 104 and 118 degrees on average during the height of July and August.

True, some genius decided to establish the colony relatively close to the planet's equator. The area of Earth where she used to live occasionally saw temperatures in the hundred-teens at the height of summer, too, but had almost no humidity. While the government destroyed information about past nations, she knew it had once been a desert before the creep of city took over. High heat *plus* humidity would be dreadful.

At least the Center and her residence had cooling systems.

No more sitting around in underpants, dripping in sweat.

Sima much preferred civilization.

Though, she did miss swimming in the river. Perhaps if the day ever came where someone could travel a short distance outside the colony and not need an armed escort, she'd consider taking the kids swimming again. However, the fitness room in the Center had a pool. Much safer there, if not as magical as a natural river surrounded by forest.

A few minutes into her walk home, the mood in the air turned threatening. Certain someone stalked her, Sima peered back at the darkened street. Every third building—give or take—had an exterior light attempting to illuminate the path. Nimbuses of white reflection glared up at her off the metal sidewalk. Indigo and black filled in the spaces between the lit areas, offering any would-be attacker plenty of room to hide.

She stood still, staring, listening. Signs of people moving around sounded too distant to be a problem, but also too far away to help if something happened. It didn't help that every nearby shadow and alley gave off the sense of a presence watching her.

It's probably just Kurosawa and his 'booze gang' trying to scare me. Sima took a breath. *Or I'm about to become Progenitor Colony's first victim of a random crime.*

Paradoxically, rather than afraid, she became angry.

"Dammit," she muttered, "I thought I left this BS on Earth."

She pulled her knife out from behind her back, but left it in the sheath, clutching it close in front of her. Avoiding fights whenever possible and hiding kept her alive on Earth. It should work here, too. The knife would only matter if someone cornered her.

After another minute of not seeing anyone, she resumed walking home, hurrying along.

The scuff of a shoe behind her confirmed she hadn't imagined a threat. Someone *did* lurk in the shadows, tailing her. In mere seconds, eight months of adjustment crumbled. Sima mentally leapt back to being on Earth. All her old survival instincts kicked in. She scanned the area for hiding places and alternate routes, refusing to lead the threat back to her safe place.

Unfortunately, the colony had *far* too much open space. On Earth, buildings stacked on top of buildings, crammed up against each other in a tangle. No matter where she went in the city, she'd be within seconds of reaching any of a thousand potential hiding places a grown man couldn't even fit in.

Here, she had only relatively wide alleys for cover... or climbing on top of a single-story prefab building. The mall had some mazelike parts where she might be able to lose someone, but an equal chance of stumbling into a dead end, trapping herself.

Every few seconds, she peered back over her shoulder. Twice, she caught a glimpse of a dark figure ducking behind a structure. Visual proof she didn't imagine the threat had the paradoxical effect of calming her down. A real, living, dangerous person scared her less than the idea she might have cracked and become paranoid.

Another person walked out from behind a building up ahead, coming directly toward her. She tensed, nearly baring her knife, but caught herself upon recognizing the guy approaching her: Koji. A surprised expression, a half smile, and non-aggressive body language gave her all the proof she needed to trust him entirely in the moment. She'd never pulled the 'meeting a friend' move with a boy before. Female Outcasts who didn't belong to gangs often pretended to know each other to discourage creeps, even if they'd never met before. At least she didn't need to whisper 'act like you know me' to him.

She still didn't much care for being social, but... she only preferred being alone when it wouldn't get her mugged.

"Hey." Sima ran over to him.

"Oh, hey. It *is* you." Koji smiled. "You're out late."

She resumed walking, but headed off in a random direction, not toward home. "So are you."

"At a friend's place. Was going home."

"Oh." She looked down, feeling awkward both for having no idea what 'going to a friend's place' was like as well as breaking her usual policy of ignoring everyone. "Kinda weird."

He raised both eyebrows. "What's weird about going home?"

"No." She chuckled, surreptitiously glancing back in search of her stalker while pretending to fix her hair out of her face. "Having friends. Just thinking. Before I came to Mirage, I used to kinda hate little kids."

Koji gasped. "Who hates children?"

"Not hate, really. Jealous. Little kids always got most of the glint from begging. If a pack of them decided to hang out near me, I got nothing."

"Ahh. Yeah, I can understand."

"So... I mean it's funny that after I got here, what do I find but three small kids in big trouble. The girl who couldn't stand children ended up risking her life for them." She squeezed the knife. "Now, I'd be destroyed if anything happened to them."

Koji leaned back, gazing up at the stars. "Proves you never really hated kids. So, what's weird about having friends?"

"Just having them." She exhaled. "I'm babbling. Had a couple friends when I was little. Just not after being on the street. Everyone's worried about themselves, trying not to starve or get dead. Didn't have time for friends. Couldn't trust anyone. Don't say sorry."

"Wow."

"Or wow." She narrowed her eyes at him. "That 'wow' meant sorry."

He stood there looking clueless for a moment before blurting, "Random nonsense."

"Huh?" She blinked.

"No idea what to say so..." He grimaced while scratching the back of his head.

She didn't have a response, so continued walking, having no particular idea in mind of where to go other than *not* home. The colony center offered the biggest sense of security due to there being no residences, lots of buildings, and a larger presence of security. Of course, intentionally going *to* a Security officer felt all kinds of wrong. She still couldn't find the ability to trust them.

As they passed a side street, the glow from a flickering blue-and-purple sign caught her eye, five buildings down. The fast food place 24-6 was—as its name suggested—open twenty-four hours a day plus six minutes. Seemed dumb, but some critical personnel *did* work overnight shifts in the Center. Someone had to feed them.

"Idea." She tugged on Koji's sleeve, then turned right. "Want to grab something to eat?"

"Uhh..." He stared in shock. "Sure."

She led him down the street to the smallish restaurant. The place had maybe twelve booth tables and a counter with eight stools. Most people who got food here picked it up and ate elsewhere. Two men in brown engineering jumpsuits sat together at the counter munching on a late dinner. A tired, middle-aged woman behind the counter looked up from her tablet, giving them a 'what are you kids doing out at this hour' stare. Sima hurried to the table farthest from the door and sat on the side putting her back to the wall.

"Do you usually get random cravings for food after ten?" Koji slipped into the other bench seat opposite her.

"Umm, sometimes. I actually forgot to eat dinner. Was at the resource room and got absorbed." She stood. "Be right back. If the woman comes over, order me a titan burger, okay? Need to hit the facilities."

"No problem." Koji fidgeted, seeming unsure of what to do or say.

She ducked into the bathroom and held her left wrist up near her mouth to whisper, "Send a message to my parents. Tell them someone's following me and I ducked in the 24-6 to avoid leading whoever it is home. I don't want them knowing where we live."

‹Your parents will most likely contact Security.›

Grr. Her stomach knotted up. Dealing with them made her as nervous as a potential mugging… but at least she had parents to complain if the officers roughed her up. Maybe they wouldn't even rough her up right in front of her parents. "Fine."

‹Shall I mention Koji?›

"Erm. Tell them I, uhh, made a friend… and forgot to eat dinner. Will eat here and go home as soon as possible."

‹Done.›

"Thank you." She patted the bracelet and returned to her table.

"Never did say what you're doing outside so late." Koji grinned. "Oh, I ordered you a burger."

"Thanks. And, uhh, didn't I? Resource room. Studying for a test."

He biffed himself in the forehead. "Right. You did. What test? I don't remember any class having a big one coming up."

She explained having to take remedial instruction for sixth-to-ninth grade material she missed while living on the street. "It's kind of embarrassing, honestly."

"Nah. You're not stupid."

"The word 'remedial' feels like it."

The bracelet vibrated, then opened its screen. ‹Your parents have notified the Security team and your father is on his way here.›

Ugh. She squirmed, conflicted. Having a dad willing to drop everything and rush to her side felt weird. It also eased—mostly—her fear of the Security officers. Maybe it wouldn't be too bad dealing with them if she had her father there, too. Even the EGSF treated Citizens okay. Only the Outcasts got the abuse.

He waved dismissively. "Life got in the way of your ability to go to school. Wasn't your fault. Hey, you're already in high school and got skipped ahead to sophomore year before you officially finished the remedial work, right?"

"Yeah, but I'm seventeen. I *should* be a junior."

"Who cares about age?"

She pointed at him. "Hang on. You're seventeen, right?"

"Yeah."

"And in the same class as me. But you're not an Outcast."

"Nope."

"You definitely didn't fail a year."

Koji shook his head. "I didn't. The Separatists set off a bunch of bombs. I don't remember much more than walking down the street past some shops and then somehow being in a hospital. My parents told me I'd been in a coma for four months. Felt like minutes. Then I got this infection... The school felt bad for me, but I'd only been two months into my first year of high school and missed the rest, so I had to start over."

"Ack. You don't know what happened to you?"

He shrugged one shoulder. "Pretty sure a flying gee-vee, or a big piece of one, hit me. Stuff got real crazy after the bombing. Even after the doctors let me go home, the EGSF practically invaded the area. One of them for every five people. The biggest bomb hit one of their offices. Like kicking a hornet nest."

Sima shuddered.

"Yeah, it was bad. Anyone who even gave them a dirty look ended up being strip searched. They interrogated everyone they could track down who'd been in the area during the days before the blast."

"Bastards," muttered Sima.

Koji leaned back. "I used to think Outcasts made up stories about them for sympathy. Never believed it until I saw them beating the hell out of people right in front of me... who weren't even Outcasts."

"Citizens are like that... don't believe what happens in the shadows and alleys to Outcasts they couldn't care less about."

"Did they ever do anything to you?"

She rested her elbows on the table, most of her attention on the front door. "Not really. But it only takes once. I never gave them attitude. They like feeling powerful, and I wasn't too proud to act small and scared."

The woman from the counter—Allie—arrived with their food. A titan squash hamburger for Sima and French fries for Koji. She appeared curious what a pair of teens were doing in her restaurant at the late hour, but didn't ask.

Despite being called a 'titan burger,' the sandwich wasn't particularly huge. Titan referred to the squash, not the burger itself. Still, she'd come to rather like the flavor, especially after whatever they did to it in order to make it taste like a hamburger.

"Here you go," said Allie. "Let me know if you two need anything."

"We will." Koji swiped his Omni bracelet at the reader to pay for their meal before Sima could.

"Thanks." Sima shot him a look, then smiled at Allie.

Once the woman walked away, Sima whispered, "You didn't have to pay for mine, too."

He shrugged. "It's okay. If you want, you can cover it next time."

Next time? She bit her lip.

"So, how'd they get you? The EGSF, I mean... or did you volunteer?" asked Koji.

She told him about the day a shootout between moving geevees caused a transport truck to flip, spilling food packets. "I was stupid and tried to grab as many as I could out of the street. Got arrested because the stupid driver started shouting about me being a Separatist."

Koji gasped. "Wow, what an ass. It could've gotten you killed… for taking food."

"I know. Jerk probably wanted me to get shot. Don't know what makes people *hate* Outcasts so much he'd rather see a girl my age be shot dead than eat."

"They are afraid because they're one really bad week away from becoming Outcasts themselves." Koji ate a fry. "And some people are just cruel."

She told him about the arrest, sitting in a plain white cell for days waiting for them to take her to the spaceship while technically not being an inmate. 'Protective custody' didn't feel much different. "Might've been a tiny room, but I guess it was clean. And they gave me real food. It really surprised me no one hit me or did anything really horrible. I mean, they could've done *anything* they wanted to me and no one would've noticed or cared."

"I don't think *every* EGSF officer is bad… just most of them."

Sima chuckled. "Or they didn't want to lose whatever money they got for putting me on the ship."

"Kickbacks?"

"I dunno." She scrunched her nose. "They didn't even put clothes in the lockers near our pods. Totally empty. Cheap bastards."

They ate in silence for a moment, then stumbled into a general conversation. He kept smiling at her, and sometimes missed his mouth when attempting to eat. Twice, he repeated a sentence from minutes ago as if he hadn't already said it.

Uh oh. He's going to think I like him. Sima nibbled on her burger. No one could ever accuse it of being real meat, but it didn't taste bad. *Well… I don't dislike him. Seems smart and nice.* She exhaled hard, looking around at the empty tables. *Mirage is so different from Earth. Maybe I should try to make friends.*

Dad rushed in, along with a Security officer.

"Crap," whispered Sima. "Here goes."

"What's wrong?"

She flicked her gaze over his shoulder.

He twisted to look. "What are they doing here?"

"My father. You know, adoptive. But… never had one before so he's like my real father as far as I care."

"Why are you unhappy to see him if you like him?"

"I'm not. I'm…" She looked down. "Scared of Security officers." Realizing she'd admitted it to someone other than Dr. Bystrova or her parents made heat rush to her cheeks. "Yeah, I'm just a big ol' bag of mental problems."

"I understand. EGSF are cretins. I'm scared of parked gee-vees."

"Really?" She stretched up and waved so her confused father noticed them all the way in the back. "Parked?"

"The bomb. If being outside kinda looks like the street before the blast, I have anxiety attacks. Haven't had one here. Probably because there are no gee-vees—or actual roads. The rovers and Nomads don't look anything like them. Uhh, why is your dad here with a Security officer?"

She bit her lip, guilty at being caught in the lie of not telling him about the person following her. Why hadn't she wanted him to think she only hung out with him for protection? She'd ducked into the bathroom to send the message home so he didn't know about it. It would've been easy to ask the bracelet to send a message right from the table… but then Koji would've become aware of the stalker. After all, she *had* only decided to spend time with him for protection in the heat of the moment, right? Admitting it to him should have been easy. Why should she care what he thought of her? Why did it bother her that he *might* feel used?

"You helped me tonight and didn't realize it. Someone followed me, but they ran off when they saw you." She managed a weak smile. "I'm so glad you ran into me."

He tilted his head. "You didn't say anything?"

"Didn't want to freak you out, and I'm still not completely sure it really happened."

"Sima!" Dad jogged over to their table, nodding once at her friend. "Koji."

"Hi, Mr. Akbar." The boy straightened out of his slouch.

Whoa... Dad knows him? She shrank a little, wondering if her parents eavesdropped on her somehow. But... Koji also acted as if he'd met Dad before. *Weird.*

The Security officer, a late-twenties guy, approached the table in far less of a hurry. "Ms. Nuvari?"

"Yes, sir." Sima clasped her hands in her lap.

"I understand you've been threatened?"

She bit her lip. "Not exactly *threatened*. I was at the resource room late, doing some extra schoolwork. While walking home, I noticed someone following me. They kept hiding whenever I looked back. Only saw a bit of an arm or leg."

"Any idea why someone would be following you?" asked the officer.

Sima stared at the name 'Merrick' on his light armor vest. "No, sir."

"Not a clue who it might've been?"

"No. I'm sorry. It could've been a man or a woman. They had a hood and a mask or something. Guessing. Didn't see a face, just dark. I took a few random turns and they kept following me. Not sure what they wanted to do."

Officer Merrick thumb-typed into his tablet. "All right. I'll document the report, but without anything more to go on, there isn't really much we can do at this point other than to beef up our monitoring of the area around the Center. If you can think of some reason beyond the obvious ones someone would follow you, let us know."

"Yes, sir." She swallowed, having a fairly good idea what an 'obvious reason' for someone to follow her at night would be.

"Are you comfortable returning to your residence, or would you like me to stick around?" asked Officer Merrick.

Wow... She stared at him.

Dad gestured at the little bit of burger remaining on her plate. "Go on and finish your dinner. Let's get you home. Your mother is worried. No sense bothering Officer Merrick any more than we have already. I doubt whoever followed her is sitting outside watching this place."

Sima scarfed down the last two bites.

"No bother at all, Mr. Akbar. I'll give a look around outside, just in case."

"Thank you." Dad shook the officer's hand, then looked at Sima. "Ready?"

"Yeah." Eager to get home to the safety of her room, she jumped to her feet, then flashed a grateful-guilty smile at Koji. "Thank you for coming out of nowhere at the perfect moment. You probably saved my ass tonight."

The boy fidgeted.

"Next time, I'll cover the food." She waved at him and took Dad's hand. "Hey, why don't you walk with us?"

Koji nearly tripped himself trying to stand up.

12

OLD HABITS

To avoid leaving Koji alone, Sima and her father walked him home first.

They couldn't come up with any explanation for *why* someone followed her. Officer Merrick made some assumptions based on Sima being a girl. However, Sima had seen enough crazy Scathers to know boy or girl didn't matter, especially if they simply wanted to kill for fun. Neither she nor her father felt right about leaving him to go off by himself.

The whole way to his residence building, and then home, Sima felt like she'd been drawn straight back to District A019F4. She kept her head up, obviously watching her surroundings. This dissuaded casual predation. If she spotted a Security officer, she did the exact opposite: looked down and conveyed timidity. Gang members wanted easy victims. Anyone who looked like they'd put up a fight or make them run, they'd ignore. The EGSF, however, bristled at defiant Outcasts.

She watched every shadow, every alley, and every bit of motion in her periphery. Having her father beside her made the difference between trusting her knife to stay tucked behind her back or having it in her hand. For the first time since arriving on Mirage, she missed her old tunic. The big front pocket could conceal a knife comfortably while still allowing fast access. One of the stores here probably sold them by now. Maybe she'd get one. Lots of people on Earth wore them, not only Outcasts.

By the time they arrived home, she felt confident the person who'd tailed her gave up, most likely as soon as she and Koji went into the 24-6. The exhaustion of hypervigilance wanted to pull her straight to bed, but the look on Mom's face demanded further delay.

Her mother sprang from the sofa, rushing over to them the instant they entered the apartment. "What happened?"

Sima hugged her, then returned to sit beside her on the couch. "I don't really know."

She explained everything—except her odd guilt at being mildly dishonest with Koji.

"Hmm." Dad rubbed his chin. "Perhaps those people you observed selling alcohol?"

"Maybe." She flicked at a fold in her baggy pants. "Not sure why they'd wait over a week and try to scare me. I'm not going to cause trouble for them. It's probably someone new from the second ship. The EGSF didn't exactly screen me for sanity. They could've picked up a Scather or something, not realized it, and sent him up here."

Mom brushed at Sima's hair. "Could it be someone who knows you from Earth?"

"Uhh. Don't think so. I didn't exactly have friends... or enemies, really. And if they knew me, why hide and sneak around?"

The parents exchanged a glance.

"This concerns me," said Dad.

"Will you stop going out after dark for a little while at least?" Mom kept fussing at her hair.

Sima tensed, unsure how to process physical affection. It didn't bother her as much as felt odd. Not wanting to make Mom feel bad, she decided not to squirm away and redirect the feeling of awkwardness into being mildly angry at her birth mother for never being affectionate. "I have one more late class tomorrow, then the test on Friday. If I pass it, I'll be done with the remedial sessions and won't have to go out after dark anymore."

"Good." Dad set his hands on his hips. "Tomorrow, I'll meet you at the Center and walk with you."

"You don't have to. A kid doesn't stay alive for four years as an Outcast without learning how to ditch a tail."

"Non-negotiable." Dad smiled. "Also, not an inconvenience. I'll be home by then anyway."

As much as she adored having parents, catching herself feeling ever so slightly annoyed at his overprotectiveness made her smile. *Normal. Maybe I'm not a head case after all.*

Mom appeared placated at the compromise. "Are you prepared for the test?"

"Yeah. It's why I stayed late today."

"Speaking of late." Dad tapped his Omnicomputer bracelet. "It's almost midnight. You should go to bed."

"If anything like this happens again..." Mom took her hand. "Please find the nearest safe place and call Security."

Sima grimaced. "Umm. Okay. I'll try."

"Try?" asked Dad.

"Maybe you guys don't know how it was on Earth. EGSF could be so horrible to us. At first, I didn't know any better... and being twelve, they *were* kinda nice to me. But it didn't take long before I saw what they did to older teens and adult Outcasts. They scared me more than the gangs. At least the E86ers, Pluggers, and Zap-Fiends sometimes hesitated before attacking someone because they feared the EGSF. The EGSF had nothing to be afraid of. They'd do whatever they wanted to whomever they wanted whenever they wanted, and nothing would ever happen to them."

Her parents hugged her.

Sima choked up. "I don't know if I will ever be able to *intentionally* contact Security officers... but, I guess my life has kinda changed. Okay. I'll try."

13

TRASH

few moments in Sima's life brought tears of happiness.

By far the strongest had been when Lissa woke up in her arms after she'd assumed the child suffocated to death. She couldn't claim getting real parents who cared about her as one of these moments because adjustment to the reality of it happened gradually over months. The emotional impact of such a huge change didn't hit her all at once.

Other times positive emotions made her cry generally included finding good food, a kind Citizen giving her a large amount of glint, or passing her educational equivalency exam. It didn't make a lot of sense for her to lose her composure when told she'd passed a test she had every expectation of passing. Dr. Bystrova called it a 'sense of validation,' and thought she internalized success on the exam as a badge of legitimacy. As in, she fully put being an Outcast behind her. Eight months of busting her butt erased four years of sleeping in alleys and sewers.

Whether or not the doctor had it right, Sima didn't know. Acing the exam *did* greatly reduce her constant worry people might mock her for being a 'dumb Outcast' or 'street trash' or some such thing.

She technically now had the same education as any Citizen. From Friday forward, she'd attend high school like any other kid who'd never eaten food out of an ORC bin.

If two years of travel at .877 percent the speed of light didn't put Earth far enough behind her, the test did.

For the first time since being on the street, she had a Saturday entirely to herself.

She'd even mostly forgotten about the person following her last Wednesday. No sign of any threats showed up Thursday night, but Austin swore some things in the boys' bedroom had been moved and he didn't do it. Juan denied doing it and Austin didn't doubt him. Lissa denied it as well, and also said someone moved her bed.

This, of course, concerned Mom and Dad. A thorough search of the residence found no evidence anything had been stolen. Sima couldn't imagine why a person might break into their home, rummage around, and leave without taking a single item. Predictably, the parents involved Security. The building's access logs showed a maintenance worker named Lao Zheng entered the apartment at 10:03 a.m. Friday when no one had been there. However, Security found the man unconscious on the floor of his residence and determined he'd taken a near-fatal dose of gamma-hydroxybutyric acid mixed with alcohol.

Sima suspected someone knocked him out to steal his access card. Maintenance workers, fire control, Security officers, medical responders, and command staff had cards capable of opening every door in the colony. An attack on a maintenance worker would be the one least likely to be noticed fast.

Question being: *why?*

Between being thrilled over the test results and learning someone had been in her home, she didn't sleep much Friday night. Late morning on Saturday, she groggily pushed herself up out of bed and went to the bathroom. Head in her hands, hair draped almost to the floor, she stared down at her feet as the discomfort in her bladder lessened.

With relief came clarity of thought.

Theof, one of the older Outcasts from the last Crash she lived in, often waxed poetic about toilets being 'thrones of thought.' She used to sneer at him for it, but having an idea fly into her brain while in the bathroom made her question reality.

They're not after me. It's Mom or Dad. They were gonna kidnap me to make my parents do something. She sat up and flung her hair behind her back. *Someone searched our home looking for something they didn't find. Research? Plans? Dad's a senior person in Engineering. Mom's a doctor, but she's not treating people, she's evaluating native plants for potential medical use. Not exactly spy grade stuff.*

"Ugh. Fail. Not an epiphany."

Hah. Used one of those big new words.

Once finished in the bathroom, she hurried down the hall to the kitchen to pay the price of sleeping in: making her own breakfast. Her parents both relaxed in the living room, Dad watching the holo-TV, Mom gazing at her tablet. On Mirage, television presently had three uses: watching recorded movies from Earth, one news/announcement station that tended to play a repeating twenty-minute segment, and video games.

She put breakfast on hold. "Mom? Dad? I thought of something."

They looked at her.

"Someone followed me, but what if they weren't after *me* so much as maybe hoping to abduct me to make you guys do something? I bet the same person or people are the ones who attacked the maintenance guy and broke in here. Are either of you working on anything special or secret someone might want to steal?"

Their clueless expressions answered without words.

"Right, so no top-secret research project hidden under your pillows."

Dad laughed. "Not unless someone is highly interested in wiring diagrams on how we're going to connect the *Progenitor II* into the existing colony structure from an electrical power perspective."

"I do not bring my work home with me. Don't want the kids to end up growing fur," said Mom in such a serious tone Sima almost worried... until her mother chuckled.

Juan ran in. "I can have fur? I want fur. How do I get fur? Is it gonna be blue or green?"

Mom shot Sima a 'see what you started' look, then tried to explain to Juan she'd been joking. The boy cried over not being able to turn into a 'wolf child' as if he'd been told he'd never be allowed to have food again.

SIMA SAT at a table in the mall's food court a little after one in the afternoon.

Sadly, Dad got called in to work despite it being Saturday. The administration wanted to hurry up and establish connectivity between the colony and the second ship. Her father happened to be the head of the team assigned to produce the design schematics for the second half of the colony. This meant they needed to work with the people planning out the locations of all the prefab buildings yet to be unloaded.

As a celebration for passing the exam, Mom took Sima and the kids to the Mall for a 'fun day.' She'd seen—and begged in—a few malls on Earth. All had been much larger, far more crowded, and *way* filthier. Making good on her idea from the other day, she bought a hooded tunic similar to the one she used to wear on Earth. They didn't have pink ones, so she settled for pale green. It also lacked built in electronics for connectivity to Dreamland. However, it *did* have the big front pocket she missed.

A little over an hour into their time at the Mall, they happened upon Koji, who'd been there to see if any of the shops had new electronics or video games brought in on the second ship. Alas, if the *Progenitor II* brought anything of the sort, it hadn't been unloaded yet. Mom suggested he join them for lunch, so they headed to the food court.

Her mother clearly overestimated Sima's desire to spend time around Koji. Her father no doubt told her about meeting him at the restaurant. She still had no idea why he appeared to already know the boy, nor had she asked. Talking about him would probably send the wrong message, make her father think she *liked* Koji. If she made a big deal about her mother suggesting he join them for lunch, she'd definitely confirm to her parents she liked him. Despite the awkwardness of a semi-forced social encounter, she didn't fully object to it either.

Mom went off to the bathroom some minutes ago. Koji and the kids talked about video games while Sima twirled her Omnicomputer bracelet around her wrist, pondering the oddity of having money. Only former Outcasts used the term 'glint' for money, and most of them abandoned it in an effort to blend in. She could tell who came from the middle class and up compared to 'normal' Citizens depending on if they used the term 'oomoo' (UMU - Universal Monetary Unit), or 'cows.' Lower middle class to poor people favored the slang. Not wanting to come off as aloof, she'd been training herself to think of 'glint' as cows.

In spite of the relatively low population of Mirage, the governor decided they would continue to use a traditional form of currency rather than simply work on a communal distribution model or even ration assignments. All the money here existed as numbers in a computer anyway, just like on Earth. If the Separatists ever succeeded in blowing up or hacking the system, they could wipe everything out. No more rich, no more poor. Everyone would have zero. It sounded scary, but much more difficult to pull off. The government must have backups on top of backups. The Seps might delete money information and cause a few days of chaos, but since UMU represented nothing tangible, the government could simply set the numbers back to whatever they wanted.

Life really is a video game. Everyone's trying to accumulate points.

"I heard they're planning to build between the colony and the new ship, making it into one big city," said Koji.

Sima looked up, not having noticed the moment their conversation switched away from computer games.

The boys attacked their lunch, some manner of burritos, while Lissa sat there in front of an empty plate. Considering the amount of food on her face and the table around her, it appeared as though her burrito exploded. Upon realizing Sima noticed the mess, she grinned.

"What did you do?" She whistled. "Eat it or try to crawl inside it?"

"I had lunch. It was good." Lissa wiped her cheeks, then licked strands of printed chicken and sauce off her hands.

"She's still feral," muttered Austin past a mouthful.

Lissa stuck her tongue out at him.

The weight of Koji's expectant stare became too much to keep on 'hold.'

"Umm, yeah. I heard that, too." Sima nodded at him, deciding not to mention Governor Harland said so when the ship landed.

Koji had a habit of making obvious statements around her, even worse than her bracelet. For a boy who had some of the highest grades in their class, he frequently sounded a bit like an idiot. Unless, of course, they got to talking about something science-related, or video games, art, or even reading. The *Progenitor* had multiple terabytes of electronic books, some older than the End of Nations, though those had been edited by the EGSF to remove references to names of countries or individual locations. It would probably be a long time before anyone on Mirage made new movies or video games, established professional sports, and so on. The next several generations would likely either read a ton or become incredibly sick of the same video games and movies.

At least she had a real day off.

"This is really weird but nice." She stretched.

Koji blushed. "Weird? What is? Something wrong?"

"No. Having a day off and not *needing* to do anything. I've never really been able to just be a kid and loaf around all day not worrying. I mean... maybe when I was super little... but like, right now? I don't have to think about school until Monday. Don't have an OT—yet."

"People think street kids just party all the time." Koji rolled his eyes.

"The stupid ones do. Everyone else is basically working fourteen hours a day... begging or stealing, trying not to die." Sima rubbed both hands down her face. "Trying to forget."

"Sorry."

"You should be." She stuck her tongue out at him.

His eyes widened.

"Wow. Teasing." She nudged him.

Koji practically collapsed over the table in relief.

Austin looked at him, then Sima, and raised his eyebrows.

She interpreted the boy's expression to mean he thought Koji *liked* her.

Her cheeks reddened, which sent the exactly wrong message to her little brother.

Austin grinned impishly. The way he looked at her said, 'I'll keep quiet if you pay me.'

Before she could come up with anything to change the subject to, Mom returned. She also appeared to misinterpret the blush on her face and awkwardness radiating from Koji.

"Looks like you'd enjoy some time with your friend." Mom beckoned at the kids. "C'mon you three. We'll be at the zero-g place."

"Yay!" cheered the kids at once.

Dammit, Mom. Sima hid her face in her hands, too embarrassed to say anything as her mother and siblings crossed the food court to the amusement center. The place had various real-world games, trampolines, bounce pits, climbing walls, and so on. Basically, fun —and active—stuff geared for children younger than Sima. Even Austin verged on being a little too old for it, but didn't appear to mind. It sounded like a strange thing to include on a deep space colonization ship, but perhaps it served more purpose than simple fun. Keeping kids active kept them healthy. Maybe it also doubled as a day care.

Koji sat up straight, hands in his lap, seeming nervous.

"Dr. Desai sent me an email a couple days ago. He's been analyzing the cellular structure and DNA of the botanical samples we took."

"Cool." He relaxed, half turning in the chair to face her. "What did it say?"

"It's still pretty much over my head. I haven't hit university-level science yet. DNA sequencing is an entirely different language. He did comment the plants are basically using the same genetic materials as Earth plants, merely arranged in slightly different ways. It's why we can eat some of the native vegetables and fruits and not die."

Koji gave a thumbs-up. "Not dying from what you eat is a big plus."

"Yeah." Sima laughed. "*So* glad I had my Omni. It saved our lives."

The bracelet vibrated affectionately.

A group of eight teens crossing the food court in a pack caught her eye. All looked to be a year or two younger than her and wore the basic plain grey jumpsuits issued to minors under eighteen. In spite of their new and pristine attire, the kids carried themselves as if they owned the mall, scowling around at everything. A few looked directly at her. The wariness in their eyes betrayed the fear lurking beneath their outward bravado. Sima knew the routine; she used it plenty of times.

"Know them?" whispered Koji.

"Nope. But they're street kids. Former anyway. Gotta be from the new ship." She sighed. "How much more garbage is Earth going to dump here?"

"Garbage?" Koji glanced at her.

"People like me. Outcasts. Kids no one wants."

"Hey, Sima..." He elbowed her. "You're not garbage. Okay, maybe Earth didn't want you, but Mirage does."

She smirked at him, but the sarcasm brewing on her tongue evaporated at his smile. "Little lame, but thanks."

"Maybe I sound lame, but it's sincere. Earth has outcasts because of massive overpopulation. People blame the rich, but it's not their doing."

"I know. They're confused. Three percent of people owning ninety-six-something-percent of all wealth is what started the war leading to the End of Nations. Now that we're up here, I can say this out loud. It's really weird how human society went from two hundred or so individual countries using various methods of government to one global society ruled by an emperor or empress."

"The empress doesn't get upset if people criticize her." Koji scratched his head. "She never claimed to be perfect."

"Not that. The government doesn't like people talking about individual countries." She twisted in the chair to face him. "Ever wonder why? If a single government is really the best way to exist, why would they be so afraid of even talking about the world before it happened? They don't want anyone to know Earth wasn't *always* run by a unified government. What are they afraid of?"

Koji shrugged.

They discussed the question for a little while before getting bored and switching from politics to the plant studies Dr. Desai sent her. Sima thought he wanted to tempt her into pursuing an OT as a biologist, which *did* still sit at the top of her list. Since he happened to be here and talking at the moment, she discussed her indecision regarding what to do as a career between biologist, robotics, or electrical engineering like Dad.

While he pondered, faint weeping drifted in from the left.

Sima held a hand toward Koji. "Shh."

"I'm not making a sound."

"You hear that?"

He tilted his head. "Some kid's crying."

"Don't say the world doesn't have a sense of irony or karma."

"Huh?"

Sima stood. "Back on Earth, I'd have heard a little kid crying and thought something like 'hah, good,' if I had a bad day, or 'not my problem' any other time. Now, I'm going to go check on them and see what's wrong. This is karma biting me in the ass for being nasty to little kids for two years."

"You weren't nasty. You were desperate."

"I tossed a little kid in an ORC bin because she kept insisting on begging in my spot."

Koji blinked. "Okay, that's nasty."

"Yeah... wish I could find her. Really want to apologize." Sima sighed. "Be right back. Hey, maybe this will be her."

"Hah. That would be weird." He got up.

Sima followed the crying along the edge of the food court to a cluster of ORC bins. They all bore the word 'ORC' stenciled on them despite Omni Recycling Corporation not existing on the planet. A small person in a grey jumpsuit hid behind them, curled up in a ball and crying. Long, white hair tinged pink at the ends, plus painted fingernails—no two the same color—probably meant girl. Sima guessed her age around eleven or twelve. The way she cried sounded like a young Outcast spending their first night on the street.

Sima crept past the bins and crouched in front of her. "Hey, sweetie. You okay?"

The girl jumped, scrambled back a little, and stared at her, deep blue eyes widening in fear. Her cheeks reddened in shame, and a second later, her expression hardened into a 'who you calling sweetie, bitch' stare.

"Oh, crap..." Sima gawked. "Oema?"

"Tell anyone you caught me crying, and I'll cut you," whispered Oema.

"Easy. I'm no snitch. Wow, what happened to you? Did you get smaller when they froze you?"

"I dunno. What's that supposed to mean?"

"When I saw you hiding back here, I thought you were like eleven."

Oema held up her left arm, showing off a bracelet. "Nope. Thirteen. They put this stupid shock restraint on me. Won't come off. It took four of them to hold me down and get me in the ice box." She struck a defiant, proud pose.

"I love my Omni. It saved my life more than once. Trust me, don't hate it. It's not a shock restraint. If it's zapping you, it's trying to warn you of something important. Turn your arm up so you can see the bottom of your wrist." Sima demonstrated. "It projects a little holographic screen and communicates by text."

"Aww, crap. You've gone soft."

"Soft? Nah, more like I've gone Citizen."

"Even worse."

"Come on. Don't be a dumbass. It's really not bad here. Totally rather be on Mirage than Earth."

Oema stared at her.

"I'm serious. Do I look stressed out?"

"Kinda."

Koji chuckled.

Oema looked up past her. "Who's he?"

"Koji. We're in the same class."

"Huh?"

"School?"

"Oh, crap. They're gonna make us go to *school*?"

Sima shook her head. "What's worse? Going to school or being chased down an alley and cut into a dozen pieces by Scathers ripped on Nightmare Fuel?"

"Umm..." Oema tapped a finger to her cheek. "Hard choice."

"No, it isn't. Look, I get it. You're still young. The world feels way different at twelve than it does at sixteen. Trust me. Back there, everyone treats you different as soon as you stop looking like a little kid."

"She *is* a little kid," said Koji.

Oema glared at him.

"Nah. *Lissa* is a little kid. Oema's somewhere in between. Kinda hard to grow up when you only eat once every few days." Sima sat on the floor. "So… why are you hiding back here 'not' crying?"

"I'm not."

"You are. Hey, I wanna help, okay? Promise nothing you tell me will go anywhere unless you want me to tell someone else. Did someone hurt you?"

Oema shook her head. "No. Just being a wimp. Got lost and couldn't deal. It's freaky being on a different planet. The stupid trees are blue! Why are the damn trees blue?"

"A tiny difference in one chromosome causes Mirage plants to produce a form of chlorophyll that reflects blue wavelength light instead of green."

"Sima?" Oema blinked at her.

"Yeah?"

"What did they do to you? You're talking like a robot. And what's wrong with him?"

She peered back at Koji, who smiled in a weird sort of way. "Good question."

"I love talking about science stuff." He grinned.

"Oh no." Oema grabbed her head in both hands. "Is this what 'school' does? Makes everyone talk weird nonsense?"

Sima laughed. "Kind of. But… you did ask why the trees are blue."

"It's not supposed to have an answer!" Oema flailed. "I'm complaining."

"Seriously. You should be happy you got away from Earth when you did. You're still young enough not to have seen anything really awful."

Oema gave her a flat look. "Floating idiots who overdose isn't awful?"

"Umm." Sima cringed. Sure, a thirteen-year-old should probably not watch people throw a dead seventeen-year-old in a river of human waste, but… far worse *could* have happened to—or in front of—her. "It is, but there's other stuff even you wouldn't want to see. You're pretty tough for a kid. Still got the Minicube you nabbed from Draz?"

"Maybe."

"You don't know?"

"It might be in my stuff. Had it on me when the cops grabbed me."

"Where's your stuff?"

"At the place."

"Which place?"

Oema shrugged. "I don't know. They made me talk to this woman who was gonna sell me to someone. I jumped out the window and ran."

"Wow. Not how it works here. They aren't selling us. Just assigning us new parents."

"No way." Oema waved both hands while shaking her head rapidly. "Last ones tried to kill me. I don't need or want parents."

Sima grasped the girl's shoulder. "Your last parents were psycho drug addicts who had a bad trip and thought you were a demon. They are not normal. I mean, wow. *Your* parents make my birth mother look like a good option. It's totally different here."

"They're gonna lock me up."

"For what?"

"Sneaking away."

"No, they won't." Sima started explaining about her new parents and how happy it made her to feel safe.

Oema calmed, uncurled from a ball, and sat with her legs to one side. "You sound like a Citizen."

"There's no such thing as Outcasts here. Forget Earth. Forget everything. You're not an Outcast anymore, either."

"They arrested me for being an 'unaccompanied minor' or some bullcrap like that. Asked me where my parents were. Didn't like me saying, 'Hope they're dead.'"

Sima winced. "Did they hurt you? I mean the EGSF. I know what your parents did."

"Not really."

"Not... *really*?" Sima raised an eyebrow.

"They were pretending to be nice, but I didn't trust them. Tried to run away, so they put handcuffs on my legs so I couldn't escape. Told me I had to get on this spaceship and I'd be all happy and stuff. Sounded like *such* a lie."

Sima nodded. "Yeah, I got the treatment too when I tried to run. Now it feels so stupid. Coming here was the best thing I ever did."

"They sent us all over here to the first colony, 'cause they didn't want us in the way." Oema frowned. "Doesn't feel like the Citizens are happy we're here."

"Umm." Koji held up a finger. "It's not because they don't want you. The colony here already has schools and residences set up. We can deal with kids too young to work. They still have to unpack everything."

"I guess." Oema stared at her lap. "They tried to find my parents, but couldn't, so here I am."

"Hey... it really is better here."

The girl stared at the floor for a moment, then sighed. "I'm really scared. If you tell anyone, I'm gonna stab you."

Sima chuckled. "Everyone here is scared. Even the adults. Change is scary. But this is good change. Hey, wanna hear something super crazy?"

Oema peeled her gaze off the floor. "Sure."

"I think we can trust the cops here."

"Bull." She gawked. "They really did replace your brain with a potato."

"Don't be so scared. You're still little enough even the cops on Earth wouldn't have been too bad to you."

"I'm thirteen."

Sima quirked an eyebrow. "So... elderly."

Oema smirked, giving her the finger.

"I said 'little,' not 'young.' You could pass for eleven easily. Maybe ten if you worked on it."

Oema waved the finger back and forth.

Sima chuckled. "EGSF officers are piles of crap. But... think about it. They abuse Outcasts. We're not Outcasts anymore." Sima told her about Officer Merrick and his offer to walk her home. "The Security team here are mostly to protect us from dangerous stuff outside the colony."

"Huh?" Oema went platter eyed. "What are you talking about? Dangerous stuff?"

"Giant cats. These other things like bears. Some deadly plants. These big red ones tried to eat my little brother. There is even evidence of a prior civilization being here."

"Aliens?"

"Not technically, since this was their planet." Sima chuckled.

Oema fidgeted at her bracelet. "How do I make this thing stop zapping me? It hurts."

"Like this." Sima grabbed the girl's left arm, twisting it to expose the underside.

The bracelet projected a holographic panel. Text scrolled into view with a familiar electronic pattering noise. ‹Oema, you should return to the Center so Ms. Wade can assist you. I can help you navigate the Colony, or you can ask any Security officer in a blue jumpsuit for assistance. They are trying to help you. Also, I am sorry for the shocks, but you weren't paying attention. I do so loathe how they neglected to give us speakers.›

"Whoa," whispered Oema, gawking at the shimmering panel of light.

"It's an AI. They're smart. You can talk to them like a person. And, believe it or not, their primary mission in life is to protect whoever's wearing them. If you can trust anyone on this planet, it's your Omni."

The one on Sima's wrist vibrated affectionately.

"Why won't it come off?" Oema tugged at it. "I don't like that it's locked."

"Because we're not eighteen yet. They don't want us to lose them and wander off to be eaten by a quill cat."

"What's a quill cat?"

By the time Sima finished explaining her experiences with them, Oema could only stare.

Sima stood. "C'mon. You can hang with us until you decide to go get a family."

"There's nowhere to hide here," whispered Oema. "Everything is so open."

"Yeah." Sima led her back to the table where she'd been before and sat in the same spot. "You'll get used to it."

Koji planted himself next to her.

"Sure..." Oema gazed around in nervous awe.

Sima held out her bracelet. "Wanna swap codes?"

"What's that mean?"

"Means we can call each other to talk, either using the bracelets or our tablets." Sima shrugged one shoulder. "Sorry if it's lame. You're the only person I know on this whole planet from before."

Oema gingerly lowered herself into the chair on Sima's right, still looking around like she expected the cops to show up at any second and grab her. "Umm, that would be cool. I mean, we didn't really know each other, but I remember seeing you in the Crash a few times. Thought you didn't like me."

"Sorry. I had a bad habit of giving nasty looks to kids. Just jealousy."

"Jealousy?" Oema fluffed at her hair. "Well, I am perfect. Makes sense."

Sima laughed.

"Seriously, though... why?"

"You look younger than me. That's it. Easier to beg. It's stupid. But doesn't matter here."

Oema touched her bracelet to Sima's. "Okay. How do we do it?"

"Umm. I don't know. Never tried to do it before."

Sima's bracelet vibrated, so she turned her arm to look.

‹You ask us to share information.›

"Aha. Probably happened already since we both talked about it." Sima glanced at Koji. "We could swap codes if you want."

Koji's face reddened. "Sure. Yes. Great idea."

"You really like it here?" whispered Oema.

"Not at first. Had a scary landing… but now? Yeah."

"Scary landing?" Oema scrunched her nose. "How did you even know? They didn't let us wake up until after the ship landed."

Sima took a deep breath. "Long story…"

STUPID CREATURES

Tuesday, a little past noon, Sima sat on the grass under a tree, nibbling on her lunch.

The park behind the Center made for a nice break from a day spent inside classrooms. Somehow, a modest copse of trees around a stream survived the first ship landing so close. It had to be a miracle. She could step across the little stream and not get wet. Not even the smallest kids could swim in it. The big river she and the children swam in months ago passed about a quarter-mile away on the east side of the colony, throwing off a handful of such streams. One happened to mostly cut through the middle of town.

She daydreamed about what might have happened if they decided to try making a boat and seeing where the river went. Certainly, they'd have spotted the colony after however long it took them to go roughly 160 miles.

Occasionally, a spray of sparks spat out from the giant form of the *Progenitor II* in the distance, wherever workers cut away squares of hull to use as sidewalk tiles. Her time as an Outcast made it uncomfortable to watch a 'useful' object be torn down... but her feelings about Earth counteracted any sympathy she might've felt toward the dying starship.

The number of people on the planet she knew longer than eight months increased to two.

According to Oema, Pim—the eleven-year-old boy who gave her attitude because she swatted a Pixie inhaler out of his hand— had been arrested in the same raid as her. *Unlike* Oema, the boy considered the idea of going on a spaceship the 'most awesomest thing ever' and didn't fight or resist once they told him about it.

Yesterday, once Mom and the kids returned from the amusement place, they'd all escorted Oema to the Center. She didn't get in trouble for running off, merely asked to 'please not do that again.' Of all the things a traumatized former street kid could do in response to forcible interplanetary relocation, suffering an anxiety attack and fleeing ranked as pretty mild.

Being done with remedial classwork allowed Sima to enjoy the idleness of a lunch period and not feel as though she wasted time. Some of the other students complained about it being 'too warm for May.' She thought it fine, if a little cool. Her old home on Earth tended to be quite warm during the day and cold at night.

At some point hundreds of years ago, the Earth had been as beautiful and untamed as Mirage. She didn't believe the majority of humans intended to ruin it, merely did what they needed to do in order to survive. *Some* humans definitely exploited the planet for money, but most of the pillaging occurred long before the End of Nations. By the time war broke out, there hadn't been many natural resources left to exploit. Perhaps the scarcity on top of massive civil unrest at such an imbalanced distribution of wealth had something to do with the war happening in the first place. Since she knew the Earth Government censored or erased history, she didn't really trust anything they said about the past. However, she'd seen enough greed among Citizens to accept some people had likely poisoned the planet for profit.

I'm not going to let them do it here, too.

Sima chuckled at herself. Even if the absolute worst-case scenario of humanity ruining Mirage were to happen, it wouldn't reach anything close to a crisis point for multiple generations.

She'd be *long* gone by the time anyone even worried about this planet ending up polluted. History class mentioned fossil fuels being a large contributor to the damage done to Earth. Humanity only ceased using them because they ran out. Such fuel may not even exist here. Even if it did, technology surpassed it centuries ago. Self-contained fusion reactors handled what solar and wind power plus superconducting batteries couldn't. Large things like the starships or big cities (on Earth) harnessed antimatter reactors.

We shouldn't need to make a mess of this place, too. She gazed up at pinkish-orange clouds. *This planet is so beautiful. Deadly as anything, but beautiful.*

Text patter emanated from the bracelet.

She glanced at her arm.

‹You have 00:19:51 remaining before you need to return to class.›

"Thanks. Remind me at ten minutes? I'm enjoying the sun."

‹All right.›

Barely a minute later, rapid approaching footsteps intruded on her serenity.

Koji ran over to her, seeming a bit out of breath. "There you are."

"Here I am." She held her arms out to either side.

"Thought you were in the resource room when I couldn't find you in the cafeteria."

She puffed out her chest. "I'm all caught up. Don't have to spend fourteen hours a day or more studying… at least until I get to university level classes. Heard some girl in the resource room complaining about ten-hour days. It's going to feel like a vacation to me."

Koji laughed, then flopped to sit cross-legged beside her.

"Umm…" She pointed at the burrito in his hand. "You didn't even eat yet? We've only got like twenty minutes left."

‹00:18:12.›

"Thanks." Sima waved her arm at Koji. "My Omni lacks the

ability to process a socially convenient lack of specificity for conversation."

‹I am aware that, to a teenager such as yourself, 'like twenty minutes' can vary in meaning from fifteen minutes to twelve hours depending on the desirability of the upcoming event.›

"What?" Sima blinked at the screen.

‹'I will be there in like twenty minutes' translates to approximately fourteen-point-eight minutes when a teenager is being summoned to a friend's residence for entertaining activities. 'Give me twenty minutes' translates to multiple hours if the teenager is being asked to perform a task they deem unpleasant.›

Sima and Koji laughed.

She held her arm up. "He's not wrong."

"Seem…" Koji's eyes widened. "Someone tried to break into my residence last night."

"What!?" She sat up out of her relaxed slouch.

He opened the thermal paper around his burrito, took a bite, and chewed fast.

"Broke into your residence? What happened?"

"It's okay. I kinda feel bad for them." Koji grinned.

She cringed. "Uhh, why? Did Security hurt them?"

"Nah. They had to see my father in his underpants waving a gun around."

Sima whistled. "Wow… your father has a gun? Is he Security?" *There's irony… me and the son of a Security officer.* "Heh. Wouldn't that be messed up?"

"Messed up?" Koji hesitated before chomping another hunk off his lunch and mumbling, "Why would it be messed up for him to be security?" past a full mouth.

"Uhh. I mean…" Sima's cheeks warmed. "I mean. Umm. You know."

While chewing, Koji shrugged in a 'no, I don't know' manner.

Sima looked off to the side, hoping he didn't catch her blushing.

"No, he's not a Security officer. Just has a gun. Why would it be messed up?"

"Umm. You know. I've been like terrified of them for years. Be kinda messed up to date a security officer's son."

He almost choked.

"Ack." She swatted him on the back a few times, until he waved her off in an 'I'm okay' manner.

"Date?" he rasped.

Crap! What the heck is wrong with me? Why did I say that!? "Umm... well, we did go out the other day. It's... I mean, someone seeing us having dinner together might've assumed... and I like hanging out with you. And, uhh. I umm, promised to cover it next time we went to 24-6, right?"

"Sorry for embarrassing you."

She gave a nervous chuckle. "You're not doing that. I'm totally embarrassing myself right now. So, uhh, what does he do if he's not a cop?"

"He's the head of the Engineering team from the *Progenitor*." Koji smiled weakly. "Your father's boss, basically."

"Oh, wow. That kinda..." She almost said 'complicates things.' But didn't want to think too hard about what 'things' meant yet. "Umm. Wait, was he standing next to the governor when the second ship landed?"

"Yeah."

"Guess it explains why he kinda looked like an older version of you." She chuckled.

Mouth full again, he nodded.

"Crap!" she yelled.

Koji frantically looked around. "What's wrong?"

"Nothing here. The break-in..." She grabbed his arm. "Someone broke into our residence, too. They stole an access badge from one of the maintenance people and went in when we weren't home. Didn't take anything, but it's like they searched around for something. Don't know if they found it or not. My parents didn't recognize anything as missing."

"That's a strange coincidence."

"Yeah!" She biffed herself in the head. "Your dad and my dad both work in engineering. There has to be a connection. Dad isn't doing anything strange or secret. No idea what anyone might want to steal or spy on. And really, what would anyone do with it? Not like they could sell it to a rival company or put it up on Dreamland to the highest bidder."

Koji laughed. "True. Doesn't make any sense. My dad isn't doing anything people would want to steal even back on Earth, just managing the colony's power system. No cutting-edge R&D."

"Huh. Maybe it isn't related to their OTs then." Sima rested her elbows on her knees, chin in both hands. "Dad's not the big boss but he's close to the top. Maybe whoever is breaking into residences is looking for something they think high-ranking people have? Not specifically engineers."

He made a weird noise—probably agreement—while stuffing the burrito in his mouth.

She laughed. "What are you doing? Trying to eat it in three bites?"

"Mmm." He nodded.

"Whose fault is it you waited until the last few minutes of lunch period to *start* eating?"

He pointed at himself, still chewing the giant mouthful.

"I can't figure out why anyone would want to steal here. Like, at all. We have everything we truly need and there isn't anything rare, expensive, or nice enough to swipe."

Koji gasped for air after swallowing. "Lots of people forced to come here who don't want to work?"

"You know I'm one of those kids who they forced onto a ship." She glanced sideways at him.

"Not saying they all think the same way. You're trying to figure out why someone would want to steal in a place where they'd have no way to sell stuff they took. They'd do it because it's what they're used to doing, and they're too freaked out at being on another planet to think, just following their same old habits."

"Hmm." She rocked side to side, thinking. "Maybe."

"Could've been a little kid breaking into your place and

snooping around for fun." Koji ate another huge bite, chewing as fast as he could.

"Doubt it. Unless a little kid drugged a maintenance worker to take a universal access card."

Koji almost choked again.

Her bracelet screen opened. ‹Ten minutes left.›

"Thanks." Sima unfolded her legs and stood. "Time to start walking back to class."

"Okay." Koji jumped up. "Sorry if I made you angry. Just saying, if they force kids from gangs to come here against their will, those kids are going to cause problems."

She started across the park toward the Center's secondary entrance. "It's fine. You didn't make me angry. Only messing with you. I don't think they put gang members on the ship. A detective talked to me and kinda screened me. Not like they jumped me in an alley and I woke up on Mirage. They raided Crashes and popular areas for begging, not gang hideouts."

"Right." Koji jogged to catch up. "You might've been on the street, but you're nothing like them. *You* haven't given up on yourself. Even back there, you tried to survive without drowning in the hopelessness and evil of it."

Wow. Umm. She stopped walking and pressed a hand to her chest, a little choked up. "Thanks." She cleared her throat. "Any former Outcast here would be pretty stupid not to take advantage of a do-over."

"Yeah, but you know…" He ate the last hunk of burrito.

"What do I know?" She smiled at him.

"As a species, we humans are exceptionally talented at doing stupid things."

Sima laughed. "Yeah…" For a moment, she considered taking his hand, but decided against being exceptionally talented. "C'mon, we're gonna be late."

15

STORM

A fter school Tuesday, Sima took advantage of having free
time to spend some with the kids.

Due to the 'heat,' they went to the fitness room at the
Center and hit the pool. Swimming proved fun, but she couldn't
help but prefer the quiet serenity of the river out in the wilds to a
crowded rec room. The colony's pool had two big advantages:
bathing suits and no chance a randomly wandering large animal
would try to eat them, so she put up with the crowd.

Her bracelet, by request, sent a message to Dad regarding the
attempted break-in at Koji's residence. She figured the elder Ito
probably mentioned it to him already, but decided to bring it up
anyway. It bothered her not to be more worried about the coincidence of two engineers having their homes attacked. Compared to
getting up close and personal with a quill cat, she couldn't find it in
her to be afraid of a person who simply wanted to snoop around.

Eventually, the bracelet reminded her they needed to return
home for dinner, so she gathered the kids from the pool. By the
time they returned to the residence and she'd taken a quick shower,
the aroma of Dad's cooking already filled the place. She volun-

teered to help, taking the opportunity to talk about the break in attempt at Mr. Ito's house.

Duh. No wonder Dad knew Koji. He probably goes to the engineering room to see his father all the time.

"Yes. We're aware of it." Dad patted her back. "So far, it seems only the two of us have been targeted."

"Did Mr. Ito recognize the person?"

"I don't believe so, or they would've made an arrest. Dark, baggy clothes, night time, face covering..." Dad stirred the contents of a large pot. "You know, it is remarkable how well some of our spices work with native vegetables. I'm rather fond of these titan squash."

"Spaaaaace cucumber!" yelled Lissa from the living room.

She chuckled at the girl, then rolled her eyes at Dad. "We're going to become *so* sick of them. They're in everything."

"The flavor is so mild, its entire character changes depending on how you prepare it. Firm, mushroom-like texture also lends itself to a variety of dishes."

"I'm still not sure I want to know how they make the titan burgers taste like meat."

Dad chuckled. "They don't. Have you ever actually had meat?"

"Just printed chicken... maybe I ate some goat or beef a long time ago before running away, but I don't remember."

Sima felt rather proud of her passable attempt at making naan bread and showed the tray off to him while grinning.

"Those smell amazing." Dad leaned closer, sniffing long and deep.

"*Not* made from titan squash powder." She put the second tray in the oven. "Two trays enough?"

"As delightful as those smell? I could eat six myself."

"So, three trays..."

He winked. "Teasing. I *could* eat six myself, but I won't."

FOR THE REST of the week, Sima dwelled on the break-ins.

Wednesday after school, she hung out for a few hours with Koji. The way he described his father charging out of their residence in his boxers, waving a giant handgun around while screaming made it sound like a scene from a cartoon. The man chased whoever tried to hack the lock on the door halfway across the colony before losing them near the mall.

Fortunately, Mr. Ito happened to be something of a pacifist and didn't fire a shot. According to Koji, he'd only have *used* the gun to stop someone from committing murder, and even if he had to shoot, he'd still try not to kill the person. Unfortunately, the would-be thief dressed to conceal their identity in a mask, hooded tunic, and baggy pants. Mr. Ito suspected it had been a woman, due to height, stature, and gait, but couldn't say for certain.

The next two days, Sima constantly took note of every woman around her, alert for anyone paying unusual attention to her or seeming inexplicably nervous. No one stood out as acting strange until science class on Friday. Ms. Taylor bounced around as though she'd consumed multiple pots of coffee. The woman always had high energy, as if perpetually excited. She became *more* energetic whenever she sensed her students enjoyed science. Every time they did a practical experiment, she appeared as thrilled as if seeing the 'science' work for the first time.

She had to be the youngest of the teachers, only like four years into her thirties. Though she spoke GANSEC like every other human on Earth, her language had some peculiarities in certain words not being the same. For example, she called cookies 'biscuits' and referred to the bathroom as a 'loo.' It had to be a product of where she lived, the same way Juan retained a few Spanish words.

This would have baffled Sima six months ago, but thanks to her being a fully educated student, she understood the global language retained regional nuances, typically slang. Some areas added no detectable variances in language while others—especially where Ms. Taylor came from—clung tenaciously to local vernacular.

Sima adored it, imagining the language issue as the final act of rebellion by centuries-ago people against a global government. She didn't necessarily think nations should return, but the government should absolutely not try to homogenize culture and stomp out all traces of what came before. Whatever they couldn't erase, they absorbed—like food. Apparently, meals she took for granted: ramen, spaghetti, pizza, tacos, tika masala, burritos, hummus, falafel, khoresht, tahchin, quiche, hamburgers, lo mein, and so on had once all been associated to particular regions.

It sounded too weird to possibly be true. Not all the rumors from the past made sense. Why would only people in one particular place eat something?

Ms. Taylor's excessive happiness Friday came from receiving amazing news: the administration approved the field trip to the 'alien' site.

As soon as Sima entered the classroom, the teacher rushed over and burst into a geyser of words.

"… trying to arrange it for tomorrow, Saturday. I know all of you have been dying to go for so long!"

We might be dying if *we go.* She swallowed the sarcasm since she didn't intend it as a complaint. The idea of visiting another place made by the civilization here before humans excited her, too. Not quite 'bouncing off the walls' excited as Ms. Taylor, but certainly enough to take the risk.

"Wow. Short notice." Sima hugged her tablet against her chest. "I still want to go, but my parents might not be too happy at it being tomorrow."

Ms. Taylor exhaled. "I understand. There's a good chance we'll push it out to *next* Saturday. Unless everyone who signed up is able to make it tomorrow, it will be next week. Still… it's happening!"

"Awesome!" Sima bounced. "I can't wait."

"I'm so thrilled you decided to go along. Would you mind stopping back here after your last class? I'd like to hear about the other location you found. I've been studying the information your Omni scanned. No one else is really paying much attention to it, but I am —at least it feels like it—getting close to cracking the language."

"Wow. Really?" Sima tried to remember what the writing decorating the walls of some chambers looked like, but her memory hadn't held onto it too well, given all the other stress she had at the time. Fortunately, the Omni recorded pictures… which she hadn't looked at. No point since she didn't have the first clue how to go about translating an entirely inhuman language. Her teacher's feat of intellect stunned her into gawking.

Ms. Taylor twirled a hand around. "Oh, I'm not there yet. Haven't even figured out one word yet, but patterns are emerging. It's a puzzle. Once we find the critical key, everything else should fall into place reasonably soon after. Ahh well. Excited. We should probably get started with class before I waste the whole period talking about the field trip."

Sima's bracelet vibrated. She looked at her arm, but it didn't display anything.

Up to mischief? What are you doing? She kept quiet and took her seat.

MS. TAYLOR'S expression looked so much like a child, Sima almost laughed.

She'd stopped by after school to discuss the time Juan fell down the slippery tunnel into the underground chamber. The teacher gawked at her, making faces like Lissa hearing an exciting story over a campfire. No surprise how anyone convinced such a young teacher—and mother of a teenage daughter—into picking up and moving to a new planet. This woman *adored* adventure and science.

The site she and the kids accidentally explored was over a hundred miles away from the colony. Ms. Taylor doubted the administration would approve a field trip for students to go such a distance. However, a small team of scientists might go… and might permit *one* student—specifically Sima—to accompany them, considering her prior experience.

"It's up to my parents. At least, if you want to go there before I'm over eighteen," said Sima. "Maybe before twenty."

Ms. Taylor chuckled. "All right. It's something to keep in mind. Please talk to your parents about tomorrow and let me know if they have any reservations."

"I will. Thanks, Ms. Taylor."

The teacher waved, then gathered a few items off her desk. "I'm going to stay up too late studying their writing."

"Sounds fun."

"To me, it is." Ms. Taylor smiled.

"Wasn't being sarcastic. Alien languages are *way* over my head, but if you haven't noticed by now, I like academic stuff."

Ms. Taylor beamed at her. "The world needs more kids like you."

Sima continued talking to her about the water-filled tunnels while they made their way down the hall to the Center's main atrium. Upon noticing a torrential downpour outside, Ms. Taylor groaned, clutched her case to her chest, and sprinted out into the rain.

Wow. Sima hesitated at the threshold, peering up at the dark grey sky. *The last time it rained this hard, I didn't have any clothes on.* She had zero interest in recreating a moment from her feral days, but couldn't deny nudity made rain less annoying. Being stuck in wet clothing had to be the most uncomfortable sensation in the world. Still, she intended to go straight home. She could dry off and change right away.

She stuffed the tablet into the front pocket of her new tunic, sealed both zippers, then waved at the door to trigger the sensor, opening it. "Here goes…"

Within four seconds of her dashing outside, the ridiculous storm soaked her to the skin. Deciding it wouldn't make any difference to run as she'd already become as drenched as possible, she huddled protectively over the tablet and walked. Being pelted by such a heavy downfall of warm water felt like she'd hopped in the shower fully dressed. The colony appeared deserted, no surprise.

Intense rain striking the ground and metal buildings made so much noise she'd have to shout in order to converse with a person right next to her. Not even 4:00 p.m. yet, and already it had become as dark as late evening due to the heavy clouds and thick precipitation.

A handful of scattered stores and restaurants gave off light in the distance, giant lanterns hung from random trees deep in a gloomy forest. Awnings on some structures offered occasional small areas of shelter. She didn't bother stopping; she'd already become as drenched as if she'd gone swimming. A Security officer standing under one awning waved at her.

She returned the gesture without thinking, for an instant, afraid of punishment if she ignored him. Catching herself, she relaxed and added a second, more sincere wave. After passing two more 'light islands' in the gloom, she stopped to look around, confused at unfamiliar surroundings.

"Dammit. Am I going the right way?"

‹Yes. You've walked home from the Center so many times, you remember the route even though you cannot see well. Continue following this sidewalk for another 104.4 meters, then turn left.›

"You are aware I can't magically tell when I've gone '104.4 meters' right? Please buzz or something."

The bracelet vibrated.

"Thanks."

She kept her eyes on the metal sidewalk, trying to figure out how many square tiles equaled the distance she needed to travel. "A girl is walking in a storm and can only see the ground. Each tile is a square 1.5 meters long on every side. How many tiles does she need to cross before reaching her turn? Gah. I've become a math problem. Sixty... no, seventy. Wait. Sixty-nine and a point some-thing. Five? Six?"

Rapid splattering footsteps rushed up behind her.

Instinctively, Sima ducked while spinning, raising a defensive arm. A dark figure in a hooded tunic lunged at her. Her sudden turn appeared to catch her assailant off guard. Still, the person grabbed a fistful of her tunic, shoved her against a metal building, and held a knife to her throat.

"Where is it?!" rasped a voice like a woman trying to disguise her gender.

Sima stared into the opaque, black lenses of a rebreather mask partially shrouded under a hood. The person threatening her had only an inch of height advantage… and didn't look terribly big. Dry, the pants would be baggy; wet, they revealed a distinctly feminine shape. She angled her eyes down at the gloved hand gripping the blade.

The woman clutched it like a four-year-old learning to use silverware for the first time.

Sima narrowed her eyes, gave a war cry, and shoved the bitch away with both hands.

Slippery metal sidewalk did the rest of the work, throwing the woman off her feet into the bluish grass beyond. Mirage grass flattened like wet hair during storms, the softer leaves turning into a soupy morass similar to a bowl of wet pasta. Water sprayed everywhere as the woman splashed down and went sliding. Still screaming in anger, Sima dove after her. In an instant, she became the twelve-year-old version of herself who tried to fight off a pack of slightly older girls trying to steal her nice 'Citizen' dress soon after she ran away. She had, of course, *lost* that fight, but didn't go down easy.

In four years, she'd learned how to fight much better than her second week on the street.

She landed on the woman, grabbing the wrist of her knife arm in one hand and punching her repeatedly in the rebreather mask with the other, landing three hits before the woman appeared to process being on her back. Sima raised her hand for a fourth punch, but the woman threw her off to one side and scrambled to her knees. Sima slid over the waterlogged grass, tumbled once, then spun out. The woman slipped and fell when she tried to chase. Sima attempted to stand in the muddy grass but ended up on her side again. Her attacker lurched upright, raised the knife, and rushed in. Snarling, Sima lunged up to one knee, catching the woman's forearm in both hands, stalling the knife. The woman's attempt to get her arm back pulled Sima upright. Growling, she slammed her left knee into the bitch's stomach twice before wrenching the knife out of her grasp.

"You pull a blade on an Outcast, you better know how to use it." Sima tossed the knife up in a fancy twirl, catching it in a combat grip. "Let me show you."

The woman bolted.

Sima chased, shouting, "Bitch, don't run from me!"

Her attacker pulled a hard left turn unexpectedly—and wiped out in the grass, landing on her chest in a sliding flat spin. Sima swerved after her, but the instant her sneakers hit the grass, they shot out from under her, dumping her face-first into the muck, logrolling. By the time she scrambled back to her feet, the woman had already resumed running, fast disappearing into the murk. Sima darted after her—and fell on her chest again, getting a mouthful of muddy water. Snarling, she bounced back up.

A squishy splat in the distance gave away where the woman fell yet again. Unable to see her through the driving downpour, Sima ran toward the sound, screaming as an unexpected downhill slope threw her into a tumbling fall.

She stopped rolling in a two-foot-deep pond gathered in a low spot, a pond that didn't exist earlier that morning. Sitting there, chest-deep in warm water, she fumed in rage. The rush of the falling rain masked any sound of the woman's flight, the gloom concealed her from view. Roughly sixty meters to her left, another Security officer stood under an awning in front of a food storage building, peering in her general direction.

Screw it.

Grumbling to herself, Sima stood out of the giant puddle and trudged over to the man.

"Wow, this weather," said the guy, casual as anything. "Have you ever seen rain like this before?"

"Yes, once. I want to report a crime." Sima scooted under the awning and stood beside him, dripping. "Or... what am I supposed to say? I don't usually talk to cops."

His relaxed demeanor faded to a more familiar 'cop seriousness.' "What happened?"

She held up the knife. "Someone tried to jump me. I... this is going to sound bad, but I think they believe I stole something from them."

"You didn't."

Wow. She blinked. "No, I didn't. But... wow. You didn't even question that."

"Nah. I know you. The kid who saved herself and three little ones after your pod fell off."

"So you know I'm a street rat."

"Were." He patted her shoulder. "Okay, so... any idea who it was?"

"No. A woman. Definitely a woman. Probably the same person who broke into our residence last week. Most likely the same person who tried to break into Mr. Ito's residence. Same clothes. I really have no idea what she's looking for. She threw me against a wall and asked, 'where is it?'"

He pulled a tablet out and began filling out an incident report. "What did this woman look like?"

"Couldn't tell. She had on a rebreather mask, hooded tunic, baggy pants... grey. Only thing I know for sure is, definitely a woman. She also didn't know how to fight. Probably never got into a fight before in her life. So... *not* one of the street rats, someone officially on the *Progenitor*. Can't tell which ship. This stuff didn't start happening until after the second one arrived, but it doesn't prove it's someone from the new ship."

"Good logic. Ever thought about being a Security officer?"

Sima laughed.

"I didn't mean that as a joke."

"Yeah. No. I couldn't. Too many bad experiences. I'm trying not to freak out talking to you right now."

He cringed. "Understandable."

"I'd say I'm over it, but it's a work in progress." She handed him the knife. "Probably no prints on it. Rain, mud, and gloves."

"Thanks." He tilted the weapon over, giving it a quick examination. "I'll add it to the file."

Sima took a deep breath. "I'm about to say something I never thought would ever come out of my mouth."

"Do I want to ask?"

"Heh." She fidgeted. "Nothing bad. Will you please walk me home?"

16

NEW SPECIES

Sima stretched out on her bed, video chatting with Koji and Oema courtesy of her bracelet.

They gawked at her from the flickering hologram screen after she finished telling them about the attack. Both appeared to be in their bedrooms—no surprise considering the time. At thirteen, Oema might get in trouble for staying awake so close to midnight, but didn't appear concerned about her new parents catching her. She hadn't said much about them other than both worked in the hydroponics facility.

For the past twelve minutes, Sima had been trying to convince them she was okay.

"So, what did you get?" whispered Oema. "Total secrecy, I swear. Won't tell a soul."

"Nothing. I legit have no idea what she meant." Sima rolled onto her back, raising her arm to keep the screen in front of her. "Crazy bitch must have me mixed up with someone else. Honestly… I'm not a thief, even back on Earth. It causes way too many problems. People get a rep for stealing and even other Outcasts don't wanna be around you."

"Only if you get caught," said Oema in an overacted innocent voice.

Koji opened his mouth to say something, but paused.

"Change your mind?" Sima grinned.

"No. Just had a thought."

"Did it hurt?" asked Oema.

Koji didn't react to her comment. "Could someone have planted a stolen item on you for some reason?"

"Umm…" *What the heck for?* "Not that I know of."

"Duh. Obviously you don't know about it." Oema rolled her eyes.

Sima got up and began searching all the clothing she'd worn since the last time she did laundry. "I really doubt anyone could've reverse pickpocketed me without me noticing. Especially if it's the same woman who came after me tonight."

"Being awesome at picking pockets doesn't mean you can fight," said Oema in a strange tone.

Koji's expression gave off obliviousness, but Sima caught the girl's meaning. Not every young Outcast resorted to begging. Some had too much pride. Even though she only knew the girl in passing on Earth, it thrilled her she'd come to Mirage. Unless the kid had *phenomenal* skills, she probably wouldn't have lived too much longer. Eventually, even the most careful thief would put her hand in the wrong place. The EGSF wouldn't bother investigating the murder of an Outcast, even a girl Oema's age.

This planet is completely messing me up. I'm getting emotional about a kid who'd have scavenged my corpse naked in seconds and not hesitated about doing it. She bit her lip. Admittedly, she hadn't felt much over Draz beyond fear it could be her someday getting tossed in the sewer, though she didn't take any of his stuff after he overdosed to death. Felt wrong to steal from the dead.

"Nothing." Sima tossed the clothes back in the 'to wash' storage bin.

"So, guess you're not going on the trip tomorrow." Koji exhaled.

She walked over to the bed and let gravity pull her over backward. "I'm going."

"What?" blurted Oema and Koji at the same time.

"Yeah." Sima raised her left arm over her face so she could see the screen again, laughing. "Shocked me, too. Figured my parents would order me to stay inside for months after I told them about the bitch grabbing me. I'm not really scared of her. Anyone *I* can beat in a fight isn't dangerous."

"Truth." Oema flashed a strange hand sign in the screen.

"Hah," deadpanned Sima. "I *did* beat a quill cat... but had a ton of help."

Koji raised an eyebrow. "Help? You told me you took it on by yourself."

"Not literal help. It dragged Lissa off and half killed her. I was in like this really weird mental place. Fearless, desperate, so damn angry I didn't care what happened to me. Nothing mattered but keeping that monster off Lissa. Without such an extreme situation, I'd probably get shredded."

"Oh." Koji winced. "But your parents are letting you go tomorrow?"

"Yeah. Mostly because the crazy bitch didn't bother me at all. Told them I wanted to go, and Dad thinks I'll be safer out of the colony. Mom's not objecting because we'll have Security people with us. Can't miss an opportunity to be part of something important because some freaky woman thinks I have something she wants."

Oema whisper-gasped, then dove out of frame. Her portrait became a close-up view of sheets.

Koji and Sima waited in silence.

A moment later, Oema whispered, "This is *so* lame. I have to pretend to be sleeping. What kind of loser goes to sleep when someone else tells them to?"

"Normally how it works for little kids." Koji chuckled.

Oema's hand—and middle finger—slid into view on her video frame.

"Losers with a future," said Sima.

"Ugh. She's a lost cause." Oema's face reappeared, tinted green by the light of her Omnicomputer's holo-screen. "Total Citizen mind-control. Umm, I should probably drop off the call and go to sleep before they catch me." She made a sarcastic, cross-eyed face. "Wouldn't want to be *grounded*. Woooo."

Sima smiled to herself, suspecting the girl really didn't protest as much as her words implied. She waved. "Night. And, give them a chance. Couple nights in a real bed might change your mind."

"Later," said Koji.

Oema's window disappeared, allowing Koji's video to double in size. "We should probably try to get some sleep, too. Tomorrow *is* Saturday, but Ms. Taylor wants us to be at the Center by 9:00 a.m."

"Yeah. Night, Koji."

"Night." He smiled, stared at her for a few seconds, then dropped off.

She let her arm flop to the bed beside her and sighed at the ceiling. *Having friends is weird.* She idly scratched at her stomach, questioning herself. Seven-ish years ago, she had a few friends. Tonight hadn't been the first time in her life she spent an hour on a video call with friends, but it *had* been the first time merely looking at one of them made her feel strange... and want to keep looking at him.

Nope. I don't have time to think about anything right now. Gotta sleep.

SIMA WOKE a few minutes before the bracelet's alarm went off.

Going on a field trip to an 'alien' site came close enough to academic work she decided to wear her grey jumpsuit and the basic black utility boots. More professional, and if she ended up covered in slime again, no big deal. The colony had tons of jumpsuits. Those, she could get for free. No sense ruining any of the clothing she bought using her allowance.

Once dressed, she paused to fidget at the silver Omnicomputer bracelet, checking her balance: 104 UMUs left. Her brain still translated the number into 'five to eight meals.' Depending on the amount of grit and/or rat meat she'd be willing to put up with, she could eat back on Earth for as little as twelve glint a meal. If moldy stuff or pet food happened to be available, sometimes eating cost as little as four, but Sima had never risked either. Better to eat once every two days than die alone in an alley after seventy-two hours of erupting from both ends.

She shuddered at the memory of one poor guy she'd seen puking himself to death after eating moldy street meat, then scoffed at some kids from school who complained they didn't get enough money in their allowance. Here on Mirage, Sima didn't need money. At least, not yet. No one still under eighteen *needed* it. Her parents bought food, so she didn't have to. Even if they ran out of money, the administration would issue people the basic edible slime. Same went for clothing. Sima bought some stuff to wear because it looked nice, not because she needed it. Hearing other kids at school whine about *only* getting fifty a week—for nothing— when at their age, money went entirely to fun stuff irked her.

Out of habit, she attached her knife to her belt, then checked herself in the closet door mirror. Carrying the weapon openly didn't look anywhere near as strange with a jumpsuit as when wearing a skirt or leggings. The pale grey garment, a little bit of her white undershirt visible at the collar, made her feel like an 'official' starship crewmember. A visible knife on Earth would absolutely cause the EGSF to mess with her... but not here. Security officers or not, every colonist had a more than minor chance of encountering hostile creatures. People probably wouldn't think it strange if Austin carried his axe around. Lissa or Juan might get odd looks for being armed, though.

Going to visit an alien site didn't necessarily offer promises of discovering anything of interest to a biologist. However, she decided to bring two of the small sample kits she'd been issued as part of her supplies for biology class. The black nylon cases, about the size of a bar of soap, each held three empty phials. On the off chance she encountered some new plants in the area around the site, she could bring pieces back. Even if her biology teacher didn't want them, she could visit Dr. Desai.

Is it still extra credit if I'm not even in his class yet?

Restless energy sent her to the kitchen to get started on breakfast before anyone else woke up. Soon, the rest of her family emerged from their rooms, following the siren call of food cooking. Her parents, as expected, appeared to be on edge, though worried more about the mysterious woman than the trip. Lissa wanted to go with her, as did Juan. Austin claimed 'alien caves' would be boring, but the look in his eyes gave away he didn't want to leave the colony due to fear.

Another nice part about having parents. I don't have to be the bad guy saying no.

Dad insisted on walking her to the Center. "You look excited."

"I am." She grinned.

He smiled back. "You also look quite professional this morning."

"It's a jumpsuit." Sima chuckled. "I look exactly like pretty much everyone."

He winked. "Adults. You kids and your fancy clothes."

She laughed. Most people wore jumpsuits during the day at their OTs. People her age and younger generally didn't like 'wearing uniforms,' and preferred 'real' clothes as soon as they became available. Garments made on Mirage tended to be softer due to reliance on plant fibers instead of synthetics. If not for the two-year trip, they'd likely sell for serious glint on Earth.

As if the attack yesterday never happened, Sima and Dad talked about fashion, school, the future of the colony, and—of course—her schedule for the day. Ms. Taylor intended to be back by 3:00 p.m.

When they arrived at the courtyard in front of the Center, Dad's good mood faded. Two Nomads—the larger six-wheeled vehicles—sat near a group of eleven people: Ms. Taylor, her daughter, Marley (the only person there not wearing a jumpsuit), Koji, two other boys from her class, Mial Tanner and Rann Bryson, three seniors she didn't know, a freshman boy, and two Security officers. She recognized Evie Ruiz, one of the soldiers who rescued her and the kids. The other soldier, she hadn't seen before. He appeared to be about the same age as Evie, mid-twenties, and radiated a sense of boredom.

"Two? That's all?" Dad gestured at the officers.

"It's only eighteen miles away from the colony. Half the distance compared to Dr. Desai's sample site. It isn't like we're going into a dangerous area full of gangs. At worst, we meet a stray quill cat or one of those bear things." She swiped her hair off her face, holding it against her neck to stop the wind from throwing it around. "Two officers with rifles can deal with a whole pack of quill cats. We probably won't even see one."

He chuckled. "The way it works, right? Go prepared, don't have any problems."

"Yeah." She hugged him. "Ms. Taylor is giving me the look. I should go join them."

Dad waved at the teacher. "All right. Have fun out there and learn as much as you can."

"I will."

Sima jogged over to the group of students. Marley Taylor, a willowy blonde sylph, already appeared quite 'thrilled' at the whole idea of the trip, arms folded, foot tapping, a *so done with this* air to her entire presence. Instead of a jumpsuit, she'd worn a plain peach-colored skirt, white off-the-shoulder clingy top, and pink flip-flops. Her attire worked fine for a warm day around the colony… for exploring alien ruins, not so much.

Ms. Taylor had undoubtedly insisted her daughter go along. Sima didn't understand the girl at all—for reasons beyond her habit of referring to cookies as 'biscuits.' Marley wasn't even close to dumb, but appeared to hate everything to do with academics. Most days in class, she'd be daydreaming, sneakily playing video games on her tablet, or doing anything other than paying attention. Marley, Koji, Veesa Langley, and Mial Tanner belonged as sophomores, all being sixteen and having attended school without inter-ruption their whole lives.

Rann, a former Outcast, ended up like Sima, another seventeen-year-old sophomore. She didn't know much about him other than he'd only missed one year, ending up on the street at sixteen. He'd been one of the first to get out of the remedial class, but still ended up a year behind.

None of the seniors paid much attention to her—or anyone not a senior—standing together and discussing whether nor not they believed actual aliens lived here. When all three of their bracelets simultaneously opened their screens, Sima laughed.

We are the aliens here.

The freshman—she assumed he had to be in high school due to his being allowed on the trip—had the stature of a sixth grader. Short for his age, and skinny, he totally looked like one of the kids who would probably be done with university before turning eigh-teen. Sima winced a little inside at the idea of him ending up on the street, one of the few times she'd ever not regarded a Citizen with resentment.

He'd have been lucky to last a week.

"All right." Ms. Taylor waved one hand back and forth in the air. "Everyone's here. If there's anyone who needs a last-minute restroom break, I suggest you go now."

No one moved.

"The prior civilization site we are visiting does not have bath-room facilities, at least none compatible with our anatomy." Ms. Taylor looked over the students.

"What are we supposed to do if we have to go while we're out there?" asked Veesa.

Sima folded her arms. "We're on an untamed, largely feral planet. What do you think we're going to do if we have to go while out there? Darn. Maybe the jumpsuit was a bad idea. Now, the short skirt makes sense."

Some of the boys laughed.

Veesa gawked. Marley's face turned scarlet.

"If I can interrupt." Evie raised a hand. "The nomads have toilets. They're not large nor are they comfortable, but privacy is still privacy, even if you can barely move."

Everyone relaxed.

"Well, since we are bringing facilities with us, no point in further delay." Ms. Taylor grinned.

She divided the students into two groups, one per Nomad. The large vehicles sat so far off the ground on 'legs' tipped with fat tires, a person could walk under the body and not touch it. Sima climbed the ladder built into the middle wheel leg to the cabin and took a seat in the back. The Security man she didn't know—Mors, N. according to his name tag—headed for a narrow passageway connecting the cockpit to the seating area.

Koji sat on her right, Marley Taylor on her left, Ms. Taylor beside her daughter nearest the window. Mial took the seat on the far side of Koji. The rest of the students went to the other Nomad. Marley kept her head down, playing a game on her tablet.

Compared to the little rover, the Nomad rode like a slow-moving aircraft. On the relatively flat grasslands near the colony, the six flexible legs absorbed the ground contour, keeping the vehicle's body level and shielding it from bumps. Only the motion of scenery outside the windows gave any sense they didn't simply sit still.

This thing could run over boulders the size of gee-vees and not even notice them.

Koji kept fidgeting his fingers together, not looking up.

A bit of warmth flooded Sima's face. Wildlife aside, they had no reason to be nervous about visiting one of these… places. Leaving the colony did present a logical reason for anyone to be on edge. Most likely, his stress came from the danger of the trip and not because they sat so close together their legs shared warmth. She leaned forward a little, trying to make eye contact.

He either didn't notice or pretended not to.

"You okay?" asked Sima.

"Yeah."

She half smiled. "Excited or scared?"

"Both." He finally looked up, managing a tenuous chuckle.

She let her gaze fall onto his hand, and contemplated grasping it, saying 'I'll keep you safe' or something lame. He'd totally take it the wrong way, and besides, the teacher could see them.

Don't want her to think I'm not taking this seriously. Not like we're really dating or anything. Oh, no. I'm blushing again. Dammit! What is wrong with me?

Sima looked to her right, past Rann, staring out the window and thinking of quill cats, giant birds, and Lissa making flower bracelets… anything but questioning why her 'other people are all dangerous' mental wall had a Koji-shaped hole in it. She absolutely didn't think about seeing other students, even ones at university level, who all seemed to have plenty of time for academics *and* boyfriends.

THE NOMADS CAME to a stop beside a giant hill fourteen minutes after leaving the colony.

As soon as the vehicle lowered itself, a process the Security people referred to as 'sitting,' Ms. Taylor rushed to open the side door, then stood beside it advising everyone to be careful climbing down. Marley appeared intent on trying to stay in her seat all day. Sima descended the ladder, jumping the last few feet to land in grass up to her waist.

"Seem, look," whispered Koji. "What are those?"

She turned toward him, noticed he pointed to the right, then glanced where indicated. Hundreds of giant oblong puffballs dotted the meadow, starting roughly ninety feet away and continuing for a long swath. Hard to tell from the distance, but she guessed them to be approximately as big as sheep. Three quarters of them sported fluff in a pale pink hue, like a few of Mom's formerly white jumpsuits she'd 'helpfully' washed with Dad's new red shirt.

She blamed the education system for teaching her about centuries-extinct animals, but not how to separate colors.

The remainder of the creatures had a dull beige coloration. Like the quill cats, their eyes glowed green, but they only had two. Each walked upon four stilt-like legs, largely hidden by their puffy hair or fur. Based on the way they moved, she estimated fairly long legs under the pastel-colored floof. The animals intermittently munched on grass. None paid the least bit of attention to the presence of giant vehicles or humans.

One surprising thing this particular location lacked: alien ruins. Other than the animals, every direction contained miles upon miles of wavering grass. Watching the iridescent grass shimmer in the wind, cycling from sky blue to deep sapphire and back *was* mesmerizingly pretty... but not terribly educational.

"Uhh... space sheep?" Sima shrugged. "No one's seen these before."

A few of the other students laughed.

Wait, they have to be larger than sheep... their whole bodies are above the grass. Long legs.

"How? They're like right next to the colony."

"Eighteen miles is not 'right next to' the colony." She nudged him.

Koji started walking toward them, but stopped when she grabbed his arm.

"Don't stray off. This grass is so high there could be cats hiding in it." Sima whistled. "I bet these are their primary prey. Much easier to take down than an aurak."

Marley begrudgingly came down the Nomad's ladder, followed by her mother.

"Ms. Taylor?" Sima pointed at the grazing animals. "New species."

"Ooh." Ms. Taylor bit her finger. "Drat. It's out of scope for today's trip, but we should document them since we're the first to spot them."

Sima looked around at grass. "There's nothing else here. Are we in the right place? I don't see any cave openings."

The teacher tapped her tablet, activating the screen. "Yes. We picked the site up during the landing operation. Viewed from the air, this large hill next to us has an obviously unnatural square shape. The aerial pictures made me suspect some manner of buried structure. Found the entrance a few weeks ago when I came out here alone. It's on top of the hill."

"No space sheep were here then?" asked Koji.

Ms. Taylor shook her head. "Nope. They must migrate around the plains. I can't ask students to approach unknown species. Please wait here." She waved at the Security officers. "Nahan, would you follow me for a few minutes?"

Sima and the other students waited, watching while Ms. Taylor and Nahan walked over to the herd. The 'space sheep' remained indifferent to their approach. It soon became apparent Sima's revised opinion of their size had been closer to accurate. When the teacher stood next to them, she only came up to their shoulders. They reminded her of horses covered in sheep's wool.

Shorses?

She cringed, vowing never to suggest the name to anyone. If she successfully became a scientist, no one would ever let her live down the ignominy of unleashing a word like 'shorses' on humanity.

Neither sheep nor horses had existed on Earth for around 300 years, but she'd studied them in two different classes. Once in history and once in biology, both part of the remedial stuff. Ms. Taylor took several photos, went so far as petting one, then returned. The animal didn't even move when she touched it, continuing to stand there chewing on bundles of long blue grass dangling from its mouth.

"All right, everyone. Apologies for the delay." Ms. Taylor continued walking past the group and hurried up the side of the hill. "The entrance is right up here."

17

MALICIOUS INTENT

Ms. Taylor led the group of students and two soldiers up the giant hill.

On the way, Sima looked around. This 'hill' did have an odd shape, almost as if the bottom third of a pyramid three times the height of the Nomads lay buried under soil and grass. The top turned out to be suspiciously flat. The teacher stopped at the edge of a hole surrounded by grass.

A ramp wide enough to accommodate one of the small rovers led down to a pair of sliding doors largely covered in dark blue moss… or a plant quite similar to moss in appearance. An area near the bottom had been cleared, revealing bare silvery metal. The removed moss lay in curled sod patches on the floor nearby.

"Ms. Taylor?" Sima pointed at the strips of plant matter on the ground at the bottom of the ramp, one hand on her sample case about to open it. "Did you take samples of the… moss?"

"I did." She raised one finger. "An excellent question. So far, we have determined this plant does not photosynthesize, but leeches nutrients from other plants. In this particular location, it's drawing from the grass."

"Parasitic moss..." Sima nodded, letting her hand fall away from the case. No need to take a sample if the teacher already did.

"Those are doors," whispered one of the senior boys, sounding shocked. "Metal."

Various expressions of astonishment came from the students at 'aliens' being real.

"I don't think those doors formed naturally," said Marley in an aloof tone.

Mial looked at her quizzically.

Ms. Taylor glanced conspiratorially at Sima, stifling a laugh.

She grinned back.

"Hey, what's with the attitude?" asked the same senior. "Like you knew this stuff was real already?"

Marley huffed. "If you had read the documentation packet my mother sent to everyone about the trip, you'd know Sima here already explored and documented another underground complex showing obvious signs of being constructed by sentient non-human life." She smirked at him. "Why did you even sign up for this trip if you couldn't be bothered to do the pre-reading or didn't believe a prior civilization really existed?"

The eighteen-year-old loomed at her, brows knitting together.

If his attempt to intimidate her worked, Marley didn't show it. "What's your plan, exactly? Hit a girl two years younger and a third your size because she caught you being lazy?"

"You don't know we didn't read the materials." He ceased looming, but folded his arms.

Marley examined her fingernails. "If you read it, you wouldn't have been talking about the aliens, wondering *if* they're real."

"Do you realize it's possible to read something and stay skeptical until there's proof? We have no idea how the place she found was made."

"So, you think some other group of humans invented manned space flight thousands of years ago, came here, and built the place Sima found?" Marley raised an eyebrow. "Or do you think she dug the caves out using her fingernails in a few weeks, then covered the walls in a made-up alien language to fake the whole thing?"

Muted chuckling came from the students.

"All right, everyone." Ms. Taylor held her hands up. "I'd prefer we let the evidence speak for itself."

The senior shook his head. "Why are you even here if you are so bored? You've been rolling your eyes all morning."

"My mother." Marley gestured at Ms. Taylor like a girl from a holo-advert showing off a prize. "She's the one interested in staring at incomprehensible squiggles on the walls and old clay pots, but this is *science*, so I am obligated to go with her even though it's boring and pointless."

Ms. Taylor appeared sad for an instant, a slight enough droop in her posture that only Sima appeared to notice. She shook the doldrum off and headed down the ramp, once again excited, though her smile had a new, insincere quality.

The students trailed after her, except Marley, who dawdled, perhaps hoping to be overlooked and allowed to wait outside.

"Hey, Marley." Sima doubled back and walked over to her, speaking a touch louder than a whisper. "It's pretty messed up to tell everyone you don't want to spend time with your mom while she's *standing right next to you*. Ms. Taylor usually has the energy of a betarabbit hopped up on Nova Dust. This is the first time I've *ever* seen her stop smiling. Don't gotta love exploring ruins, but you shouldn't crap all over her in front of everyone."

"Why do you care?" muttered Marley, taken aback. "You've never so much as looked at me, now you're reaming me out?"

Sima stared at her, unable to come up with an answer for her sudden, inexplicable annoyance. "Umm, honestly? No idea. Normally, I stay out of other people's business, but the way she looked so... *defeated* when you said that kinda pissed me off. Citizens always have everything they need and they always bitch about it. My bio-mom hated me. She wouldn't even make food for me when I was little. Had to cook for myself. She could've given me a hunk of bread with fruit paste smeared on it and I would've been thrilled. What you did here? It's like your mom gave you food and you threw it on the floor while she watched."

"Okay, okay. Relax." Marley swiped a hand at her hair. "This is just so damn boring to me. Walking around old places? I don't care what happened here thousands of years ago. We should be worrying about our survival, developing tech we can use to, I dunno, not go extinct."

"Fair enough. I'm not saying you have to like going on this trip. But—and this is going to be hard for your Citizen-brain to grasp—either you or your mother could die tomorrow. Back on Earth, I learned life could end randomly at any second within the first week of being on the street. Maybe a normal person would've taken that and treasured the people they knew. Me? I didn't know anyone, so I took it in the other direction and kept away from people so I wouldn't have to care who died. You're smart. What is a population of 20,000 humans compared to an entire planet? Have you seen quill cats? Or any of a thousand other things that might wander into the colony and eat someone?"

Marley turned half away, sighing. "I know… just nothing gets through to her. She's like a giant six-year-old super excited over *everything*. She does a simple experiment for her fifth-grade class and it's like *she's* the one seeing the reaction the first time. She acts the same way in *our* class and we're not eleven-year-olds. I don't get how she's interested in such lame stuff. I don't hate her at all… just wish she'd stop forcing me to do stuff that's so easy it's boring."

"You're going to end up by yourself in a lab with thirty-four cats slicing quantum nuclei in half with a laser someday. I get it. Honestly, I do. I had to attend remedial classwork. Most of it was super basic and extremely boring. Just deal with it. You won't have your mom forever, and I dunno… watching her make that face after you said what you said… last time someone kicked a kitten in front of me, I stabbed them."

"What?" Marley gasped. "Someone kicked a kitten?"

Sima sighed at the sky. "No. I'm lying. Didn't stab anyone… for that, anyway."

"Fine." Marley rolled her eyes. "I get it. You're going to cut me if I don't apologize to my mother because you never had one and it's making you sad."

"Why are Citizens always so melodramatic? You freak out if your food's not hot enough, never once wondering *if* you'll eat."

"Why do you have such a problem with Citizens? It's not *my* fault you were a street rat. You're not one anymore. Can you please stop acting like one?"

"A street rat wouldn't have gotten on your case."

Marley narrowed her eyes. "Fair point. So, can we just call each other bitches now and get on with the rest of our Saturday?"

Sima narrowed her eyes.

They glared at each other for a moment before cracking up at the same time.

"Marley? Sima?" called Ms. Taylor from the bottom of the ramp.

Both girls turned their heads to look at her.

Ms. Taylor peered out the gap between the doors. Her smile still looked insincere, but had a hint of hopefulness.

Sima nudged Marley, then jogged down the ramp. Ms. Taylor ducked back inside as she neared, allowing her to slip between the doors into a large, rectangular chamber lit by a strange, sourceless light. Bluish metal walls definitely gave off an 'alien spacecraft' vibe, though the sixteen square stone columns arranged in a perfect grid pattern definitely didn't belong in a high-tech setting. They made the room appear to be a museum containing artifacts from an ancient dig site. The columns reminded her of various places back on Earth in her district where *ancient* relics sat out on public display.

How weird would it be if these aliens had discovered the remains of an even older civilization on this planet? Oh, this is probably stuff from their past. Aliens didn't make the artifacts in the museums on Earth.

The students split up into several groups to examine and photograph the columns. Carved writing covered all four sides of each one from the eight-foot-tall mark down to the floor. The upper three feet contained small bas-reliefs of humanoid figures. Sima, again feeling a bit antisocial, headed for an unattended column close to the middle of the chamber. When she spotted Koji and Mial working together at the farthest column in from the door, she kept going past her 'target' toward them.

Marley stopped at the entrance to have a murmured conversation with her mother, starting with, "Look, Mum, I'm sorry."

Sima smiled to herself, slowing to eavesdrop a little. Sure, Marley told a bit of a lie, claiming to be upset at the senior for not caring enough about the trip to read the materials, but she apologized for hurting her mother's feelings and said she didn't mean to.

I am such a meat sack.

Meat sacks said 'hello' to Outcasts they didn't know, expecting they'd be friendly. Meat sacks didn't put up armored walls around their emotions or act like nothing mattered. Meat sacks didn't know how dangerous the world really was. Meat sacks didn't live more than a few days on the street.

Twelve-year-old Sima *had* been a meat sack, inside. Living with her mother hadn't been fun, but at least it equipped her with the ability to keep her emotions hidden. Had anyone noticed how terrified she'd been those first few days, she wouldn't have made it.

Grr. I really have to stop thinking about Earth. She mockingly 'blamed' her new parents for destroying her 'armor,' and Dr. Bystrova for convincing her to try going outside without it. Tuning out the other students, she hurried across the remainder of the room toward the boys. The last time she walked up to Koji in a strange place, he helped her avoid a crazy person. Approaching him in *this* strange place helped her change the subject in her brain.

For some reason, the boys had gone all the way across the room to the last column, which stood about ten feet away from a short dead-end corridor where the walls had an almost organic appearance due to rippled carving in the stone. This 'alien site' appeared to consist of only one, huge room. Given the standing stone columns, perhaps the former residents of Mirage used it as a storage facility, some manner of museum, or a temple.

Sima stopped half a step from standing between Koji and Mial, peering up at the bas-reliefs, which resembled crude renditions of humans. "Wow, are those people?"

Koji and Mial both jumped.

"Uhh, not exactly." Koji pointed at the left side of the column. "Some of the figures on this column have two arms, a chest, and a head, but the majority have four arms. Only a few are depicted with legs. Most have... I think it's supposed to be a tail."

"Mermaids?" asked Mial.

"Or slugs... maybe serpents." Sima leaned up on her toes, bracing a hand on the column while peering up at the images. "The other place we found had all sorts of tunnels. Water everywhere."

Mial stepped around to the next face. "Wonder if this planet might once have been covered in water? Do you think whoever they were, they died out when the planetary ocean dried up?"

Koji shrugged.

"I don't know. Where would all that water go? A planet can't be entirely covered in water, basically one giant ocean, then all of a sudden not be. It's gotta go somewhere." Sima scratched her head. "Planet's don't have giant drains."

Mial pointed. "On the other side, there's a thing that kinda looks like a comet or an asteroid fireball. If a big ass rock fell from the sky and hit the planet, could it have vaporized the water? Or enough water to allow land to emerge in places?"

"There are oceans still. We've seen Mirage from orbit," said Koji. "Except for the shape of the continents, it's pretty close to Earth in terms of appearance."

Marley walked up and bumped Sima. "Thanks for that, by the way. Now, Mom's going to be extra. She thinks I adore this stuff as much as her."

"Let her be happy." Sima brushed her fingers down the column over the carved symbols. "Figuring out what this writing means is seriously over my head. If you're looking for an extreme challenge, you could help her decode this."

Marley pursed her lips. "Some things are *too* difficult. And besides, it serves no purpose other than to give archaeologists warm fuzzies. Ninety-nine percent of humans won't care what this civilization had to say."

"What if they left a warning about what not to do?" Mial grinned. "Like, hey we had this cool planet but Jim did that thing we told him not to do and wiped out our civilization. Don't be like Jim."

Koji, Sima, and Marley chuckled.

Her bracelet vibrated.

Sima lifted her arm, allowing the hologram screen to scroll open above the sleeve of her jumpsuit.

‹I have decoded the file.›

"File?"

‹The file from the resource room terminal. The encoded attachment.›

Sima blinked. "Wait. What? You copied it?"

‹The file contains a series of highly suspicious program instructions. In my estimation, this software is intentionally malicious.›

"A virus?"

Koji leaned closer. "What are you talking about?"

She pointed at the screen.

‹I do not believe it is a virus, rather a subroutine intended for a reactor control system. The effect of running this software could be severe.›

Sima raised both eyebrows. "What—?"

A brilliant red flash went off, accompanied by a thunderous buzz. Sima instinctively jumped back, raising her arms to shield her face as a blast of heat rolled by. Koji grabbed her and Marley, pulling the girls behind the column and squishing them into Mial. Frightened screams—and smoke—filled the air. An older boy gave an agonized wail. Veesa shrieked in terror.

"Everyone, behind a pillar, *now*," shouted Evie Ruiz. "Stay down!"

Sima coughed on a billow of smoke.

The buzz happened again; a bright red energy beam lanced

across the middle of the chamber and left a glowing orange crater in a column near the middle of the room, the same one she almost decided to study alone. Sima clung to the stone, sheepishly peering around the corner on the left. The beam sliced the column in half, the upper part now lying flat on the ground atop of one of the senior boys' legs. Both edges of the cut glowed orange from heat.

Whirring noises came from a spot near the ceiling on the left about halfway down the length of the room. A silver metal dome, slightly larger than a human head, had extended downward from a previously concealed nest. It twitched back and forth, rotating like a cat watching a room full of terrified mice, unable to choose which one to go after. Intense red light glowed from within a round opening on the side of the dome next to a flat bright green panel.

"Laser turret," whispered Mial.

An inch-thick shaft of red light appeared in an instant, connecting the turret to another column, cutting it in half mere inches above Veesa's head. The upper section slid on a layer of molten rock, following the downward angle of the beam. Fortunately, Veesa noticed it coming and dove out of the way before the huge block of stone crushed her.

Sima gasped.

Both Security officers opened fire on the turret, covering it in sparks. Bullets ricocheted around the room, pinging off the walls, columns, and the floor. However, the turret appeared impervious to their assault. Students screamed and ducked for cover.

"Stop firing!" yelled Nahan. "We're gonna hit one of the kids."

The gunfire ceased.

"No, more like a plasma turret." Koji shook his head.

"Who cares about technicalities!" yelled Marley.

As if reacting to the girl's shouting, the turret rotated, pointing straight at Sima. She stared into the barrel at a spot of red energy as bright as a dying star.

"Crap! Run! Stone's not gonna stop it!" Sima sprinted for the only place that made any sense: the short dead-end corridor behind them.

The loud buzz went off as she ran. Scrambling footsteps and screaming followed. She leapt past the corner, ducking a spray of molten metal from a second plasma blast clipping the wall. Unfortunately, the corridor didn't go far, being more of an alcove. Sima crammed herself into the innermost left corner, putting as much stone between her and the turret as possible.

Koji, Mial, and Marley crashed into her, huddling close.

After four seconds of sustained buzz, a third beam pierced the wall at head level, roughly two feet in from the corner—straight through dirt, rock, and half-inch-thick metal wall plates.

Sima gawked.

Marley screamed.

Koji looked as though he wanted to scream but couldn't.

"We should be safe here," rasped Mial.

The buzzing started again.

"Or not..." Koji appeared close to fainting. "Solid stone isn't stopping it. It's gonna get us in a few seconds."

Sima scowled at the too-short passage. Standing there waiting to die didn't seem like a great plan, but the alternative... charging *into* the room sounded way, way worse. "Guys, get down." She squatted.

Koji, Marley, and Mial all ducked as well.

The beam pierced the wall nine seconds later, also at head level —directly over Marley.

She screamed again.

... and the buzzing resumed.

"We gotta do something!" yelled Mial.

"Thank you, Commander Obvious," barked Koji.

"What exactly are we supposed to do? Phase through the wall like ghosts?" barked Sima.

The second the words left her mouth, she re-noticed the strange rippled, almost organic texture decorating the innermost wall of the alcove. A large egg-shaped ridge at its center looked exactly like the door Juan accidentally opened when he fell into the underground complex. Giving it no further thought, she rushed over, patting around the spot where she expected the button would be.

Koji grabbed her. "Stay in the corner or it'll—"

The oval slab of rock inside the ridge snapped downward the instant Sima touched the hidden switch.

"Here!" Without hesitation, she dove forward into a familiar-looking tunnel.

Striations of purple and blue on the tunnel walls blurred by. Running water plus clear, slippery slime on glass-smooth rock sent her rocketing downhill so fast she rose up on the left side while shooting around a turn. Eight seconds later, she flew headfirst into a water-filled room.

Despite expecting the bath, she still screamed out a giant bubble in response to the cold, her body reflexively curling into a ball. Three more splashes happened around her. Once the shock of icy cold passed and she could move again, she righted herself and discovered the underground lake to be only waist deep.

The others, all soaked, gathered close to her, gazing around in bewildered awe.

"Eww," whispered Marley, making a horrified-slash-disgusted face.

Much like the last alien site she and the kids discovered, this chamber appeared to be a centralized room with multiple passage-ways leading off. Quite *unlike* before, two openings led to actual corridors as opposed to round slime-lubricated tunnels. Metal walls, inexplicable light from no visible source, and bizarre cleanli-ness made the passages look like they belonged on a spacecraft rather than a catacomb.

"Whoa," said Mial. "We found the aliens' swimming pool."

"Seriously, eww." Marley cringed. "This is disgusting. The floor is slimy."

Sima shuddered at the memory. Waterlogged boots were annoy-ing, but she'd take them over walking barefoot in this muck again. "This is why reasonable people don't wear flip-flops to unexplored ruins."

"Ha. Ha." Marley huffed. "I'm not wearing them now. Lost them on the water slide. Or should I say, slime-slide? Ugh. So disgusting. Is this stuff harmful?"

"There they are." Mial pointed. "Your shoes are floating away."

Everyone looked where he indicated. Two flip-flops glided like tiny boats toward one of the rounded openings, though they didn't exactly race off.

"I got 'em." Mial sloshed after them.

"No. It's harmless. Merely disgusting." Sima blushed. "When we found the other site, I didn't have shoes at all."

Koji tilted his head. "Why'd you take them off?"

"I didn't. All we had was our underwear, and we only had it because we'd worn it in the stasis pods. The EGSF was so damn cheap they didn't put *any* supplies in the lockers for us. No jump-suits, shoes, food... nothing."

"Wow, seriously?" Marley cringed. "So wrong... but I don't think they expected the escape pods to deploy. We were going so far away from Earth, if the pods activated, we'd have much bigger problems than nothing to wear... like floating off in the middle of space. Where, exactly did they think the pods would go if some-thing happened to the ship halfway here?"

"Ugh." Sima swiped wet hair away from her eyes. "Good thing Mirage is warm. Once I got over being mortified, it ended up not actually being all that bad."

"Not much different from a swimsuit, really." Marley shrugged.

"Yeah." Sima kicked her boot toe idly at the muck.

Koji looked up from the glowing screen above his left forearm. "Whew. The bracelets are waterproof."

"How many times have you showered wearing it?" Sima laughed. "And you're only now figuring out they don't care about water?"

"It's seriously lame how they lock them on us." Marley folded her arms. "We're not toddlers. They should trust us to be responsible."

Her screen lit up. She glanced down.

"Oh, go to hell."

"What'd it say?" asked Sima.

Smirking, Marley held her arm out to read.

‹They do trust you to be responsible… once you turn eighteen.›

Sima chuckled. "Are all Omnis sarcastic?"

All four bracelets activated screens. Sima's typed, ‹Yes.›

The boys laughed.

"Here…" Mial handed the recovered flip-flops to Marley. "Wouldn't try putting them on until you're out of the water."

"Thanks. Didn't really need you to point out that foam floats. I'm blonde, not stupid."

Mial grinned.

"Now what do we do?" asked Koji.

"Well…" She looked at the two metal-walled corridors. "The first place I found had multiple tunnels leading back up to the surface room. Like here, the upstairs only had one room. This site's upstairs room is a *lot* bigger than the last one, and rectangular. Only saw the one alcove… I don't think we're going to find another way up to the same room, but there might be an alternate way out."

"Did the other place have a back door?" asked Marley.

"No." Sima pointed at the two hallways. "But it also didn't have spaceship corridors or giant stone blocks. It might've been more of a small village. This site feels totally different in purpose."

Marley whistled. "Wow…"

Sima smiled to herself, gesturing at the finished corridors. "I don't think those formed naturally, either."

"Hah." Marley gave a nervous laugh. "Umm… totally never expected anything like it down here, just a bunch of old dusty rocks and cave writing."

"All this water…" Mial splashed off to the side. "Was the other place flooded, too?"

"Yeah. The main chamber looked pretty much the same. I remember it being a bit deeper, like up to my chest. Water ran into all the tunnels, almost like the aliens used it to help get around. If those tails are slug-like, they might have needed the water to stay alive."

Koji ducked under for a moment, coming back up holding a glop of dark purple muck. "Maybe you're right about them being slugs. What do you think this is? Algae of some kind? Stuff the aliens might've secreted? Dead skin?"

Marley retched.

"It's probably the decaying remains of 10,000-year-old alien poop." Sima opened one of her sample phial cases.

Marley retched harder. "Did you *really* have to say that?"

"I said the same thing when the slime squished between my toes." She scooped some of the muck from Koji's hand into the tiny bottle. "No idea what it is now, but we'll find out when we get back to the colony. If this ever was actually poop, it's decayed well beyond recognizable by now."

"*If* we get back," muttered Mial.

Marley whined out her nose. "Don't talk like that."

"Easy. We just wait here for the Security team to get rid of the turret and we go back up." Koji pointed at the hole they flew out of. "It's basically a U-turn. We are directly under the upper chamber."

"Dude." Mial cringed. "Did you see when the Security officers shot at the turret? Didn't even scratch it."

"Yeah, I saw." Koji shrugged. "They just need to get something bigger... like a missile. We're only eighteen miles from home."

Sima tilted her head. "Did they even bring missiles?"

"Of course they did." Koji flailed his arms. "They're the military. They bring missiles to everything."

Marley clutched her flip-flops to her chest, shivering. "We should go back upstairs. What if it's dangerous down here? I have to find my mom, make sure she's okay. I don't want to stay down here."

"We can't." Koji pointed at the ceiling. "The crazy plasma turret will kill us."

"But my mother's up there..." Marley sniffled, giving Sima a pointed look.

Ugh. She's going to hate me if anything happened to Ms. Taylor. I said any of us could die at any minute.

Mial sighed at his left arm. "Omni doesn't have a signal down here. Too much dirt and rock in the way. Relax. We're safe from the plasma gun. Just sit here and wait for someone to yell into the tunnel that it's safe."

"Half a column fell on someone!" yelled Marley. "It's shooting at us. What if it hit someone? They could all be dead! You guys are talking about water aliens and taking samples of purple snot like it's no big deal? My mom..." She buried her face in her hands, crying.

Sima sloshed over and grasped her by the shoulders. "I'm pretty sure no one got hit." *At least, not before we fell down here.* "There would have been a lot more screaming. No one screamed like they saw someone get vaporized."

"Uhh...." Marley lifted her face from her hands to gawk at her. "Vaporized?"

"The beam melted stone in seconds," said Koji. "However, I don't think it would vaporize an *entire* person if it hit them... only wherever the beam touched would turn to ash in an instant."

Everyone stared at him.

"You aren't helping." Sima exhaled. "Just... Marley... don't panic. It kept shooting at us when we ran for the alcove. We gave everyone a chance to get out."

"Except for that kid stuck under the rock." Mial gazed up. "Think they dragged him out?"

Sima cringed. "Not sure. Didn't get a good look at him. If we go upstairs now, we will definitely get killed."

"This is some kind of facility." Mial sloshed across the flooded chamber toward the nearer of the two finished corridors. "Maybe there's a control or something to turn it off?"

Koji paled. "What if there's more turrets down here? Any idea what made the first one turn on?"

Marley resumed crying.

"No idea what activated it... and there are no turrets in this room." Sima whistled innocently.

"How do you know that?" whimpered Marley.

"Because we haven't been shot at." Sima shrugged.

Mial held a finger up. "She makes a good point." He stepped out of the water at the start of the corridor. "Looks like we're inside the *Progenitor* again. Kinda. Obviously alien, but same basic design as us. Floor. Walls. Ceiling. Doors... they're kinda egg-shaped, but still doors."

"C'mon. We should get out of the water at least. It's too cold." Sima grasped Marley's arm and tugged her along, following Mial.

"Keep your eyes on the ceiling." Koji sloshed past the girls, rushing to catch up to Mial. "We can't let a turret ambush us. Stop at every corner and look first. Everyone be ready to run."

"Okay." Marley wiped her face. "I'm okay. Just... scared and worried."

"So am I." Sima offered a reassuring smile. "The other site had nothing in it. Totally abandoned. We'll be fine."

"Did it have a plasma death turret?" asked Koji. "Or high-tech corridors?"

Sima sighed. "Guys, I'm trying to help her feel better. Umm. No idea about the turret. There *might* have been one, but it never activated."

Marley struggled up the seemingly natural stone ramp leading up from the water-filled pit to the corridor. The instant her slime-coated foot hit metal floor, she slipped, flailing around in a crazy dance for a second until stabilizing herself.

"Nice moves." Mial clapped.

"Stuff's slippery." Sima paused at the edge of the water to scrape the unknown bio-slime from her boot soles.

Marley wiped her feet off, then stepped into her flip-flops. "Yeah."

"So, umm..." Mial chuckled. "What are we looking for? A big red button marked 'off'?"

"Something like that." Sima grinned.

18

EMISSARY

Somehow, Sima ended up taking the lead after the first three rooms.

Neither Koji nor Mial appeared overly frightened of surprise pop-down turrets, so perhaps they unconsciously deferred to her having 'prior experience' in alien facilities. The rooms they'd explored along the first section of hallway contained empty shelves and a few tables, nothing of any use or containing any information regarding the former occupants of Mirage.

Other than the odd shape—generally oval but wider at the bottom—the doors easily accommodated humans. Their size, however, suggested the natives had been taller and wider. Unable to help herself, Sima took some pictures, documenting the openings as eleven feet tall at the narrowest part of the oval and eight feet wide at the widest part.

Marley shivered constantly, peering back toward the water room every so often.

Lissa didn't act half as scared down here as her. Sima crept up to the next room. *But... she's also too little to really understand danger she can't see.*

As all the previous doors had before it, the next one she approached slid into the wall sideways when she approached it.

"Anyone else thinking it's strange a place abandoned for thousands of years still has electrical power?" asked Mial.

Sima peeked into the room. "You're assuming they use electricity as we understand it. Who knows what makes this stuff operate?"

The room contained six large, boxy objects bearing a striking resemblance to freestanding closets. A seam down the middle of each one divided the front into two apparent doors, but they had no obvious handles, buttons, or other controls. Nothing in there appeared relevant to the mission to turn the turret off, merely storage.

"Whatever it is, it works." Koji continued down the corridor to the next door on the right, which opened with a soft hiss. "Still weird. This place doesn't look like it's been empty for ten thousand years. There isn't even any dust. Nothing's broken."

Ignoring the room of 'cabinets,' Sima walked past Koji to a four-way intersection. "They made a beam turret our bullets bounced off. Maybe they were good at building things to last."

Every direction appeared the same, seemingly endless shiny metal hallways and egg doors.

Mial walked up behind her. "Wow, this place is huge."

"Uhh, guys?" whispered Marley. "I just had a really scary thought."

"Found a weird chair," yelled Koji.

Marley shifted her gaze to the right. "Forget the furniture. We're in big trouble."

Sima peered back down the hall at her. "What's your thought?"

"What if this place is so nice because the aliens are *still* here?" whispered Marley.

Mial scrunched up his nose.

"Nah," called Koji. "A civilization advanced enough to make a plasma beam weapon would have noticed our ships land and come out to say hello already."

Or kill us. I hope the urge to destroy what one cannot control or understand is a uniquely human trait.

"Yeah," said Sima in a less-than-confident tone. "He's right. If the… Mirrans still existed and posed a threat, we'd know by now."

Koji poked his head out of the room. "What the heck is a Mirran? And… check out this chair."

"I'm tired of my Omni complaining at me every time I say 'alien.'" Sima hurried over to him. "Natives of Mirage are Mirrans. Just made it up. It's easier than saying 'the civilization that existed here before us' over and over."

Mial laughed.

"Seriously," grumbled Marley. "You're checking out a chair? We're trying to survive here, not shop for furniture."

Sima peered into the room.

The supposed 'chair' resembled a stand to hold a nine-foot-long banana. A curved, cushioned part on the floor connected to a frame topped by a silver console containing multiple buttons. Two subordinate keyboards attached to small movable arms stuck out on either side. Their arrangement made her picture a four-armed creature using one hand per keyboard. The 'chair' had two pairs of armrests, each at a different height.

"Oh, wow…" Sima approached, holding her bracelet up. "Get some pictures of this, please. This has to be some kind of workstation. Unless the Mirrans needed to store giant four-armed bananas, this has got to be a chair for a creature like a mermaid, only serpentine rather than fish."

"Can see that." Koji grinned. "The tail goes in the curved part, but it's not really like sitting for them. Just a padded sling to, uhh, 'stand' in."

Mial walked up to the 'chair,' examining the console. "They must use holographic screens like us. There's nothing here to display output."

"Maybe they plug it straight into their brains." Koji pantomimed connecting a wire to his head behind one ear. "Or have implants like Dreamdots."

Marley, still in the hallway, rubbed her hands up and down her arms for warmth. "Guys, can you stop being jealous of their furniture? We'll have plenty of time to check this stuff out once we don't have to worry about *dying*."

Ack. Looking at her shivering is making me *feel cold.*

"Marley." Koji faced the doorway. "Do you think the Mirrans developed cybernetic implants?"

She sighed. "It would entirely depend on if their species has the same inherent feelings of inadequacy as humans and wanted to improve themselves by any means necessary."

Beep.

Sima whirled. "Who touched what?"

"Uhh, sorry. My fault." Mial stepped back from the 'chair.' "Poking random keys. It's kinda strange to see a keyboard. Only read about them in history class. Why's a civilization capable of making plasma turrets still using tech from 200 years ago?"

"Why are they arranging giant stone blocks in their lobby?" asked Sima. "The other place was almost *all* stone. Looked like primitives lived there... except for a few metal objects."

"Possible they couldn't talk?" asked Koji.

Marley's teeth started chattering. "Maybe they don't trust AI so they never developed computers you talk to. Or maybe they never even thought to make AI. Whatever. I don't care. You guys shouldn't care. We have to find a way out."

Hiss.

Sima, Koji, and Mial spun to the right.

A panel in the wall opened, revealing a closet-sized alcove containing a nine-foot-tall shiny silver being—or Mirran in a fully enclosed armored suit. Its spindly legs and arms seemed far too narrow to have living limbs inside them. The creature's wide head —or helmet—possessed a distinctly insectoid shape, reminiscent of a praying mantis without the giant eyes or protruding mandibles. Five small glowing red dots along the front could be its eyes, or simply sensors.

Unlike the 'chair' suggested, the being only had two arms. In one claw-like hand, it held a narrow silver rod. A helix of blue coils covered the upper half of the three-foot staff, connected to a pod on one end. The hole in the tip looked quite a bit like a smaller version of the plasma turret. A part at the opposite end resembled the rubberized grip of an e-bike's handlebar.

Everyone stood still, open-mouthed.

The Mirran stepped out of the alcove, panning its head back and forth.

When its gaze fell on Sima, she raised a hand.

"Hello?"

"I think it's a robot," whispered Koji. "People—or Mirrans—don't stand in tiny hidden compartments until someone pushes a button."

Mial nodded. "I agree with him. Definitely a robot."

"*Glzt nihh ek obt kzlcht,*" said the robot, its voice a harsh crackling buzz.

"Do you understand GANSEC?" asked Mial.

The robot gripped the rod in both hands—exactly as one might hold a rifle—and pointed it at him. Red light welled up in the hole.

Sima screamed, "Look out!"

Koji hurled himself at Mial an instant before the robot fired a small plasma beam.

Time appeared to freeze, an instant burned into in her perception: the blinding streak of crimson light passing through Koji's left thigh, into Mial's abdomen, and out his back into the wall behind them. Koji's jumpsuit leg burst into flames around the wound. Mial's jumpsuit caught fire on both sides as well.

Overcome by a mixture of rage and need to stop it from killing them, Sima rushed at the robot, hoping to knock the skinny machine on its metal ass long enough for them to run. She jumped at the last second, hurling all her weight into its body—and stopped hard, as if she'd thrown herself at a wall. The robot swayed back barely an inch.

"Oof!" she barked, bouncing off its chest and landing on her feet in front of it.

Somewhere behind her, Marley shrieked, then yelled, "You're on fire!"

"I noticed!" shouted Koji.

The robot swung its left arm up and seized her throat in a three-fingered appendage somewhere between robot claw and insectoid pincer. Gurgling, she grabbed its 'hand,' struggling to pull its grip open. It dragged her around to the left, holding her aside while pointing its weapon at the boys.

Sima kicked the rod, redirecting the second plasma beam into the wall. The blast melted a squiggly hole in the metal wall, fringed in glowing orange.

Koji and Marley dragged Mial out into the corridor, smoke wafting from their extinguished jumpsuits.

Sensing its arms didn't have too much strength, she twisted into its grip, forcing the elbow joint of the arm holding her to hyperextend, and yanked at the claw. Metal scraped over her neck as the metal grippers lost their hold.

Again, she rammed her shoulder into the robot, but may as well have tried to tackle one of the stone blocks upstairs.

Damn. This thing has something else keeping it upright... it's not that strong.

Marley grunted from exertion, Koji in pain. Mial, partially unconscious, moaned.

The robot swung the rod at Sima.

She ducked, then stomp kicked its leg. The seemingly frail limb buckled, dumping the robot over on one side.

"Hah!" Got you!"

Of course, falling over didn't appear to damage it at all.

She stepped both feet on the rod, pinning the weapon to the floor so the robot couldn't shoot anyone. "Hurry up! Get Mial out of here."

The robot made a series of angry buzzing noises, attempting to yank its weapon out from under her boots. She slid an inch or two at a time, waving her arms for balance. The machine refused to let go of the weapon, and almost appeared confused as to why it couldn't pick it up.

"We're trying!" shouted Harley. "He's heavy!"

Mial grunted.

Sima glanced at the doorway, wanting to run, but afraid to move. Out of desperation, she pulled her knife and jabbed at the machine's eyes… succeeding only in making a few small scratches. *Dammit!*

The attack appeared to remind the robot of her existence. It looked at the plasma rod, up at her, back at the plasma rod, then grabbed her right ankle in its free left claw-hand. She lurched forward as it yanked her foot away from the plasma rifle. Subconsciously, she flung her arms out and grabbed the armrest of the weird chair to stop her face from smacking into the floor.

She dangled suspended between her hands on the chair and the robot's grip on her leg. The instant the machine pivoted its rifle up toward her, she screamed a war cry and pulled at the chair while trying to kick its hand away from her boot.

Creaking metal accompanied the bizarre chair teetering toward her. A plasma beam appeared in front of her face, slicing the armrest she grabbed in half between her hands. The ponderous Mirran furniture collapsed over sideways, landing on the robot with a loud metallic crash. Sima stumbled backward, staring in shock at the smoldering plasma burn on the chair as well as the ceiling. Her cheeks and nose tingled from the heat of an energy beam passing so close. She didn't even notice the robot still held her right ankle until it tripped her over backward.

Falling seated on the floor redirected her attention from the near miss to the more immediate problem of a murderous robot holding her leg. She stomped her free foot at the claw hand, trying to dislodge it. Metal grippers left small cuts in her boots, proof this machine had been designed for combat and not utility. Even its hands served as weapons.

The fourth kick knocked the gripper claw loose. She flipped over onto all fours, then scrambled into a run out the door, leaving the machine to struggle under the weight of the toppled chair. A surprisingly sparse trail of blood smeared to the right, though she didn't need it to find the others. They'd only managed to go about thirty feet down the corridor. Koji lurched along at a severe limp, putting no weight on his left leg. Marley appeared to be doing most of the work supporting Mial, though the reedy girl struggled to do so.

Sima ran over to them. "I got him. Your leg…"

Koji collapsed to the floor as soon as Sima took his place. "Aww, dammit. This hurts."

"Did you kill it?" grunted Marley.

"No. It kinda pulled the chair over on itself." Sima grunted under Mial's surprising weight.

Except for the other girl being an inch or so shorter than her, they were roughly the same size. Sima credited her scrawniness to barely eating for the last four years rather than entirely genetics. However, her body tolerated physical stress quite well, being accustomed to running from gang punks, navigating ruined buildings, or literally climbing walls to avoid having to walk near EGSF officers. She didn't hold her life against Marley. If she could've spent all day sitting by a computer in a nice, cushy residence, she would have.

Sima stared at the floor, watching where she stepped, entirely focused on getting Mial—and herself—as far away from the killer robot as possible. His legs dragged limp. Marley lost her flip-flops again—probably ran straight out of them in a panic—and didn't seem the least bit interested in going back to the 'robot room' to pick them up.

How does such a smart girl do something so stupid? Who wears foam slippers on a field trip like this? We're not going to a damn museum.

Crashing, banging, and angry machine buzzing filled the hallway behind them.

Koji forced himself upright again, hopping on his right leg. Watching a boy with only one usable leg easily outrun her made Sima growl and throw her all into dragging Mial forward.

"It's coming!" yelled Koji.

Marley made a noise part scream, part whimper, part grunt of exhaustion.

Text patter came from her bracelet. The screen's light glow filled her peripheral vision.

"They *really* need to give you a speaker or something," grumbled Sima. "I can't see what you're trying to tell me unless I let go of Mial. Send it to Koji."

Koji's bracelet activated. He looked at the screen. "Uhh, it says turn left up ahead, take the first right, then go to the third door on the left side."

"Do it!" yelled Sima.

A plasma bolt going by an arm's length away from her face had been bad enough. She didn't want one coming any closer. Whatever the bracelet knew, she trusted it. Having some semblance of a plan gave her hope. For the first time in her life, she feared something more than the EGSF. Cops wouldn't always kill her. Big eyes and tears had a chance to work on them. A Mirran robot wouldn't care what she said or how deferential she acted. It probably had no idea what humans even were. To it, some manner of vermin got into the building and needed to be eliminated.

Dread gave her strength. She surged up to a normal walking pace, probably carrying about seventy percent of Mial's weight.

Koji hopped around the first corner. Sima channeled the desire to check on him into extra motivation. She couldn't leave Mial behind to freak out over the hole in Koji's leg. Marley would get confused and stand there by him, and they'd both end up dead when the robot broke loose. The constant metallic banging and buzzing served as the countdown to a ticking bomb. They had mere seconds to find a hiding place before it hunted them down.

Sima's legs quivered from exertion, yet she pushed herself onward. Koji hopped down an agonizingly long stretch of corridor. Sima and Marley closed the distance gradually, being only ten feet behind him when they dragged Mial around the final corner.

The hallway ahead of them showed the first signs of anything having gone wrong in this place. Scorch marks on the walls suggested a plasma gun fight happened there. A twisted mass of warped metal, loose earth, and rock blocked off the hallway a mere fifty feet from the corner. Her bracelet wanted them to go to the third room on the left side, but the corridor only had two doors.

Too afraid of the robot to stop, she kept moving. "There's no third room!"

"In the rubble." Koji pointed ahead.

"I'm…" Marley gasped, stumbling. "I can't…"

"You have to!" whisper-shouted Sima. "Almost there. Stay quiet or it'll hear us."

Koji fell to all fours a short distance from the cave-in and crawled under a tangle of metal beams, screaming in pain past a clenched jaw. Marley collapsed. Mial's weight dragged Sima to her knees. He jolted back to consciousness, gurgling in agony.

"Hurry! Can you crawl?" rasped Sima.

He groaned. "Maybe…"

She guided him to the debris. Under the cave-in, Koji crouched in a doorway mostly blocked by junk. He took Mial's hands and helped pull him in. Marley curled up on the floor where she fell.

"Get over here," whispered Sima. "If it sees you, it'll know where we went."

Marley didn't move.

"Come on. Don't give up. How's your mom going to feel when they show her your charred skull?"

The girl lifted her head off the floor to stare at her. Sima expected her to start sobbing or curse her out, but Marley surprised her by doing neither and dragging herself closer. She and Marley hastily scurried under the rubble, following the boys into a cramped space where a big metal table resisted the cave-in, creating a small pocket of space. Soil scattered across the floor scraped whenever anyone moved, making far too much noise for comfort. Koji and Sima rolled Mial onto his back. The boy promptly passed out. Marley, now safely hidden, surrendered to her emotions and curled up in a ball, trying to sob without making a sound.

Koji looked up from Mial to Sima, mouth open as if to talk, but he froze at the repetitive thump of metal footsteps echoing in the hall. The mood in his eyes shifted to dread. Sima reached out and took his hand. Marley lifted her face off her knees, her expression asking, 'Are we going to die?'

Sima shook her head, offering the girl her other hand.

Marley grasped it and scooted closer.

They huddled together in the dark, the footfalls of the robot hunting them the only sound louder than their breaths.

19

A QUESTION OF IF

Clattering metal footsteps grew louder out in the corridor.
They echoed in an odd manner, making it impossible to tell how close the robot came to their hiding place. It certainly couldn't be too far away, probably checking each door as it passed. Sima stared transfixed at the patch of light under the mangled wreckage, waiting for any sign of a shadow falling over it.

Why am I watching? It's not gonna matter if I see it coming or not. If it finds us, we have nowhere to go.

Somehow, despite being terrified, she neither trembled nor cried. Her only outward reaction took the form of complete still-ness. Her old fear of being trapped in a dead-end alley while EGSF officers machinegunned Outcasts down in a hail of bullets paled in comparison to this moment. Even the worst cops might hesitate before killing children. Granted, EGSF officers wouldn't consider anyone her age a child, but she'd become good at pretending a few years off her face.

The only reason a Mirran robot would hesitate before killing a child would be to compensate aim for a smaller target. A spike of dread tightened her grip on Koji and Marley's hands at the thought this place might contain an army of similar robots. If Mial somehow activated all of them, Progenitor Colony would soon be wiped out.

Assuming the robots had the ability to climb out the slimy water tunnels.

Sima used the funny mental image of the robot slipping down the tunnels to stall her panic spiral. The Security officers' bullets didn't bother the turret, so she initially assumed the robot would be immune as well. But it also hadn't been *too* strong. Even if it took her using both hands, she overpowered its skinny arm. Maybe the turret had a force field or some other defense requiring a power source impractical to put on a walking robot. It stood to reason that if her knife scratched its face, bullets would shred them. Maybe, just maybe, the colonists could kill the robots.

For a tediously long few minutes, no one moved. Finally, the tromping footsteps became quieter and quieter.

It's AI brain is going crazy trying to explain how we disappeared. Wonder if it thinks we're a glitch?

Marley wiped her face, sniffled, and stared into nowhere. Her expression reminded Sima of a young Outcast who watched the EGSF gun their parents down in front of them. Of course, a Citizen would be traumatized by something as basic as running away from a person—or robot—trying to shoot them. Sure, it bothered Sima, too, but after a few months, running away from killers had become a routine survival skill.

Mial, Koji, and Marley were all in her class. She'd been spending six and a half hours a weekday with them for a few months, but up until this morning, hadn't directly spoken to or much acknowledged Marley or Mial. Until Koji sat beside her for lunch not long ago, she hadn't spoken to *any* other student, old habits and all. Talking to an unfamiliar person was a great way for an Outcast to end up bleeding out naked in an alley after someone stole *all* their stuff.

Life on Earth had been scary, but the streets had nothing on an alien robot with a plasma rifle.

This girl she'd barely acknowledged looked at her almost the same way Lissa did when they'd been stranded out there, as if begging her to do something to 'make it all better.' Marley had to be one of the smartest kids in the entire school, but all her intelligence didn't mean much if her brain shut down in a crisis.

Sima didn't think she managed too well either, but given a choice between sitting there and dying or *trying* to escape alive, she'd for damn sure take option two. Possible death beat definite death.

After a minute of total silence in the hallway, she looked at Koji's leg.

Char ringed a hole in his left thigh about the size of her index finger. A tunnel went completely through his leg, the insides burned black. Surprisingly, it only bled a little near the edges where motion cracked the char-scab. The wound didn't appear to have hit bone at least, and probably missed the big, important artery as well.

"Can you feel your foot?" whispered Sima.

"I don't think it's numb, but the hole is kinda distracting." He closed his eyes, exhaling out his nose. "Trying not to move and it still feels like I've got a burning hot needle in my leg."

When Sima let go of their hands, Marley crawled around to check on Mial. The girl still trembled somewhat, but appeared to have regained some control of herself.

Koji gasped and squirmed as Sima peeled the fabric of his jumpsuit away from the injury, examining the area using the light of her bracelet's screen.

"You're not really bleeding. I know it hurts a lot, but the doctors can definitely fix this." *I hope.*

"We have to get out of here first," whispered Marley. "Mial is bleeding."

Sima shifted around to look at him. He'd been shot in the abdomen. A similar char-edged hole offered a grotesque view of stuff moving around inside him. Probably intestines.

‹Mial needs medical attention within hours or he will die.›

"Yeah…" Sima stared at the text. "Thanks for finding this room."

‹U R welcome.›

"*How* did you find this room?"

‹This facility has an active network. It is using a radio frequency at the extreme end of my capabilities, but I've managed to achieve sporadic connectivity and translate some of the data. Enough to discover this collapsed section.›

"Map? Do you know if there's another way out where no turret's going to melt us down?"

‹There is a section I am unable to evaluate due to missing data or garbled transmission. Based on a few assumptions, I estimate there to be a 62.788 percent chance of an alternate exit. It would be unusual for a sentient civilization to make an underground facility this size with only one way in and out.›

Sima looked at Mial, then Koji. No way should they drag Mial all over the place on a mere sixty percent chance of an escape. Koji couldn't really walk at the moment. While Marley hadn't been injured, she looked terrified and would certainly panic if anything happened. Also, if more of the place had caved in, debris posed a danger. Running around barefoot sounded like a bad idea.

"What were you trying to tell me about some program before?" asked Sima.

‹The encrypted file you discovered on the terminal in the resource room. It appears to be a command sequence for a power management system.›

Koji grunted, but leaned closer. "Let me see it?"

Her bracelet screen blanked, then stretched larger, roughly half the size of a standard desk terminal screen... covered in program code.

Koji brushed his finger at the holographic display, scrolling the code upward as he read. "Uh oh. This is... bad."

"What do you mean by 'bad?'" She blinked. "It's just a bunch of text."

"I'm not exactly an expert, but I've looked over my father's shoulder enough to make sense of an existing program. I think this is a routine capable of causing a power reactor to overload and blow up." He stopped reading and stared at her, looking far more worried than he'd been when the robot appeared. "It's compatible with the reactor on the *Progenitor*."

Marley squeaked. "Who would be crazy enough to do that? We're 1.754 light years away from Earth with no lifeboats!"

"Umm." Sima swallowed dry. "Someone's trying to blow up the Center?"

"No!" whisper-shouted Marley and Koji at once.

He rested a hand on Sima's shoulder. "Seem... if someone were to upload and run this software on the control system, the reactor would enter an irrecoverable state within an hour. This program disables the first two levels of sensors and alarms. By the time the situation became dire enough for the hardware alarms to start going off, it wouldn't be possible to stop it. We'd have maybe fifteen minutes before the reactor core vaporized everything within roughly twenty miles."

Marley leaned back as if afraid of her. "What are you doing with that?"

"Uhh... I just found it on a terminal in the resource room. Didn't even realize my bracelet downloaded it."

"You should delete that right away!" Koji grasped her forearm and shook her bracelet at her. "This is as dangerous as a Q-bomb."

She shuddered. History class went over ancient weapons of mass destruction, including nuclear bombs. As far as anyone knew, none of them still existed. Humanity now had Q-bombs, which admittedly hadn't been much of a leap ahead in power over nuclear weapons from 400 years ago. However, a Q-bomb capable of flattening a twenty-mile radius could fit in the palm of her hand. What little she knew of them involved quantum physics, some manner of antimatter reaction spanning multiple theoretical dimensions. The same way quantum computers supposedly crossed such boundaries to perform calculations, these devices crossed dimensional walls to find more atoms to tear apart.

"Yeah." Marley plucked at her top, still soaked and stuck to her skin. "If anyone finds you having it, you could get in a *ton* of trouble."

"What about evidence?" Sima looked back and forth between them. "I have to show it to Security so they believe me if I tell them someone's trying to wipe us out. I, umm... won't get in trouble for bringing it straight to them."

"You don't sound confident." Marley pulled one foot into her lap and fussed at it. "Ouch. Think I stepped on a metal splinter."

Sima held her bracelet close to give her light. "It's the Outcast coming to the tip of my brain again. EGSF would be crappy to us, even if we tried to do the right thing sometimes. Much better to stay out of everyone else's business and never go near the cops. But this? I have to risk it."

"There's no risk," said Koji. "Security here isn't like EGSF. Besides, you aren't an Outcast."

"I'll go straight to them when we get back."

"*If* we get back," rasped Mial.

Screw it. We don't have time to hesitate. She crawled toward the exit. "You guys wait here. I'm going to go see if there's a way out in the part of the map my Omni can't read."

"What? No..." Koji kept holding her arm. "You can't go out there alone."

Sima tugged at her arm. "You can't walk. Mial can't even stand." *She's too scared.* "Marley needs to stay here and keep an eye on you two."

Marley gave her a grateful look, likely for not insisting she go with her to scout around.

"Bracelet, can you use the Mirran's network to communicate with their Omnis?"

‹Yes. We are already working on it... though Mial's is not helping much, too worried to think straight.›

Oh, wow. The AI is panicking?

Sima dragged herself into the debris pile, shimmying along the floor until she could see out into the corridor. Empty. No robot. *What the hell am I doing?* She came close to backing up, but a pained grunt from Mial worried her too much to simply wait for help to find them. Not only would the boy die in a few hours, someone apparently wanted to destroy the entire colony and kill everyone on Mirage.

Including her family.

Hell with it. I'm already in the hallway.

Sima pulled herself out the rest of the way and stood.

‹What is your plan for dealing with the robot if it finds you?›

"Same as my plan for dealing with a pack of Scathers." She took a deep breath and started down the hall. "Run and don't look back."

20

REPRIEVE

Omnicomputers could do a great many things, hence the 'omni' part of their name.

However, hacking into non-human technology hadn't been on the marketing presentation. Granted, Sima didn't decide to buy an Omni. She *did* want to hug whoever came up with the idea of issuing them to everyone. Her bracelet kept her alive when she'd been stranded. It found them a hiding place, and now, it gave her as much of a map as it could.

Even Outcasts occasionally played video games, whenever they found or stole a system. Some people with cybernetic implants could experience a game world as if in an alternate reality, but she'd never done so. For one thing, she didn't have any implants. For another, she didn't *want* any implants. Even something as simple as a neural interface to let her log on to Dreamland like 'telepathy' made her feel as monstrous and inhuman as Magdalena. The woman mostly looked human, but like some kind of techno Medusa, could transform from ordinary to a terrifying creature in an instant. Blades in her fingers, glowing eyes, a body more machine than not. Rumor on the street claimed she'd existed for over 200 years.

Sima felt as if she experienced one of those video games over a cyberlink. Having a map display floating above her left arm as she walked added an unreal quality to the Mirran base. The more she saw of its various rooms and corridors, the more she suspected the site to be military in nature. Perhaps the Mirrans had a different concept of interior design, but the layout of long, straight corridors and a complete lack of anything even close to decorative made it feel clinical.

The Mirrans didn't come to this place for fun. This doesn't look like a residence or a prison or a factory.

She didn't waste much time investigating rooms, rushing toward the southeast portion of the map. Based on what the Omni downloaded and estimated, the facility spanned a little over three square miles. The west and northwest portion consisted mostly of water rooms and natural tunnels… perhaps where the Mirrans slept or lived. All the furniture she glimpsed from brief glances while jogging along appeared to be designed for beings with serpentine lower bodies instead of legs.

If the planet at one point had more ocean than it did now, it could explain how the aliens died off… assuming they'd died off. She also couldn't explain how water levels could drop. Planets didn't have giant drains pulling water underground. It didn't seem possible for Mirage to have ever been entirely covered in ocean. Then again, perhaps a big enough asteroid smacking into the planet could have been responsible. Water clinging to the outside of a sphere in zero gravity would go flying away from the sphere if something hit it hard enough. An asteroid impact forceful enough to fling ocean water off into space would probably do horrible things to the planet itself, so she discarded the theory.

Of course, Mirage didn't *need* to be entirely covered in water for the Mirrans to exist. Humans exist on Earth and it's not *all* dry land. A comet, asteroid, or something could've hit the planet and triggered environmental changes the aliens couldn't cope with. Or perhaps a massive volcanic event blasted all sorts of ash and sediment into the air, blotting out the sun for decades.

"Bracelet?" she whispered. "Do you think the Mirrans are all gone?"

‹Most likely. Given the technology level around us down here, they would certainly have become aware of our arrival. This equipment also appears to have been idle for a long time.›

"How is everything so nice? Except for the obviously smashed parts."

‹Automated cleaning processes. Humans have robots that clean. I suspect these systems have been maintaining themselves for perhaps thousands of years.›

She whistled.

Forty-six meters into the unmapped area, Sima peered in a doorway to a large room containing a row of giant cylindrical tanks filled with pale blue fluid. She started to move on since the room didn't offer a way back to the surface, but stopped upon noticing dark grey bones on the bottom of the second to last chamber. Momentarily taken by curiosity, she darted in for a closer look. While jogging by the line of tanks, she glanced past them at a row of padded slabs against the innermost wall. They resembled beds, each with a console similar to the one she'd seen on the chair before the robot attacked. A pod at the head end contained an array of extendable robotic arms, some as thin as needles.

"Is this a medical facility?"

‹It appears to be so, yes.›

Sima crouched by the cylinder containing the bones. They had a faint silicon shimmer reminiscent of the quill cat's claws. Except for a skull and vertebra, she couldn't readily identify the other bones due to how they'd fallen completely apart. The Mirran lacked obvious femurs or leg bones and had a whole bunch more vertebra than a human, adding to her opinion they slithered around on snake-like tails.

Could Mirrans have visited Earth a long time ago and started stories of mer-people?

She stared into the eye-sockets. Other than being half again the size of a human skull, it generally had a similar shape... though much wider in relation to its height. The teeth looked nothing like human teeth, being pointy and curved inward. Based on the design of the chair, looking at the bones also suggested the creatures had two pairs of arms with one set being larger. The presence of teeth sticking out of other bones helped identify a two-piece lower mandible rather than a single jawbone like most Earth creatures. She pictured its mouth opening downward as well as outward, each half of the lower jaw most likely capable of independent motion.

"Ick. Scary." She pushed herself upright. "Can gawk at bones later. Mial is dying." Sima blinked. "Wait. Mial is dying…"

‹Why did you say it twice?›

Sima hurried over to one of the beds, eyeing the cluster of creepy tools on robotic arms. "Is this machine a surgical tool? Can you connect to it?"

The bracelet vibrated intermittently over the next fifteen seconds.

‹Left mini keyboard. Push the third button in from the left on the second row. It has a symbol like an upside-down trapezoid sitting on top of a circle.›

"Okay." She located the key and pushed it. "This isn't going to activate another robot, is it?"

A curved holographic screen appeared above the machine, displaying three blank boxes of varying size and a bewildering array of alien text.

"Uhh…" Sima blinked. "What was that about translating Mirran writing being useless?"

‹Lol. I am analyzing this device based on programmatical connections between the individual keys and the apparent function of the mechanism they are associated with. I may be able to achieve an operational level of understanding of this text.›

"Whoa… Ms. Taylor will be thrilled. This is the contextual key she's been missing." Sima bit her lip. "Do you think she's still alive?"

‹What you told her daughter makes logical sense. The reactions of other students did not sound extreme enough for them to have witnessed a death.›

"Great. How long is it going to take you to translate this? Or… can you?"

‹Possibly. I will know for sure in about thirty minutes.›

She fidgeted, debating if it would be worth it to stand there so long instead of searching for a way out. No guarantee the unmapped area even *had* a door out, so roaming around could be a total waste of time while standing here could give them a usable surgery machine to save Mial's life. The 'clinic' hung in such total stillness, the faint electronic hum from the hologram emitter became noticeable.

"Thirty—"

Pssht.

The pneumatic hiss of the door opening startled her like a bomb going off. Sima whirled around, years of street living having trained her not to scream. Soft clicking footsteps accompanied the robot entering the room… and looking straight at her. She locked stares with the robot's five glowing red eyes. Despite its inhuman, silver praying mantis face, it somehow radiated satisfaction at having found her.

We don't have thirty minutes. "Crap!"

21

FROM BAD TO PLASMA BEAMS

The robot hesitated, for some reason not firing at her.

Sima tolerated gazing into the barrel of a Mirran rifle for roughly a quarter second before rushing to cover behind one of the giant tanks. Hopefully, a column of fluid eight feet across and fourteen feet tall would protect her from burning energy.

Unless this stuff is explosive...

She doubted the Mirrans would be reckless enough to store such vast quantities of a dangerous liquid in clear tanks. Considering the bones, the tanks' purpose didn't appear to be preservation of remains. It had to be some kind of medical device, which implied a benign fluid. Putting a big wall of liquid between her and plasma made sense.

A series of vocalizations came from the robot, sounding more like an electronic device dying in a hail of laser beams rather than any attempt to speak. Sima huddled low, trying to watch the homicidal machine via its warped image in the fluid.

"You don't have to shoot us. We'll leave and go back outside."

The robot stepped into the room as if to come after her, but hesitated... then backed up to the door.

Crap. It doesn't want me getting away. "Please tell me this thing isn't calling for backup."

‹I am not detecting any unusual activity in their network. However, I might not be capable of recognizing it.›

Sima peered around the side of the tank.

The robot aimed for her head.

She ducked before it fired.

"Dammit!" She grumbled. "At least it doesn't want to shoot the tank. Can you tell if this stuff is explosive?"

A pyramid of laser beams shone from the bracelet, penetrating a few inches into the fluid.

‹The substance in the tank is predominantly water. I am detecting trace amounts of unknown chemicals and one recognized chemical. Basic analysis indicates this liquid cannot combust.›

"Recognized? What?"

‹The violet dye the children smeared all over themselves.›

"From the huge root?"

‹Yes. My assumption for its inclusion in a device of this type is it may possess antimicrobial properties, and possibly be toxic to molds and fungus as well.›

"That's awesome but it's not helping me right now."

The robot moved into the room, walking toward her. Sima waited for it to reach her tank, then dashed around the other side. It chased her around the tank three complete times before the realizing and abruptly reversing. Sima backpedaled, feeling dumb for letting fear take over her brain and keeping her going in circles. She slalomed between the tanks, heading for the exit... but stopped two cylinders away upon noticing the clanking of robot footsteps ceased.

Pressed to the clear plastic-like wall of tank three, Sima looked around. Tanks of fluid played tricks on light, hiding the robot from view. She edged to her left, closer to the way out, peeking around the cylinder a little at a time—until she spotted the robot standing in the open space between the tanks and the wall, plasma rod poised.

It's going to shoot me as soon as I make a run for the door. Grr. What am I going to do? Am I faster than an electronic targeting system?

She retreated a step, turning to put her back to the tank wall. Either the robot knew firing into the tank would do nothing, or it had been programmed in such a way as it *couldn't* fire at the tanks. If they once served a medical purpose, it made sense why the Mirrans would prohibit their guard robots from shooting in here.

Another question hit her: who or what did the Mirrans need armed robots to protect them from?

Duh. Humans kill each other all the time. I shouldn't assume aliens on another planet are all one big happy, friendly, unified society. Maybe they wiped each other out. The robot's not going to let me leave. If I get shot, Mial's going to die. No one will find us in time.

She tossed idea after idea around in her head. Charging the robot wouldn't work. It had some manner of technology making it impossible to knock over. But... taking its leg out from under it worked. So, it resisted force rather than had a powerful gyroscope or awesome sense of balance. Spindly arms gave it the distinct disadvantage of lacking strength. If she could somehow get close enough to grab the plasma rod without it slicing her into pieces, she might be able to tear the weapon from its grasp.

Of course, it might also rip her throat out.

The robot appeared to grow impatient and rushed forward. Again, she waited for it to reach the tank she hid behind, then circled it. This time, she recklessly tried to overtake it and come up from behind. Unexpectedly, the strategy worked. As soon as the robot calculated the futility of going in circles after her and stopped to turn around, Sima pounced on it, grabbing the plasma rod in both hands.

Emitting an angry buzzing garble of speech, the robot pivoted at the hips, swinging her off her feet. She flew around sideways, crashed into the tank, and fell flat on her front, losing her grip on the plasma rifle.

Snarling, Sima sprang upright before it could aim down at her, again grabbing the weapon and pushing it off to the left. Like a pair of small children fighting over a toy, she and the alien machine spun in circles, pulling back and forth on the plasma rifle. No matter how hard she struggled, she couldn't get the damn thing to slip out of the robot's grasp. One of three metal claw fingers hovered over a pushbutton on the grip near the back end, likely the trigger.

Being practically chest to chest with the robot scared her to death, but extreme proximity made it difficult for the robot to shoot her with a rifle-length weapon. The killer bot appeared to remember her last success in taking its leg out, and avoided her attempts to kick its leg out from under it with maddening precision. It avoided her sixth try to stomp its knee, then shoved off the tank, swinging its rifle side to side in an effort to throw her off. They stumbled in circles away from the row of giant cylinders, heading for a bank of storage shelves.

Grunting, Sima struggled to control the energy rifle so it didn't point at her. It took *all* her strength to stalemate the robot, but the damn thing would never get tired. She had maybe thirty seconds left before her muscles gave up whether she wanted them to or not.

An electrical buzzing snarl came from the robot. It lurched forward, twisted, then hurled her into the air. She barely noticed her fingers slip off the weapon before she crashed into the storage shelves and landed in a jangling pile of long metal pipes. A hastily fired plasma beam scorched an orange melt line in the wall above her head, leaving a haze of smoke around her. The taste of burnt metal filled her mouth. Screaming, she grabbed a random pole, sprang to her feet, and swatted the rifle aside.

Its second shot melted a trench in the floor.

In a moment of random, barbarian inspiration, Sima roared, grabbed the quarterstaff-sized pipe in two hands, and clobbered the robot over the head.

The hit bent the pipe, but had no visible effect on the machine.

This thing's going to rip my head off.

Unamused, the robot raised its weapon again.

"Crap!" Sima javelin-tossed the pole at its face, then ran.

Metal clanged to the floor behind her. She timed two seconds, then dove to the ground, sliding on her chest. A plasma beam passed harmlessly over her as she slid out the door into the hall. She scrambled upright and ran in the direction she already faced, having no time to think about where to go—only the need to keep walls between her and a plasma rifle.

Angry digital growling and clanking footsteps resonated in the corridor behind her. Heedless of direction, Sima ran for intersections, skipping every door. Going into a room meant death if it had no other exits. Long, open passages also meant death. The occasional plasma blast scorched the corners behind her, sending sprays of molten metal into the air as she raced around turn after turn, no care whatsoever for direction other than wanting to keep walls in the way of energy beams. Thirteen turns later, she raced into a wide but short passageway that dead-ended at a huge, sealed door.

Sima had never been certain of her imminent death before... and did *not* like the feeling of *knowing* she had seconds left to live.

Her bracelet vibrated—and the massive door split into two halves, sliding away from each other.

"Yes!" shouted Sima.

She dashed forward, turning sideways to shimmy between the two separating pieces a split second before the robot appeared at the corner behind her. It fired a plasma blast past her, missing by such a thin margin she screamed as if burned. Smoke peeled off the front of her jumpsuit.

Gasping for breath, Sima stiff-legged it into a massive four-story-tall chamber. Hundreds of boxes ranging in size from tiny to bigger than gee-vees turned it into a veritable maze.

‹This facility is significantly larger than the last complex.›

"True, but that isn't helpful information right now."

She ran in among the stacks of boxes, seeking cover in the winding pathways between whatever materials the Mirrans stockpiled here. Alas, the doors delayed the robot for only fifteen seconds before a pneumatic hiss warned her it got in. Hoping the machine relied on sound to track her, Sima forced herself to stop running. The reverberating *click* of robotic feet tapping the metal floor in the huge chamber sounded simultaneously close and nowhere near her.

Stacks of shiny metal boxes and an immaculate floor looked nothing like anywhere she'd ever been on Earth. However, crumbling buildings, cargo box towns, and bombed-out areas often felt like mazes. Cleanliness aside, she'd played this game before. And here, she didn't have to worry about running away from one gang and stumbling into another punk or vagrant who happened to be there.

Feeling better about her odds, she weaved around the maze, favoring stealth to speed. If she could hide somewhere, the robot would probably lose interest and wander off as it did once already. None of the gaps in the stacked boxes offered shelter. Every spot with enough room for her to squeeze into left her exposed to the robot's vision.

Still, she had a massive room to work with and a maze to deny the robot the ability to attack from long range. As long as she kept moving, she might stay alive. Somehow, the robot's clicking steps sounded angrier and angrier each minute they played cat and mouse. Lack of hiding spots wore on her confidence. The robot sounded a bit too close when she skidded to a halt in a dead end, so she decided to climb up and over the stacked containers into the next aisle. They almost formed steps, being far easier to scale than crumbling Earth buildings. Upon reaching the top, she perched cat-like for a quick look around.

The robot had wandered off in the wrong direction, being much farther away from her than its footstep sounds made her believe. It also had its back turned. Out of breath, she sat still for a moment, trying to give her body a bit of a break. All the running, the wrestling, and being smacked into walls or weird alien medical tanks started to catch up to her.

She considered lying flat on top of the boxes as a means to hide, being two stories up. A better idea hit her a few seconds later when she noticed a series of walkways overhead, near the ceiling.

People don't look up. Maybe robots won't either.

Sima crept along the wall of cargo boxes, eyeing the strange trackway above. She passed two metal support columns, dozens of which formed a grid pattern throughout the room, holding up the ceiling. The overhead walkway passed close enough to the third support to be worth risking the climb. Various gaps and reinforcing spars on the column made for passable handholds. After a quick look to make sure the robot hadn't spotted her, she scaled the column the remaining twenty feet or so up to the walkway.

Unfortunately, the Mirrans didn't believe in handrails. Also, catwalks—what few she'd seen—had all been mesh or gridding. This path consisted of a solid metal ribbon, thicker at the middle than the edges. Sima crawled onto it, then stretched out flat, peering over the side at the robot still patrolling the maze. Grateful for a fairly safe place to rest, she held absolutely still and tried not to breathe too loud.

‹I am not detecting any path out of this chamber from this elevated walkway, which by the way, is sorely lacking in safety standards. It is quite dangerous for you to be up here. A forty-foot fall can be fatal.›

She stifled a chuckle, then whispered, "It's quite dangerous for me to be shot by a plasma rifle, too."

Ten minutes later, the robot showed no signs of giving up, continuing to roam the maze.

"Ugh. As if being stuck underground isn't bad enough already… I don't need a stubborn killer robot after me. Come on, you hunk of crap. Give up."

‹I do not advise direct confrontation.›

"Gee, thanks. Figured that one out already."

‹What are you intending to do?›

Just gonna sit here until it gets bored and goes away."

‹You are not sitting. You are prone.›

"Thanks," she whispered, then kissed the bracelet. It's habit of saying obvious things had gone from extremely annoying to comforting. Good chance, it said it on purpose to soothe her. "And thanks for opening the big door. You are awesome."

‹^_^›

22

GOING DOWN

Another eight minutes passed.

Still, the robot patrolled.

‹It does not seem probable the robot will discontinue its pursuit. This material storage chamber has three exits. All at ground level. Two reinforced doors, one of which you entered from, and a smaller side door... but it appears to lead to a sub area that does not offer escape.›

"Where does the other big door go? Maybe outside?"

‹Unlikely, considering how far underground we are. However... it would make sense the Mirrans had a means to transport large items to the surface. It is reasonable to conclude the second door wide enough for the cargo pods may contain an elevator or a surface access tunnel large enough to accommodate the pods.›

"Sounds like a plan. Where is it?"

‹147 meters ahead as you are facing.›

"Ugh."

She pushed herself up on all fours and crawled. It didn't take long for the glacial pace to get on her nerves enough to risk standing up. Navigating a metal ribbon barely the width of a sidewalk hanging four stories off the floor without railings stirred a sick, swirly feeling in the pit of her stomach... but it frightened her less than the robot.

As long as I don't try to go too fast, I'll be fine.

Arms out for balance, she crept forward.

Why is this even here? Mermaid-shaped aliens couldn't have slithered on this. Maybe it's for cargo-moving robots?

Sima scurried around several intersections, following the catwalk down the long axis of the rectangular chamber. The whole room had to be 200 meters long by about eighty across. She pushed the precariousness of her situation out of her thoughts, forcing herself up to a normal walking speed, then a light jog. Mial's life depended on her finding some way out of here. The robot presented a thorny complication. Even if she *did* locate an exit, how in the hell could they get him past it alive? The only answer she came up with involved finding Security officers and bringing them here to shoot it.

As she neared the middle of the room, the purpose of the elevated walkway became quite clear: six enormous machines clamped onto it like monorail cars riding *below* the track. Each had a retractable gripper bigger than most gee-vees. Clusters of thick black cables dangled from each machine, draping halfway to the floor before looping back up and connecting to the gripper portion.

"Ooh. Can you hack into the system and use one of those loaders to smash the robot?"

‹Testing.›

The cargo-movers clustered on the rails near the center of the room, above an empty area inside the maze. A large, square opening in the floor piqued her curiosity. She kept walking until she stood directly over it—and peered down a vertical shaft several stories deep. Before vertigo made her fall off the side, she let herself drop to kneel, holding her stomach.

"What is that?"

‹I require a more specific query.›

"The giant hole in the floor."

‹This installation is quite massive. I am unable to access any data in their network, but it appears to go down another six levels.›

"Can you take control of one of those big claws, maybe knock the robot into the hole?" She looked left at the opposite end of the room. Another large, armored door in the wall *might* be a way to the surface. "It's our best chance of getting Mial to the surface alive. We have to take the robot out. If we don't, there's no chance we can get him past it."

‹I am having some difficulty translating the interface.›

"Please keep trying. We—"

A plasma bolt pierced the walkway inches from her hand.

Screaming, "Craaaaap," she lurched to her feet. Another beam sizzled by her arm, missing by inches. She ran four steps before a third shot came up through the metal in front of her. Sima tried to stop short, slipped on a blot of molten metal, and tumbled off the side of the walkway.

A mass of black cables flew into her from the side. Instinctively, she grabbed on, not questioning where they came from. One second she fell, the next, she slid down a bundle of insulated cables. No thought more complicated than 'I don't want to die' existed in her brain for the few seconds it took her to come to a stop, arms and legs wrapped around squishy hoses, wires, or whatever.

Her Omnicomputer must have taken control of a cargo-mover claw and sent it racing into her path.

She dangled thirty feet or so above the floor, swaying back and forth on the rubbery tubes with no clear idea of how to get down or go back up. Still, it beat going splat.

I am never taking this bracelet off.

Clanking came from below.

Sima peered down at the robot stomping angrily into the clearing at the center of the maze, aiming its rifle up at her. Despite her hopes, it didn't stupidly walk into the hole, seeming aware of it without the need to look.

"Uh oh."

An instant before the robot fired at her, the cargo claw zipped to the right. The sudden motion ruined her grip, causing her to slide a few feet down. Again, the robot fired, but her claw zagged the other way. Helpless to do nothing but cling to the fat wires, Sima held on as the enormous cargo mover lurched back and forth, swinging her around like a toy tormenting a cat.

Six or seven shots later, a red energy blast sliced the cables above her. Screaming, she plummeted straight down, still clinging to the rubbery lines. At the end of their length, they slowed her in the manner of a bungie cord, stretching. The cargo unit overhead moved again, swinging her across the room in an arc a hundred feet wide. Being flung around in a circle at dizzying speed almost made her close her eyes and wait for it to stop... but closing her eyes while a robot tried to shoot her would be the dumbest thing she ever did, except possibly run out into the street to grab food packets one day.

No... if I didn't do that, Lissa, Juan, and Austin would be dead.

Plasma beams filled the air every few seconds, none coming any closer than fifteen feet or so. The Omni had to be swinging her around, but how long could she hold on. Any second, she'd lose her grip and go flying to a painful—and probably fatal—meeting with the floor.

The bracelet vibrated in two distinct pulses.

No way could she look at the screen without falling. It would have to know this, so it couldn't be asking her to. The cable came to a midair stop and careened back in a wide curve. As soon as the wind pushed her hair out of her face, she realized her Omni manipulated the crane to swing her directly *at* the robot... which stood at the edge of the hole. The cargo gripper dropped without warning; she plummeted under another plasma beam, rubber-banding on the flexible cable, flying toward the robot mere inches above the floor.

Sima raised her legs, aiming both feet at the skinny left leg. Hitting the chest would be like smacking into a stone wall. The robot, evidently oblivious to her plan, stood still and kept trying to shoot her. Another beam singed the cable less than a foot above her head an instant before her boots collided with the robot's knee, sweeping its leg out from under it.

The hit stopped her Tarzan swing short, knocking her into a puke-inducing spin, dangling over the sixty-foot pit. A shock of pain hit her ankle as a metal hand closed around it, jerking her spin to an abrupt stop. The robot teetered over the side and fell, dragging her with it. Sima shrieked in panic as the robot's weight pulled her down the cable, her hands slipping.

All of a sudden, the squishy black substance no longer pulled out of her grasp. It took her a second to understand why: the cable snapped above her where a plasma bolt singed it. She, the robot, and about twenty feet of cable above her free-fell down a six-story vertical shaft.

Something clanked overhead.

The cable snagged on a boxy component sticking out of the wall. Again, she bungied, her freefall slowing until the material reached its stretch limit. At the sudden jerky stop, the robot's claw snapped off her boot. The abrupt loss of a several-hundred-pound ball and chain attached to her leg slingshotted her straight up. She became weightless, then fell again.

Every swear word she'd ever heard on the street screamed across her brain.

A loud metallic *whud* came up from below.

She bounced off the side of a fat, vertical pipe, then narrowly missed a horizontal beam. The cable wrapped over it, rubber-banding her to a near stop. She bobbed up, then fell, bouncing to a halt.

Before she could even think 'whew, I'm still alive,' the cable began to unfurl from the crossing beam overhead. She kicked her leg, flinging herself toward another horizontal beam. She overshot, flying toward the same fat vertical pipe she'd hit earlier. Her primal lizard brain took over. Without conscious thought, she abandoned the cable and koala-grabbed the foot-thick pipe. Crashing into it mostly knocked the wind out of her, but she managed to hold on and not bounce away. Overjoyed not to be falling, swinging, or flying at all, she clutched the pipe with all the strength her muscles could summon.

It took her a moment to find the courage to look around.

She clung a little more than one story away from the bottom. Below her, a wide corridor extended in two directions from the shaft. The robot she'd been running from lay near the center of a group of dead Mirrans littering the floor. It looked like a food canister run over by a gee-vee. Distorted, somewhat flattened, but not entirely smashed.

Over a dozen pale yellow suits contained the bones of bipedal beings similar in proportion to the robot—beefy chests, large heads, but narrow arms and legs. Five larger skeletons appeared to have four arms and long tails.

Plasma rods lay on the floor near each corpse.

The robot twitched, then struggled to get back to its feet.

"Oh, no. No way…"

Sima loosened her grip on the pipe, sliding down to the floor. She kicked a yellow-suited alien out of the way, grabbed its plasma rod, and pointed it at the robot. The device had only one apparent control… a single button on the handle at the end opposite the barrel.

When she pushed it, a red plasma beam connected the front end of her weapon to the floor beside the robot. Sima corrected her aim and fired again, burning a hole clean through the stupid machine that had been trying to kill her for the past twenty minutes. She shot it repeatedly, slicing off all four limbs and drilling multiple holes in its body until it stopped moving and burst into flames.

Smoke peeled up from the half-molten killer. Steaming dark green fluid leaked out, forming a puddle beneath the scrap.

"Hah!" She grinned, standing there wild-eyed, breathing hard.

Light shimmered on the wall from her bracelet's screen activating. She pivoted her arm to look.

‹Are you all right?›

"No. Not even close. If I think about what just happened, I'm going to pass out." She hefted the plasma rifle. "But I just found our key to the front door. Bet this thing will get rid of the turret."

‹A dangerous… but likely effective plan.›

She crouched to examine the remains. The beings in the yellow suits had decayed to bare bones. Their skulls bore a striking resemblance to praying mantises with four eye sockets in a horizontal row and no bug mandibles.

"They look like the robot, but without the big eye in the middle."

‹Perhaps the Mirrans made robots to look like them the way we made androids.›

"Yeah." She moved to one of the other 'mermaid' skeletons.

Nothing had disturbed the remains since they died. Though the bones lost all connective tissue, they lay on the floor in the approximate shape of the creature it had once been. Considerably larger than the legged ones, these aliens had a shoulder width roughly equivalent to two large human men standing side by side. No way to know the true 'height' of a being that slithered around on a fish, snake, or slug tail, but she estimated they approximated a 'standing' height of nine or ten feet.

"Studying these guys can wait. Time to get out of here." She kicked the dead robot. "No more problem. Umm… is there a way up without climbing this shaft?"

‹Searching.›

"I'm in the middle of a corridor." She peered up at the shaft, then to either side. "There are only two ways to go…"

She stood there for a moment, waiting… until the all too familiar clicking of an approaching robot made the hairs on the back of her neck stand on end. "Ugh… not another one."

Sima aimed her plasma rifle down the corridor toward the sound.

The instant a robot came around a corner forty feet away, she blasted it, putting a glowing melt hole in the almost center of its chest. Its limbs locked rigid in an instant and it fell over like a bumped mannequin.

"Not so tough now, are you?"

Another robot rounded the corner, followed by three more, then another five.

"Oh, go to hell…" Sima backed up. "I think I know which way I'm gonna go."

23

EXTINCTION EVENT

S ima sprinted away from an army of Mirran robots, shooting back at them as rapidly as the weapon could cycle.

She aimed for the front row, trying to cut them down before they could return fire. Thirty feet from the vertical shaft, she rushed around a corner on the left. More dead Mirrans lay slumped behind portable barricades, others out in the open. Both bipedal and tailed appeared to have fought on each side. The corridor made a ninety-degree turn to the right roughly sixty meters ahead.

Must be something important at the end of this hall if they went to war over it.

The lay of the bodies suggested two opposing factions of Mirrans clashed in battle. The bones of the defenders, behind the barriers, wore the same yellowish suits, while no trace of clothing accompanied the—much more numerous—bones in the hallway. Also, the 'non-uniformed' remains had far fewer plasma rifles among them. A haze of ash around each group of bones made her suspect whatever they had been wearing burned away. Simple fabric. The boys' jumpsuits ignited when it shot them…

A bunch of civilians fighting an official army? Rebellion?

An approaching horde of robots had a serious negative effect on her curiosity. Sima sprinted onward, hurdling barrier after barrier. She made it within twenty feet of the corner before plasma beams started coming down the hall, so she dove to the floor. Six waist-high barricades spaced at twelve-meter intervals behind her would block any shot they had on her as long as she stayed low enough. Hopefully, the robots couldn't jump over them. The one chasing her all afternoon didn't seem too agile, but she didn't want to sit there and wait to see what happened.

She belly-crawled to the corner and slipped around. The next section of corridor only went a short distance to a huge, round vault-like door. A vast array of bones lay on the floor in front of it. Electronics in the walls appeared scorched as if a bomb had gone off, but inflicted only superficial damage. Two massive half-disks comprising the door either hadn't completely closed or stopped short in the process of opening. The space between them looked tight, but doable.

"Grr. This is totally not fair."

‹Sixty against one is never fair.›

"No… I thought the robot was like this unstoppable killer I had to run away from or die. Find a plasma rifle. Kill it. Think I'm safe. Now there's a million of them."

‹Only 61, that is 999,939 less than a million.›

She sighed.

Clicking continued. She looked back. The robots didn't *jump* the barriers, but managed to gingerly step over them.

"Dammit."

She forced herself up on exhausted legs and hurried to the strange door, walking over bones and the plastic-like yellow alien suits. Wedging herself into the gap required breathing out all the air in her lungs. Being stuck between a pair of three-foot-thick metal slabs didn't thrill her, so she shimmied as fast as possible.

The room on the other side of the massive door made her gasp.

Rows upon rows of much smaller tanks held hundreds of Mirran bodies in various states of decomposition. Some appeared close to preserved while others had decayed to bones floating in rancid muck. Roughly three-quarters of the tanks held the larger 'mermaid' aliens. She'd been right—their tails resembled slug bodies more than serpents or fish, their skin mostly dark blue with patches of black or lighter blue. A vertical seam down the center of their chins matched what she'd seen of the split lower jaw.

The bipedal aliens also had dark blue skin, but more insect-like heads.

Neither species had any obvious clues as to male or female. For all she knew, women had tails and men had legs—or the reverse. Perhaps the bipedal ones were a juvenile form, or two completely unrelated species lived together. Earth only had one species—humans—evolve to sentience. No rule demanded *only* one species could become smart on a planet.

Robots clamored around outside the door.

She twisted to look at the gap. "Please tell me they can't open that."

‹I have insufficient data. There is a large interface terminal at the far end of the room. Can you move closer?›

"Might as well since I'm, you know, trapped in here by an army of killer robots."

At the opposite end of the chamber, some 150 meters away from the door, she found a sunken area resembling a control room. Multiple terminals had chairs—both for bipedal Mirran and the others. She approached the largest terminal in the middle. Her bracelet vibrated in a series of pulses, reminding her of when it sent the distress signal to the colony without telling her it did so. The Omni didn't know at the time if anyone would receive the signal, so it kept quiet, not wanting to get her hopes up.

‹I am able to access some information in this terminal. Translating and guessing.›

"Are you translating or guessing?"

‹Yes. Much of what I am about to communicate to you is the result of interpreting images rather than processing their text. It appears civilization on this planet died out thousands of years ago. This facility was likely intended as an underground shelter, perhaps one of multiple such shelters the Mirrans hoped would allow them to survive whatever extinction event occurred.›

She glanced back at all the tanks. "I don't think it worked."

‹Agreed. They perished. I do not see any information here to explain the signs of warfare. Perhaps those who were not allowed into the shelter rebelled and attempted to force their way in.›

"Sounds about right… they killed everyone trying to save themselves."

‹I do not think it fair to blame them for this destruction. We have insufficient data to determine why this stasis system failed. It may have simply been too much time passing. I am seeing evidence of an extraterrestrial projectile—comet, meteor, or unknown object —hitting the planet. Translating. One moment.›

"Not to be a bitch, but we don't really have a moment. I need to figure out a way to get back upstairs and help Mial before he dies."

‹The unknown object from space contained enough material to effectively change the composition of the planet's atmosphere. By my calculations, this event made Mirage suitable for humans but fatally toxic to the Mirrans.›

"Oh, crap… Do you think we sent a missile here to wipe them out so we could steal the planet?" Sima cringed. "Earth Government is pretty evil to its own citizens. They'd totally wipe out a whole planet for more real estate."

‹I estimate the comet or meteor struck this planet during approximately 7,800 BCE Earth time.›

"Whoa… so, like over 10,000 years ago?"

‹Yes.›

"I'm fairly sure prehistoric humans didn't have a space program."

‹Unlikely. Unless, of course, you believe the unsupported theory another civilization of humans came before us but wiped themselves out via nuclear war and we are the result of re-emerging from primitive tribes.›

"Umm, no. Don't believe that. Are you sure about the timing?

Nothing here looks like it could possibly be ten thousand years old."

‹Superior Mirran craftsmanship.›

She smirked at the glowing screen floating above her arm. "Right. There is a ton of data in this system that will completely change humanity's perception of the universe. Aliens exist. Yes, I know, we are the aliens on this planet. But to people on Earth... Anyway, another team can come back here to grab all this data another time. Mial can't wait... and Marley's probably about to have a nervous breakdown. Is there a way out of here that does not require me getting shredded?"

‹Yes. If you do not mind climbing a maintenance conduit.›

"Dark, claustrophobic shaft with constant fear of falling to my death or an army of killer robots... Hmm. Climb it is." Sima plucked another plasma rifle from a pile of bones. "Lead the way."

24

FINAL STAND

A few shots from the plasma rifle opened an otherwise immobile hatch.

The maintenance passage turned out to be a narrow shaft packed with cables, pipes, and other tubes. After a long horizontal crawl, the passage bent upward. Most likely, the Mirrans only dug one vertical shaft down to the shelter. This duct likely paralleled the same large shaft down from the 'warehouse' room. Fortunately, Sima didn't need to worry too much about falling due to the tight confines. Even if she lost her grip, she would only slide downward at a reasonably slow speed due to being wedged between pipes.

Scurrying up a confined passage didn't leave her mind much to do, so she thought about the water-filled areas. Had the other place she and the kids found been a shelter of some kind, or had the Mirrans always preferred to live underground? Perhaps they'd constructed the shelter near one of their larger cities? Her Omni discovered information suggesting a giant comet of frozen oxygen hit the planet millennia ago. It would have needed to be quite big to change the composition of the atmosphere globally, but even a small percentage difference could have been devastating to existing life. Many of the plants and animals on the surface now likely came about after the impact, evolving over ten thousand years to tolerate the higher oxygen levels.

In the time of the Mirrans, the planet probably looked completely different—nothing at all like Earth.

"Hey, you translated their big computer. Can you make the medical table work?"

‹Insufficient data. I am too far away to connect to it.›

She shimmied upward until the duct bent ninety degrees again, becoming horizontal.

"Point me to the nearest way out of this tunnel, please. All the robots are downstairs." Sima collapsed on her stomach, exhausted. "In a minute… My arms are jelly."

Once she caught her breath, she followed the bracelet's directions. The passage hadn't been designed for regular access. She had to use the plasma rifle again to cut open a plate where a pipe bundle exited the duct, then squeezed herself past the hot metal into a room packed with large machinery. None of it looked obvious in function, being quite visibly *not* of human design. Somehow, it all appeared to be running… doing whatever it did. The soft thrum of electronics or magnetic motors surrounded her.

The bracelet displayed a map again, leading her across the facility to the caved-in passageway where they'd taken refuge from the robot at first.

Sima stopped at the edge of the debris. "I'm back. Are you guys still in there?"

"Sima!" yelled Koji. "Yes. We're here. Mial's drifting in and out. He's still alive for now."

"What happened?" called Marley. "Did you find a way out?"

"Sort of. Have a different idea. I found like a medical clinic or something. My Omni has kinda figured out their language. We might be able to use their robo-surgeon to fix him. C'mon out."

Marley crawled into view first, dragging Mial behind her while Koji pushed him.

Sima randomly decided to hand the second rifle to Koji.

"Whoa. You got the robot's gun?" He examined the device. "Looks more like a giant magic wand."

"Not the same one. There's tons of them downstairs." Sima helped lift Mial mostly upright. "But, the robot is dead. I blew it up."

"Tons of them?" Marley blinked. "Wait... *downstairs?*"

"Yeah. Long story. No time now. I am beyond exhausted. No idea how the heck my legs still work. It's a huge facility, a shelter they made to survive an extinction event... but it didn't work."

Upon hearing of the robot's demise, Marley went back to radiating confidence. She supported at least half of Mial's weight, making the task of moving him much less arduous. Sima shuffled along, glancing occasionally at her bracelet's display map.

"You guys should probably know, there's a bunch more robots down there. I have no idea if they have any way to come after us, but these rifles kill them fast."

"*Eep!*" Marley stared at her. "Define 'a bunch more.'"

"Sixty-one. They're probably still trying to figure out how to open this giant door, thinking I'm inside the stasis room. I climbed up a duct."

"How?" whispered Koji.

"Not that difficult."

"I mean, how did you do all that and you're not passed out?"

Sima laughed. "Ever get so damn tired you're not tired anymore?"

"Not really."

Clicking came from a hallway up ahead.

Marley stopped short. "Is that a...?"

"Probably." Sima struggled to balance Mial's weight on her shoulders and raise the plasma rifle.

A robot ambled out into the hallway from an intersection up ahead.

She and Koji blasted it simultaneously, slicing the metal body into three twitching pieces.

Marley darted over to grab its rifle. "How do these work?"

"Button at the back end. Real simple. Just be careful where you point it," said Sima.

"Okay." She scurried back and pulled Mial's right arm across her shoulders.

A few minutes and three melted robots later, they dragged Mial into the medical room and got him onto one of the beds.

Sima's bracelet screen opened. ‹One moment. All four of us are co-processing the translation algorithm I started.›

"My Omni's doing something." Marley glanced at her arm. "It makes me nervous how they sometimes do stuff all by themselves."

"Your paranoia is unfounded." Sima patted her bracelet. "Mine saved my life again, like *three* times just today. If your Omni does something, it's trying to keep you alive, happy, or safe."

Koji leaned against the table to take weight off his injured leg. "Yeah. They are amazing."

The screen appeared above Sima's arm. ‹I have good news and bad news, but I will spare you having to decide which to hear first. The good news is, we have managed to translate enough of the Mirran language to determine the bad news, which is this device is completely incompatible with human anatomy.›

"Damn," muttered Koji.

"You expected it to work?" asked Marley in a defeated tone, far from snotty. "I would have been really shocked if alien tech could fix us. Still, my mother is going to be super thrilled about the translation... if she's alive."

"She is," said Koji and Sima together.

Clicking footsteps approached in the corridor outside.

Sima, Koji, and Marley all aimed at the door.

Two robots barged in... and dropped under a barrage of plasma bolts.

"This is just like a video game," said Marley.

"Those things are getting irritating." Koji huffed.

Sima shook her head. "I am totally done with them."

"We were scared of *one* of those?" Koji gestured at it.

"They're terrifying when you don't have an alien ray gun."

Marley held hers up. "But… space guns aren't going to do Mial any good."

"Yes, they will." Sima gathered the boy's arm. "Help me get him up. Time for plan-B, the dangerous option."

Marley stared at her. "How is a death ray going to help him? He's dying!"

"Simple. We're stuck down here because of a laser turret, right? A laser turret the Security team's guns bounced off." Sima hefted the plasma rifle. "We're not trapped anymore. These will definitely fry the turret."

Koji cringed. "Agreed… but it might kill us before we can hit it."

"I know. It's why I called plan-B the dangerous plan, and tried to use the surgery robot first." Sima caught herself gazing longingly at the next cushioned bed. It might not be of any use as a surgeon, but something soft would be a *great* place for a nap.

"You okay?" Koji jostled her.

"Yeah… just tired. Marley, gonna help me with him?"

"Ack. Yeah. Sorry." She grabbed his other arm. "Sorry, Mial. I know this has to hurt… but we're almost out of here."

He grunted.

A sign of life made Sima's chest swell in hope. Assuming they could shoot the turret before it noticed them, they had a reasonable chance of escape. Of course, if they couldn't beat a computer's reaction time, they might also die.

25

DISASSEMBLY

Periods of light-headed giddiness faded in and out of Sima's mind.

She struggled to keep holding Mial up. Her left shoulder, ribs, and left knee throbbed, probably from crashing into the pipe while falling sixty feet, or from when a giant rubber band yanked her to an abrupt stop out of free fall several times. Without the adrenaline of a robot soldier hunting her down, pain and exhaustion threatened to rob her of consciousness.

Koji limped along in front of them, alert for any additional robot surprises. He didn't move fast but had both arms free for the plasma rifle. His Omnicomputer bracelet helped them navigate the Mirran complex to the water chamber they first arrived in. It took them twelve minutes to go from the 'hospital' room to the spot where high-tech corridor became bare, slime-covered stone sloping down to the underground pool.

Koji started into the water.

"Wait!" yelled Sima. "Koji!"

He whirled, aiming the plasma rifle past the girls down the hall. Water lapped at his legs a little above the knee, mere inches from the wound in his left thigh. Upon realizing no threat existed, he lowered it. "Uhh... what?"

"You have a hole all the way through your leg. Mial has an open wound." Sima glanced at Marley. "The two of you should stay out of this water. We don't know what's in it. The slimy muck at the bottom could be dangerous if it gets inside you."

"Eep," whispered Marley.

"So... what? We stay down here and die?" Koji flapped his arms.

Sima helped lower Mial to the floor. "No. I'll go up the tunnel, shoot the turret, then send help down to bandage you guys before you get wet."

His annoyance faded to a resigned slouch. "You really think there's bad stuff in the water? I want to get out of here."

"I don't know." Sima rested Mial's arm by his side, stood, and walked into the water beside Koji. "The muck kinda looks like algae, but it could be anything. Please, just... don't risk it?"

"Fine. Fine..." He backed up the ramp to dry hallway. "Just hurry up, okay?"

Marley clutched her plasma rifle. "I'll go, too. We'll have a better chance of disabling the turret."

Wow. Sima raised both eyebrows. "Are you sure?"

"Yeah. I'm scared of getting shot, but I'm more scared of being down here and can't stand not knowing if my mother's okay."

Koji grabbed Sima for balance and lowered himself to sit on the floor beside Mial without bending his wounded leg. "Don't do anything stupid. If these rifles don't hurt the turret, back off."

"I will." Sima crouched and took his hand. "Thanks for trusting me. It's been a long time since I really had a friend, and I don't want to lose you to some aggressive, mysterious alien fungus."

He fidgeted, unable to look directly into her eyes with her face so close to his. "Wow... never had a friend before?"

"Just, you know, some kids I sometimes hung out with when I was small. Not really friends. Too young to understand real friendship back then, but..." Warmth filled her cheeks. Out of nowhere, a weird urge came over her—and perhaps due to her exhausted state, she didn't fight it.

Sima kissed him.

Koji stared up at her in absolute shock.

Marley opened her mouth but shut it without saying a word.

Crap! Why did I do that? Now he's going to hate me. No more friend-ship. It's gonna be weird.

"I think I'm hallucinating angels," whispered Koji, before smiling.

Relief fell on her like a blast of cold water. Still, she continued blushing. "Yeah, well… umm, let's make sure you don't see any real ones. At least, not for like another eighty years." She stood. "Here goes."

He kept holding her hand, letting his grip slide away as she walked into the water. Expecting the slime, Sima deliberately 'surfed' down the curved stone floor instead of attempting to walk. She sloshed to a stop in frigid water a little higher than her waist. The numbing effect it had on her legs offered welcome relief, and the cold shock jolted her awake better than coffee.

Marley stopped short with a yelp the instant she put one foot in the water. "I forgot how cold it is. Oh, heck…" She clenched her jaw and tried to tiptoe forward, but her feet shot out from under her and she went completely under. She resurfaced horizontally, swimming a few seconds later. "I totally meant to do that."

"It's not so deep you have to swim," said Sima, trudging toward the exit tunnel.

"I know. I'm swimming so I don't have to put my feet in this mess on the floor. It feels *so* disgusting."

Sima sloshed along. "What were you going to say before? You like opened your mouth, then changed your mind."

"Nothing… just… was going to ask if you could make out with your boyfriend later, but I guess you were, like, *having a moment* or something and I didn't want to ruin it."

"Thanks," rasped Sima, mortified.

"You okay?"

"Long story. We don't really have time, what with being trapped down here."

"Ahh." Marley chuckled softly. "Never kissed a boy before?"

Sima didn't answer.

"It's okay. I haven't either. Don't have time for boys yet. They're like dogs you can't ever housebreak and sometimes start arguments. Expensive, make messes, suck up all your free time. Not going to worry about one until I'm done with university."

"I said the same thing..." Sima exhaled out her nose. "It's a little different when you almost get killed four times on a field trip and are about to play chicken with death again. I, uhh, had to do that in case this turret fries me."

Marley sputtered water. "Do you think it's gonna kill us? Really?"

"It's definitely going to try. It's not perfect, though. We can probably fake it out and hit it before it gets a good shot." Sima stepped up into the tunnel. "Honestly, going up this tunnel is going to suck more than dealing with the turret."

"Why?" Marley swam up to the edge.

"Because it's a perfectly smooth uphill slide covered in slime with water running down it." Sima grabbed Marley's hand and helped her up into the tunnel. "When we got stuck in the other place, the kids kept losing their balance and falling... and they'd take everyone with them back down."

"Any suggestions?"

"Yeah. Try to keep your feet in the middle. Water flows harder there, so the slime is thinner. The sides are more slippery."

Marley nodded.

"Also... we're going to need our hands for the climb." Sima opened the zipper on the front of her jumpsuit and stuffed the plasma rifle inside.

Marley stuck hers down the back of her shirt.

Sima went first, bracing her hands against the tunnel walls and walking one foot in front of the other. Thankfully, this passage had less slime than the other site, and perhaps a shallower angle. A long, curving arc looped around to the left, bringing her to the chamber on the surface directly above the water room.

Six feet away from the door into the outer chamber full of giant stone blocks, the 'slide' came close to being flat ground. She lowered herself to crawl and drew the plasma rifle out of her jumpsuit. Marley padded up behind her, dripping and shivering. Waterlogged clothes clinging to her body made her look even skinnier. Her wide hazel eyes gave off desperate terror like an Outcast kid backed into a corner—right before they stabbed someone.

"Last chance. You still want to do this? You look like you're about ready to faint."

Marley shivered. "I'm shaking because I'm cold. Yeah. I'm okay."

"'K. Dunno for sure if it can hear us, but we should stay quiet." Sima crawled up to the door and felt around for a moment to locate the trick rock.

As soon as she touched it, the door snapped down into the floor, revealing the outer chamber. Everything looked the same as before, except for there no longer being a boy trapped under a cut-in-half stone block. Repetitive whirring—a turret rotating back and forth—came from the left.

"It's still active," whispered Sima.

"Yeah." Marley crept up alongside her.

Sima clenched her grip on the plasma rifle. "Do we try to sneak up to the corner and hope it doesn't notice us, or do we run forward and try to nail it before it gets us?"

"Umm… I say sneak," whispered Marley. "If it senses us, it'll start trying to shoot through the wall. We'll have time to run back."

Sima nodded. "Okay…"

Distant shouting broke the silence. Several men appeared to be arguing, though she couldn't make out what they said, only that they screamed it.

Marley squeaked.

"They're still outside." Sima grinned, nearly fainting from a strong wave of relief. "Wait… Bracelet, can you get a signal up here? Send a message to them and let them know we're alive and have a way to deal with the problem?"

‹Yes. Transmitting.›

A moment later, a female voice wailed in sobs. The men stopped shouting at each other. Sima stared at the little four-by-eight-inch screen floating over her forearm, hands trembling from anticipation or fatigue. People outside the ruins now knew the four of them survived, and likely that Mial needed medical help fast. Any second, a reply would appear.

"Bracelet," whispered Marley. "Tell Mom I'm okay. Please tell me she's okay."

A few seconds later, she covered her mouth and collapsed against Sima, crying silent tears.

Worried, Sima grasped the girl's arm and turned it so she could see what her bracelet said.

‹Already did. The sobbing you heard outside is your mother being happy you are okay.›

Sima hugged her. "See. Told you she's fine."

"I was such a bitch to her all morning… I thought she died, and you guys were just saying stuff to make me feel better." Marley sniffled.

No response yet showed on Sima's screen. "Bracelet, what's going on? Hey… Idea. Suggest the Security team start shooting at the turret to distract it. Once it aims away from us, we'll blow it up."

‹They are asking for more of an explanation. I've been filling them in on the vital details.›

"Umm…. Tell them we found alien ray guns that will destroy the turret. You told them Mial's hurt bad, right?"

‹I did. They are asking for the medical team to return. Should not be long. Several others were injured earlier. No one died.›

"Whew…"

‹The Security team has agreed to distract the turret. They are waiting for you to be ready.›

Sima pushed herself up to stand. She crept past the door into the alcove, scooted left, and pressed her body against the wall, three feet away from melt holes in the stone... evidence of the turret's attempt to kill them earlier.

Marley emerged from the doorway, squishing herself into the corner while clutching her rifle. She nodded once in a 'ready' gesture.

Sima raised her alien weapon, put her thumb over the fire button, and tried to picture the silver dome sticking out of the ceiling halfway down the room on the left side, then whispered, "Send a go."

A few seconds later, scuffing footsteps echoed in the outer chamber.

"Sima?" called a man. "It's Nahan."

The repetitive whirr-whirr of the turret sweeping back and forth didn't change.

"Hey," yelled Sima.

"Gonna waste some ammo on the count of three. You ready?"

"Yes!" Sima bounced on her toes, the need to be with her parents and family growing painful.

Nahan yelled, "Three... two... one..."

Sima waited a half-second longer, then rushed the corner.

A short rip of automatic gunfire thundered from the far end of the enormous rectangular chamber, drowning out the *buzz* of the turret's plasma weapon. Marley ran around her on the right, passing around the corner at the same time.

As the dark grey stone moved out of her field of view, Sima took aim on the shiny silver dome. It swiveled toward her as she pushed the button. A red beam, half the thickness of the one from the turret, appeared in a brilliant pulse, connecting the tip of her weapon to the dome. A second beam from Marley struck it a split-second after.

The turret exploded, showering the floor in a hail of tiny metal fragments and crimson sparks.

"Holy shit!" yelled Nahan. "You really *did* find ray guns."

Sima glanced toward the exit.

An assault rifle stuck around the corner, pointed in the direction of where the turret had been. He'd no doubt aimed by video camera. A glowing hole in the wall suggested the turret had tried to shoot him through cover.

"Mom!" yelled Marley, sprinting for the exit.

Sima rushed after her.

Officer Nahan Mors dropped his rifle onto a shoulder strap and caught them, one girl per arm. Marley struggled to get away, pedaling her feet in the air. Sima didn't particularly care who she hugged; seeing another human felt awesome.

Once Marley calmed, he escorted them up the ramp to the surface, then let go of Marley—who dropped the plasma rifle and bee-lined for her mother. Both burst into tears, clinging to each other. Sima picked up the second rifle and handed them both to Officer Mors.

"Here... I don't need these. They're super dangerous and I probably shouldn't be allowed to have them at my age." She pointed at the door. "Koji and Mial are at the bottom of a tunnel. It's really slippery, has water running down it and some kind of slime."

"Any threats?" asked Officer Mors.

"Sixty-one hostile robots are all over the lowest level, but I don't think they can get up to the exit. There are also a few dozen more of those plasma rifles all over the place at the very bottom."

"Sima!" shouted Mom.

She twisted toward the voice.

Her parents ran over from a third Nomad. The sight of them brought her to tears. She stumbled toward them, managing only a few steps before they grabbed her in a tight, protective embrace. In the safety of their arms, Sima finally stopped trying to avoid thinking about how close she'd come to getting killed in there... and broke down.

By the time she regained her composure enough to process reality again, a group of Security officers and medics emerged from the site carrying Mial and Koji on stretchers. They hurried them to the nearest Nomad.

"Are you hurt?" asked Mom, looking her over.

"Bruises and scrapes." Sima exhaled. "Nothing serious. Mostly exhausted."

Dad pulled her close again, smushing her face against his chest. "I am so grateful you are all right."

"Sorry for scaring you guys." Sima sniffled. "It's *so* awesome to have parents."

Mom brushed a smudge of something off Sima's cheek. "You don't have to apologize... but you did give us the scare of our lives."

"I don't think there will be any more field trips." Dad exhaled hard. "Dangerous and foolish, and for what?"

Sima shrugged one shoulder. "After this trip, I'm definitely going to focus on biology or botany—maybe both. Screw robotics. The only thing I want to do to robots is disassemble them."

Her parents gave her quizzical looks.

"Oh, there's also a ton of information down there about the Mirrans... and I got a sample of this weird gooey algae. Might be poop. Might be plant. Don't know."

"Sima?" asked Dad, concern in his voice. "Are you hanging on me because your legs are injured?"

"No. I'm *that* exhausted. A killer robot chased me around a huge room, then I fell down a six-story shaft, got chased by more robots..."

Dad scooped her up and started carrying her over to the Nomad. "We are going to have a doctor take a look and make sure you are okay."

"Okay." Sima rested her head against his shoulder. "Wake me up when we get there."

26

A HIDDEN THREAT

S urrounded by warmth, Sima awoke under a pile of children. Austin curled up against her left side. Juan clung to her right arm. Lissa lay on top of her, chest to chest, cheek on her shoulder. Both boys wore blue pajama pants. Lissa borrowed one of Sima's shirts for a nightgown.

Her entire body ached, refusing to produce the amount of strength necessary to dislodge her siblings. Between the effort required to move and the comfort of her bed, she decided not to bother trying.

It took her a minute or so to reboot her brain and process everything. She didn't remember the drive back to the colony or much of her time at the medical center. Everything after she and Marley blew up the turret all blurred into one continuous sense of relief. At some point, she'd visited Koji, who they had hooked up to some machine to regenerate the muscle fibers and blood vessels scorched away by plasma. If she visited Mial, she didn't remember doing so. Chances were, she didn't. He'd been in much worse shape and probably couldn't even have visitors yet. She'd given Mom the sample she took of the slime to analyze—or pass along to Dr. Desai if she couldn't use it for any of her research.

Being home in her bedroom implied the medics hadn't found any serious problems with her.

A vague memory of explaining everything to her parents drifted in and out of her thoughts.

Oh, that's right. I passed out in the medical center.

"Ugh. Bracelet… *when* am I?" She wriggled her left arm out from under Austin.

‹It is currently Sunday, May 14, 2410, 9:44 a.m.›

"Wow… only the next day. Feels like a week ago."

‹You were treated for several hairline fractures in your left shoulder, ribs, and right forearm, plus given a dose of pain medication. That is when you lost consciousness.›

"Broken bones?"

‹Hairline fractures. Easy to fix. Your bones are intact, but may be sore for a few days.›

"Great…"

She put her arm around Austin.

The kids woke up after not too much longer. Predictably, they alternated between freaking out she'd been in danger and demanding to know *everything*. She tried to sneak off to the bathroom first, but Juan outran her. Eventually, she and the kids sat in the kitchen having a late breakfast while she gave them a less scary version of the story—which continued after everyone finished eating.

"Sounds awesome." Austin grinned. "I wanna see a plasma rifle. What kinda sound did it make?"

"Like a combination of a hum and buzz. Pretty sure my Omni recorded some images of them." She blinked. "Crap!"

All three kids leaned back, wide-eyed.

"Dad!?" yelled Sima.

"In here," called Dad from the living room.

Sima leapt from the chair and ran through the arch connecting the kitchen to the front room. "Dad… we have to go to the Security office right now and talk to the highest-ranking person they'll let us talk to."

"Whoa," whispered Austin.

Dad quirked an eyebrow. "Is this about the... uhh, Mirrans?"

"No. They're all dead. This is something way worse. More dangerous."

"Sima?" Dad tilted his head. "What are you talking about?"

"My Omni found and copied a program that can—" She glanced back at the three kids watching from the kitchen archway. "Do something really, really bad. With the, umm"—she lowered her voice to a whisper—"reactor."

Dad waved her closer. "Show me."

What? Oh. Duh! He's like the second most senior person on the engineering team. She hurried over and sat on the sofa beside him, holding her left arm out in front of him. "Bracelet, please show him."

The screen activated, expanding again to full size.

Dad perused the lines and lines of instruction code, his cheeks gradually going from brown to ashen. He looked over at her, seeming on the verge of fainting in shock. "Where did you get this?"

"My Omni grabbed it off a terminal in the resource room. The place was full, only one seat open, so I sat there. Someone using the terminal before me left so fast they forgot to log out. When we were stuck down in the Mirran site, the Omni told me it broke the encryption. Koji looked at it and figured out what it does."

"What's it do?" asked Austin.

"Something bad." Sima shivered. "Something really bad."

"It's gonna kill everyone," deadpanned Juan. "Dad's scared. An' he's never been scared before. Seem said reactor. We're probably gonna be blowed up."

Lissa ground her toes into the carpet, her hands swallowed by the long sleeves of Sima's shirt she'd slept in. "I don't wanna be blowed up. It doesn't sound nice."

"No one's blowing anything up." Sima turned her head back to Dad. "Koji knew what it was, and he wanted me to delete it right away. I only kept it to show Security for evidence. To prove someone here is trying to… well, you know."

Dad stood. "Pai?"

"Yes?" called Mom from the master bedroom—where she had a computer workstation.

"Sima and I need to head over to the Center for a little while."

"All right." Mom poked her head out into the hall. "Is something wrong? You sound worried."

"There's an issue of some urgency, yes." Dad beckoned for Sima.

She stood.

"I'll explain everything once we're back."

Mom did a weird slow-motion nod. "Ooo-kay."

SIMA SAT on a black bench outside the office of Commander Anlon Yos, fussing at the bracelet.

No way would Dad have let her bring the program here if they'd punish her for having it. Koji thought the Security team would shoot her, or put her in a cell for the rest of her life. All her past history with EGSF officers agreed with him. Sima kept telling herself the cops would listen to reason. Someone intending to use it would *not* bring it to the Security office and show it to them.

Because Dad came along and requested it, they got to skip past the desk officer and went straight to the man in charge of the entire Security team on Mirage. Not terribly impressive considering the human presence amounted to roughly one-twentieth of a single district back on Earth.

Still, for Mirage, the highest-ranking Security officer. It made him one of the few people on the planet with the authority to decide someone deserved to be executed. Maybe they wouldn't even use the death penalty here, given the low population.

The door to their left opened.

A late-forties man stepped out into the hall. He appeared a little older than Dad. Age tinted his otherwise jet-black hair grey above his ears, the white spreading down into his facial hair. Something about his ice blue eyes and thin jawline beard suited a former starship captain. Despite his position, he gave off a friendly air. Usually, EGSF officers who acted friendly and smiled did the worst things to Outcasts, but this man didn't make her feel uneasy at all.

"Manoj," said the man. "What's so urgent you had them page me here on a Sunday?"

Dad stood. "Anlon… this is my daughter, Sima. She has something critically important to show you. It is… sensitive."

"All right then. Let's not waste any more time. Please, come in." Commander Yos walked into his office.

Sima got up and followed her father after him. Dad closed the door.

"All right, hon." Commander Yos nodded once at her. "This must be pretty important if you're asking to see me and not one of the investigators."

"Yes." Sima clenched her jaw. *He's not going to be mad at me. I'm not going to get in trouble.* "I found this program…"

She explained the day in the resource room, the logged-in terminal, the email with the attachment on an account belonging to a twelve-year-old boy, her Omni copying it… and what the program would do.

Commander Yos made the same face Dad did when reading the program. "Is this true, Manoj?"

"I looked at the instruction set. The only way to know for sure if it will work is to run it, but… there is no way I am going to let this code module anywhere near the reactor room. Merely from reading it, I think there is an extremely high chance it will result in a catastrophic critical failure and vaporize a thirty-to-forty-mile radius."

Whoa. Koji said twenty miles… but, I think Dad knows better.

The commander's expression darkened. He shifted his gaze to Sima.

"I swear I only kept it for evidence. Didn't write it. I don't want it and I *definitely* don't want it used."

"Relax, Sima." Commander Yos raised a hand, his expression softening a little. "You aren't in any trouble. Everyone on this colony owes you their lives for bringing this to our attention."

"Thank my Omni." She fidgeted at the bracelet. "It grabbed the file. I didn't even know it did. Total dumb luck I happened to go to the resource room and find a terminal someone left logged in."

"Allow me a moment..." The commander tapped his Omnicomputer bracelet. "Tell Tadashi Ito I need to see him immediately in my office."

Sima looked at Dad.

"It's fine. He doesn't doubt me. Probably needs two witnesses before telling you to destroy the program." Dad patted her shoulder. "At least I am hoping he will tell you to destroy the program."

Chuckling, Commander Yos nodded.

Sima sat on the chair facing the desk, waiting in awkward silence. A few minutes later, a knock came from the door.

"Anlon?" asked a man outside. "What's so important you demanded me right away?"

"Come in, Tadashi," said Commander Yos.

Koji's father, the guy she'd seen standing beside the governor the day the second ship landed, strode in, seeming annoyed.

"I need your expertise and your official statement as a verifying witness." Commander Yos gestured at her. "Please, show him."

"Mr. Ito." Sima rose to her feet and held her arm out.

Her bracelet's screen opened. Mr. Ito examined the text scrolling by, no discernible expression on his face until he finished, at which point he cut his gaze to her. "What are you doing with something like this?"

She repeated the explanation, adding more detail about hiding from the robot next to Koji when he saw the program.

"Tadashi, I need you to say on the record what you saw on her Omni." Commander Yos tapped his bracelet.

"The software appears to be designed to induce a severe criticality incident in the *Progenitor's* primary reactor. It would set off an antimatter reaction capable of vaporizing everything within approximately thirty-five miles of the core."

Commander Yos nodded at her. "Sima's Omnicomputer, you are to delete the dangerous contents of that program but preserve the metadata and trace information."

She glanced at the silver band around her left wrist. "You don't need the program itself for evidence in a trial or something?"

"No." Commander Yos shook his head. "We have both Tadashi and Manoj—the two most senior engineers—vouching they analyzed this program and confirmed its purpose. It is far too dangerous to allow to exist. The metadata information is enough to show the existence of the program without it being any threat."

‹Done,› typed Sima's bracelet.

"It's gone." She slouched in relief. No longer having to worry what Security would do to her for having it felt as good as finally shooting the first robot.

"Good." The commander smiled at her. "You will, of course, go to technical before leaving the Center so we can verify the software's alteration."

"Yes, sir."

He set his fists against his hips. "Now all we need to do is figure out who made it."

Oh crap! She gasped.

All three men looked at her.

"Sima?" asked Dad.

"I kinda know... but, not really." She grabbed her father's hand. "Someone broke into our home and didn't steal anything. Someone *tried* to break into Mr. Ito's residence."

Mr. Ito raised both eyebrows.

She looked back and forth between him and Commander Yos. "This crazy woman attacked me on my way home one night. Threw me into a wall, put a knife to my throat and asked, 'Where is it?' I had no idea what she wanted... since I didn't know my Omni even took the file then. She must have been after the program."

Mr. Ito and Dad gave sighs of relief.

"That means they don't have it." Dad clapped.

"Why would they try to break into Mr. Ito's residence? Did they think *he* deleted their program?" Commander Yos scrunched his nose in disbelief.

Sima shook her head. "No. They were probably looking for access badges. Both Dad and Mr. Ito have complete access to everything in Engineering. They're the two bosses. In order to even use the bad program, they'd have to physically get to the reactor control system, which is not open to the outside network. Once inside, they would need full access to the control computer—meaning Mr. Ito or Dad's credentials."

Mr. Ito and Dad exchanged a glance, patted their badges at the same time as if to verify they still had them, then looked at Commander Yos.

"I believe someone may have been following me," said Mr. Ito.

"What did the woman look like?" asked Commander Yos.

"No idea." Dad frowned. "She had a rebreather mask on."

"Only reason I even know she's a woman is her voice. She's definitely not an Outcast. Sounded older, like late twenties. Also, couldn't fight at all."

Commander Yos shifted his jaw side to side in thought. "What are the chances this woman can recreate the program?"

"I don't think she wrote it." Sima bit her lip, not entirely confident in her theory, but pressed on anyway. "The email she sent sounded like she got the program from someone before they left Earth. Since we have no way to communicate between planets, she probably can't ask the source to send them another copy. And… she's obviously working with at least one other person here. Who'd she send the email to? If they could recreate the software, they wouldn't be coming after me to get it back."

"Yes. Good points." Commander Yos smiled at her. "All right. We'll all sleep a bit easier hoping this woman does *not* have the overload software. For now, we'll increase security at the reactor room here and the engineering section of the *Progenitor II*. Chances are, the recipient of the email is a bogus account, which may already be deleted. I'll have our technicians scan the system to see if they can connect the activity to anyone on the ship's roster."

Sima held up a finger. "I think the woman arrived on the second ship. This all started happening after it landed."

"A reasonable conclusion," said Commander Yos. "Ordinarily, I'd say we begin investigating the background of all women aboard, but we are slightly out of range of Dreamland. No access to the EGSF criminal database, so our information is pretty much limited to any crimes they might have committed after arrival."

She smirked. *Lucky me. Food thief. If I ever go back to Earth, I go straight to jail. Yeah, no. Not happening. This is home.*

27

STREET RAT

L ittle happened out of the ordinary all week.

By Friday, Sima's anxiety grew to what it had been during her life as an Outcast. Every time she left home, she expected an attack from every corner or dark place. She refused to go outside after dark... and even balanced a wrench on her bedroom door so it would fall and make noise if anyone tried to come in while she slept.

Fortunately, several bits of good news prevented her from descending into complete paranoia. For one thing, the Security team hadn't made an obvious show of knowing anyone plotted to blow up the reactor. Additional officers stationed at the control room dressed like engineers to blend in. Others watched the entrance via camera, checking the identities of anyone approaching the area from afar. Most likely, the crazy woman didn't yet realize they'd been discovered.

She may or may not think Sima knew the purpose of the program or merely 'stole' it. She'd wondered how the woman even found her until she came up with two possibilities. Either she traced the connection to her Omnicomputer's ID, which meant the woman had decent skills hacking into the local version of Dreamland... or she'd broken into the resource room after hours and checked the logs to see who logged into the terminal.

Security confirmed the boy associated to the account hadn't entered the resource room on the day Sima's bracelet grabbed the program. He'd been running around the second ship pestering workers in the process of breaking it down to build the second half of the colony. The woman had undoubtedly stolen or hacked into his account and used it to conceal her identity.

Another bit of good news helping keep her sane: Koji got out of the hospital in time to be in class on Tuesday. His leg remained sore, causing him to walk stiffly, but the doctors expected him to recover with no loss of mobility in a few weeks. Mial remained in the hospital. No one said directly he'd been perilously close to death, but their grim expressions did. Last she heard, he'd likely be released from the hospital by the end of the month.

Considering no one had any reason to expect any danger from an ancient 'alien' site beyond potential collapse, Ms. Taylor didn't get in any trouble for bringing high school students there. She, and the academic community, decided to adopt Sima's term 'Mirran' for the former residents of Mirage. Based on her explanation of the shelter, the corpses, and everything else, multiple scientists pressured the governor to allow them to return and conduct a proper study in spite of the high likelihood of at least fifty or so killer robots remaining. Thus far, nothing happened. She expected they would eventually send another expedition there once the Security people finished playing with the new guns.

Marley decided to become friends, hanging around her at school and so far twice after. The initial oddity of going from never speaking to her to buddies overnight gradually wore off over the past week. Sima figured she could trust the girl. After all, she hadn't said anything to anyone about her kissing Koji.

Speaking of... on Wednesday after school, she met Koji in the park behind the Center for an experiment. How did it feel to kiss a boy when she *didn't* expect to be killed in ten minutes? He appeared to share her feelings and he already proved himself different from the boys she'd been around on Earth who wanted only quick hook ups. So, she decided to let the 'boyfriend' situation play out to see where it went.

Friday afternoon, she sat on a bench at the western edge of the colony, watching Austin, Juan, and Lissa run around the grass kicking a ball with a group of other kids their age. School ended a little less than a half hour ago. She had no remedial work to worry about. No OT to demand her time—yet—and only a mild case of crushing anxiety that some crazy terrorist would attack her at any minute.

Not only am I in school, I have a family, I'm happy, I've got a boyfriend and *two friends.* She didn't entirely know where she stood with Oema, who kept her emotions guarded. Given the girl was thirteen and unusually small—so she looked more like eleven—being around her felt more like having another child to take care of. Depending on the moment, Oema could appreciate the protectiveness or become resentful at being thought of as a help-less kid.

For the first time in months, Sima stared down the barrel of an approaching weekend and had nothing on her schedule demanding attention. She could have, if she wanted, stayed in bed until Monday. She didn't, though… too boring.

Sima reclined on the bench, watching the kids play, enjoying the idleness of finally having a break. Lissa raced around at a full sprint almost constantly. Sometimes, she slipped in the grass and took a tumble, but bounced back up every time laughing. The children appeared to be trying to play soccer, but the exact boundaries of the goals remained a mystery.

At the sound of someone running up behind her, she spun to look while grabbing the knife concealed on the back of her belt. A short white-haired girl wearing a pink dress ran down the metal sidewalk toward her. Upon recognizing Oema, she relaxed and let go of the knife. In addition to the new dress, she also wore white leggings and purple boots. If the girl disliked being thought of as a child, she certainly did *not* show it by her choice of outfit.

Out of breath from running, Oema crashed into the back of the bench for support, and gasped.

"Wow." Sima looked her up and down. "Someone spent all their allowance. Are you sure about the pink, though? It makes you look like you're ten. Adorable."

"Easier..." Oema wheezed. "Easier to get away with stuff if I pretend to be cute."

"What did you fail to get away with that you're running so hard?" Sima cocked an eyebrow.

Oema jumped over the backrest, landed on the bench next to her, and shook her arm frantically. "Seem! I overheard some people talking about wanting to blow everyone up. Dude sounded seriously nuts. Crazier than Blanks. And he's *huge*. This is serious!"

She winced at the word. Nothing creeped under her skin like Blanks, especially the stories about people having their brains replaced with computers.

"Did you see them?"

Oema bit her lip. "Yeah, but I can't tell anyone."

"Why not?"

"Umm... 'cause I broke into their place and they came home while I was in it." Oema looked around, then scooted closer. "I snuck out after they left."

Upon noticing the girl trembled, Sima put an arm around her. She had to be *genuinely* terrified. No Outcast ever showed fear openly unless they couldn't control themselves. It asked for too much trouble.

"Why are you sneaking into people's residences?"

Oema shrugged. "I dunno. It's fun."

"Hey..." Sima grabbed her shoulders, staring into her eyes. "One: stop breaking into places. We don't have to steal anymore."

"We?" Oema raised both eyebrows. "Since when did you steal?"

"I didn't. I begged. You know what I meant. 'We' as in former Outcasts. And two: we come up with a story to explain how you heard them without breaking in, then we go to the Security team so they can find these lunatics before they hurt someone. They already know someone's trying to blow us up. I doubt they're going to care about you sneaking into someone's residence even if they find out. If they do, just blame your 'traumatic past life' and swear you won't do it anymore. Crying helps."

Oema stared at her as if she'd suggested lighting herself on fire. "You *want* to go *to* Security? Are you crazy?"

"Nope. They won't be mean to you, especially if you wear this outfit. Makes you look innocent."

Oema grumbled. "I *am* innocent. Never touched Pixie or any other drugs. Never killed anyone. Never did… you know, the other thing."

"Good."

"One thing I am *not*, is dumb. Going to Security is stupid." Oema jabbed a finger at her. "You're totally soft."

"Says the cute little girl in a pink dress."

Oema stuck out her tongue. "I like pink. People don't expect the cute little girl is gonna take all the glint in their pockets."

"Seriously." Sima shook her by the shoulders. "You don't need to steal anymore. Even for fun. You're gonna get in trouble."

"Yeah, yeah. I know." Oema looked down. "Seriously, though. You're not kidding about going *to* Security? They hate us."

"Mirage Security is okay. EGSF officers suck. It feels strange to say, but we really aren't Outcasts anymore. We're normal here."

Oema shrank in on herself. "I'm scared. I think someone's been following me."

"Where?" Sima twisted to look back at the colony and put an arm around her.

"What are you doing?" Oema sounded annoyed, but didn't squirm. "I'm not a little kid."

"Sorry." Sima withdrew her arm.

"You didn't have to stop. I *am* scared, kinda." Oema narrowed her eyes. "If you tell anyone, I will cut you."

Sima froze when she noticed three people lurking in a narrow space between two one-story storage buildings, as close as anyone could get to the edge of the colony here without being out in the open. A muscular bearded guy, a skinny, frazzled man, and an annoyed dark-haired woman appeared to be watching them. All three wore large, drab beige tunics. The woman also had baggy pants... and a rebreather mask dangling loose at her chest.

Crap. "We need to go. I see them. On the right, sixty feet away, hiding by those buildings."

Oema squeezed Sima's arm and gasped. "That's them! Big bearded guy, crazy tweaker, and the screamy woman. I heard them arguing. Both guys wanted to 'just do it the hard way,' but the woman tried to talk them out of killing 'the girl.' Big guy sounded like the boss... and he's *totally* freakin' crazy. Kept talking about the Will of the Cosmos or some really out there nonsense. He thinks outer space told him to kill everyone on Mirage."

Sima swallowed hard. "They're probably talking about me when they say 'the girl.' They think I have their, uhh, bomb."

"You have a bomb?"

"No, my Omni swiped a computer program from the woman... and it's gone now. Deleted. But... they're not going to believe me saying I don't have it, and if I tell them it's destroyed, they'll assume I know what it would've done and try to kill me so I can't identify them to Security." Sima stood and yelled, "Austin!? Juan!? Lissa!?"

Something in the tone of her voice made the kids stop in their tracks. They all stared at her for a second or two before running over without hesitation or dawdling. Other kids continued playing, ignoring their departure. Lissa zoomed straight into a hug, shivering.

"What's wrong?" asked Austin, clenching his hands into fists.

Juan looked around; somehow, he ended up staring at the three people as if recognizing them as a threat.

"We have to go, right now. Bad people are watching us," said Sima just above a whisper. "Oema, stay with us. Bracelet, send messages to Dad and Security. C'mon. Let's go. Everyone act casual."

28

THE COSMOS COMMANDS

O nce again, it felt like Sima wound up back on Earth.

She didn't see much difference between crazy people who thought the 'cosmos' spoke to them and gangers like Scathers or E86ers who'd start fights for fun. Staring at any of them while appearing to be worried made people a target. Not watching them made people vulnerable to surprise attacks. She'd become fairly good at keeping an eye on people without being obvious about it. Such a skill came in handy both in avoiding predation from gangs as well as scoping out people to beg from. It probably would've helped her pick pockets, too... but she'd never learned how—or cared to.

Oema could probably swipe the jumpsuit off a Citizen and they wouldn't notice.

"This way," whispered Sima while taking Juan and Lissa by the hand and walking along the sidewalk away from the three suspicious people. Going straight into the colony would've taken them to the Center faster, but also require they move toward the crazy people. If they didn't follow her, she'd turn right soon. Ironically, despite being named 'The Center,' it didn't sit at the middle of the colony, rather at the northeast corner. Construction spread mostly southwest from where the ship landed.

"Should I start carrying my axe around?" asked Austin.

"No. You're still too small. You should run away, not look for a fight."

Austin stuffed his hands in his pockets. "Not those losers. What about wild animals?"

"Same. You run... unless they're in our residence."

He chuckled.

"Or they're small like those bugs." Juan grinned. "Smashin' them was fun."

"Eww," muttered Lissa.

"Getting bit wasn't fun." Sima cringed.

Oema hovered close by, constantly looking around. Her eyes couldn't get any wider. Though irrational, her fear made sense to Sima. The younger girl hadn't been on Mirage long enough to process her new reality, and *still* dreaded cops. Being stuck between them and dangerous people offered a no-win scenario in her mind, like running from a pack of Scathers into a group of EGSF officers. Getting slapped around and arrested for simply existing would be preferable to the Scathers playing murderball with her.

Come on. What's taking the Security people so long?

No one appeared to be following her, so after walking for a little while, she turned right, ignoring sidewalks to cut a straight path northeast into the heart of the colony. Some swaths of grass remained damp from the heavy rain, but the mud no longer swam like soup. They weaved among small buildings, single residences, workshops, and storage boxes. Urgency pulled Sima up to a fast walk once they had cover and the crazy people couldn't see them.

Lissa screamed as she lurched backward to the side, her hand torn from Sima's grip.

Sima whirled toward her. The skinny frazzle-haired man had come out from behind a parked rover, ambush-grabbing the child.

"Let go! Get off me!" shouted Lissa, flailing and kicking.

The man made a hesitant attempt to grab a large knife from his

belt—presumably to threaten Lissa with it, but the little girl struggled so furiously, he needed both hands to keep holding her.
Blinded by instant rage, Sima let go of Juan's hand and rushed the
guy. She shoved him—and Lissa—back, yanked the man's knife out
of its sheath, and rammed it into his abdomen.

"Don't you dare touch her!" roared Sima, grinding the knife
back and forth in him.

He wailed in pain.

Lissa slipped out of his weakened grip and scrambled away.
Austin rushed the man, flying into a barrage of frantic punches.
Oema stood still, stuffing one hand up the back of her cute dress—
probably grabbing a knife.

The man caught Sima in the jaw with a wild flailing arm,
knocking her back. She refused to let go of the knife, tearing it out
of him as she stumbled to the side. He clutched the bleeding
wound, slumped to his knees, and fell over sideways. Austin
continued kicking at his face, hitting his defending arms or chest
most of the time.

Overcome by protective rage for Lissa, Sima snarled and
stomped toward him, raising the knife—but stopped herself.

What the hell am I doing? Not a killer. He's down. Time to run.

"Rane, you are an idiot," said a woman. "Kid, get away from
him."

Sima shifted her gaze from the wounded man to the source of
the voice.

The 'rebreather mask' woman stood by the corner of the next
building, a large handgun pointed at Austin. She didn't look very
old, probably mid-twenties with a deceptively innocent rounded
light-brown cheeks. The instant Sima made eye contact, she
doubted the woman had any intention of shooting him. Good
chance she'd never killed anyone before. Definitely a Citizen. She
didn't have any distant hardness in her stare.

Her companion, however, appeared utterly out of his mind, his
eyes wide and full of the sort of fervor she'd only seen in Blanks
before. Whatever sanity remained in his skull had to be frag-

mented. The top of the woman's head didn't quite reach the height of his shoulders. Long hair and shaggy beard made him look like a well-groomed bear walking on two legs. Older, perhaps forty, he appeared to be the group's leader.

Austin stopped kicking Rane, staring at the gun.

The woman aimed at Sima. "Toss the knife."

"At who?" asked Sima.

"Funny." She frowned. "Off to the side."

"Guys, run." Sima still had *her* knife hidden behind her back, so she chucked the big one in her hand away.

"No," said Austin. "Not gonna leave you."

Juan and Lissa moved closer to her, both glaring defiantly at the woman.

"I'm serious, guys. Get out of here. She won't fire a gun. It will make too much noise. Security will be all over her."

"Shoot the bitch," rasped Rane, still clutching his stomach. "She stabbed me."

Austin moved in front of Sima protectively, glaring at the woman.

"Your dumb fault for not waiting for us to be in position." The woman sighed, then sighted over the gun at Sima's face. "Hand it over."

Her confidence the woman wouldn't dare fire a handgun in the colony had a few cracks, but still held off panic despite her being able to see the bullet inside the barrel. "Okay, relax. You're talking about that encrypted file, right?"

The woman narrowed her eyes, though her cheeks reddened slightly. "Like you don't know."

Rane groaned. "Shoot her."

She knows she screwed up forgetting to log out. I wouldn't even have the file if she wasn't careless. "At least tell me why you're doing this."

"Ahh." The bearded man held his arms out to either side, flashing a crazy grin. "Humanity has broken the covenant. We are to stay contained on one planet, not infect others like the virus we are. They defy the will of the Cosmos. Mirage does not belong to us. It is wrong to even force a name we created upon this land not belonging to us."

"See..." Oema twirled a finger around her right ear while crossing her eyes. "Told you."

"Oh." Austin nodded. "You're trying to blow us all up because you're just crazy. Got it."

The big man roared, "The Cosmos commands our actions!"

Lissa tilted her head. "He's silly."

Austin pointed at her. "She's only seven. She believes in faeries and *she* thinks you're nuts."

The man growled at them.

Lissa clung to Sima, hiding from him.

Now would be a great time for Mama Aurak to come out of nowhere and bite him.

"Zaro," whispered the woman. "Relax. They're only little kids. We don't have time for this."

Rane groaned in agony. "Laina... shoot the bitch already."

"What about you? Are you nuts, too?" Sima glanced at her.

"Obviously," whispered Oema.

Laina stepped closer, keeping her gun trained on Sima. "No. Zaro and I each have different reasons but a common goal. I'm part of a movement that objects to the forced export of Outcast orphans against their will. Destroying this colony will send a message to Earth that their mass-kidnapping won't be tolerated."

"Wow." Austin whistled. "Did they slam the stasis pod on your head or something?"

"Kill the brat, too," grumbled Rane. "Hurry up, I'm bleeding out."

Laina glared at Austin.

"So..." Sima pointed at her. "Because you think it's cruel to kidnap us and send us to another planet, you're going to... what? *Murder* us all? Oh, sure, blowing up the reactor and vaporizing the entire colony is totally saving us from the cruelty of the EGSF. You have huffed *way* too much Pixie."

"Pixie doesn't cause brain damage. She's totally on E-Rad," said Oema.

The woman's grip on the gun tensed.

"Didn't really think about that, huh?" Sima quirked an eyebrow. "If you three blow up the reactor, it's going to kill everyone here. Including you, and all the children you think didn't deserve to be kidnapped. In case you haven't noticed, Earth is a trash heap. We weren't any safer there than here."

"It's safer here," said Austin. "Even with giant cats trying to eat us."

Sima rested her hands on Juan and Lissa's shoulders. "We're actually happy here. She couldn't breathe before. They had to carry her onto the ship because she was so weak. She'd be dead now if she'd stayed on Earth."

"My bad parents made Pixie, and it hurt my breathers. I ammost died." Lissa took a huge breath. "I got new breathers."

Rane groaned, rasped, and came close to whimpering. "Come on already."

Zaro nudged Laina. "Get the software."

"Laina…" Sima eased Juan and Lissa behind her. "You're looking at five kids who basically got abducted, but our lives *are* better here. Do you honestly think anyone on Earth would give a crap if you killed us? They'd laugh and send another ship full of Outcasts. If we survive here, die on the way, die after we land, it doesn't matter to them. They only wanted the street trash not to be their problem anymore. As soon as the ship took off, they could forget about us. They've already forgotten about us. If you blow up the reactor, you're only helping them. Murdering innocent children you claim to care about, plus everyone else here."

"The cosmos demands!" shouted Rane in a pained wail. "We are a virus!"

"You are an idiot," said Austin.

Rane dragged himself along the ground toward the boy, reaching up with one hand as if intending to strangle him.

Zaro stormed toward Sima, stepping on Rane—who stopped

crawling after Austin to scream. She wanted to run from such a big, angry man, but had to keep herself between him and the kids. He grabbed a fistful of her tunic in his left hand, pulling her up on tiptoe. Even mostly off the ground, she still felt short, having to look up at his face.

"We know you have the program. It's not in any of your terminals, so it's gotta be in that Omnicomputer on your arm. Take it off."

She offered a momentary thought of thanks to quill cats and killer Mirran robots. Next to them, this guy didn't scare her much. He still frightened her, but didn't *terrify* her. Sima managed to keep her voice from sounding fearful. "It's locked. Same for anyone who's under eighteen. They don't want kids taking them off and losing them. Doesn't matter what you threaten me with, it's not possible for me to open it."

A wicked gleam shone in Zaro's eye. "No problem, sweetie." He flipped his tunic out of the way and drew a large machete from a thigh sheath. "I happen to have the right tool for the job. That bracelet *will* come off. Laina, shoot them all. We have two minutes." He held Sima out to one side like a target. "I'll be nice and wait until you're dead before I chop your hand off."

Laina raised the gun at Sima's face.

29

WITH A BANG

Austin shouted, "No!" and ran at Zaro.

Sima grabbed Zaro's hand, struggling to peel his fingers open out of her tunic.

Laina's expression softened. Sima locked stares with her, summoning her best 'please help me' face.

"Do it, Mendoza," barked Zaro.

"This is wrong." Laina aimed at him. "We shouldn't do this. I'm not shooting four little kids. Killing them isn't going to solve anything. The girl's right. EG won't care. All we'll do is make ourselves into worse monsters than them. Put her down."

Zaro spun on Laina, swinging the giant knife at her gun arm, swatting the weapon so hard it went flying out of her grip. She staggered back, clutching her arm to her chest. Lissa started screaming for help, her voice high and piercing. Austin jumped on Zaro's back, grabbing two handfuls of beard and letting all his weight hang on it.

The big man roared, sounding angrier than hurt, as he spun in circles. Fearing a machete to the face at any second, Sima drew her knife and stabbed it through the back of Zaro's hand. He snarled, angrily hurling her at Laina, knocking both of them to the ground in a heap.

Lissa kept screaming.

Zaro started after her, but stopped when Austin braced his knees against the man's shoulders and pulled on his beard. Laina shoved Sima off. They stood at the same time. Sima dropped into a combat stance, knife poised, glaring at her.

Laina shook her head, then pointed at Zaro. "I was wrong. He's out of his mind. Rane, too."

Zaro reached up over his shoulder and seized Austin by the arm, tearing him off his back and swinging him hard into the ground. The boy barked a noise like a startled aurak, and lay motionless, apparently stunned. Zaro raised a leg as if to stomp on his head. Enraged, Sima charged, crashing into his back hard enough to make him stumble away from the boy.

Rane wobbled to his feet. Cradling his stomach, he shambled after Lissa. "Shut the hell up, brat!"

Lissa backed away from him, still screaming for Security.

Oema cowered away from Rane, whimpering, but as soon as he went past her, she pulled a knife out from under her dress, jumped on his back, and slashed him across the throat. Rane gurgled, collapsing to the ground, one hand clamped to his neck, the other on the gut wound.

"She said stay the hell away from Lissa!" yelled Oema.

Zaro swung a tree trunk of a left arm backhand at Sima. She ducked, backpedaling while swiping the knife at him—more so he saw she had it than trying to hit him, hoping he paid attention to her instead of Austin. Laina ran in and tried to punch him. He caught her arm and shoved the woman aside effortlessly before slashing his machete at Sima. She jumped back, tentatively jabbing the knife in a taunting manner. This guy knew how to fight, so she didn't want to put her hand close enough to be grabbed—or cut off.

Laina came at him from behind, thrusting a large combat knife at his back. Zaro sidestepped, then caught her by the forearm, about to pull her into his machete—until Sima risked a serious attempt to stab him. The big man rammed an elbow into her fore-head, knocking her into a stagger, but doing so cost him his grip on Laina's arm.

Woozy, Sima stumbled to the side, trying to keep a safe distance from the blurry figure until her vision cleared up. Zaro came after her, but Laina kept getting in the way; the two traded a series of knife swipes, each scoring a few superficial cuts.

"Hey!" shouted Austin, right before a gunshot went off.

Zaro and Laina stopped swiping at each other.

Austin stood a short distance away, holding Laina's gun in both hands, aimed at Zaro. "Drop the weapon. You're under arrest."

The big man gave a contemptuous grunt, palmed Laina's face, and shoved her into Sima, knocking them both over. In complete disregard of the firearm pointed at him, Zaro stalked at Austin.

No! Don't you dare force him to kill! Sima scrambled to shove Laina aside and get up.

Austin fired a shot over the man's head, perhaps intentionally to scare him rather than missing.

Undeterred, Zaro continued stomping toward him. Sima leapt into a run, coming up behind him. Zaro threw his machete at Austin, making him duck. In an instant, he'd ripped the gun from the boy's grip and grabbed him around the neck. Zaro lifted Austin off the ground, slammed his back against the building, and raised the gun toward his head.

Lissa's screaming grew even louder.

Sima pounced on him, ice-picking her knife down into Zaro's right shoulder as savagely as she could. "Get off him!"

The big guy groaned, lurching to the side while dropping Austin and clamping a hand around Sima's wrist. The boy jumped on his back; Juan ran in and tried to bite him on the leg. Laina grabbed his right forearm in both hands, keeping the gun pointed up at the sky.

Zaro grunted, kicking his left leg to launch Juan off to one side. He elbowed Austin in the gut, dropping the boy to the ground, gawping for air, apparently unable to breathe. Sima twisted her knife deeper into his shoulder, dragging him in a swoon to the right. Zaro howled in furious rage; he hammered a brutal punch into Laina's face, knocking her flying. She hit the ground, rolled over a few times, and lay still, either unconscious or close to it. Zaro yanked Sima's arm, peeling her off his back. He swung her into the building, pinned her against the wall by a hand around her neck, and raised the gun toward her face.

She desperately clutched his forearm in both hands, struggling to hold the weapon away. Spots danced in her vision. The tight grip around her didn't let her breathe, but she'd hold that damn gun away until she blacked out. She refused to give up. If she could speak, she'd yell for the kids to run.

Darkness seeped into the edges of her vision, collapsing into a tunnel around the huge, hairy face.

Sima stared into the eyes of insanity, refusing to allow such a sight to be her last, refusing to give up.

Time seemed to freeze still. Two or three seconds felt like thirty.

Zaro abruptly flew to the side.

His hold on her neck released, allowing a rush of air into her lungs.

Sima collapsed to all fours, choking and gasping for breath. Somewhere to her left, an electrical buzzing crackle accompanied a man's scream. *Breathe. One… two…* Sima pushed herself up to kneel. Six Security officers piled on top of Zaro, who twitched and convulsed under repeated shots from an electro-stunner. Laina remained unconscious. Austin had curled into a ball on the ground, holding his stomach. Juan grinned from ear to ear despite having a bloody nose. Oema peeked around the corner of the building, trying to hide from the Security officers.

Lissa finally stopped screaming.

Security officers wrestled Zaro into handcuffs—and had to bind his legs. The man kept fighting while screaming about the will of the cosmos and how the Security team were all 'doomed pawns.' It took five of them to drag him off.

A female Security officer approached Sima. "Are you all right, kid?"

"Yeah. What's a little more mental trauma?" She coughed. "Just a bruise or two. He hurt Austin."

"I'm okay," rasped the boy. "Just don't wanna move."

"Wow…" A Security man patted Lissa on the head. "Some set of lungs on this kid."

Lissa beamed up at him. "They're new!"

Sima allowed the woman to help her up, deciding not to make a sarcastic remark along the lines of 'took you guys long enough.' They probably had to run most of the way across the colony, then search a maze of buildings. Honestly, the whole confrontation with Zaro had taken less than two minutes. Two security men examined Rane, who surprisingly *hadn't* bled to death yet.

Guess Oema cut him shallow. Wasn't really trying to kill him.

Austin groaned and sat up. "Ow."

Sima hugged him. "I'm not sure where brave stops and stupid starts with you."

He squeezed her back. "He was gonna kill us, anyway."

"Yeah." She shuddered. "And everyone here."

The Security woman put a hand lightly on Sima's back. "C'mon, hon. You're safe now. Going to bring you to the medical center to get checked out, then we'll need to talk about what happened. As soon as you feel ready to."

Oema crept out of her hiding place. She no longer appeared terrified, merely afraid of getting in trouble. Of course, since the three idiots attacked them openly, she wouldn't have to identify them. No one had to know about her break-in.

"Thanks. Never thought I'd be so happy to see Security officers." Sima gathered her siblings close, hugging all three of them, nearly overcome with emotion.

"Can we go play soccer now that the bad guys are gone?" asked Juan.

"In a bit." Sima wiped blood off his upper lip. "We need to talk to the Security people first… and get your nose looked at."

UNCHARTED TERRITORY

Two days later on Sunday, Sima sat in a booth at 24-6, explaining what happened to Koji.

They'd decided to meet for lunch today. She'd been stuck dealing with Security people and overprotective parents all day Saturday, and didn't feel right talking about stuff like this over Omnicomputer text or video call. Koji's usual awkwardness around her when they didn't talk science resulted in a few amusing mishaps, such as a French fry going up his nose.

Over lunch, she explained what happened Friday.

"… so, yeah. That woman is definitely in some trouble, but I think they're going to be fair. Worst thing she did was break into my residence… and try to break into yours. The Rane guy attacked Lao Zheng and got the card for her."

Koji wagged a fry at her. "And threaten you with a gun. And conspire to commit mass murder."

"Yeah, I know." Sima nibbled on her titan burger. "But she changed her mind and tried to protect us from that crazy idiot. I asked Commander Yos not to be too harsh on her and maybe even have her see a psychologist or something. She meant well, but she's kind of a moron."

Koji laughed.

"Still not sure why she used a resource room terminal instead of her Omni... or how the email she sent never got to wherever she tried to send it."

Her bracelet vibrated.

She glanced at her forearm.

‹You're welcome.›

"Huh?"

‹The file had not been accessed by the recipient yet. An encrypted file sent from a little boy's account calculated out to a ninety-eight percent probability of something illegal or dangerous, so I recalled the email and downloaded the file prior to deleting it from the colony network.›

"You are amazing." Sima kissed her bracelet.

"So, what are they going to do with them?" asked Koji before stuffing a hunk of general's chicken in his mouth.

"Laina said she doesn't want to blow us up anymore. She's probably going to sit in jail for a while until the psychiatrist is certain she's not bluffing. Mr. Crazy and the son of a bitch who grabbed Lissa might be executed or just be in jail for a super long time. Depends on if they are legitimately nuts or merely fanatical."

He nodded.

"Hey there, Koji," called Corbin Mays.

Sima twisted to look behind her.

Corbin and a few other boys she recognized from class but didn't know walked by their table, all carrying trays.

"Hot date with your *girlfriend*?" asked Corbin in a taunting tone, before laughing.

His friends chuckled.

Koji blushed.

"Yeah. So what?" asked Sima, casual as anything. "Something wrong with having a girlfriend? I notice you don't seem to."

Corbin stopped laughing. He stared uncomfortably at her for a few seconds before walking away. His friends snickered at his expense while following him.

Satisfied, Sima turned back to face the table.

Koji blinked. "Did you just say that to get him to leave me alone?"

She picked up her burger again. "Not entirely. Never had a boyfriend before. It's gotta be more fun than fighting a quill cat."

"Umm."

"Probably not as dangerous." She smiled over the burger at him. "Might as well see what happens."

---

fin

ACKNOWLEDGMENTS

Thank you for reading Out of Mind!

I'd also like to thank Lee Sheridan for editing, Merethe Najjar for proofreading, Jackson Tjota for the cover illustration, Ricky Gunawan for the title page illustration/chapter art, and Alexandria Thompson for cover formatting,

ABOUT THE AUTHOR

Originally from South Amboy NJ, Matthew has been creating science fiction and fantasy worlds for most of his reasoning life. Since 1996, he has developed the "Divergent Fates" world, in which *Division Zero, Virtual Immortality, The Awakened Series, The Harmony Paradox, and the Daughter of Mars series* take place. Along with being an editor at Curiosity Quills press, he has worked in IT and technical support.

Matthew is an avid gamer, a recovered WoW addict, Gamemaster for two custom RPG systems, and a fan of anime, British humour, and intellectual science fiction that questions the nature of reality, life, and what happens after it.

He is also fond of cats.

Visit me online at:

Facebook: https://www.facebook.com/MatthewSCoxAuthor

Pinterest: https://www.pinterest.com/matthewcox10420/

Goodreads: https://www.goodreads.com/author/show/7712730.Matthew_S_Cox

Email: mcox2112@gmail.com

OTHER BOOKS BY MATTHEW S. COX

Divergent Fates Universe Novels

Division Zero series

- Division Zero
- Lex De Mortuis
- Thrall
- Guardian
- Harbinger
- The Shadow Fixer

The Awakened series

- Prophet of the Badlands
- Archon's Queen
- Grey Ronin
- Daughter of Ash
- Zero Rogue
- Angel Descended

Daughter of Mars series

- The Hand of Raziel
- Araphel
- Ghost Black

Virtual Immortality series

- Virtual Immortality
- The Harmony Paradox

Prophet of the Badlands Series

- Prophet's Journey

Divergent Fates Anthology

(Fiction Novels - Adult)

The Roadhouse Chronicles Series

- One More Run
- The Redeemed
- Dead Man's Number

Faded Skies series

- Heir Ascendant
- Ascendant Unrest
- Ascendant Revolution

Temporal Armistice Series

- Nascent Shadow
- The Shadow Collector
- The Gate to Oblivion
- The Queen of Discord

Vampire Innocent series

- A Nighttime of Forever
- A Beginner's Guide to Fangs
- The Artist of Ruin
- The Last Family Road Trip
- The Phantom Oracle
- How Not to Summon Demons
- Ordinary Problems of a College Vampire

- A Vampire's Guide to Surviving Holidays
- An Introduction to Paranormal Diplomacy
- A Vampire's Guide to Adulting
- How to Stop a Vampire War in Six Easy Steps
- Ancient Vampire Death Cults and Other Annoyances

Standalones

- Wayfarer: AV494
- Axillon99
- Chiaroscuro: The Mouse and the Candle
- The Spirits of Six Minstrel Run
- Sophie's Light
- The Far Side of Promise anthology
- Operation: Chimera (with Tony Healey)
- The Dysfunctional Conspiracy (with Christopher Veltmann)
- Of Myth and Shadow
- The Girl Who Found the Sun

Winter Solstice series (with J.R. Rain)

- Convergence
- Containment
- Catalyst
- Catacombs

Alexis Silver series (with J.R. Rain)

- Silver Light
- Deep Silver
- Silver Quarrel
- Silver Crucible

Samantha Moon Origins series (with J.R. Rain)

- New Moon Rising
- Moon Mourning
- Haunted Moon

Vampire For Hire series (with J.R. Rain)

- Moon Master
- Dead Moon
- Lost Moon
- Vampire Destiny
- Infinite Moon
- Vampire Empress

Maddy Wimsey series (with J.R. Rain)

- The Devil's Eye
- The Drifting Gloom
- Dark Mercy

Samantha Moon Case Files series (with J.R. Rain)

- Blood Moon

Immortal Operative (with J.R. Rain)

- Broken Ice

Four Elements series (with J.R. Rain)

- The Elementalist
- The Black Rose
- The Wakefield Curse

Young Adult Novels

The Eldritch Heart Series

- The Eldritch Heart
- The Cursed Crown
- The Sapphire Soul

Evergreen Series

- Evergreen
- The World That Remains
- The Lucky Ones
- Nuclear Summer
- The Nuclear Frontier

Progenitor Series

- Out of Sight
- Out of Mind

Diary of a Teenage Fey

(Short story series)

- Elder Horror
- The Hag of Barrow Falls
- Babysitter's Nightmare
- Lharakki
- Bauble for a Soul
- Simulacrum
- Amorphous
- Manticore

Standalones

- Caller 107
- The Summer the World Ended

- Nine Candles of Deepest Black
- The Forest Beyond the Earth

Middle Grade Novels

The Adventures of Ubergirl series

- My Dad is a Mad Scientist
- Aliens Ate My Homework
- The End of all Halloweens
- Dr. Infinity and the Soul Smasher

Tales of Widowswood series

- Emma and the Banderwigh
- Emma and the Silk Thieves
- Emma and the Silverbell Faeries
- Emma and the Elixir of Madness
- Emma and the Weeping Spirit

Standalones

- Citadel: The Concordant Sequence
- The Cursed Codex
- The Menagerie of Jenkins Bailey

www.ingramcontent.com/pod-product-compliance
Lightning Source LLC
Chambersburg PA
CBHW051939220626
47052CB00004B/720